DANCING IN THE DARK

A woman's search for her identity leads her to confront a series of disturbing truths in this enthralling psychological mystery

Abandoned at the age of eleven by her beautiful, capricious mother, Theodora Cairns, twenty years on and with a painful divorce behind her, is still struggling to get over her childhood abandonment. With the urging of her new love interest, Fergus Costello, and a chance discovery, Theo becomes determined to find her mother and demand answers to the questions she should have asked years ago. Her search for answers leads her to Vermont, USA – but will she be able to handle the disturbing truth?

A Selection of Titles by Susan Moody

LOSING NICOLA *
DANCING IN THE DARK *

DOUBLED IN SPADES
DUMMY HAND
FALLING ANGEL
KING OF HEARTS
RETURN TO THE SECRET GARDEN

writing as Susan Madison

THE COLOUR OF HOPE
THE HOUR OF SEPARATION
TOUCHING THE SKY

* *available from Severn House*

DANCING IN THE DARK

Susan Moody

Severn House Large Print
London & New York

This first large print edition published 2014
in Great Britain and the USA by
SEVERN HOUSE PUBLISHERS LTD of
19 Cedar Road, Sutton, Surrey, England, SM2 5DA.
First world regular print edition published 2012 by
Severn House Publishers Ltd., London and New York.

British Library Cataloguing in Publication Data

Moody, Susan. author.
   Dancing in the dark. -- Large print edition.
   1. Vermont--Fiction. 2. Romantic suspense novels. 3. Large
   type books.
   I. Title
   823.9'14-dc23

   ISBN-13: 9780727896667

Severn House Publishers support the Forest Stewardship Council™
[FSC™], the leading international forest certification organisation. All
our titles that are printed on FSC certified paper carry the FSC logo.

MIX
Paper from
responsible sources
FSC
www.fsc.org   FSC® C013056

Printed and bound in Great Britain by
T J International, Padstow, Cornwall.

He stood by the window, looking down at the girl in the wide-brimmed straw hat as she paced the perimeter of the garden. The planting was formal, geometric. In the explicit sunlight, the clipped hedges seemed almost black. If he were to push open the long glass doors and step out on to the narrow balcony, the air would be filled with the aggressive scent of box, and the sweet-smelling plants which crowded the beds. The fountain in the middle caught rainbows from the air. White wooden benches were set in the exact middle of each hedge, with white planters on either side of them, each containing a single white agapanthus. Sorrow occupied him. And apprehension. But not, perhaps surprisingly, guilt.

Guilt would have demeaned them both. Until this young woman who waited for him in the garden, he had never known doubt. His way had always been clear, a simple matter of setting one foot in front of the other until he reached his expected destination. He had always had just a single ambition. Now the purity of his purpose had changed. Now there were choices, and he was afraid. Damned if he did, and damned if he did not.

The woman seated herself on one of the white-

5

painted benches at the far end of the garden. She took off her hat, and for a moment, the ribbon tied around its crown trailed over the shoulder of her pale dress before she lifted it free. To him, she seemed entirely beautiful.

Somewhere a bell tolled, sombre and coercive. She looked up at his window and their eyes met but neither of them smiled. He did not know if they had reached the end of one thing, or the beginning of another. He was not sure which he would rather it be. What he wanted, he admitted wryly to himself, was to have both the end and the beginning. But that was the one thing not allowed.

She bowed her head, and he saw the white part in her black, black hair. This is a moment trapped in time, he thought. A fly in amber, a bubble in ice. This may be all I shall have to hold on to for the rest of my life. Whatever we decide – she decides – I must remember this always: white flowers, green hedges, a woman walking, holding our future in her hands.

ONE

My mother went mad when I was eleven. I didn't tell anyone, of course. Even at that age, I knew enough to be aware that if I asked for help, they might split us up, put me in a home or her in an asylum. Who'd look after her then?

We were living in Rome at the time. It was Easter Monday and she'd gone to the Mass being celebrated at St Peter's. I usually went with her but that day I didn't because we'd been only the day before. She came back limping, her tights ripped, her face white, a large gash above one eye.

'What on earth happened?' I demanded.

'He pushed me,' she said, shuddering. 'He tried to kill me.'

She was dragging our bags out from under the bed, and my heart sank.

'You should go to the hospital,' I said. 'You need at least three stitches in that cut.'

'Off the pavement,' she said, as though I hadn't spoken. 'Deliberately. Right into the traffic. Oh God, a car just missed me.' Her teeth were chattering. 'Thank heavens you weren't with me.' Tears rolled down her face. 'I always knew he would.'

7

'Would what?' I was suspicious. This wasn't the first time she had spun some wild story about someone trying to kill her. 'Do you even know?'

'I saw him. I ... recognized him.'

'Are you sure it wasn't an accident? Maybe you just slipped or something.'

'I didn't slip.' There was a tight white line round her mouth. Just looking at her made me feel ill. 'We have to leave.' Pulling things out of the drawers, she began piling them into the suitcases. 'We must get out of here right away.'

'But *why*?' I could tell that this wasn't like our other departures.

'Because,' she snapped. She snatched up the postcard of the Virgin of the Rocks, which she carried with her everywhere we went.

'That's not an answer.'

'It's all the answer you're getting,' she said. 'You might be indiscreet and then what would happen?'

'Indiscreet about *what*?'

'Anything.'

'So where are we going?'

'Anywhere that's not here.'

I didn't want to leave. I liked Rome; I'd found Italian an easy language to master, which made me less of an oddball at school, and for once we'd been somewhere long enough for me to make a friend. 'Can I at least say goodbye to Francesca?' I asked, and that's when I knew something terrible must have happened inside her head.

'No!' she screamed. Running across the room, she pulled the limp curtains across the dirty

8

panes, snap, snap. 'You're not to leave the apartment, do you hear? Don't even look out of the window.' She was as tense as a guitar string; the tendons of her neck stood out like wings.

'Why not?'

She didn't quite rock backwards and forwards making strange noises, but she kept plucking at the front of her blouse, the way crazy people do in films, and I could see white all round her eyes.

By late afternoon, we were on a train heading south out of Rome, she with her big battered suitcase full of tatty costumes, I with the few clothes that still fitted me, some books, and my father, wrapped in a blanket.

Before that, she'd always been eccentric, though I'd never minded about that. I'd grown used to the way she kept changing her name – Astarte, Jasmina, Yolanda, Lilith, names which had no connection to her staid English upbringing – but they were the sort of names you'd expect a dancer, an *artiste*, to use. She had other quirks too, like, when we went to Mass, she would insist on walking on the other side of the road, as though she and I were unattached. Or she'd tell me to meet her somewhere and then she wouldn't show up, and I'd know that if I looked around, I'd see her lurking in a doorway or hiding behind a parked car.

She hated crowds. She preferred canned food to fresh. Sometimes she kept the curtains closed all day long, saying the light was bad for her eyes. I was only allowed to call her Luna, never Mother or Mummy.

I was used to her bad days, too, when she

9

would start weeping for no reason at all that I could see, and then I would have to hold her against my chest, or brush her long black hair, sometimes for an hour or more, until she was soothed. At other times, she was so bad-tempered and ugly that I would simply sit in a chair with a book until she got over whatever was bothering her, and would come to kneel at my feet, saying how sorry she was, what a terrible mother she was being. I always assured her that she wasn't, though sometimes I agreed with her.

I'd become accustomed to our poverty, and to the disorder with which she surrounded the two of us. I used to see it as something actually tangible, a savage animal sniffing at the windows, clawing at the door, trying to break in and gobble us up. In self-defence, I tried to maintain some control over our lives by hanging up the clothes she dropped on the floor, tidying the newspapers she left around or scrubbing down the hotplate on which we cooked.

It worried her. 'I'm sorry, I'm sorry,' she would say ruefully, ranging round whichever cramped quarters we were occupying at the time, scarves floating about her like pennants. 'You should be grabbing at life, chewing it up and swallowing it down in gulps. Not plumping up cushions, folding newspapers, *dusting*.'

I didn't answer. There'd have been no point. Chewing up life, let alone swallowing it down in gulps, isn't really an option at the age of six, or eight, or ten.

'You're such a good girl,' she said once. 'Maybe you're a changeling. Maybe the fairies

10

stole away my real daughter and left a middle-aged housewife in her place.'

Such remarks didn't upset me. Of course I was her real daughter. Put us together and our likeness to each other was as strong as a rope. But almost from birth, our roles had been reversed. I was the one who looked after things, who handled the day-to-day business of our peripatetic lives. It was I who dealt with landlords, or charmed shopkeepers into extending our credit. By the time I was six I'd learned to iron; at seven, I could fry chops, cook spaghetti sauce, make an omelette. I had never wished to be, but I was the one who held our chaotic world together.

In spite of that, we were happy. The only thing I couldn't stand was her restlessness. We didn't have any kind of social life, in the generally accepted sense of the phrase, because we were never in one place for long enough to get to know anyone. Occasionally we stayed put as long as a year, but mostly it seemed that no sooner had we settled somewhere than we were off again. Sometimes, I wanted to stay so badly I could almost taste it. I longed to put down roots and make friends and not be eccentric any more.

But that was OK. If she wanted to keep moving, I could handle it. People are weird, I knew that. I didn't like it, but I went along with it because I loved her. Because we were best friends. Because we were everything to each other.

After that time in Rome, she grew crazier and crazier. We never stayed anywhere longer than a few weeks, and everywhere we went, things happened to her. One night she started screaming and I woke up from my mattress on the floor to see her flapping at a spider which was crouched on her pillow.

'Don't touch it!' she shrieked. 'Whatever you do, don't touch it.' I picked it up by one leg and dropped it out of the window, but she was trembling as though it really had been poisonous.

Another time she shook me awake, demanding to know if I smelled burning, and it took me nearly an hour to convince her that the building wasn't on fire. She was always looking over her shoulder as though she could somehow forestall the next bad thing about to happen to us. I'd wake sometimes and find her standing over my bed staring at me with tears rolling down her face. When she caught me eating a chocolate bar which the man at the corner shop had given me she snatched it away, saying it could be poisoned.

Because she was so obviously unhinged, it seemed easier to go along with her. The pace of our travels accelerated. Morocco, Turkey, India, Mexico, California; it seemed like every week she was pulling out the suitcases and we were off once more. In Mexico, she fell again and sprained her arm, though luckily it wasn't bad enough to prevent her from carrying out her engagements. Of course, she claimed that *he* had tried to kill her again, but she would never explain who *he* was, so I ignored it.

My poor mother. I loved her, but living with her was exhausting. It was hard to cope with her.

If I could have taken on some of her burden, I would have done, but I didn't know how. As it was, all I could do was be there in case she needed me.

And then, one evening, she dropped the bombshell which brought everything to an end. 'I'm going to India,' she said. We were in Warsaw at the time, living in a room at the top of a tall, pockmarked building which had once been painted yellow. She was doodling in her sketchbook.

'India, again?' We'd been there a couple of times before – I'd even been born there. I remembered standing on a quay somewhere and watching our bags swing down into the hold, labelled *Not Wanted On Voyage*.

'I could rent a houseboat, somewhere isolated,' she said. 'I can easily get work, there's a rich maharajah who'd do anything for me.'

To me, India was long hills reflected on still water, chimes ghostly in the dusk, crimson silks and tarnished cushions, polished brass and the smell of incense, and along with that, too much diarrhoea and not enough loo paper, scavenging, importunate traders, people, payment demanded, discomfort. 'Can't we go to Russia instead? India's full of horrible flies. And I'd love to see some of the paintings in the Hermitage.'

She put down her pencil. 'Darling ... don't be upset ... but I'm not taking you with me this time.'

'What do you mean?' My mouth hung open with surprise.

'It's time you went to school.'

'I do. Every day, in case you hadn't noticed.'

'A *proper* school. An English boarding school. All this chopping and changing, moving about. You're almost twelve years old and it's time you got an education.'

'I've already got one.'

'Only the other day you were saying that you've been to nine different schools in six different countries and you never have any friends.'

It was true. 'But I've always got you.'

'Of course you have. But you need girls your own age. You'll make *lots* of friends. Didn't you say just yesterday that you wished we could be normal?' She leaned towards me. 'That's why I've enrolled you at a convent school. The same school as my friend Terry Cartwright's youngest girl. Jenny, she's called. She's the same age as you; she'll be starting at the same time.'

I could see she was serious. I banged a fist on the table. 'You're trying to get rid of me!' I screamed. I didn't think I could bear the pain of being separated from her. 'Is it because ... don't you love me any more?'

'Darling, don't be silly.' Tears came into her eyes. 'Of *course* I love you.'

'If you truly did, you wouldn't make me go to horrible England.'

'It's not horrible.' She tightened her mouth. 'Besides, you're English yourself and it's time you lived there.'

She wasn't going to change her mind, I could see that. How did she think she was going to manage without me to look after her? Who'd see

14

that she ate properly, or press her costumes before a performance or supervise her new routines? 'So that's it,' I said. 'No discussion, no arguments. Just, boom! Theodora Goes To Malory Towers?'

'It's called St Ursula's.'

'I don't care *what* it's called. I'm not going.'

'You are. You have to.'

Tears welled in my throat. 'No! No! Don't make me go, Luna!' It was all too much. I began sobbing. 'Don't send me away.' I'd never been away from her in my life.

'I promise you that once you've settled in, you'll love it,' she said.

'Please let me stay with you. *Please*.' Hard as I tried to hold them back, the tears carried on coming.

'Oh, darling. Don't you think I want you with me?' She was crying, too. 'Of course I do. I can hardly bear the thought of being without you. But racketing round the world with me isn't doing you any good. And school is something we all have to do.' Out in the street a car back-fired and she pressed her hand to her chest, half starting out of her chair. 'My God! Was that a gunshot?'

'Of course not.' I forgot my own fears and once more set about soothing hers.

Five days later, we took a taxi out to the airport. 'Don't worry, darling,' she said, staring round the crowded concourse and then holding me tightly against her. There were tears on her cheeks. 'Oh, Theodora,' she murmured. 'I love you *so* much.'

15

'If you really did, you'd let me stay with you.'

'I can't. One day you'll understand.'

I recognized the finality in her words. 'You'll look after my father, won't you?' I said resignedly.

She stared at me, blood draining from her face. 'Of course,' she said, after a pause.

'I don't want to go.' I began to cry.

'You'll be OK, my darling. Remember ... remember that I'll think of you every single day.'

'When? What time?'

'Five o'clock, sweetheart. Every evening at five o'clock. Now, don't worry, when you get to London, someone will meet you.'

'How will I know who they are?' I said, but she was already hurrying away towards the exit.

As she had promised, someone did meet me when I arrived at Heathrow. The man who claimed me was wearing a suit which even I could see was of superb cut and material. The pink rose in his buttonhole perfectly matched his silk tie. 'You must be Miss Theodora Cairns,' he said, holding out his hand. 'I'm Hugo, a friend of your mother's.'

He took me off to a big London hotel for the kind of tea I'd only ever imagined: tiny savoury sandwiches, scones and clotted cream and strawberry jam, plates of cakes. I'd never seen so much food in one place. 'If you can't eat it all,' he said, 'we'll ask them for a paper bag and take the rest with us.'

'Where are we going?'

'To the Cartwrights,' he said.

'Are they the ones with a girl the same age

16

as me?'

'Jenny,' he said. 'Yes. Didn't your mother say?'

'She didn't tell me much.' I reached for another scone.

'I wonder why that was.'

'Because I might be indiscreet,' I said. 'That's what she said, anyway.'

'Indiscreet? What about?'

I shrugged, reached for another sandwich. 'Are you English?' I asked.

'No, I'm from Boston, Massachusetts.'

'My mother's from Canterbury-in-Kent, so how did you meet her?'

'I met her years ago, when she was a little older than you are.'

'What was she like?'

'Funny. Interesting. Pretty, just like you.'

Was I pretty? I stored the possibility away, while Hugo poured another cup of tea. 'She was always dancing,' he said. 'We used to call her the Dancing Queen.'

'That's a song.'

'Yes. She and her parents were staying with some friends who had a house in France, with a pool and a lake and tennis courts and everything, and I was there too, with my parents. I remember one day, your mom was dancing along a tree branch which hung out over the lake – and suddenly it broke.' He leaned back and sipped his tea, watching me.

'What happened?'

'She fell in with this almighty splash.'

'Honestly?'

'Cross my heart. And what a splash that was! It must have been one of the biggest splashes ever seen in France. There were eels and ducks and herons and minnows flying all over the place. Frogs, too. Even a couple of boats, with people who'd been fishing.'

I recognized a brilliant storyteller. 'What did she do then?'

'Just went right on dancing.'

'Even in the water?'

'Not in it, on it.'

I could see it clearly, the heavens dark with birds and frogs, fishing lines trailing from the clouds, black-bereted men in the sky peering over the edge of their boats to see what had happened. And Luna dancing on tiptoe across the sparkling surface, her supple hands catching rainbows from the sun. 'That's typical of my mother,' I said gravely.

'I think you may be right.'

'I wish I was back with her.' I tried not to cry. 'She really needs me. I don't know why she's sent me away, or what I did.' I dabbed at my eyes while Hugo tactfully looked away.

'You did nothing, Theo. Absolutely nothing,' he said, wiping his mouth on his napkin. 'Just remember that she loves you more than anything in the world.'

I didn't see or hear from her again for more than ten years.

18

TWO

The dream is frequent, the place familiar. I am alone in a garden bounded on three sides by yew hedges, on the fourth by the many-windowed stone frontage of a house. Elaborate parterres surround beds of white pebbles or, sometimes, white flowers. Always, the thick, aggressive smell of box fills the air. As I stare up at the house, I am aware that someone I can't see is looking down at me. Spying on me. A man. Sinister. Malevolent. Always dressed in black. In the dream, I've never met him, but I know who he is.

There is no way into this garden, no way out. What lies behind those blank windows? What lies?

For weeks, England has been sweltering through a heatwave. Hosepipes have been banned, drought officially declared. Every day, the newspapers publish images of dried-up river-beds, parched fields, cracked earth. Pundits pronounce on the dangers of global warming and the rising incidence of melanoma. Sales of sunblock rocket. Gardens die.

I've been away for three weeks, visiting clients in the States. Now, I let myself into my silent house. It's early evening and the musty unused

19

air still holds the day's breathless heat. Dropping my bags, I push open the French windows and step outside. Although I am prepared for damage, what I see is even worse than I'd feared. My herbaceous borders are dry and dishevelled. Flowers hang listlessly from sagging yellow stalks. There are ominous patches of bare soil, which will mean gaps next spring. Brown-edged roses droop; leaves wilt. The meadow-grass in the orchard, once the refuge of crickets and grasshoppers, larks and field mice, lies flat, veldt-coloured against the dry earth. There's no need to visit the bog-garden I've been working on for the past year; it's all too easy to visualize the scummy rim of the pond, the stink of stagnant water, dead fish floating.

I feel physically sick. At least Marnie, my part-time secretary, has watered the tubs outside the French windows; I can see that the containers of white pelargoniums, the pots of herbs, are green and healthy. But everywhere else, the water-butts are long empty. Unless we get some rain, it will take me weeks to bring the garden round.

And suddenly, as though I've personally conjured it out of nowhere, a drop lands on my shoulder. Followed by another. Amazed, disbelieving, I look up at the sky. A swell of dark cloud is rolling in from the west. The weather is breaking at last. More beads of water fall, heavier this time, and almost immediately become a deluge. Raindrops whack and drum against the path, bounce up and fall back. Within seconds, the stone flags are streaming with water. Rain plunges steadily from the sky.

Eyes closed, I raise my face and let it stream over my head. In minutes, my silk blouse is soaked. I slip off my sandals and stand barefoot on the path, relishing the wet until at last, as the temperature drops, I run shivering back into the house.

So far this has been a lousy day. Hot, sweaty weather, the heaviest day of my period, one of those crazy I-hate-the-world New York cab drivers who got me to Kennedy with only just enough time to check in. Not that it mattered because after we'd boarded the aircraft, one of those spuriously reassuring airline voices announced that there would be a short delay while the engineers rectified a minor technical fault. Don't even *think* about stapling those wings back on, I wanted to shout. Load us on to a different plane, and let some other poor bastards plunge to their deaths over Greenland. But of course I said nothing. I just sat there, in the stifling heat, with a splitting headache and menstrual cramps, longing to get back to my Cotswolds home.

The flight attendant passed round newspapers. Headlines flashed in and out of my head like summer lightning – BUSHFIRES IN SYDNEY, FLOODS IN OHIO, RAIL DISASTER IN BENGAL. I read a piece about the joys of being a mistress (*'How the Other Half Loves'*), an article on the giant panda, the well-connected wife of a banker going public about her cheating lover. I'm in too much discomfort to concentrate. There are more reassuring noises from the cockpit, more dull aches in the pit of my stomach, temperatures

21

soaring.

And, to top it all off, my car developed a flat on the way home from Heathrow and the AA man took ages to come and change it.

Not a good day at all. But at least it's now raining. There's a towel in the downstairs cloakroom and I wrap it round my hair before I pad into the kitchen and pour myself a glass of wine.

In the office, I check the answering machine. There's a message from Regis Harcourt, with yet another brilliant new idea she wants me to incorporate into the design for her town garden. There are three commissions for a Decoration, one of the miniature tabletop container gardens which I've developed into a lucrative extension of my garden design business. A couple in Kent wants a change of date for a meeting I've set up with them. A man from Yorkshire asks me to go up and advise on revamping his garden. Bob Lovage, my contractor, has rung to say he's hurt his back. And Jenny Hill wants me to call her urgently, the absolute minute I get back; it's a matter of life or death. She's my best friend and probably just wants my recipe for strawberry shortcake.

The mail consists of notifications of already-paid bills, a postcard of the Acropolis from a client telling me when she'll be back and hoping we can get together over her garden, a letter from someone I'd known at university, an excitable communication from *Reader's Digest* informing me that I've been specially selected to win at least two million pounds and, failing that, a set of steak knives. There's nothing much else, except an invitation to a gala night in Stockholm, at which a trio of specially commissioned inter-linked modern dance ballets choreographed by Lucia Cairns would be performed. Choreograph-ed? Has my mother finally turned respectable? It's hard to believe. Since the event had taken place two weeks earlier, I drop the invitation into the wastepaper bin.

I go upstairs, dry my hair and finally, I go into the sitting room and look up at the portrait hanging above the fireplace.

'I'm back,' I say.

As I speak, the doorbell rings. Visitors, Jehovah's witnesses, double-glazing: whichever it is, I don't need it. All I want is a small whisky, a hot bath, an early bed.

I open the door and, to my irritated surprise, find Liz Crawfurd, one of my clients, standing there. She holds an umbrella over her head, and there is a tentative smile on her face.

'Hello,' I say. Coldly.

'I do hope you don't mind me dropping in,' she says.

I do. 'That's OK,' I say, not attempting to sound gracious. I hate the unexpected, the un-planned, being caught unawares. And why has she come to the front door, when a sign on the wall of the house quite plainly directs visitors to the office at the back of the house? Why is she here at all, when it's way past office hours?

Behind her, the rain is tipping down. I can almost hear my thirsty plants sucking up the moisture. I remind myself that Liz and her hus-band have recently bought an Arts & Crafts-

designed manor house down in Somerset and
have lucratively commissioned me to help them
restore the gardens. That certainly doesn't
bestow on them the right to barge in unannounc-
ed. What it *does* mean is that I have to be nice –
not something I'm particularly good at. 'I've just
got back from the States,' I say. 'But do please
come in.' I'm so sweet, you could put me in a
centrifuge and spin me into candyfloss.

It's unfortunate that the reception room is still
being refurbished by possibly the most incompe-
tent builder in the world, which gives me no
choice but to take her into my own sitting room.
That's another thing I dislike: uninvited people
leaning against my cushions, eyeing the books
on my shelves, the *objets* on the mantelpiece, the
contents of the eighteenth-century chinoiserie
cabinet. My home may also be my business
premises, but I prefer to keep my personal life to
myself.

As soon as she's in the room, Mrs Crawfurd's
eyes swivel towards the painting which hangs
above the fireplace and then back again to me.
She smiles. 'What an interesting place,' she says.

I launch into a brief description of how the
house was once three separate farm cottages,
now knocked together and how I bought it five
years earlier because just over an acre of
paddock and copse came with it, offering me the
challenge of my own wilderness to tame.

What I *don't* tell her is that the thing I'd liked
best of all was not the land, nor the orchard full
of gnarled old trunks of apple and plum, but the
fact that it would be *mine*. That it sat rooted in

the earth, solid as a tree and nobody would ever be able to make me move on. That stepping over the threshold for the first time, I'd already felt my roots sprouting, burrowing down through the stone-flagged passage and into the ground beneath, strong and fibrous, permanent.

Why is she here? Even though there is nothing in the least ominous about her smartly styled grey-blonde hair, her green linen slacks and short-sleeved white blouse, I am disturbed by the way her eyes march about the room, leaving footprints on my possessions, my painting, the blackened beams of the ceiling, the exposed brickwork of the hearth. *Leave my house,* I want to say. *I don't want you here.* The words sound so strongly in my head that I am not entirely sure I haven't spoken them aloud.

I pull myself together. 'How can I help you?'

She hesitates. 'Look, the chances that you can do it at such short notice are slight, I know that, and it's a bit of a cheek even to ask, but my youngest daughter's twenty-first birthday is coming up and we're planning a celebration for her, very small, nothing fancy. I'm wondering if you could possibly find time to make one of your Decorations for her.'

Couldn't she have telephoned? 'I'm really awfully busy at the moment...' I interrupt.

Mrs Crawfurd spreads her beautifully manicured hands. The big emerald on her fourth finger exactly matches her trousers. 'You probably get booked up years in advance, and I wouldn't have asked except that...' Briefly, she closes her eyes. 'You see, my daughter Holly is

... is very special. She suffers from a form of cerebral palsy and she was never expected to live this long. As it is, she's confined to a wheelchair and, although she shares our pleasure in the garden, it's difficult for her to do much, even though we've built special beds for her. But the sort of thing *you* do, those amazing tabletop gardens – it's something I think she could really enjoy.'

My instinct is to tell her the truth: that I won't have time. Then I try to imagine what it must be like never to walk through summer grass, never to kneel at the edge of a border and drink in the scent of lavender, or lie beneath a plum tree on a late summer's afternoon and see the purple fruit heavy against the sky.

I open my engagement diary. 'What date are we talking about?'

'You'll do it?' Her face lights up. 'Oh, thank you so much.'

With the date in October written down, I move towards the front door and am reaching for the latch when she stops in the middle of the room. She puts her head on one side and says, 'I love your painting.'

'So do I,' I say.

'Funnily enough, a friend of mine has one very similar.'

'Really?' I open the door but she stays where she is.

'In fact,' she continues, 'his is almost a companion piece to yours.'

'Is that right.'

'As I'm sure you're aware, Barnes has come

right back into fashion,' she says. 'Not that he ever really went out of it.'

'Barnes?'

She looks surprised. 'You did realize it was a Vernon Barnes, didn't you?'

I shake my head.

'But...' Her voice is disbelieving. 'You must know that it's an extremely valuable piece of work.'

'As far as I'm concerned, any value it has is entirely sentimental.'

'I hope I'm not being impertinent if I ask how you came by it?'

She knows perfectly well that she is. Impertinent *and* intrusive. 'My mother gave it to me for my eighth birthday.' I am distinctly frigid.

'Eighth?' Her careful eyebrows rise a little. 'That's an unusual gift to give a child.'

'My mother's an unusual woman.'

'And where did she get it?'

I recall myself, aged seven, nearly eight. I remember my whining, repeated questions. 'Why haven't I got a father? All the other children have – where's mine? Why doesn't he live with us? I want a daddy, like everyone else.' And Luna, her voice trembling, saying, 'Oh, darling, you know your daddy's dead, I've told you often enough.'

And then, on my eighth birthday, she presented me with this painting, said I was old enough now to take charge of it. 'That's John Vincent Cairns,' she said, looking at the portrait, reaching a hand towards it as though to brush away the lock of hair on the man's forehead. 'That's your father.'

27

'I never asked.' I give Mrs Crawfurd a fac-simile of a smile. 'Children don't, do they?' I pull the front door wider, feeling like someone trying to get rid of a blowfly, but she still doesn't move. 'Do you have any idea who the subject is?' she asks.

'Of course I do.'

'Who?'

Again, I can't see what it has to do with her. 'It's my father,' I say.

'Your...' She frowns.

'Colonel John Cairns.'

'Are you sure?'

Laughing at the absurdity of the question, I step outside on to the rain-wet step, 'I'm one hundred per cent positive,' I say. 'And I ought to know.'

'I suppose so.' She sounds very uncertain.

Why can't she just *go*? 'Look, I'll be in touch about the miniature garden for your daughter nearer the time, and we can discuss the details then, all right?'

'Fine.' Mrs Crawfurd steps towards her BMW in the drive. 'Thank you so much for your time.'

'Just part of the service.'

The rain has eased off, but the shrubs and bushes which surround the front of the house are still dripping. Water drops hang from the laurel leaves which, now that the summer's dust has been washed away, shine like polished green leather. As she opens the door of her car, Mrs Crawfurd turns to where I'm still standing under the porch and gives me a speculative look. She climbs into the front seat, turns the key in the

28

ignition and drives off.

I gaze after her. What was *that* all about? As the sound of her engine dies away down the lane, I breathe in deeply. The rain has brought out the perfume of growing things and I fill my lungs with leaf-flavoured, flower-scented, fruit-laden air. Then I turn back into the house. *Are you sure?* For some reason, I feel a vague unease, as though I have meekly offered a lighted match to someone holding an open can of kerosene.

It's obvious her interest in my painting has nothing to do with aesthetics. Does she want to buy it? Too bad; it isn't for sale, and never will be, since it's just about my most precious possession – certainly the one I love best.

Crude initials are splashed in the bottom left-hand corner, VB in careless red paint. It's executed in what my mother told me was the *faux-naif* style. It shows my father standing to one side of a long window, his face in three-quarter profile, as though he has just turned away from gazing down at the garden below, which is all white pebbles and box-edged parterres. A small fountain plays in the centre; there are stone urns in the four corners. In the background, a girl sits on a white-painted bench, her pale dress sprigged with green, a straw hat on her knee. Although I've never been there, I know the garden well. It's my father's garden. It's the place of my dreams.

To one side of the middle distance is an orchard full of fruit trees. Not just apples, plums, cherries, but oranges and lemons, mangoes and pineapples. If I look carefully, I can see a small tree laden with silver nutmegs and golden pears. On the right-hand side of the canvas is a dark wood where, between stiff lines of tree trunks, a unicorn lurks. Beyond them, the landscape stretches across fields and hills towards a faintly suggested sea on which rocks a full-rigged ship flying a skull and crossbones.

In the foreground a slice of grand piano is visible. The letters STEINW are on the lid, shining brassily in the light from the window. A Siamese cat sits beside the pedals. Next to the cat is a mouse; next to the mouse, a ladybird. The man's open-necked shirt is tucked into white flannel trousers which are held up by a red-and-white schoolboy's belt fastened with an S-shaped clasp. Holding a book, he seems on the verge of crossing the parquet floor towards me, on his way to engage in some manly pursuit: fencing or cricket, or riding a high-spirited horse across the fields beyond the garden.

His face has always moved me: grey eyes, a slick of blond hair, a thin and aristocratic nose, a full mouth. I love him more than anything in the world. Colonel John Vincent Cairns. My father.

Are you sure?

Of course I'm sure.

I dial Jenny Hill's number and wait for her breathless voice to answer. Jenny, wife of Richard, is my closest friend. A model of everything I would like to be.

'It's me,' I say, when she picks up.

'Darling, how lovely! Did you have a good time in the States? Did any gorgeous males come on to you?'

'I was there for business, Jen.'

'I realize that, but you never know your luck.'

I smile. 'So what's the life-and-death thing?'

'Life rather than death. I wanted you to be the first to know – apart from Richard, of course. Even before Mum.'

'Know what?'

'I'm pregnant again! Isn't that wonderful?'

'Fantastic! Brilliant. Jen, I'm *thrilled*. And if all goes according to your life-plan, this will be my god-daughter Laura, right?'

'Right.'

'And after that, all you have to do is carry on living happily ever after.'

'You got it.'

'Congratulations! I'll come for a visit as soon as I can.'

'Don't leave it too long. We don't see enough of you these days.'

'Too much work.'

'Well, don't forget to make time for your friends.'

'Jen ... as if.'

'But in any case, we'll see you on Sunday, won't we?'

'Sunday?'

'Caro and Charlie's lunch party, Theo. You'd better not miss it.'

Charlie is Jenny's brother. 'Sorry, sweetie, it's jet-lag,' I say. 'I've only been back a couple of hours. Of *course* I'll be there. I've got a new frock and everything.'

Putting down the phone, I'm suddenly despondent. It's not something I'd ever talk about, but I want a child, too. More than I dare let myself imagine. I want the chance to be the most wonderful mother in the world, and sometimes I'm terrified by the possibility that it will never come. I'm already over thirty. Occasionally, in my head, I can almost see those children I don't have. One thing is certain. They would be the very centre of my world, and would know it. They would always feel secure. I would never leave them, disappear for ten years of their lives, hand them over for someone else to look after. Never.

Upstairs, I strip off my clothes and gaze briefly at my reflection in the long cheval glass. I'm in pretty good shape. And while the people from Revlon or L'Oréal aren't likely to run after me imploring me to be the face of their latest range, neither does anyone cross themselves when I walk down the street. In other words, I'm fairly average looking.

For once, even my black hair looks good. There's not much I can do about my heavy eyebrows but my eyes have always been unusual. Icelandic eyes, my mother calls them, inherited from my paternal grandmother. With shorter hair, they seem even more remarkable.

Lying in a Floris-scented bath, I sip cold wine while my muscles slowly unknot. It's raining again. Water gurgles in the gutters, streams down the drainpipes into the empty water butts, dashes wetly against the windows. There is a distant rumble of thunder.

My thoughts drift. Though I'm unwilling to count chickens which may never hatch, I allow myself a brief moment of cautious satisfaction. The trip to New York was very rewarding. My business, begun five years ago on a shoestring, is really starting to take off. There are full order books, a gradually swelling bank balance, a growing reputation.

I reach over the side of the bath for my cordless phone and dial Luna's flat in Rome. Although I let it ring for minutes on end, and then redial in case I got it wrong the first time, there's no answer. I don't know why I expect there to be. Long ago my mother had abandoned me and I'd learned to live my own life. I recall how I used to cry myself to sleep every night, wondering where she was, what she was doing, who she was with and whether she loved him more than she loved me. Because as I grew older, it became increasingly clear to me that she must have traded me for a man. I never imagined that she might be dead; the set of her back as she walked away from me at the airport was too determined, she'd planned this betrayal for months, must have; otherwise how could she have enrolled me at St Ursula's, or made arrangements with Jenny's mother, Terry?

Strange that she should have returned to Rome, after all these years. I've often wondered whether she remembers her paranoia, her insistence that someone was after her. These days, she and I lead separate lives. As we should. Which is fine by me. She has her career to follow and I am much too old now to need a maternal bosom to weep on, or a motherly kiss goodnight. Besides, she abandoned me for ten years. I will never be able to forgive her for that, even though she had been right about St Ursula's. I learned to love the safety of my school uniform, the gentle voices of the sisters, the rules, the expectations we were supposed to live up to. Above all, I adored the complete predictability of school-life.

From time to time, I would imagine I'd glimpsed Luna from the edge of my eye or seen her turning the corner at the end of the street. I'd fancy I saw her standing at the end of the school playing fields where they merged into woods, or walking rapidly away from the gates on Saturday afternoons, when we were allowed to visit the town or stroll on the Downs. But I never went after her, to see if it really was her. And gradually, as the years went by, I didn't even think about following; I was afraid that it *would* be her.

Suddenly I'm sniffing back tears. Which is ridiculous, when I have nothing to cry about. I'm probably working too hard. I need to take Prozac, take a holiday. Take a lover.

I consider the possibility of a holiday, a proper one, without any responsibilities. But it's impossible. I can't afford to take the time off. I reach an arm over the edge of the bath, grope around and find the wine bottle, refill my glass.

Despite the rain clouds, it's still light outside. I look at my watch and see that it's five o'clock. Magic time. The hour when I used to think about my mother. When I hoped that she was thinking of me.

I'm getting sleepy. Gardens float behind my

eyes. So many gardens. One in France, full – the way I remember it – of blue roses. An elaborate topiary garden in Maine. Italian gardens, all shrubs and statuary. Gardens the size of handkerchiefs, rolling acres, Zen gardens, Mediterranean gardens, imaginary ones. And my own. My beloved acre of earth, where I can express myself in any way I choose, where I can look into the future, plant for posterity, put in an acorn and know with a gentle sense of content that I shall never see the mighty oak it will become.

I recall another garden, and Luna, with her scarves and her beads and her floaty dresses, dancing in the damp green dusk, with five ropes of artificial pearls around her neck and her hennaed hair tied up in a white cotton veil. Wooden chimes thonked flatly between the hissing leaves, and the bird which hung in a cage from the upstairs balcony sang a few sad notes behind the bars of its bamboo cage. Eight years old, I was crouched on the flat roof, watching her glimmer like a moth in the warm darkness. Loving her. Wishing with all the strength I had that she would put down roots somewhere and be still.

It's one of the reasons I don't like doing things on the spur of the moment. I've seen at close range the kind of havoc that giving in to impulse can wreak. Because there can't have been anything but impulse behind the restless way in which she was always moving on, dragging me behind her. The fact is that there are women who missed out on the maternal instinct, women who should never have had children, and Luna is one of them. Nothing wrong with that – unless you happen to be the child who should never have been had. I used to worry about it. Not any more. The best way to describe our relationship these days is to call it fragile, like a house of cards is fragile, or a rose on the verge of dropping its petals. From a distance, it may look solid enough, but breathe too heavily and it disintegrates.

We're civil to each other, of course. She refuses to come and stay with me, or allow me to visit her in Rome, but very occasionally we meet in London for lunch. I'm only too aware of how little I matter to her.

Trouble is, in spite of the way she left me, all those years ago, she still means the world to me. And who wants to settle for civility when what they really crave is love? But these are old wounds, and by now they are well scarred. Really they are. I'm not bothered any more. Half asleep, I ease out of the bath and reach for one of the thick towels piled on the shelf above the bath and drape it round myself. I love towels, the bigger the better.

And, hey, I'm light-years away from the confused child I was once. Only rarely do I mull over memories which by now have grown as soft and faded as well-washed linen.

THREE

Once a week, I help to landscape an urban garden, working with a team of enthusiastic adolescents from an inner-city school in Swindon. The idea grew out of a sixth-form science project where the students were set the problem of designing an ergonomically sound compost box which wouldn't need constant attention. Invited to judge the results, I was offered a glass of warm sherry in the head teacher's office and, one thing leading to another, found myself involved in the transformation of a forbidding piece of derelict land at the back of the school premises into a delightful and innovative garden.

Benches have been built by the woodwork class from donated or reclaimed timber, there is a pond where the kids taking Biology can observe the habits of frogs and newts – not top of my own personal must-do list, I have to say, though I have nothing against the occasional tadpole. There is even a little fountain which the Metallurgy class knocked up out of recycled tin cans.

The garden has produced a real sense of community. OAPs sit on the benches on their way to the shops or their yoga class. Young mums take a few minutes out to contemplate something which doesn't need feeding or changing. Even the odd businessman can be seen there at lunchtime, going through the *Financial Times* with a sandwich in a paper bag beside him. Someone is always dropping by with a cutting from their own garden, or a plant in a pot which they've got cheap at the market. One kid brought in a couple of goldfish he'd won at the fair and now there are a dozen of them. Local shops donate compost or loan tools. The garden is a symbol of community and hope in an area with very little else going for it.

'It's amazing that we've only been vandalized once,' Mick Haigh, the teacher overseeing the project, tells me, as we take a well-earned break. 'And that was right at the beginning, when we'd just got started.'

'I know.' I look round at the oasis of shady trees and shrubs, the rough-built stone walls and crowded lily-pond. Several kids are working on the flowerbeds, even though the summer holidays have already begun. It is nearly a week since Liz Crawfurd dropped by my house.

'It's good of you to spare the time to work with us,' he says. 'Not many people bother about kids like these. It makes all the difference to have someone high-profile like yourself involved. The fact that Theo Cairns, off the TV—'

'Oh, please, Mick. I was only on a couple of times.'

'That's enough for most of them. Watching programmes about gardening is so much easier than doing it yourself. The point is, to this generation, television is the great god. You've been

38

on it, ergo, you must be *Fame*-us. Having you on board lifts the project right off the ground, as it were. Nurseries all over the city are rushing in to give us free plants, compost, potting soil. It's great.'

'Best of all would be if some of the kids, even *one* of them, developed an interest in gardening.'

'Funny you should say that.' He wipes sweat from his high forehead. 'Trina Hawkins came to see me the other day and asked if there was any chance of her doing work experience with you.' He gazes at me hopefully from behind his pebble-lensed horn-rims.

'Which one's Trina Hawkins?'

He grins. 'Guess.'

'Oh, no...' I groan theatrically. '*Not* the blue dreads with all the piercings.'

'Bullseye.'

'What is she, sixteen?'

'Almost seventeen.'

I think about it. 'Look, Mick, I'll be frank: I work damned hard, and I value my privacy. Apart from anything else, when I'm alone is when I think out my projects and commissions.'

'She's not at all what you'd expect – I think you'd find her quite a surprise.'

'Is it the telly, or the gardening which attracts her?'

'The gardening, no question.'

'If I agreed – and she'd have to work hard, if I did – how's she going to get out to my place? It's miles from here.'

'She could stay with her aunt in High Wycombe. There's a bus goes every hour which could drop her off at the end of your lane.'

'I see you've obviously done your homework.'

'Not me. Trina. She researched it all very thoroughly before she even suggested asking you. She's dead keen.'

A dead-keen almost-seventeen-year-old would-be gardener is already a surprise. 'Let me think about it and get back to you. I need to work out where she'd fit in.'

'She'll be horribly disappointed if you won't take her on. Her heart's absolutely set on it.'

'Why do I suddenly feel as if I have no choice?'

He spreads his hands and grins again. 'I can't imagine.'

The following Saturday, I'm sitting at my desk, working on a new plan for Regis Harcourt, the interior designer. She first called me up about five months ago and though she speaks so fast that half the time I can't understand a word she's saying, I gathered she felt that, by working together on her town garden, the two of us could raise our individual profiles by several notches.

'I want lots and lots of green,' she gabbled, when I showed up at her London home for the first planning session. 'Bushes and trees, and winding paths, and a fountain so I can hear the sound of trickling water, and maybe a pergola thing at the end, painted white with vines trailing all over it, *so* Mediterranean, and possibly a reflecting pool.'

'A bit of a tall order for such a small area,' I said. 'The space could get very crowded. And remember that lots of green means lots of maintenance. You'll have to spend hours pruning and trimming, just to keep things under control.'

'I can do that.' She flexed her long, crimson-tipped fingers. The Gertrude Jekyll of West Hampstead. 'And nothing but white flowers, what do you think, it could be wonderful, couldn't it? I'm definitely into monochrome at the moment.'

Since then, she's changed her mind twice. When I returned the call she'd made while I was in the States, she'd babbled enthusiastically, 'I want a vista, Theo, I must have a vista! I've just sourced this amazing marble statue of Cupid and Psycho, I thought a plinth or something would look rather stunning at the end of a green avenue, can't you just see it?'

'You're not going to get much of a vista in a fifteen-foot garden. You can certainly achieve a sense of space, but avenues are out. And,' I add, 'isn't that Psyche, not Psycho?'

Now, I'm working at the zoning plan of the site. I've already drawn up my survey, checked the orientation, soil quality, condition of those elements already in place, such as the silver birch set to one side of the rectangular space. I've made a rough list of background plants, and another of perennials and evergreens intended to provide something of the sylvan atmosphere which Regis wants. It will be great when it's finished, even if not precisely as she imagines it. I've provisionally rebooked my construction crew for early next month; once they've started work, she won't be able to change her mind so drastically. Everybody but Regis is ready to go.

But I'm not giving this project a hundred per cent of my attention. I keep remembering my eleven-year-old self, the hopes and expectations I had then, and the way my mother so abruptly opted out of my life. And suddenly my face is crumpling, there is an almost intolerable weight in my chest; I am crying and I don't know why.

The doorbell rings.

I stay where I am, hot tears falling on to my drawing board, my heart throbbing like an abscessed tooth. After a while, the bell rings again. Dammit! Why can't people take a hint? Grabbing a paper tissue from the box in my drawer, I scrub at my face. The bell rings yet again as I go through the sitting room to open the door.

'What do you want?' I say, aggressively.

'Hi.' A pinched-faced waif, barely five feet high, stands on the doorstep, dressed from head to toe in rusty crone-black garments, as though she'd just finished playing the First Witch in *Macbeth*.

I pull myself together. Blue dreadlocks, metal-studded face. 'It's ... uh ... Trina, isn't it?'

'That's right. I was spending the night with my Auntie Sheila, down the road, and I thought, if I was going to, like, do work experience with you, it'd be a good time to drop by, just on the off-chance.'

'Off-chance of what?'

She looks faintly disconcerted. 'I dunno. Catching you in, I s'pose.'

'I don't like people dropping by,' I say.

She frowned. 'OK then, I'll just bugger off out

of it, shall I?'

'Don't be silly. I'm just saying that I prefer to have advance warning.'

'I'm like that, too,' she says. The elaborate hair is blue, but it is also clean, and the piercings – eight round the edge of her ear, two in her eyebrows and a stud under her lower lip – while fairly grotesque, aren't entirely unattractive.

I am aware of my own unbrushed hair and red-rimmed eyes. 'I haven't really had much time to think about your work experience yet.'

'You been crying?' she asks.

'Um, well, yes, as a matter of fact, I have.'

'Boyfriend trouble?'

'Something like that.'

'Bastards, the lot of them, that's what my auntie says.'

'Does she indeed?' Since Trina obviously isn't going to go away any time soon, I open the door wider. 'You'd better come on in, and we can talk things over.'

'Just a sec.' She bends down and picks up an old enamel washing-up bowl by her feet. 'I brought this to show you.'

I look down and gasp. 'My goodness! That's simply beautiful.'

'Thought you'd like it.' She grins and steps inside the house. I smell cigarette smoke on her clothes.

I lead the way to the kitchen. 'Want a coffee?'

'No, thanks. Water will do. I don't touch stimulants – unless you count boys.' She gives a horrible raucous laugh, full of the kind of know-ledge someone so young oughtn't to possess.

43

She makes me feel terribly prim.

I look down at the bowl which she has set on the table, feeling a stir of excitement. She's filled it with earth and then created a miniature garden on top of it. Beds full of tiny flowers, a patch of lawn, a diminutive birdbath. OK, so it's a pseudo-Theo Cairns garden, but it has some lovely individual touches. For instance, there is a tree at one end, with a Lilliputian tree-house skilfully put together from twigs and bits of bark. In the middle, a pebble pathway leads between flowering shrubs to a sandpit and a paddling pool, all in perfect proportion.

'See the nest?' she says. 'Took me ages, that did.' She points to a little beech hedge where a nest of twigs and moss, containing three minuscule eggs, snuggles among the leaves.

'This is really amazing.' I bend down to look at it more closely.

'It's for my little brother,' she explains. 'He turns five next week.' She lifts one shoulder, as if she couldn't care less, but her blue eyes – the exact same colour as her hair – watch me intently. 'So ... what do you think?'

'How long did it take you to make the tree house?'

'Ages. Bit of a bother, that was. Holding it together till the glue dried. The nest was much easier.'

'I'm really impressed.'

She shrugs again. 'Keeps me out of mischief.'

'So what would you hope to get out of working with me?'

'Dunno, really.' She twists one of her locks.

44

'The garden project at school ... that's been really good fun – I mean, I really, really liked it. So I thought if I could tell my mum that I was working for you, someone off the telly and everything, she might let me find a job at a commercial nursery, instead of down the supermarket or hairdressing or something.'

'Why doesn't she want you to get a job with a nursery?'

''Cos the pay's shitty.' She starts patting herself, and brings out a packet of cigarettes.

'If you're going to smoke – and it's extremely bad for you, in case you didn't know – you'll have to do it outside,' I say. *'And* clear the butts up afterwards.'

'Fair enough.' She puts the packet away again.

'When do you leave school?'

'I already did, end of the term.'

'What about your GCSEs?'

'I done that,' she says. 'Got ten of them, didn't I?'

'Ten?' Mick Haigh said I'd find her surprising. 'That's pretty good. Shouldn't you stay on, think about going to university?'

'My mum wouldn't go for that. And anyway, my boyfriend wants us to get married—'

'But you're only sixteen!'

'Seventeen next week, but that's what *I* say. There's a lot of things I want to do before I start settling down and having kids.'

'What sort of things?'

'Travel. Earn some money, real money. I got a nest egg already, but nobody knows about that, not even me mum.'

45

'Where do you want to travel to?'

'All over. Egypt – I'd really like to see the pyramids. And the Great Barrier Reef, all them sea creatures and coral and stuff, we did that in geography. I want to go round the world, get some memories stored up, because if my mum's anything to go by, it's all downhill after the first baby.'

'It doesn't have to be.'

'Not for people like you,' she says. Again the defensive shrug. 'People like me ... well...'

'What kind of people is that?'

'You know ... Nothing much going for them.'

'Where did you pick up such defeatist ideas?'

'You try living with my older brothers. You'd be defeatist, too.'

'You've got *everything* going for you. You can be anything you like.' I feel like one of the self-help manuals which fill my bookcases. *Anyone Can Do Anything. 10 Steps to Personal Fulfilment. Moving Forward.* 'You don't have to live up – or down – to anyone else's expectations of you. Do your own thing.' I take her by the shoulders. 'Trina, you're sixteen years old—'

'Almost seventeen.'

'And your whole life is in front of you. Do what *you* want to do. And though I haven't got any myself, plenty of my friends have children. *They* don't see it as a downhill step at all.'

'No, well, it's different for them, innit? They probably got money, for a start. Look, about this work experience ... are you going to take me on or what?'

'To be honest, I don't want to.'

46

'OK, suit yourself.'

I can see by the intensely nonchalant look on her face how much it means to her. There is a neediness to her which I can't ignore because I recognize it. I guess that, like me, she sees a garden as a sanctuary, the secret enclosed space, the *hortus conclusus* where nothing can get at you, where the wild beasts can raven outside all they like but aren't able to break in, where silver unicorns lay their gentle heads in your lap.

'OK,' I say reluctantly, wondering what on earth I'm doing. 'Why don't we give it a month's trial, see how we go?'

'You mean it?' Her thin face lights up.

'I rarely say things I don't mean,' I say. 'I'll pay you, too.'

'You don't have to, you know. It's supposed to be work experience.'

'If you're doing a job, you should get paid for it. I'll also cover your expenses. Bus fares and so on. You'll have to bring your own lunch. I eat mine on the run, or alone at my desk, when I'm here. I'm not going to sit around gossiping over coffee.'

'Suits me,' she says.

'And you'll have to work bloody hard.'

'Not a problem.'

'I'm talking about shifting earth about and carrying gravel, digging in compost, lifting stones. You might be a bit small for that kind of thing.'

'Less is more,' she says. Maybe she reads self-help manuals, too. 'Trust me. I know all about hard work.'

47

'Four weeks only, is that clear?'

'As crystal.'

'We'll review the situation after that. And you'll have to lose the piercings. Change the hair. I have clients coming here all the time, and you aren't exactly the kind of front-woman they expect to see.' I'm wondering what Marnie will say when she meets this new addition to the work force.

'Front-woman? You mean I'd have to meet people and stuff?'

'Of course.'

'I thought I'd just be watering the flowers and putting in plants, shifting stones like you said, seeing how you start designing a garden.'

'Not much point learning about garden planning if you're not going to have any clients,' I say briskly. 'And looking like that, trust me, you won't.'

'Why not?'

'Because people who hire garden designers are people with money. And people with money...'

'OK, boss. But I'm not going to start licking anybody's bum, just because they're rich.'

'And I'm not going to start asking you to.'

She sighs heavily. 'My boyfriend really likes this blue.'

'What do *you* like?'

'I liked it better green.' She grins at me.

'You can't live your life according to someone else's dictates,' I repeat firmly. 'Believe me, I've tried it and it doesn't work.' I touch the tree house in her bowl-garden. 'This is really good, Trina.'

'I read your new book,' she says. 'Borrowed it from the library. *ReDecorations*. It started me thinking about the things you could do. Gave me all sorts of ideas.'

'Let's go and look at what I'm doing in the big gardens. And I'll show you some of the long-term preparations needed for the miniatures. After that ... we can work out what your duties will be.'

'Duties! Great.' She looks about her. 'You got some nice things.'

'Too much clutter.' I don't really mean it. I wouldn't say I was a shopaholic exactly; in fact, I hate spending money when I don't have to. But I do like *things*. Possessions. Growing up with nothing that couldn't be packed into a suitcase at a moment's notice, my Mughal miniature, the Limoges jardinière, the lamps, cushions, dishes from France, jugs from Portugal, all emphasize the permanence I've achieved. I never forget how, when I was a child, the sight of our bags being pulled from under Luna's bed could reduce me to tears, signalling as it did that we were once more on the move. Objects reassure me.

'It's ever so tidy,' Trina says. 'Don't suppose I'll ever have enough money to live in a place like this.'

'I don't see why not. I started out with nothing, built the business up entirely on my own,' I say. 'If I can do it, so can you.'

Before she leaves, we arrange that she will start work the following week. 'Here's an assignment for you to work on at home,' I say.

'Thought I'd finished with homework.'

49

'Think again,' I say firmly. 'In October, I've got to make a tabletop garden for a girl who's confined to a wheelchair. It's her twenty-first birthday. I want you to think about what kind of a miniature garden...' An idea strikes me. 'Or any garden, for that matter, that would be suitable for her.'

When she's gone, I pick up a hand-mirror with a heavily chased silver frame and run my fingers over strategic vine leaves, rounded buttocks, dimpled knees. Lifting it, I stare dispassionately into the bevelled oval, and see my face floating below the surface of the glass – strong black hair, a full mouth, strange grey eyes surrounded by thick lashes and haunted by fear of the past.

Theo Cairns. Gardener. Woman. Daughter. As always when I look at myself, I see my mother.

I'm blending my bog-garden into an au naturel wildwood planting: huge dramatic growths of giant hogweed, tangles of cow parsley, gorgeous blue-grey thistles, thick hedges of rambling rose and trails of old man's beard, euphorbias, fatsia, verbascum, feather-duster plumes of astilbes. I've planted thickets of bamboo, rheums and more hostas. Azaleas, too – I much prefer them to the more pushy rhododendrons.

I'm currently building a pathway through this carefully planned wilderness, using stone flags and edging them with bricks recycled from the rubble that used to clog up the spring. It's sweaty work; those flags weigh a ton and I'm grunting and cursing as I transfer the rectangles of limestone from the wheelbarrow to the sandy bed

I've prepared for them.

'Can I give you a hand with those?'

I nearly drop a slab on to my foot. I carefully ease it down to the ground then shade my eyes to peer in the direction of the voice. Standing in the undergrowth, backlit by sunshine and the brilliance of sun-edged leaves, is either the Great God Pan or an extremely fanciable youth. Tall, well-built, longish blond hair tied back in a ponytail.

'And you are?' I say.

'Harry Lovage. Son of Bob.'

'I didn't know he had one.' Bob Lovage, my contractor, is a good-looking bloke, if you like them weathered.

'He does, and it's me. Let me take that.' He lopes down the chip-wood lane between the overhanging bushes and effortlessly picks up the slab leaning against my leg. 'Where do you want it?'

'Just settle it there, please.' I point, pressing my hands into the small of my aching back.

Efficiently he eases it down, adjusts it, tamps it into place with his boot. 'That should do it.' He straightens up and looks around him. 'This is nice.'

'There was already a hazel coppice down here, and a may tree,' I say. 'I've just added to it over the years.'

'I love the smell of may. When I was a kid, my mother used to tell me it was the smell of summer. I've never forgotten that.' He smiles at me. 'You can't rush a garden.'

'Very true.'

'Dad told me you'd probably be down here.'

51

'How's his back?' I'm not a personal-hygiene fanatic, but I am suddenly very conscious of the rings of sweat under my arms.

'Worse. He's hoping you'll take me on in his place. I'm free until October.'

'What happens in October?'

'I start my final year at uni.'

'Where are you?'

'Sheffield.' He grins. 'Oxford seemed a bit too close to home. I didn't want to reel out of the pub and find the old man glaring at me.'

'Any experience with landscaping?'

'Quite a bit. Helping Dad in the hols and so on.'

'OK, Harry. I've got about thirty minutes more work here and then we'll go in, have a cuppa or a drink and I'll show you what we've got on in the next few weeks.'

'Can I give you a hand?'

I prefer to work on my own, thinking about the next project, but it's been a long afternoon and I'm tired of heaving things around. 'Are you quiet?'

'When need be.'

There are no obvious signs that he has a personal CD player strapped to his body. Nor does he look as though he is about to start doing card-tricks or somersaults in a bid to attract my attention. 'OK, thanks.'

With his help, most of the path is laid by the time I call a halt. When I've cleaned myself up, the two of us settle down in my office and go through the schedules. 'It's more or less full-time between now and October,' I say apologetically. 'Is that OK?'

'Great. Just as long as I can get back home most days, so I can spend some time with Dad. He doesn't like being on his own.'

'What about your mother?'

'She's not around.'

Seeing the way his mouth closes over the words, I don't pry any further. But I feel ashamed as I watch him drive away in his father's truck. Although I've worked closely with Bob over the past few years, I've never asked him a single personal question.

I walk out to the water garden I've built to one side of the house, and sit down on a stone bench. People with gardens seldom give themselves time to sit and enjoy the beauty they have created, which is why I have benches placed at strategic points all over my grounds.

It's peacful here, specifically designed for contemplation. Fish, like slices of orange and lemon, slide between the water lilies. A dragonfly darts. I gaze into the pool and remember Luna's white hands, fluid as honey as she danced, the scent of jasmine, hot summer nights, the voices of men playing cards in another room, cicadas beating the air. I remember, too, white spires, the black mouth of an arched doorway, a dark interior full of candles. Was it in Córdoba? Mexico City? Florence? There were always men in black robes and white surplices, their faces sour. Sometimes, seeing them, Luna would turn away at the door into the church and walk hurriedly away. More usually, with our heads covered in lace, we watched the officiating priest in white-and-gold-embroidered robes conducting the Mass. When he held out his arms on either side of his body, his robes hung straight down, like a beautiful waterfall. There was a purple ring on his finger that kept catching the light. I wanted to ask Luna if this was the same priest we'd seen before, in another cathedral somewhere, or if it was just that this one was wearing the same kind of robes as the other. But she was always looking straight ahead, her hands pressed against her chest as though she were trying to staunch a wound. Her eyes were wet, and I didn't dare interrupt whatever it was she was thinking of.

Now, the sun beats down on my head while an aeroplane drones its way westward. Ever since Liz Crawfurd's visit I have been agitated. My certainties have been undermined. I should be happy or, if not happy, then at least content. So why do I feel only despair?

FOUR

What's the best word, wonders Fergus Costello, what's the *mot juste*? Would it be melancholia? Despondency? He walks away from the Notting Hill underground, the pavement hot under the soles of his shoes. What about malaise? Whatever it is, he's got it. And it isn't helped by the fact that even on a Sunday, London is noisy, dirty, heavy with traffic and litter. He thinks of the calm spaces he's experienced in the past few years: Australian bush, Canadian wilderness, a green courtyard in Spain.

He pushes past a gaggle of minimally clad teenage girls displaying concave stomachs and pierced belly buttons. Music blares from a door, the mindless oom-pah of the bass line thrumming along his bone marrow. A blast of rancid fat covers him in droplets of invisible grease as he passes a chippy offering battered sausages, samosas and spring rolls.

A big black guy, half-recognizing him, flashes a smile, teeth hanging like a line of laundry from the douche-red of his gums. 'Hey, wossup, man?' whirling past into the jumble of the crowded street. The Knight of the Dolorous Countenance, that's me, he thinks. Tilting at windmills in search of something long since vanished. Isn't it Sidney Smith who offers twenty-two recipes against melancholy? Sugar plums are in there, somewhere. Which reminds him. He stops at a newsagent to buy a box of chocolates – *'Sorry, dear, we're right out of sugar plums'* – for Caro's boys.

Turning into her hedge-lined white street, he thinks, *What's gone wrong? Here I am, thirty-eight, closing on thirty-nine. I have everything I set out to gain and yet, for two pins, I could crumble into the gutter and caterwaul, howl, ululate.*

Is it the next book, stuck somewhere in his subconscious and refusing to show itself? Is it the solitariness catching up with him?

55

Or is it Brendan, come back to haunt him after all these years, Brendan last seen with his blue-white skin lying flat on his bones, a pile of newspapers clotted and stained with human waste, his head resting, dear God, on a cushion that was putrid with snot and vomit, clammed with it, his hollow yellow face pressed into the stink of other men's breath? Brendan gone at last to the Land of Promise, and Father Vincent at the funeral, scrawny neck emerging from stiff white collar, floggings furnace-hot at the back of his eyes, *Well, Fergus, we did all right by yez, I'm thinking*, lips pulled back over wolfish teeth, and himself, hate and rage rising in him like pus, lungeing for the man's throat, screaming, *Bugger, sodomite, sadist, all fucking right?*

Ye're at the Oxford University, aren't yez, and wasn't it us who got ye there? Yes, Father, with your hands and your canes and your fleshy pricks – yes, you got me there with the Latin and the poetry, Synge and Yeats and the rest of the sodding Anglo-Irish fraternity, and the whimpers of little boys, the plump pillows of spread buttocks, the worm-shine of their tears. Yes, you got me there.

Ah, Jesus...

Adrenalin-pumped, he presses the bell beside the smartly painted navy-blue door. Will the anger ever leave him or has it scarred him for life, like someone who's drunk Drano and painfully survived the corrosion of his entrails?

'I'm growing old,' he says aloud as it opens to reveal Caro, long and elegant in designer jeans and a cropped white top.

'Rubbish.' She reaches up to kiss his cheek.

He smells her familiar scent. Sanity and *Miss Dior*. The same as it has always been, ever since she was the girl sharing the bedsit below his, years and years ago, a medical student intending to specialize in paediatrics. He'd loved her, back then, in a hopeless kind of way, knowing that she was already half engaged to Charlie Cartwright, and in any case the last thing he wanted was anything at all that suggested settling down, mortgages and careers, all the things Charlie had embraced with relish because it never occurred to him not to. So many evenings, the sea-taste of tears on his cheeks as he drooled out the squalor of his rearing, the death of his brother. She is the only one he has ever told. He's gone on loving her, in an intensely fraternal way, standing as best man at their wedding and then as godfather to Ricky, their first child.

'Still as beautiful as ever,' he says, stepping into the wide hall, handing over the bottle of champagne he's brought with him for the party. What would he have done if she'd ever responded to his muted advances? Run a mile. Run a marathon. Run to the flat edges of the world and dropped over, clung there by the very tips of his fingers until she'd gone away. 'What are you on, the elixir of youth? You never seem to change.'

'I wish I could say the same for you, Fergus.' She gives him a quick professional scan. 'You look terrible, if you want to know the truth.'

'Ignorance was bliss.'

'Did you get another dose of malaria in

Mexico?'

'Surprisingly, no.'

'Then what's wrong? And don't say nothing.'

He longs to lean against the mother-lode of her bosom and be soothed. 'Just a little matter of my next book, that's all. Getting into it. Finding the theme, the connections.' He laughs lightly, unconvincingly, hoping the airiness of his tone will disguise his fear. 'Maybe I'm all written out.'

'"*One of the most original voices of his generation*",' she quotes. 'I don't think so.'

He moves behind her into the big drawing room. The room has been knocked through so that one end looks on to the street while the other leads out to the garden, where he can see tables set up, umbrellas, a couple of people in white jackets bustling about, preparing for the party that is due to begin in a couple of hours. As Ricky's godfather, he's been invited early.

In the ordered room there are marble fireplaces, high ceilings, deep skirting boards, a sense of permanence. Things he's not before felt any urge for. Now, there's a scorpion-scrape at the base of his gut: *whatever it is, I want some, too.*

'Wine? Gin? Whisky?' she says.

'A glass of cold white wine would just touch the spot.'

'Which spot would that be, Fergus?' She hands him a glass and raises her own.

He touches his hand to the area above his heart. 'This one, maybe.'

'It's high time you found yourself a nice girl, a girl to keep. A girl to marry.'

58

'You know something, Caro, I'm beginning to agree with you. Not that I think of marriage as a cure for all ills.'

'Quite the opposite.' She's laughing. 'And talking of ills, the boys know you're coming and they're dying to see you.'

'And I them.' He pats the bag he's brought with him. 'Afraid I've got typical bachelor presents in here. Chocs, comic-books – and this rather gruesome drum from Columbia for my godson Ricky.'

'What's gruesome about it?'

'The guy who sold it to me said it was made of human skin.'

'Fergus!'

'He only told me after I'd paid for it. And in any case, it probably isn't true.'

Charlie comes into the room and stops. 'Aha!' he says. 'Fergus the Love Rat!'

Fergus groans. 'Not you too, *please*. I've had the press camped on my doorstep for days now – not that the houseboat has a doorstep.'

'Charlie, I told you not to mention it,' says Caro.

'But is it true?' Charlie is eager.

'Of course not. Do I look like a man who can get it up ten times a night?'

'I don't know.' Caro puts her head on one side.

'It's not the frequency which fascinates me,' Charlie says, 'so much as the woman you're alleged to have been shagging. Aristocratic landed gentry? Not at all the sort I'd expect you to go for.'

'She went for *me*,' insists Fergus. 'She fancies

herself as some kind of a writer and I was leading a course at one of those summer schools. I simply passed the time of day with the creature, and the next thing I know, she's in my bed, wearing something so flimsy you could have blown it off her with a sigh.'

'And did you?'

'What?'

'Sigh.'

'Actually, before I could even draw breath, she had her tongue down my ... Look, I really don't want to go into this. All I can say is, don't believe anything you see in the newspapers. If anything, I'm the victim here, not her.'

'Is it true the husband came after you with a shotgun?'

'He threw a glass of wine over me at a book launch, if that's what you mean.'

'And now two other women have come forward to say what a heartless beast you are,' Carolyn says.

'Axe-grinders, the pair of them. One's a novelist who didn't like what I wrote about her latest book, and the other is a well-known self-publicist.'

'So not an atom of truth in their allegations of hanky-panky,' says Charlie.

'An atom, maybe. No more than that. Look, can we change the subject?' Fergus looks round.

'Come into the kitchen.'

Ah God, that kitchen. Cream-coloured Aga, Welsh dresser crowded with pretty pieces of china, double sink, magnet-cutesy fridge door covered with kiddy-art. Something to aspire to,

60

or something to shun? Fergus the Aganaut. A terrible beauty...

'Charles, don't you think Fergus is looking a bit seedy?' Carolyn asks.

Charlie, busy with bottles, blundering round the kitchen like a balding bear, considers his friend. 'I've certainly seen him look better.'

'Something must be done,' says his wife.

Charlie sighs. 'What kind of a something do we have to do?'

'Fergus here needs a stabilizing influence. We have to marry him off. For his own sake as much as for all those betrayed women,' Carolyn says, the bit between her teeth, his future assured in her capable hands. 'I mean, just look at him.'

Fergus lifts his shoulders. 'I'm probably constipated.'

'Constipation of the heart rather than the bowels, if you ask me,' Carolyn says.

'Wouldn't it be easier to prescribe me a paregoric or send me on a nice bracing visit to the seaside? Getting married seems a little drastic.'

'Drastic measures are what's called for.'

'Got someone in mind, Caro?' asks Charlie, filling three glasses and handing them round.

'I was thinking that there might be someone coming this afternoon who would be just right for him.'

'Who?'

'I don't know, but...'

'Why should there be?' asks Fergus. 'How easy is it for two totally random entities to meet in the right place at the right time?'

'Isn't that a definition of falling in love?'

'Man exists in an eternity of single atoms spinning out of the void and eventually disappearing back into it. There's no guarantee he'll ever connect to any of the other similarly spinning atoms around him.'

'Maybe today you'll get lucky and bump into another atom.' Carolyn leans forward with a brilliant smile. *'I* know! Theo Cairns!'

'Theo? The anal retentive?' says Charlie.

'If you wish to be so insensitive about someone who's practically family, well, yes.'

Charlie pulls a face. 'You know I love her dearly. She's like my second sister. But you've got to admit she's kind of –' He waves his hands in the air as though hoping the right word will fly into them – *'edgy*. Would I wish her on my friend Fergus, the freest spirit of them all?'

'She might be exactly what he needs.'

'You could be right,' Charlie says thoughtfully. 'Trouble is, she's carrying an awful lot of baggage.'

'Aren't we all?'

'Well, no, actually. Not us. Your family, my family? Not a lot of baggage there – unless you mean the expensive Louis Vuitton kind.'

'Fergus's got baggage, too.'

'That's what I mean. Between him and Theo, there's so much baggage they'd never be able to lift it off the ground.'

'Hell-*oh*-o.' Fergus taps the side of his glass. 'Anyone home?'

The two of them stare at him as though they're not sure who he is. 'What?'

'First of all, who says I need a stabilizing influence?'

'I do.' Carolyn reaches up and adjusts the complicated mechanism holding her smooth blonde hair in its French twist.

'Secondly,' says Fergus, 'over the many delightful years that I've been privileged to enjoy your friendship, you have placed before me a pot-pourri, a farrago, a veritable gallimaufry of girls so totally undesirable that a weaker man than myself might have been driven to the brink of suicide.'

'Nonsense,' Charlie says. 'What about—'

Fergus interrupts him with a raised hand. 'And thirdly, can I state categorically that despite disastrous appearances to the contrary, I am more than capable of finding my own women friends.' He looks from husband to wife. 'When you speak of Theo, do you mean that friend of Jenny's who I met here at one of your parties several years ago?'

'That's right.'

'When I say she's uptight, don't get me wrong,' Charlie says. 'She's a very ... interesting woman.'

'Exactly,' says Caro. 'Fergus needs someone intelligent, complex, feisty. Theo's all of those. And pretty, besides.'

'But is she really what he's looking for?'

Fergus leans back against the dresser. In the distance they hear the sound of little boys thundering down the stairs, calling his name. 'How the fuck do either of you know what I'm looking for?'

'Because I know *so* much better than you do who's right for you,' says Charlie. 'And because I'm a psychologist.'

'And because we love you,' adds Caro, sweetly.

'I really appreciate your concern, but I'll select my own mate, if you don't mind.'

'Be like that.' Carolyn smiles at him as her sons burst into the room.

Later, when he is left alone while Caro and Charlie occupy themselves with last-minute preparations for their lunch party, he finds himself thinking about the once-met Theodora Cairns. She had dimples, if he remembers correctly. And extraordinary eyes, the colour of pewter or of deep-packed ice, the colour of smoke, with the blackest eyelashes. Eyes that yearned. Eyes that begged not to be rejected. Smoke gets in your eyes. Makes you weep. Baggage, Charlie said. He dimly remembers something about the mother – a singer? A dancer? – who'd abandoned her when she was a child.

He walks out into the garden. White-clothed tables laden with glasses and open bottles wait beneath a leafy walnut tree. Something is being barbecued. Caro's garden gleams green and gold. Has she thwacked the nail on the head? Is that what's wrong, is it time he settled down? Trouble is, he hasn't yet found the elusive Ms Right, even though he knows that the woman he hopes for does exist somewhere, she *must* exist, even if it's on another planet, in another country, a different century, an alternative life. So where is she, why is she not banging on his door? He's

64

thirty-nine and so far has never met a woman he could imagine in his future. And what are the chances of colliding with her at Caro Cartwright's luncheon party?

He pours himself another glass of wine. Remembers the unforgettable vacation he'd spent in Corfu years ago with Charlie, at the Cartwright family's villa. Part of an unforgettable year. His first book published. Money, for the first time in his life. Freedom. A loosening of the chains which bound him to Dublin. Knowing that he had finally kissed the past goodbye. Or so he hoped.

Every day he'd got up at five and worked until the household came to life. He'd written there, fingers flying across the keys of the typewriter he'd carted out from England, desperate to keep up with the glossy thoughts oozing from him like some rich oil. Corfu had pulled the words out of him, unrolled them like scarves, like banners, thick as paint impasto'ed on to the page. His limbs hung loosely from his body, his hair shone, he grew two, four, six feet in the short time he was there.

The days rolled into each other. After breakfast, he and Charlie would swim, or take a boat out to rock on the motionless water and look down at the ribbed sea-sand below. They climbed the rocky iris-scattered hills behind the house, carrying olives and figs, coarse bread, bunches of yellow grapes. Sheep bells plunked among the rocks. Eagles soared above the crags, while the sunshine soaked through the top of his skull and trickled down into the hollows and interstices of his bones. As dusk fell, sea and sky merged and became a single velvety black.

Occasionally he'd left the others and gone in to light a candle, remembrance of things long past, thank God, sniff the familiar smells of incense and damp, kneel for a moment and let himself be transported into anonymity. When Charlie left to meet up with Carolyn in St Jean de Luz, Fergus stayed on. The heat grew. Albania shimmered on the horizon; at night they could see firelight on the hills across the water. Max Cartwright, Charlie's father, took him out in a boat one night and they fished by the light of an oil lamp, watched the octopuses squeezing themselves through the translucent water, like beating hearts, or drifted through the night-black ocean, trailing green fire from their fingertips. Iris and asphodel springing from the bare earth, the crippled mandolinist under a tree with a voice like a bird and everywhere, the sharp smell of salt and sage.

By now, thinks Fergus, the island has probably turned into some Blackpooled nightmare of beer bellies and chips, heavy metal thumping from café doorways, karaoke bars and fake Oirish pubs, hideous apartment buildings backing up the hillsides, Corfu concretized.

The doorbell rings. He hears the high, excited voices of people prepared to enjoy themselves. Anticipation sparks through his blood. Maybe, this time, Caro and Charlie will be right and this Theo Cairns will have transmuted into the woman he desires in his dreams. What he would never have admitted to either of them is the extent of the isolation he feels, the increasing

66

difficulty he has in pretending to both himself and to others that he enjoys the solitary life. His simple lack of happiness.

If he could only recapture the effortless creativity he'd known back then in Corfu. Perhaps the possibility of going back was worth looking into. If nothing else, it would get him out of London, away from the bastards of the press, the sniggers. Wherever he went, he'd carry the ghost of Brendan with him, of course, but maybe he'd finally be able to bury him there, by the citron sea. And he might find that he could write again with the same passion and intensity he'd written that summer.

'Yes,' he says now, aloud, under the walnut tree as the doorbell rings again, drawing in a breath, preparing to be sociable, to meet the knowing glances and whispered asides of those who read the tabloids. 'I should go back.'

FIVE

'You don't remember me, do you?'

He's right. In fact, I've never seen him before in my life. Or have I? Now I look more closely, he is definitely familiar in a distanced kind of way. More than familiar. Is he someone famous? Was he on – God no, surely I'd remember! – one of those TV gardening programmes with me?

'Uh ... of course I do.'

67

'Caro told me you would be here,' he continues.

I suddenly realize what this is: a clumsy Cartwright attempt to get me off with some totally unsuitable no-hoper. Though, to be fair, as no-hopers go, this one isn't bad looking. 'Ah,' I say, still trawling my memory.

'I've been looking forward to seeing you again.'

Again? Where did we meet before? I register an Irish accent, one eyebrow slightly higher than the other, blue eyes that tilt at the corners, and a shock of hair even darker than my own, albeit flecked with white. He's what, middle thirties? Is he an actor, a TV person? Have I read about him somewhere?

'So,' he continues, 'I'm disappointed that you obviously have no recollection of me.'

'Uh...'

The higher of his eyebrows flutters briefly. 'I'm Fergus—'

'Fergus Costello!' I say. 'Of *course* I remember you.' Though in truth, I have no more than a trace memory of him standing here, under this same walnut tree. And then I remember reading about him in the papers. Fergus Costello. It's not a common name; I should have made the connection between the cheating lover and the man I'd met years ago. I can't recall the exact details, but they involved other men's wives, country estates, lurid tales of his sexual prowess. Ten times a night, that had certainly been mentioned. Maybe it's just juicy silly-season scandal, but it still makes him either mad, bad or dangerous.

68

Just the sort of thing I'm *really* looking for. I step back, eyeing the crowd for someone a bit less of all three.

I see Max and Terry Cartwright over by the lily-pond. 'I must go and say hello to Jenny's parents. It's been really nice to meet you again, Fergus. Maybe one of these days we can...' I smile, give him a little wave and move off.

'Theo!' Terry inclines her cheek for my kiss. 'How lovely to see you.'

'And you, darling Terry.'

'You're looking much too thin, honey. Are you all right?'

'Of course. Are *you*?'

'I guess so.' Her cheerful face droops for a moment. Earlier in the year, her mother had died, loved and missed by all. 'I've just got up the courage to start clearing out Nancy's closets, and if you know anyone who takes size-three shoes, I'd be happy to pass them on.'

Nancy Halloran was Surrey's answer to Imelda Marcos, owner of a custom-built shoe-closet that held up to four hundred pairs at any one time.

I look down at my own size sixes. 'Can't help, I'm afraid.'

'I can't bear to throw out all those lovely hand-made shoes.'

'If I hear of any shoeless midgets, I'll be sure to let them know.'

Terry and Max are – *were*, when I needed such things – my guardians, appointed by my mother when she sent me off to boarding school. Terry had been her closest friend since their own child-hood in Canterbury. I love the Cartwrights as though they were my own parents which, in many respects, they are.

'How was your trip?' Max asks.

'Great. Very successful.'

'You've done really well,' he says. 'Getting the business off the ground the way you have.'

'There's still a long way to go,' I say.

'Your mother's so proud of you,' Terry puts in. 'She phoned last week. She's in Sweden at the moment.'

'I know. Someone sent me an invitation.'

'I expect you'll get together when she's in London next week.'

'Mmm,' I say.

'I tried to get her to come down and stay with us, but she says she prefers to be in a hotel.' Terry turns to Max. 'What's the name of that funny little place she likes on the Edgware Road?'

'Can't remember – some name that sounds like a Chinese takeaway.'

'Lotus Flower Hotel, that's right.'

I nod, hoping they don't realize that I haven't heard about this visit.

'We'll miss her, anyway,' Max says. 'We're off to Corfu for a couple of weeks.'

I smile at them both. 'You lucky things.'

'Why don't you join us, darling?' says Terry. 'There's plenty of room. And you look as though you could do with a holiday.'

'I'm far too busy,' I say, though right now, the thought of a few days in the sun, doing absolutely nothing, is incredibly tempting.

Irritatingly, Fergus Costello appears at my side

again, and the Cartwrights move off elsewhere with what seems to be over-elaborate tact.

'That's what you call a truly happy union,' he says, watching as they join Charlie and Caro. 'You look at those two and you understand what it's all supposed to be about.' His eyes slide up my face. 'Are you married, Theodora?'

'I was, but it didn't work out.'

'Why not?'

'All sorts of reasons,' I say lightly. I have to admit that sometimes I think of Harvey with regret. His reasons for wanting to get married might have been the wrong ones, but so were mine. We lasted five years before we split up; they weren't unhappy years, just rather meaningless.

'So why did you choose him in the first place?'

'He's twenty years older than I am. He offered me safety and I took it.'

'What did you offer him?'

I shrug. 'Who knows what these bargains entail?'

'Is that how you see marriage? As a bargain?'

'Isn't it? In return for security, he got a young body in bed. A dutiful hostess. A chatelaine to take care of his home. Which, let me say, I enjoyed doing.'

'So why did you split up?'

'In the end, it came down to the chains,' I say, to my own surprise. I'm not in the habit of talking so freely to virtual strangers.

'Chains? Do you mean real, or symbolic?'

'Both. Every birthday, every Christmas, Harvey gave me another chain. Solid. Beautiful.

Expensive. Red gold, yellow gold, rose gold. I started to feel as though they were a slave collar, like a badge of servitude.'

'Pretty classy servitude.'

'Servitude, all the same.' On my twenty-sixth birthday, seeing the by-now-familiar shape of the package beside my plate, I'd panicked. I have nothing against gold, but I prefer it in ingots, stashed in a bank vault, rather than hanging down between my boobs. As I picked up the package and began to tear off the wrapping, I had an absolutely clear image of myself ten, fifteen, twenty years down the line, shoulders bowed, forehead scraping the ground from the accumulated weight of all the chains I'd been loaded with. 'It was the way he looked at me when I put the last chain round my neck. Exactly the same as when he bought a new car or a new tie. I realized that as far as he was concerned, I was just another chattel. Another asset.'

'So what happened?'

'A week later I left him. It was all very amicable.'

'Where is he now?'

'Happily remarried, with a clutch of babies puking all over his Savile Row tailoring.'

'And you have no regrets?'

'Very rarely. What about you?'

'I've been in a couple of long-term relationships but nothing serious.' He looks at me quizzically and I know he's wondering if I've read about him in the papers.

I pretend I haven't. 'Does it worry you, still being single?'

'A little. No, actually, that's not true. I'm heading towards forty, and it worries me a lot. If I'm not careful, I'll end up as a crusty old bachelor. Trouble is, I'm too much of a wanderer. I never stay in one place very long – I just have to hope that one day I'll meet someone who doesn't mind.'

'It won't be me,' I say, before I can stop myself. 'I had enough of thc gypsy life when I was a child. I never really acquired the taste for it.'

'Your father was in the services, was he?'

'Erm ... yes. Do you have a base somewhere?'

'A houseboat in Chelsea.'

'Very suitable.' A houseboat is not exactly a high-powered motor boat, but there's still a sense of impermanence about it.

'I suppose even my home reflects my restlessness,' Fergus says, as though reading my mind.

'Always ready for a quick getaway, right?'

'Right.' He lifts his glass to the light and looks through it. 'How would you describe that gorgeous colour?'

'Crimson? Ruby?'

'Vermilion. Garnet. I never understand why they talk about the blood-red wine. *The King sits in Dumfernline toun, drinking the bluid-red wine* ... even in Scotland, one of the great non-wine-growing regions of the world, it can't have been anything like the colour of blood.'

'Mulberry,' I said.

'Mulberry is good.' He smiles at me. 'Yes, I'm still single because, in my experience, women don't like being on the move all the time, they prefer to settle down in one place.'

73

'I'm like that.'

'How did I guess?'

I ignore that. 'Are you working on a book at the moment?'

'Naturally. That's what I do. At least...' He rubs at his cheek. 'I'm *trying* to work on a book. This one's proving difficult to get down to.'

'What's it about?'

'Everything. Nothing. Life.' He hesitates. 'I just got back from Mexico. I'm interested in a painter called Lennart Wells. Ever heard of him?'

I shake my head.

'Some years ago Wells walked out of his house and vanished into the Mexican jungle. Every now and then one of his paintings appears on the market but nobody ever sees him. I thought it might be fun to try and track him down, see if he would talk to me, tell me why he literally got away from it all. It sounds like a story I could work with.'

'Didn't Somerset Maugham already write that one?'

The Moon and Sixpence, yeah. But I'd be approaching it from a different perspective. It could be good. But it's still very nebulous.'

'Is it difficult, being a writer?'

'A lot of the time. But when it works, it's the biggest buzz in the world.'

'It must be hard to think of new plots.'

'They say there are no new stories, only new ways of telling them. That's what I like about the job. Putting words together and ending up with a story.' A sudden glow of enthusiasm shines in his

74

eyes. 'Ever appreciated how fortunate we are to live in a world so crammed with words, where everything, *everything*, has a name? Everything. And not just one name but many, alternate names, names in every language, hundreds and thousands of them, millions?'

'Once you've named something, I guess that kind of ties it down.'

'That's exactly right.' He moves closer. 'Did you know that the English language, as spoken in the British Isles, contains more than half a million words?'

'I didn't.'

'But you know about writing yourself,' he says. 'I've got copies of your books. I especially liked the one about container gardens. That's the sort of gardening I'd enjoy.'

A woman who's been eyeing us for some time now comes over. 'You're Theo Cairns, aren't you?'

'Yes. And this is Fergus Costello.'

'Ah.' She tries to remember why she knows the name and then gives up on it. 'Forgive me interrupting, but I saw one of your miniature gardens recently and thought it was absolutely exquisite. I loved the little pagoda. And the musicians – *so* adorable!'

'They're great, aren't they?'

'I was at a banquet at the Guildhall recently,' she goes on. 'The tabletops you did there were absolutely stunning.'

'Well...' I spread my hands deprecatingly. 'Thank you. Thank you very much.'

She leaves and Fergus leans into me. 'The

price of celebrity is eternal prominence,' he says.

I can't resist. 'It's the other way round in your case, isn't it?'

It's a weak witticism, but he laughs ruefully. 'It can't be true, it was in the papers.'

I dredge up further information from my memory. In addition to his exploits in the boudoir, he's also something of a literary firebrand. Writes columns for the heavyweight Sundays. He's a Booker-prize commentator who can always be relied on to produce a controversial point of view. Is often on television arts programmes, not that I ever have time to watch, or I might have made the connections sooner. Over his shoulder, I can see Carolyn watching us with a little smile on her face.

'*Carpe diem*, that's my motto,' Fergus says, draining his glass.

'I have no problem seizing the day,' I say, 'as long as I know what's happening the day after.'

'How can anyone expect to know that?'

'If you organize yourself well enough, you ought to be able to, to a large extent.'

'You can't possibly believe such a thing.'

'Why not?'

'Even assuming that you'll never be caught up in accident or chance, you'd lose all the excitement of wondering what's going to happen next.'

'I don't like nasty surprises.'

'What about nice ones?'

'I don't like them either.'

'No leaps in the dark, Theodora? No acting on impulse, running after rainbows? Just safety,

76

security?'

'What lovely words those are.'

'I suspect you don't allow yourself to enjoy things.' He looks down at me. 'I'd much rather go on talking to you,' he says. 'But Caro will never forgive me if I don't mingle.'

After he's gone, Charlie materializes. 'Are you well, Theo?' he asks. 'You look as though you're not getting enough sleep.'

'Pressure of work.'

'Maybe you should slow down.'

'One of these days, I may be able to afford to, but I haven't got there yet.'

'How much money does one need to make one happy?'

'A lot more than I've got.' I don't think about happiness, only about security, though in my case, they're the same thing. 'It's a lovely party, Charlie.'

'Glad you're enjoying it. Uh ... how're you getting along with Fergus?'

'Charles,' I say, 'you're a wonderful father, a top-notch psychiatrist and an all-round super human being but you don't do nonchalant very well. Is this what I think it is?'

'Depends what you think it is.'

'A heavy-handed attempt to get uptight Theo together with free-spirited Fergus?'

His kind face goes red. 'Absolutely not,' he blusters. 'I didn't say anything like that.'

'But close enough, I bet. Darling Charlie, it's sweet of you and Caro to care, but he's not my type.'

Charlie goes off to fill more glasses and I

move about, too, exchanging news with people I've known – thanks to the Cartwrights – for more than half my life.

The spicy scent of the pinks in Caro's flower-beds is intoxicating. Bending down to brush a finger against the serrated petals, I close my eyes and breathe in deeply. Delicious. When I straighten up and turn back into the party, Fergus Costello is there. For a still moment, we look at each other. I have the impression that I am standing on the edge of an abyss. I am somewhere I cannot afford to be. I take a deep breath.

He seizes both my hands. 'Come to Corfu with me.'

'What?'

'Corfu ... I'm thinking of going back there.'

'To the Cartwrights' place, do you mean?'

'No, somewhere else. I don't yet know where. Why don't you come with me?'

'You don't even know me.'

'I know enough.'

'I don't know you,' I say, though for a minute, I am almost persuaded. Then I remember the newspaper scandal. 'I bet you say that to all the girls,' I say.

He ignores the feeble remark. 'Come with me.'

How tempting it is to think of taking a break. 'I don't do spontaneous,' I say. 'When are you going?'

'I haven't fixed it up yet – but if you'd agree to join me, I'd organize it straight away.' He moves closer. 'Will you come?'

I laugh. The idea is insane. 'Are you on drugs or something? Of course I won't.'

78

'Why not?'

'I have work to do. A business to run.' I take another deep breath. 'I can't just take off.'

'Don't decide now,' he says. 'I'll call you.'

'I won't change my mind.' I recall the pictures in the papers, the sexy mouth and revealing cotton T-shirt of the woman he's supposed to have been two-timing. 'But thank you *very* much for asking.'

He raises his eyebrow, gives a little shrug, turns away.

What I'd like to do is run after him, grab his arm, tell him that wherever he's going, I'll come along. But I think of my mother, of our footloose lifestyle, the way I felt every time I found our suitcases lying open on the floor, signalling that we were off again. I think of my house, my gardens, my strong roots.

Then Jenny takes my elbow. She looks at me, eyes glowing, teeth gleaming, hair shining with good health and joy. If anyone ever wants a poster-girl for happiness, Jenny's the one. When we were younger I used to imagine that if I touched her skin, the tip of my finger would gleam, as though the gold dust of her well-being would rub off on me.

'Jeez,' she says. 'You look terrible, Theo.'

'So I needn't have bothered having my hair done and spending a fortune on a new dress.'

'I didn't mean that. And I love the hair. But look at the shadows under your eyes. And you're as thin as a pin. What on earth are you doing to yourself?'

'Overworking. Undersleeping.'

'Surely you don't need to work so hard.' Her placid brow wrinkles. 'You should take a holiday.'

'I know, but I can't afford the time right now.'

'Money isn't everything, Theo.'

'Did I ever say it was?'

'No. But why else are you pushing yourself like this?'

Given her secure upbringing, her happy family background, it's not something I could ever explain to her, even though from time to time I've tried. I put my hand on the small mound of her stomach. 'How's Laura coming along?'

'Fine. Everything's just fine.' Her face grows suspiciously bland. 'Uh ... what did you think of Fergus Costello?'

'Not you, too.'

'How do you mean?'

'Charlie's more or less admitted there's some kind of Cartwright conspiracy to get Fergus Costello and me together.'

'You're being paranoid.' She laughs. 'So ... what *did* you think?'

'Nice bloke.'

'Is that all?'

'What more do you want?'

'As soon as he walked in, I thought Aha! This guy is just Theo's type. Or, rather, exactly *not* her type, which *makes* him her type, if you see what I mean.'

'If I tie a cold cloth round my head, it might start making sense.'

'He seems really nice, Theo.'

'I'm sure he is. As long as you don't read the

tabloids.'

'Tabloids?'

I gather that she doesn't, and give her a quick run-down.

'Ten times ... Are you sure?' she gasps.

'Of course not. But there's no smoke without fire, as they say. So definitely *not* my type.' I feel like Judas, saying this. But I'm not about to get involved with a gypsy. Let alone a love-rat.

Jenny steps back, looks at me with her head on one side. Sweet Jenny. My dearest friend since we'd first met. My almost-sister. Everything that I am not: grounded, settled. Happy. 'Oh, Theo darling. I just wish you could be as happy as I am.'

'Who says I'm not?'

'I *know* you're not.'

She's quite wrong. Apart from the sense of emotional disruption that Liz Crawfurd has brought into my life, I am perfectly happy. Perfectly.

SIX

The morning after Caro Cartwright's party, I lie in bed, staring at the ceiling. I've scarcely slept. Cars start up as people set off for work. A tractor is already coughing and bucking in the fields behind the house. Birds are chirping away outside in the garden. I picture them in my orchard, clinging to the branches of fruit trees already swelling with harvest. Green apples, golden pears. The dusty purple of plums. Crab apples as colourful as parakeets. Nancy Halloran, formerly of Boston and Cape Cod, sometimes used to commandeer the Cartwrights' kitchen and line us children up in aprons, to help her make jelly from their fruit, like the distilled essence of rose petals.

Footloose Fergus Costello is caught in the crevices of my brain.

The telephone bleeps and I pick it up. 'Hello?'

'Was that a great party or what?' Jenny says enthusiastically.

'Mmm.'

'Hello?' Jenny says.

'I'm still here.'

'What's with this "mmm" stuff,' she demands. 'Is something wrong?'

'Nothing whatsoever.'

'I loved your dress yesterday – Chloé, was it? Silk chiffon ... heavenly.'

'You said I looked terrible.'

'You know I didn't mean it. Not terrible in that sense. You just looked ... well, terrible.'

'You're far too kind.'

'You promise it's not a man?'

'No more than usual.'

'Nothing to do with the gorgeous Costello, is it?' Her voice is expectant, as though she hopes for girlish gushings on my part.

'I barely spoke to the man.' I'm not going to tell her about the invitation to join him in Corfu because she'd immediately start lobbying for me to go. As if he'd even meant it.

'OK, if it's not love that's making you look so run-down, then either you're heading for a nervous breakdown, or you're working too hard, or both. Why don't you take a break, go away and veg out for a week or two?'

'If only,' I say.

'Come on, Theo. You know your nice Marnie can manage perfectly well without you for a bit. All she has to do is ring round and tell your clients that you're taking a vacation.'

'Except this is my busiest time of year. I can't afford to take time off.'

'Of course you can.' Jenny speaks with the certainty of one who has never been poor, who has never had to steal a loaf of bread in order to feed herself and her mother, who's never learned to shoplift in the full knowledge that if she doesn't she will go naked or dirty. I am determined never to be anywhere near that situation again. 'You could come and stay here. You know how much we'd love to have you. Not to mention your little god-daughter-to-be.'

'I'm not very good company right now.' I'm quiet for a moment. Without really meaning to, I say, 'Jen, I'm afraid.'

'What of?'

'Cracking up. Falling apart.'

'Maybe it's about time you did. Actually acknowledged for once that all is not entirely well with Superwoman Cairns.'

'Is it that obvious?'

'Only for the past twenty years or so.'

'I hate feeling so ... *flimsy*.'

'Oh, Theo,' Jenny says softly. 'I know things aren't right with you. Is it to do with your mother?'

'I doubt it. I came to terms with all that, years ago.'

'I wish I could give you a magic kiss and make it all better, the way I do with the little boys.'

'So do I.'

'Ever thought of talking to someone about it? Professionally, I mean?'

'No.'

'Perhaps you should.'

'Perhaps I will.'

I put the phone down on Jenny's snort of disbelief then struggle out of bed. After a shower, I feel almost normal again – whatever normal is – apart from the black weight of depression hanging a foot above my head.

By the time I get home from the school project the following Tuesday afternoon, I am bone-weary. It has been a long day and I am ready for a shower and the chance to put my feet up. I'm not, therefore, thrilled to find a dark-blue four-wheel drive parked on the gravel in front of the house and a man in a Tattersall checked shirt and yellow cords leaning against it, smoking. He must be fifteen or twenty years older than I am, and very much a type: solid, ruddily handsome, the sort of upper-middle-class Englishman who takes it for granted that he will always get whatever he wants. After my years with Harvey, I recognize the breed.

As I get out of my car, he tosses his cigarette, still burning, into one of the blue ceramic pots beside the front door. Outraged, I glare first at the thin stream of blue smoke rising between the leaves of the white agapanthus which I planted in the spring, and then at him.

'Sorry,' he says, not in the least apologetic. He picks up the fag end and stubs it out against the side of the pot. About to drop it on the gravel, he sees my expression and instead tosses it over the hedge into the lane. I can tell we are never going to become friends.

'What can I do for you?' I ask in my most offputting voice.

'I'm James Bellamy.' He holds out a big hand, which I don't take. 'And you're Theo Cairns. I've seen you on the television.'

'Right.' Two appearances on a darned gardening quiz show and I'm a national celebrity.

'I'm a friend of Liz Crawfurd's.' Bellamy sounds as though he considers this more than enough reason for his presence on my property.

'So?' The front of my designer T-shirt is filthy, and my thumb still throbs from a misplaced hammer-blow delivered by an overeager young carpenter from Woodwork B. I am not inclined to be gracious.

'She tells me you own a Vernon Barnes.'

'Apparently so.'

'She also says it's one which would be of particular interest to me.'

What's the matter with these people? 'Did she also tell you that it's not for sale?'

Bellamy glances at the front door as though waiting for me to open it and invite him in. When I make no move, he looks a little less certain of himself. 'I ... uh ... could I see it?'

'I repeat: it's not for sale.'

'Miss Cairns. Let me show you something.' He walks over to his vehicle and raises the back. Easing forward a rectangular shape carefully wrapped in a horse blanket, he lays it on the flat bed of the boot and pulls back the woollen folds which protect it. Unwillingly, I go and stand beside him. Lying there is another painting. I recognize at once the reason why Liz Crawfurd has alerted him to mine.

'What do you think?' he says.

What do I think? I think I want him to leave, right now. I think I am about to learn something I do not want to know. I also think that simply dismissing this man, simply walking away from him and into my house, closing the door behind me, is not going to change any of that.

'You'd better come in,' I say.

Carrying his painting, he follows me through the door, ducking his head under the low lintel, and into the sitting room. As soon as he looks up at the wall and sees my own portrait, he stops.

'Oh my God,' he says. 'At last.'

I do not want to know what he means. I do not want any of the distress which already I sense is piling up.

'Would you like a drink?' I make the offer, not out of hospitality but because I myself need something short and strong.

'Nice idea.' He props his canvas carefully on the cushions of the armchair so that it rests against the back. 'Whisky, if you've got it.'

I pour him one, the blended stuff and another,

slightly larger and single malt, for myself. I'm not going to waste expensive whisky on a man who smokes. Both holding glasses, we stand side by side and look from one painting to another.

His shows the same parterred garden as mine does, the same girl in the pale dress with the straw hat, the same obelisks, the same white bench. There's a house of ivied stone, blank windows, a roof of lichened tiles. At one of the tall second-floor windows, is the image of a man in white.

The difference is that Bellamy's picture is painted at ground level, with a full portrait of the woman who sits in the foreground, gazing up at the windows. As I do, in my dreams.

'Of course,' Bellamy says, 'at the time this was commissioned, there was no garden there. Outside that window now is lawn and herbaceous borders, no hedges or parterres.'

'So why did Barnes paint that particular garden?' I'm puzzled.

'He was given free rein to fill in the background as he pleased, as long as there was *some* kind of garden there. I guess he just made one up. Or picked something he'd seen somewhere.'

'And the woman is...?'

'That's Connie.' Bellamy points to a little gold plaque set at the bottom of the frame. Black-painted script reads, ***Connie In Her Garden, 1968***.

'Yours and mine are obviously meant to go together,' I say unwillingly.

'Exactly.' Bellamy lifts his whisky tumbler to

his mouth. 'I can't tell you what it means to me to find this. We had no idea what had happened to it.'

'Who's Connie?'

'My mother.' He sips more of his drink, his eyes still on me. 'The Honourable Maud Constance Bellamy. The person who originally commissioned the two portraits.'

I know the name, though for the moment I can't think why. A fine tremble has started up somewhere as the base of my throat. I can feel my entire life poised as though at the edge of a cliff, ready to tumble into the raging seas below.

'Strange,' I say. I clear my throat. 'I wonder what the connection between the two of them was. The man and the woman, that is.'

He stares at me as though I've said something incomprehensible. 'Rather obvious, I would have thought.'

'I don't see why.' Nor do I want to.

'The house is clearly the Grange – Shepcombe Grange, where we live. As I said, the woman is my mother. And the man is—'

'John Vincent Cairns,' I say loudly. *Shepcombe Grange* – I know the name almost as well as my own. Constance Bellamy is a distinguished professional gardener.

'Liz said you had some strange notion about the identity of the painting.' Bellamy laughs, not unkindly. 'I'm afraid it's not your father, Miss Cairns. And I ought to know.'

'Why?'

'Because...'

He nods at the picture. 'That's Captain Thomas

Bellamy, Baronet. *My* father.'

They say that at moments of extreme stress, you can feel the turn of the globe, the earth moving beneath your feet. I certainly do. Not just moving, but splintering apart. I want to scream at this man who has come into my house and taken away something I have treasured most of my life. I want to yell that he is mistaken. And yet I know instinctively that he is not, if only because of the unmistakable likeness between the two faces, one painted, one a physical entity in front of me.

'No,' I say faintly. 'Not your father. *Mine.*'

'Look ... this is obviously a bit of a shock.'

'You could say that.' Tremors have broken out all over my body, fluttering like feathers under my skin. My lungs are seizing up. I bend from the waist, draw in gulps of air, try to catch my breath.

'I'm sorry if this has been a surprise.' Bellamy takes my arm and leads me over to a chair. He pulls up another one and sits down, facing me. 'Perhaps I should explain. I mean, even if he *was* your father, which he couldn't be – he certainly wasn't called Cairns.'

From here I can see what I've never noticed before: the mark on the gilt frame of my painting where the plaque has been removed. Who removed it and what was once inscribed there? *Tommy at His Window, 1968*, perhaps? A flap of profound grief is ripping away from my heart, leaving it raw and wounded. 'My mother said he was. Why would she lie to me?' I demand.

'I ought to explain.' Bellamy has risen to his

89

feet and is pacing about. 'My father was ... well, he was an alcoholic.' He looks at the tumbler in his hand and sets it down on the nearest surface. 'And a gambler. The races, the betting shops, Las Vegas, Monte Carlo, Aspinall's ... In those days, drugs weren't as easily available or he'd have been on those as well. My mother tried to help him, sent him to dry out at various clinics, enrolled him in AA programmes, that sort of thing. It was hopeless. Even as a boy I could have told her that. He didn't want to be helped. He was in love with his own addictions. He didn't want to lose them because then what would he do? If he ever took a long hard look at himself, he might have disliked what he saw as much as ... as much as we did.'

'We?'

'My sister and I.'

I nod, not knowing what to say.

'I suppose,' he goes on, 'that if he was going to go to hell in a handbasket, he wanted it to be a handbasket of his own choosing.'

I stare up at the portrait on my wall. So he isn't about to follow some virile pursuit after all. He is off to the gaming tables or the drinking club, the racecourse or the gambling den. That brooding gaze is not the Byronic enigma I've always believed it to be, but the addict's itch for his craving.

'He had the social cachet, you see,' Bellamy is saying. 'The name, the breeding. The place in society. All she had was the money.' He too looks up at the painting. 'We never realized when we were children how much he sneered at her. Despised her. It wasn't until we were older that it all made sense.' He turns to me. 'It's almost a cliché, isn't it? The American heiress brought in to shore up the crumbling fortunes of the English aristocracy. Extremely minor, in our case. She fell head over heels in love with him – God knows why. In return for his title—'

'And him,' I put in. He might no longer be my father, he might be a complete stranger to me. Nonetheless, I still feel protective of him.

'She paid for the restoration of the house. Laid down the gardens. Dealt with the bills. My father was far too much of a gentleman to actually work for a living.' Another contemptuous curl of the lip. 'Poor Connie; it wasn't for years that she realized he'd only married her for her money.'

I've looked at the woman sitting in her garden so many times over the years and never really wondered who she is. I've never seen her as belonging there, have assumed she is simply a shape to set off the formality of the garden. I've noted her hands – gardener's hands, like mine – holding the edge of her broad straw hat. Long ago I'd identified the splash of red lying beside her on the bench as the red-handled trowel she's obviously laid down in order to sit for the painter. To me, she was not important. It was the man who mattered.

Bellamy seems to be losing the thread of his story. 'So where did my painting come from?' I ask.

'She commissioned Vernon Barnes to paint the two portraits...' He breaks off. 'Know anything about Barnes?'

'Nothing at all.'

'He's another Yank, grew up with my mother, often summered with her in New England. When she decided to have the portraits painted, he was the obvious choice.'

'I'd never even heard his name until Mrs Crawfurd mentioned it.'

'He's pretty well known. Started out as a portrait painter, then changed to Abstract Impressionism. Getting on a bit now, but he still has a studio in New Hampshire, up near the Canadian border.'

I stand up. Beneath my grubby T-shirt, my heart beats like a dynamo. I put a hand on the back of an armchair, needing something solid beneath my fingers. 'Why,' I ask again, knowing the question is futile, 'was I told that the person you're saying is Thomas Bellamy, was John Cairns?'

'I can't explain that. Didn't Liz Crawfurd tell me you were given the picture as a child?'

'Yes – it was a gift from my mother.' Which she stored somewhere most of the time, so although I grew up with it, I didn't see it very often, which made it all the more precious to me. It arrived at the Cartwrights' house just before I married.

'Then she's the one you should ask.' Back on track, Bellamy is not to be deflected from his saga of family wrongs. 'When Mother finally refused to fund my father any longer, he began to steal from her. Money first. Then jewellery. He tried to forge her signature on cheques and would have gone to jail if she hadn't refused to

92

press charges. After that he took anything sale-able he could get his hands on. This picture was one of them. It went missing years ago. I don't know why he didn't take both of them – perhaps even *he* balked at selling his own wife to some backstreet fence.'

'I'm not parting with it.' My voice is rising towards shrillness.

'I'll pay any sum you care to name to bring the bastard back where he should have been and never was – at her side.'

'Wouldn't that be a bit hypocritical?'

'It means nothing to me, but everything to her.'

'Where's your father now?'

He waves a hand. 'Long dead. Cirrhosis of the liver. She nursed him herself to the end. My sister and I were away at school most of that time; we barely remember seeing him, after his years abroad.' Another movement of his full mouth, so like that of the man in the painting. 'Sounds like a cheap novel, doesn't it?'

'When did he die?'

He looks almost apologetic. 'About thirty-five years ago. So you see, he couldn't have been your father, could he? You wouldn't have been born for another – what, four or five years, at the earliest.'

There is a whirring in my head, as though a bee has gone berserk inside my skull. My lungs are packing up. 'I...' Deep breath. 'I can see that.'

'I don't care about the bloody thing,' he says. 'It's just that it would give my mother so much pleasure.' He shakes his head. 'It always astonishes me that she's gone on loving him all

93

these years, in spite of everything.'

'It's mine,' I say loudly. 'And it's going to stay that way.'

'Fair enough. I can't force you to do something you don't want to do.'

'Too right.'

'Just think about it, Miss Cairns. That's all I ask.'

'I'll think about it,' I say. 'The answer will still be no. By the way, what's the cat called?'

'Cat?'

'The one under the piano.'

He studies the Siamese's insolent blue gaze for a moment. 'It was probably Gin Seng. We still have his great-great-grandson, also called Gin Seng.'

Gin Seng? Luna told me the cat's name was Frankie, after Frank Sinatra, because of its blue eyes, and of course I assumed she knew. I feel like a gullible fool.

Bellamy stands at the front door, already reaching for his cigarettes. 'Look, why don't you come over to Shepcombe some time? It's not that long a drive. You might understand more then. And of course you'd get to see the gardens – if you haven't already.'

'I've been there,' I say. 'I've met your mother several times.'

It seems extraordinary that the Honorable Constance, well-known garden designer, has been hanging on my wall for years, even if only as a figure in the background. She's tall, angular, extremely snooty, beautifully groomed. A type that makes me uneasy, makes me conscious of the earth still under my fingernails, the bramble-scratches up and down my arms. She has an American drawl and a way of looking at you as though you're an invading bug.

As soon as Bellamy's gone, his big car spewing out blue smoke as he backs out of the gate, I rush back inside the house. In the cloak-room, I double up over the pedestal and vomit, retching acrid yellow bile into the bowl. I clasp my hands round my body, holding myself together while the room closes in on me, wall advancing to meet wall, floor rising to the descending ceiling. I'll be crushed if I don't get out, out – then I am scrabbling at the door handle, gasping for breath, let me *out*, slamming the door back on its hinges and stumbling into the narrow spaces of the hall, where I lean against the wall, face sweaty, head hanging, mouth bitter.

After a while, when the waves of dread have receded a little and my chest has loosened up, I stand in front of the empty hearth and look up at the portrait. Luna's lies pierce me. *Oh, darling, you should have heard him playing the piano,* she would say, *it was beautiful. Chopin, Mozart, Debussy, yes, John seriously considered becoming a professional pianist, he could have been anything, singing, oh, such a beautiful voice, Schubert lieder, Strauss, Handel,* 'röslein, röslein, röslein röt'. She sang softly, and I would glimpse a younger, happier Luna long since lost inside the sheath of her sadness. *His beautiful voice, he couldn't go anywhere without being asked to sing. Yes, he could have been anything,*

*played tennis at championship level, Wimble-
don, Roland Garros, that's why he's wearing
white in the picture,* and when I said, but those
are cricket flannels, she had continued, seamless
as a cloak of invisibility, *Tennis, cricket, you
name it, darling, he was so handsome in his
white clothes, and a hero, of course, an officer
and a gentleman. His men adored him, they
would have followed him to the ends of the earth.
He loved gardens – he created that one in the
picture and, of course, he loved cats, we'd have
one ourselves if only we were able to settle down
somewhere.* And sometimes when she hugged
me, I'd feel tears on her cheeks. *I'm so sorry, my
darling,* she would say, *so sorry that it worked
out the way it did, that he died without ever
knowing about his little girl, his precious gift
from God. I never got the chance to tell him I
was pregnant with you – oh, if only he'd never
gone out that evening, just down to the post
office with a letter, if only it hadn't been raining
or the man in the other car hadn't been drinking,
the accident would never have happened* and I
would be left with a vision of a black road, slick
with rain, a drunken monster at the wheel of an
oncoming car, the squeal of brakes, a tyre spinning off into the darkness, the sound of breaking
glass, blood sticky on the tarmac, rain falling,
falling, washing away my father's blood along
with his life...

James Bellamy's visit has annihilated one of
my very few certainties and the vacated space
throbs like a wound. My John Cairns has vanished. Did he ever exist, and if so, in what form?

Not as the father I've imagined so man
seated at the piano – the Steinway –
fingers winding through *L'Apres-m*
Faune, while tobacco plants scent the
air, or leading his home side to the top of the
cricket county championships, or presiding over
some dinner in his mess uniform, red and gold.

I never questioned her. Never asked for more
detail than she gave. Could I have been expected
to recognize that my mother was making him up,
using clues from the painting to fabricate an
entire dossier? Or did he indeed exist in some
form close to what I'd been told, and the
painting had merely provided her with a neat
way to flesh my father out?

He was a handsome officer in the British army,
she told me, *oh so handsome. It was love at first*
sight; we got married just after I graduated from
St Margaret's Junior College in Vermont, and I
flew back to England with my white graduation
dress and it doubled as my wedding-dress. My
parents were furious and never spoke to me
again, and his were dead, so we were entirely
alone, we only had a few months together, oh
John, how I miss him, I'll miss him until the day
I die.

Colonel John Cairns. The man who never was.
Over the years, through Luna's stories about
him, he's become part of me. It is because of him
that my own interest in horticulture took shape.
It is part of how I identify myself. I'm Theodora
Cairns, daughter of John. Everything I know
about myself is bound up in that fact. In that portrait. And now ... now some stranger has walked

o my house to inform me that all my certain-
es are nothing more than figments of someone
else's imagination. Losing my father, I've also
lost myself.

Lies. All of it lies that I've lived with most of
my life, never questioned, though of course I
should have done, instead of allowing her stories
to seduce me. I wanted to believe them. I needed
the reassurance. I've even manufactured for
myself a father who still exists, who talks to me,
who approves of me, encourages me.

I boil with misery and loss. How long will it
take me to prise the chunks of my past from the
precarious cliff-face of my existence? Not that it
matters. Thomas Bellamy, drunk and gambler, is
an irrelevancy. The man in the painting may not
be who I thought he was, but whatever else may
be uncertain, John Cairns, whoever he might be,
was my father.

Are you sure?

Perhaps even that basic fact is false.

I pour myself another whisky, look round my
ordered sitting room, a deliberate contrast to the
chaos in which I grew up. Her double betrayal –
first her ten-year disappearance and now this
terrible lie – is sharp as a sword. My Judas mother. My captivating, capricious, unapproachable,
unprincipled mother. I grab the phone and dial
her number in Rome.

I need to pour out my grief and anger. My
sense of betrayal. My *hurt*. The phone rings and
rings, on and on. She doesn't answer, of course.
So I have no way of knowing whether she is out,
or away, or simply lying on the sofa with a book,

ignoring the telephone, as I've seen her do so often. I press in the numbers again and then again, sobbing, my shirt wet with slobber and tears, letting the phone ring until it is cut off by some automatic reflex.

About to try again, I remember that she is in Sweden. I run into the office, root through the wastepaper basket, can't find the invitation from Stockholm. But the name of the auditorium comes back to me. When I've obtained the number from Directory Enquiries, I dial it, ask for Lucia Cairns. A polite voice, sensing my agitation, explains that she has left, is visiting friends in Copenhagen, is going on to Berlin and then England. She is, in other words, unobtainable.

Story of my life.

I hear her voice in my head. *Your father was so amazing, so charismatic, so unlike anyone else I've ever met. He could have been anything ...* I'll bet he could. A one-night stand. The milkman. A drug addict, a scoutmaster, a child molester, a murderer. Or the husband of her best friend, the *father* of her best friend, doctor, lawyer, Indian chief. Oh God, I never asked for more because I thought I knew.

I start to call Terry, and remember they're on holiday. I ring Hugo, and there is no answer. Leaving the house, I walk between the gnarled fruit trees in the orchard. Most of them are barely productive, but I love their shapes, like ancient people who have lived a lifetime of duty and are now finally allowing themselves to rest. I've never understood the mania for espaliering trees to increase their production. It's the same kind of torture as that inflicted on battery hens; it ignores their essential tree-ness and reduces them to mere producers of fruit.

He could have been anything ... Anything, anyone, except what I've always believed him to be.

In my bog-garden, I start to dig, thrusting my fork as hard as I can into the damp earth, lifting it ferociously, turning it over, frenziedly shaking the soil off the roots of the meadow grass which I am gradually replacing with plants I have nurtured in my greenhouses, have cherished and fed. In the damp scent of earth is a kind of elemental ecstasy. I plunge my hands into the living soil, squeeze it tightly between my palms. An earthworm oozes slowly past my fingers, unaware of me or my troubles. A green-and-yellow spider skitters on spindly legs across the turned clods of earth. Something flashes in the water of my pond. This is real, I tell myself fiercely, this is true, whatever else is false. I need to mourn my loss and am all the more wounded that I cannot do so because what I mourn has never existed.

When I go back inside, the house is still. Absolutely silent. No reassuring twitter from the fridge, no drip from a tap or creak from the stairs. Nothing. The rooms are full of emptiness, though no emptier than I feel. This has always been my refuge. Now, it feels more like a prison.

SEVEN

'So what did you think?' Carolyn asks.

'About what?' Cradling the phone between ear and shoulder, Fergus braces his feet against the floor of the houseboat as the wake of a coal-barge travelling up-river smacks against the hull.

'About Theo, of course. Did the two of you get on?'

'We're both civilized people,' he says. 'Even if we'd loathed each other's guts, we were never going to start throwing stones at each other.'

'So you *did* get on.'

'I don't really know.' They hadn't *not* got on, which wasn't quite the same thing.

'Are you going to see her again?'

'I very much doubt it.'

'Why not?'

'Partly because I'm not her type.' Why the hell did he fling out that invitation to Corfu, especially since he hadn't even begun to start making arrangements to go himself? The last thing he needs hanging round while he tries to work is some repressed female, spinster of this parish, divorcée, not that any of the above come anywhere close to the kind of woman he imagines Theodora might be, seems to be, *is*. 'But mostly because she's not mine.'

'Charlie said she wouldn't be.'

'Charlie was right.'

'We're very disappointed, Fergus.'

'Please let Charlie know how touched I am by your joint concern.'

'I personally thought it could fly. I hate being wrong.'

'I'm truly sorry, but I can't fall in love to order, you know.'

'Couldn't you try?'

'Caro, does it occur to you that Theodora might be in love with someone else?'

'I don't believe it.'

'She's a normal healthy female; why shouldn't she be? In her line of work, she probably meets bronzed young gods – or even middle-aged ones – every day of the week.'

'We'd have known about it. Jenny would, she'd have told us.'

'Maybe Theodora asked her not to.'

'I don't believe it.' Big sigh. 'Oh dear, we're all longing for her to get married again.'

'Maybe she's like me, not the marrying kind.'

'I don't believe it. About either of you.'

'What was the last husband like?' He keeps his tone super-casual.

'I told you all about him before, didn't I?'

'Tell me again.'

'He was OK. A bit of a control freak. You'd never believe it, looking at Theo now, but she used to sit there, listening while he pontificated, as though she had no mind of her own, did whatever she was told to do, eat this, drink that, buy your clothes at this shop, your shoes at that one. Here's fifty quid because you've been a

102

good little girl, don't spend it all at once. It was quite embarrassing.'

'I can imagine.'

'Actually, he was a pompous toad, to put it bluntly. The sort of man who would order for her in a restaurant without asking what she wanted.'

'And she lasted five years with him?'

'I think she was trying to find out who she was. As soon as she did, she left.'

'How did he take that?'

'Badly. Charlie met him at some do or other a few months back and he was still going on about it. Hurt pride, though, rather than hurt feelings. He's still coming to terms with the fact that he honoured her with his name and then she had the temerity to reject him. But since she's not your sort, you won't be interested in any of that.'

'Quite right.' He can hear her thoughts rasping against the inside of her skull. 'How's the book coming along?' she asks eventually.

'It's not.'

'If it's any help, you could always go up to the croft.'

He can hear the little boys behind her, and the undulating voice of the Swedish au pair telling them to be quiet while their mother is on the phone. 'Do you mean that little place Charlie's parents have up in Scotland? That's not a bad idea. I loved it there.'

'I'm pretty sure it's empty at the moment. I could check with Terry.'

He remembers it as rudimentary. Miles from anywhere. When they were younger, he'd been up there with Charlie several times, more or less

103

living off the land. Out of tins. Drinking from the loch. Once, stewing a rabbit Charlie had winged on the road. Drunk as lords, half the time, beating their T-shirts between two stones when they'd finally become so filthy that they stood upright on their own, delighting in their own story-book resourcefulness, detergent stain smoking across the clear water, fish-eyes bulging down among the reeds at the sudden nacreous smudging of their element.

'On the other hand, I'm not sure isolated is what I need at the moment. It was about as isolated as I could cope with in the Sierra Madre, believe me.'

Way beyond isolated. Detached from any world he'd ever known. Alienated. A five-mile trek downhill through the jungle to the nearest telephone, poverty so grinding that it made his bones ache. The jeeps which would roar to a stop right at his feet, the *muchachos* eyeing him impenetrably from under their hat-brims, hands on guns, not threatening him, not yet, just making it clear that for his health's sake he better tread carefully, keep quiet, notice nothing.

'You told me once that writers will do anything rather than actually write,' says Caro.

'True.'

'You also told me that when there's nothing else to do, in the end you have to write, however much you'd rather not.'

'Also true.'

'Well, then.'

He thinks of her as she was when he first knew her, the blonde hair short and boyish, the earnest compassion of her, the palpable sense she emitted of certainty that nothing would go wrong. 'If you want me to be brutally honest – the brutality being directed at myself, not you – I think I'm afraid to be on my own.'

'Why is that?'

'Difficult to say. Unfinished business, perhaps.'

'Your brother, do you mean?'

'Possibly.' He considers the matter. 'Or maybe my father.'

'Fergus, that's business which will *never* be finished. You can't expect it to. It's tragic, it's terrible, I've no doubt it haunts you and will do so until you die yourself. So absorb it. Let it become part of you, rather than a boulder you carry round with you.'

'I wish I could. Better men have come from the same places I have, and made far more use of it. Trouble is, read any recent Irish memoir you care to name and you begin to see that I'm a cliché.'

'Nonsense, you're a one-off, Fergus.'

'I'd like to think so.'

'Maybe I'm being terribly simplistic, but it can't hurt you to go to Scotland. You might find that the peace up there will help you.'

'I'll give it some thought.'

'Fergus! How are you?' The falsely bonhomous voice of his agent.

'Fine, thanks.'

'And the book?'

'Coming along,' he lies.

'I had lunch with Claire yesterday, and she's longing to see it.'

'Don't worry, Evan. She'll have something soon.'

'When's the deadline?' Evan asks, as though he doesn't have the exact date squarely in front of him.

'End of January.'

'If you've got any problems with it, you know I'm here if you want to talk.'

'I appreciate that. As a matter of fact, I'm thinking of taking off for Scotland for a couple of weeks to get really stuck in to it.'

'So I can tell Claire it's all systems go?'

'Absolutely.'

But in truth, it's all systems bunged. It's all systems sealing-waxed shut. Not supposed to be such a thing as a block, it's all down to boredom, laziness, no ability, no moral fibre – Father Vincent right about that at least, if nothing else. Hard to describe the gap between the strength and beauty of the luminous lines in his head and the flatness of them on the page. Hard to describe the discomfort of literary constipation, there are no little pills to sort this one out, nothing on the market to unplug, unblock, to give you go and keep you regular.

In the end, there's only you.

Theodora keeps intruding into his days. He hears her cool voice rejecting his Corfu suggestion. Thank God! How would he have been able to get out of it if she'd jumped at the idea, wanted to know when and where, times and dates, started buying bikinis, packing bags? He tries to push her away but finds himself running his mind's eye over the smooth olive of her skin, the curve of a shoulder under her dress, the shape of her arms. He thinks of the tender vulnerability on her face, the arrogant husband, never met but instantly recognizable, the chains hanging from her neck. Baggage indeed.

Why does he keep recalling the way her eyes sometimes glow, as though a candle has been placed behind them?

Even if he does get to Corfu, it won't be the way it once was, he tells himself, already prepared for disappointment, the world grown older now, paradise lost, throat-grabbed by vulgarity. Indeed, you can't go home again, not that he wants to, Jesus, no, but in Corfu he might recover the facility which currently escapes him. He sees his former fluency like a raincloud, heavy, significant, weighted with sentences, words escaping from the mass of it, dripping from it, tumbling earthwards, the gentle rain from heaven.

He could ask the Cartwrights if he could use their villa ... but that means indebtedness. And now there is suddenly a resonance, an echo of a different possibility. Someone was talking about the place just recently, someone who has a holiday home there, someone he knows. He tries to net the name but it slips further away from him. No doubt it will return.

Badges of servitude, Theodora had said ... it seems a sad epitaph for a marriage. He imagines her neck bending beneath the weight of golden chains. Did the grumpy husband realize their symbolism? Alice in Wonderland eating magic mushrooms until her neck sways like a snake above the trees, giraffe women, necks stretched by brass rings to precarious heights, remove them and their tender throats will droop like the pale stalks of crocuses, hang below their breasts, suffocate them. Badges of servitude. Crinolines, corsets, stiletto heels. A woman's place is underneath. *Kinde, kirche, küche.*

Despite the difficulties, Lennart Wells's disappearance into the jungle of Mexico is still pincered to his writer's consciousness. But the book refuses to emerge from his consciousness. If it is going to happen, he will have to go at it slowly, instead of rushing in. Ease into it. Creep up on it. Salt on its tail. Softlee, softlee...

EIGHT

'Lotus Flower Hotel.'

'Oh, hi,' I say. 'Is Lucia Cairns in her room?'

'I'll see.' After a while, the receptionist informs me that she's not.

'Do you have any idea when she'll be back?'

The receptionist doesn't, but she can take a message. I don't leave one.

Regis Harcourt telephones to tell me she's had yet another brilliant idea for her garden. Forget Sylvan, now she wants Minimalist. Needless to say, this involves trashing all the work I've already done for her and starting again.

'I've been having second thoughts about all that greenery,' she tells me, her rapid speech bouncing off my eardrums like rubber bullets. 'I'm thinking stark, I'm thinking austere, and that assistant of yours thought maybe something Zen and Japanesey might be more in keeping, given the size of the place and everything; makes sense to me, what do you think?'

'Assistant?'

'Said her name was Katrina.'

Trina must have come into the house to answer the phone while I was out somewhere. I scrabble among the files on the desk and find a scrap of paper which says, in sloping handwriting: *Ree-jus rang.*

'Zen is good,' I say. 'And of course your silver birch would fit in well.'

'I'm into meditation at the moment,' Regis says. 'And your girl suggested making the whole thing much more elemental, black slate chips, white rocks, a little waterfall type thing, very minimalist and peaceful, and God knows I need some peace at the moment, clients getting up my nose, changing their minds about the slightest thing, after I've put in hours of work.'

'I know *exactly* how you must feel.' I roll my eyes. 'We could use bamboo, a few water plants. It will definitely be peaceful.' And much easier to design. I think of the hours I've already spent on her behalf and shrug. Mind-changing doesn't come cheap, but that's her problem, not mine.

'Also, I just bought these three absolutely

fabulous urns which would look marvellous here and there, shame to waste them, don't you think?'

'These are Zen urns?'

'Not exactly, but you could incorporate them, I should imagine, very tasteful with sort of bul-rushes or an orchid growing in them or what's that stuff that koala bears like?'

'Eucalyptus?'

'No, it's not koalas, it's pandas and they eat bamboo, which is very Japanesey, isn't it?'

'Pandas? You're losing me, Regis.'

'I *think* it's pandas,' she says doubtfully.

'You're going to have to make up your mind,' I say. 'I've already spent more than enough time on your project, and my construction team's been standing by to get started for over two weeks now. I'll have one more discussion with you, but this really will have to be the final meeting. Otherwise you'll need to find another designer.'

Whereas what *I* need is to pin my mother down, hold her while she wriggles and squirms, demand the answer to questions I should have asked years ago. I may not like them, but at least I'll know. That's what I tell myself. But it won't be that simple. All my life she has managed to hide the truth. I sense that she won't easily relinquish it now.

Marnie duly arrives and finds me staring at nothing. I haven't seen her since my return from the States as she's been away, guiding her eldest daughter through her first pregnancy. 'What's happened?' she says, frowning at me.

110

'Nothing much.' Only my whole life.

'Something has.'

I shrug.

She brings me a mug of coffee. Proper coffee, continental roast, fresh-ground, dripped through a filter. 'Is it something you can talk about?' she asks.

'I'm tired,' I say briefly. Since Caro's party, I've scarcely slept; this morning I was up at first light, working in the garden, trying not to think about Bellamy's bombshell, wondering what might have happened if the weather hadn't broken that particular afternoon, if Mrs Crawfurd had telephoned before her visit, if the reception area hadn't been out of service. If it hadn't rained, Liz Crawfurd would have stayed out in the garden and never seen the picture of my father. And that might have been the end of it. Nothing would have changed. But it *did* rain, and because of that, Mrs Crawfurd *did* see the painting. And after that, it was too late to halt the unfolding of events.

'By the way, there's a new addition to the staff,' I say. 'She's got blue hair.'

'That's always useful.'

I explain about Trina.

'So, how did your trip to the States go?' she says, when I've finished.

With an effort I shake off my depression and outline the details of my visit. It seems like a lifetime ago, instead of two or three weeks. I saw two clients in Connecticut, two in Maine, one in Vermont, all of them with expensive friends who are dying to have me design gardens for them,

111

too. On top of that, Bruno Vitti, owner of a string of fancy New York florist shops, invited me out to lunch to talk about the possibility of franchising my Decorations, for what sounds like an exorbitant amount of money. 'Sounds promising, don't you think?' I say, when I've finished.

'Yes ... except that you're not in a position to take on any more commissions.'

'I know we're full but—'

'Full? We're absolutely chocker.'

'I could squeeze the schedules a little.'

Marnie shakes her head. 'They're already bursting at the seams.'

'There's always a bit of give, if we look for it.'

'Can't be done, Theo. You're cramming in far too much.' Marnie often acts as though I'm one of her children, especially when it comes to handing out unasked-for advice. 'You're not a Superwoman.'

'No, but...' I hate to think of new business getting away from me.

'You've got the same problem as most successful one-person businesses, which boils down to the fact that however efficient and energetic you are, there's a limit to how much work you can handle on your own. If you want to expand, you absolutely have to find a partner to share the load. You're starting to look like some kind of zombie. You have to accept that you're already doing as much as you possibly can.'

'Yes, but—'

'Take on any more projects, and your standards are going to fall, the clients will go elsewhere, the whole thing's going to collapse on

112

top of you, and you'll be found gibbering under the wreckage, in the middle of a full-blown nervous breakdown.'

I feel as though I'm halfway there already. 'Thank you for making it so clear.'

'A like-minded person, that's what you need.'

'Is there such a thing? I'd feel really sorry for anyone with a mind like mine.'

'It's just a question of finding him – or her. Doesn't matter which. Him, probably, because in my experience, hims usually have more money to invest. What is it they call a backer in the theatre? An angel? You need an angel.'

'It's a pleasing thought.' I see Fergus Costello, rising from a blue Aegean sea, wings white against the sun. 'But until he – or she – flies in, I dare not turn anything down.'

'Dare? Of course you dare.' Marnie takes off her glasses and massages the bridge of her nose. 'Not that you need to expand, in my opinion. You're doing extremely well as it is, and the one thing you shouldn't do at this stage is risk losing the personal service which made you so successful in the first place.'

'I still can't afford to turn clients away.'

'Of course you can.' She taps the ledger on the desk. 'I was just checking the figures for last year.'

'I *can't*, Marnie.'

She opens the ledger. 'Have a look yourself, if you don't believe me.'

'Just because we had one good year doesn't mean that we'll have another.' *Just because I have no father doesn't mean he doesn't exist...*

113

'Don't be ridiculous. You've had three good years and there's another one already shaping up.'

She doesn't understand. 'I may be flavour of the month at the moment,' I say, 'but who knows how long that'll continue?'

She laughs. 'What are you *talking* about? You're booked up for—'

And suddenly, frighteningly, I lose it. I bang my fist down on the desk. Although Marnie recoils, it doesn't stop me. Distress and anger flare crimson inside me, burning up through my gut and exiting from my mouth in furious words. 'Why do you always *argue* with me! What do you know about it anyway?'

'I know enough.'

She's never seen me like this. *I've* never seen me like this. I don't shout. I don't do angry. And here I am pounding the desk again, glaring, yelling. 'I'm not in a position to turn business down,' I shout.

'I've been doing the books for the past three years,' she says steadily. 'You own this place outright, plus the flat in London. You have no outstanding debts. People are queuing up for your services. You're doing *OK*, Theo, trust me.'

'It only takes a downturn in the economy.' I'm speaking too loudly. 'One more disaster on the stock exchange, and those orders could be cancelled faster than you can say bankruptcy.'

I see my house sold, the flat gone to pay my debts, myself reduced to some ugly little bedsit, everything I've worked so hard for gone up in smoke, my acre of garden reduced to a single plant pot on the window sill. I see a blank where my father used to be. And, in the distance, I see my mother's unforgiven ten-year absence, which I've never questioned, nor she explained.

I'm shaking. 'Taking on someone else will be expensive, and not even necessarily an improvement. I just can't take the risk.'

She's pushed her chair back from her desk, as far away from me as she can get.

'Calm down, Theo,' she says. 'Just calm down.'

Trembling, I turn away, put my hand to my mouth. All these years, I've been building myself a bulwark against the black spaces in my past, and I cannot jeopardize that. Yet if I'm honest with myself, I know that my present rage has nothing to do with my economic position.

Anger leaks from me as though someone just pulled out the plug. I draw in a couple of deep breaths. 'I'm sorry,' I say. 'I don't know what got into me.'

'You're tired,' she says.

'Wrong time of the month, too.'

But we both know it's something worse than that. For a moment we drink coffee in silence, then she says, as though nothing has happened, 'You saw your messages.'

'Yes. I've already dealt with wretched Regis Harcourt. She doesn't seem to have the slightest idea that I've had Bob on stand-by for weeks, waiting to go in.'

'That's another thing: his back problems.'

'I already met Harry, his son. He seems pretty competent.' There's a tremor running down my legs, a tremble at my wrists. I am embarrassed by my outburst.

Marnie raises her eyebrows at me. One of the reasons I'd hired her in the first place was her eyebrows. Sleek, narrow, rounded as crescent moons: I covet them. My own are of the thick untrained sort that you could weave horse-blankets out of, were you inclined that way. Over the years I must have pulled enough hair out of them to fill two cushions, and they *still* look a mess. Marnie swears that she's never plucked in her life, but I have my doubts. She gathers papers into a pile, opens desk drawers and closes them again. She doesn't look at me.

'Marnie,' I say.

'What?'

'I'm really sorry.'

She stands for a moment with files clutched against her chest, avoiding my eyes. Then she sighs. 'That's OK,' she says. 'I once had a boss who threw a glass ashtray at me.'

'Did he hit you?'

'No. I just caught it and threw it back.'

'Did you hit him?'

'Unfortunately, yes. He had to have three stitches.'

We both laugh, but I sense that our relationship has undergone a subtle change. I suspect that it's not for the better.

What makes it all so much worse is that, suddenly, I don't really care whether the business expands or folds. I'm full of emptiness. If I'm not the person I believed I was, then who am I? Everything else seems completely irrelevant.

When Marnie has left, I stand in front of the painting which is not of my father. 'Where are you?' I ask aloud. 'Who are you?'

And then I think, *If Luna's lied about so much else, maybe she's lied about the most important thing of all.*

NINE

Trina arrives the next morning, still blue-haired, still dressed in her widow's weeds. 'I've been working on that assignment you gave me,' she says, putting a folder down in front of me.

'Assignment? What did I...?'

'You know ... the girl in the wheelchair.'

'Holly Crawfurd, yes.'

'I'll show you, if you like.' She pushes the folder across the desk and leaves the room with a hopeful glance at me over her shoulder. I open it, glance through the sketches it contains.

After a while, she appears with a cup of instant coffee and puts it in front of me. Not wanting to hurt her feelings, I raise it to my lips, trying not to grimace.

Super-casual, she says, 'What do you think?'

'I think your ideas are very good. You'll have to redo your drawings, of course.'

'I already *did*,' she says indignantly.

'You'll have to do them again. These aren't nearly neat and clear enough.' I can see she is longing for more from me, but I'm too distressed to offer it. In fact, looking at anything, having to take decisions, talk to potential customers, even confronting Trina about her hair, is suddenly more than I can cope with.

'I'm off to London this afternoon,' I say. 'I'll be staying overnight. Since my secretary won't be coming in tomorrow, you'll have to be in charge of the office.'

'Dunno what I'm going to do, stuck in here all day,' she grumbles.

'You can answer the phone, rework these sketches you've done. They're good but they're still very rough.' I gesture at the filing cabinet in one corner. 'Have a look at some of my preliminary plans – filed under P for Plans, in case you're wondering – and see how I do it.'

'Don't know if I'm up to it.'

'Of course you are. I'll help you when I get back, if you have any problems. I told you already, these are good.'

'You mean it?'

'Yes. I like the way you've designed all these stone alcoves under the raised beds, so she has room to slide her chair right underneath. I know it's only for a tabletop, rather than a real garden design, but you've really thought about what it's like to be confined to a wheelchair. And this summer house with a piano in it ... where did that come from?'

'You told me to ring up the Crawfurds and find out what her interests were, so I did, and they said she plays the piano. They also said she used to be into embroidery, and the other day, I saw this little sewing table in a doll's house shop, with, like, tiny scissors and reels of cotton in it. I thought that might be fun.'

'Sounds good. Buy it, and I'll reimburse you.' I pat the sketches. 'I wouldn't be surprised if the Crawfurds wanted to incorporate some of these ideas into their own garden, to make things easier for their daughter.'

'Great!' There's a flush of colour in her usually pale face.

'If you run out of things to do while I'm gone, you can go and weed the herbaceous beds alongside the house and then draw up a list of all the plants they contain, see how many you recognize, but keep an ear out for the phone. And you can check that the seedlings in the greenhouses are watered. Also, I'd better warn you that there's a guy called Harry who's doing some work for me, just so you know he's not an intruder if you see him in the garden. By the way,' I say, 'you've turned seventeen, haven't you?'

'Ten days ago.'

'You should have told me. It'd be much easier for you to get back and forth with a car. If you learn to drive, there's an old banger in the garage you could use.'

'You serious?'

'Never anything else.'

'I *can* drive,' she says. 'My boyfriend taught me.'

'Have you got your licence?'

'Got it on my birthday.'

'I'll take you out on the road in the next day or

119

two, see how you go with the Ford, and if you feel confident with it, you can use it.'

'OK!' The grin on her face is enormous.

'Don't think it's just me being nice,' I add sternly. At least I feel I've gone a little way towards making up for my behaviour to Marnie. 'It's as much for my sake as yours. You'd be able to run errands for me. Deliver things. Pick stuff up.'

'I can do that.' She hesitates. 'I could help out with letters and that, too, if you like.'

'I thought you were interested in gardening.'

'I am. But it's not all growing things, digging and stuff, is it? I did typing at school, computer studies.'

Which reminds me... 'You already answered the phone,' I say. 'Where was I?'

'Dunno, but it was ringing and ringing. I made a note of who rang you ... didn't you find it? The only urgent one was some Donald Duck woman, wanted to see you like the day before yesterday.'

'I'm seeing her tomorrow.' I smile a little wryly at her. 'She said you'd suggested a Zen version of her garden.'

'I was just trying to stop her yacking on.' She glances at her hands. 'I also asked her if she'd realized how much all this chopping and changing was costing her.'

'Did you?' I raise my eyebrows. 'And had she?'

'Don't think so, 'cos she shut up right away and asked when you wanted to get started.'

'Believe it or not, she's changed her mind yet again.'

'The customer is always right.'

'Not this one!' We grin at each other like old friends.

Walking down the Edgware Road early the next morning, I can only think of one thing: if Luna can so easily have invented a father for me, can she also have invented his death? In other words, is it possible that the car accident which haunted my childhood never actually took place?

Between them, James Bellamy and my mother have created a void into which drops every man I pass who is the right sort of age. It could be him across the road, or that one over there, or the one flagging down a taxi with a rolled umbrella. If he's not who she has always maintained he was, he could be anybody at all. He could be married with a family. I imagine the half-siblings I might have somewhere, the aunts and uncles, the cousins.

As I reach the double doors of the Lotus Flower Hotel, I notice a man standing against the railings which enclose the gardens across the road. He's dressed in black: black suit over black shirt, like a portent of death, but it's not his dress which catches my attention, it's the fixity of his gaze as he surveys the street. He looks up and down, and up again, his handsome narrow face expectant, as though waiting for someone to appear and throw a bomb in his direction. Turning into the hotel, I feel ice between my shoulder blades. I know I've seen him before, somewhere, long ago.

The girl behind the reception-counter smiles at

me. When I ask for Lucia Cairns, she nods at the dining room, from which emanates a smell of fried bacon and a hum of breakfast conversation.

At the door, I stand looking for my mother and see her at the end of the room, back against the wall, reading the paper. She looks preoccupied, as though she is thinking of someone else, somewhere else. There are lines on her face I don't remember. How she is and how I imagine her to be when I'm not with her are two quite distinct images. Is it the white streaks in her hair, with their explicit message of time passing, of lost youth, lost hope, or is it her unguarded expression, the almost unnoticeable stiffness of her carriage, the slight droop of her shoulders, which make me see that she, too, is vulnerable? If only I could turn time back, enfold her in my arms, the way I used to. My heart unexpectedly aches. I remember the feel of her bones beneath the cover of her flesh, the warmth of her. She loved me once, I know she did. What happened to make her stop? What did I do? Why did she drop out of my life for that pitiless decade? Oh, Luna, I think sadly, if only we had not grown so far away from each other.

I make my way between the tables and stand in front of her. She looks up, her face registering terror, her hand fluttering at her chest. Her eyes dart round the room, and back to me, beyond me, as though she suspects I'm not alone.

'Theodora,' she says, half rising from her seat. 'What are you doing here?'

'It's nice to see you, too.' I bend down to plant an awkward kiss on her cheek and pull out a

122

chair.

She frowns. 'How did you know where I was?'

'Terry told me you'd be staying here.' I look round for a waitress and realize that it's self-service. If I get up and help myself to coffee, I'm afraid she'll melt away, out of the door, down the street, and I'll have lost her again.

'You've got that determined look in your eye.' She looks at me warily. 'You've obviously come about something important.'

'Yes.' There are tall windows along one side of the room and I can see out into the street, see the ceaseless passing of traffic, the gardens, carcasses in the butcher's window across the road. The man in black has gone.

I take a deep breath. 'A few days ago, a complete stranger turned up at my house, wanting to buy the painting you gave me when I was eight. He insisted that the man I've always known as *my* father is actually *his* father. He told me when his father died, which was well before I was born, so there's no possibility that we're both right. He even brought another painting with him, a companion piece, to prove what he was saying.'

She picks up her coffee cup and holds it in both hands. 'I don't know what to say.'

'But you're not surprised.'

'No.'

'Luna, I'm in shock. I'm...' I spread my hands. 'Why did you tell me it was my father when you knew it wasn't?'

She makes no attempt to deny or apologize. 'It gave you what you needed at the time.'

'So everything you told me about him was lies?'

'Not lies, Theodora. It was a story for a little girl who wanted to believe in fairytales.' She reaches for my hand. I've forgotten how soft her fingers are, how moth-like on my skin. Nor have I noticed before the way they curl inwards on themselves, like the delicate claw of a crab. She sips a couple of times then sets the cup carefully back on its saucer. 'Look, about your father ... this is not an avenue you should explore.'

I think I understand. 'Am I illegitimate? Is that what this is all about? A good Catholic girl getting pregnant outside the bonds of holy matrimony?'

She smiles. 'Who said I was good?'

I ignore this. 'Were you actually married to him? Was he really in the army? Is his name even John Cairns?'

She just looks at me.

'Luna,' I say, trying to hold on to my self-possession, 'my whole life feels as if it's suddenly been put on hold. I must find out the truth.'

'What is truth?' she asks. 'Isn't it just what you believe you know?'

'I'm not going to get into a metaphysical argument with you.'

'All right.' She picks up her spoon and stirs the grounds in her cup. 'I admit that the painting is not what I said it was.'

I reach across the table to grab her by the wrist and am taken aback by how wasted it seems, the bones lying only just below the skin. 'Luna, who is my father? Or don't you know yourself?'

'Don't be silly. Just believe me when I say there are compelling reasons why you shouldn't know.'

'I'm grown-up now, I can be trusted.'

She picks up her coffee cup again. 'You'll have to accept that I'm not going to tell you.'

My chest begins to constrict. 'But *why*?' My voice wavers. More than anything else, I want to lay my head on the table and howl.

'Who your father was doesn't matter much in the end, does it?' she says gently. Her long silver earrings turn in the light from the window. 'Darling Theodora, what matters is who *you* are, what *you've* become, not who it was that provided the genes and chromosomes thirty years back.'

'That's the whole point – suddenly I don't *know* who I am. Besides, if it doesn't matter, why shouldn't you tell me?'

Her expression grows steely. 'I have *not* spent the last thirty years doing everything in my power to—' She breaks off.

'To what?' There is an undercurrent here that I don't comprehend.

She folds her lips together. Pushes the sugar bowl further away from her then brings it back. Straightens her shoulders. 'Keep you safe,' she says finally. Reluctantly.

'Safe? What from?'

'Those who might want to harm you. Or me.' She seems absolutely serious. In the mundane atmosphere of the Lotus Flower Hotel's dining room, the words sound melodramatic. I recall the bad days, just before she disappeared. How we kept running from place to place, city to city, trying to escape from an unseen, non-existent enemy. The chocolate bar snatched from my hand, the spider on the pillow.

'Do you mean my father?'

'Not him.'

'Who then? A jealous wife? In any case, why would anyone want to harm *us*? And even if they did once – which I find hard to believe – it was thirty years ago. How can any of it – whatever it was – still matter?'

She clears her throat. 'It matters even more now than it did then.'

'*Please* tell me why.'

'I'm truly sorry, but I can't.'

'Was his name John Vincent Cairns?'

'I *told* you.'

'I know you *told* me. But was it true?'

'Yes, it was.' Her eyes shift, the concentration of their colour changes. I know she's lying. 'Look, he's dead,' she says. 'That's the important thing as far as you're concerned.'

'Is he?'

'Yes.'

'*Is* he? Truly?' Outside, the sky has turned the colour of roof-slates; rain is beginning to fall.

'Yes.' She picks up her coffee cup again. Her hand is trembling. 'Yes, yes, *yes*.'

'Then how compelling can the reasons be for not telling me about him?'

'Listen to me, Theodora. It's utterly pointless for you to go on wasting time and emotion on this.'

Behind me, a door opens, there's a murmur of voices from the hotel lobby. She starts, stares, her eyes wide with alarm. She leans her upper body towards me, as though hoping to shield me from any suffering that might befall me. I, too, begin to turn, my heart beating harder, adrenalin sparking at my wrists, before I force myself to stay as I was. Though her fear is contagious, I refuse to be sucked into her fantasies.

'He's still alive, isn't he?' I drop the question casually into the conversation and see her turn pale.

'No!' Her expression is terrified. 'I told you: he died before you were even born. He was run over. You were a post-humous baby.' She's getting to her feet. 'I don't want to discuss this any further,' she says.

'But I do.' I, too, rise. 'I can't let you get away with not telling me.'

'Theodora,' she says, sounding desperate. 'I can only entreat you – for your own good – to accept that I can't.'

'Is it Hugo?'

'Is Hugo your father? *Hugo?* Absolutely not.' With a gesture, she waves the subject away.

'Bellamy,' I say.

Her face grows still again. She raises a hand to her hair and plays with the dragonfly clip holding it together. 'What do you mean?'

'Did you know Thomas Bellamy? The man in the picture?'

'No.'

'Where did it come from?'

'I ... Oh, God.' She sits down again, passes a

hand across her eyes. 'All right, I saw it in a shop window one day. A little art gallery. I thought it might solve some problems if I gave you what you seemed to want most – a father – so I bought it. And yes,' she continues, the room emptying around us, tables being cleared. 'I made it all up, nearly all of it. Not the fact that I loved your father but ... most of the rest. It was for your own safety. If anyone ever ... ever started asking questions, you'd be able to satisfy them that you weren't who they were looking for.'

'That's a bit over the top, isn't it? Why would anyone be asking me questions?'

She doesn't answer.

I lean towards her, lower my voice. 'Was he a spy, or something? Mafia? A professional assassin? A ... a terrorist? Or was he a member of some minor royal family or something?' Each possibility I offer sounds more ridiculous than the last. I'm becoming as paranoid as she is.

'None of that.'

'Luna, for God's sake ... you're sounding like something out of a cheap thriller.' I reconstitute my father, who is no longer the army officer, the musician, the gardener, but a master criminal, an undercover agent, a hitman. Some of it even makes a weird kind of sense, it explains why we moved on all the time; maybe she's the only one who can identify him and for his own protection, he needs to eliminate her. And even as this fantasy flashes through my mind, I dismiss it. It's the stuff of spy stories and conspiracy theorists, not real life. And it all began thirty years

128

ago; it can't still be relevant. I remember the day in Rome when I realized for the first time that she was truly crazy. I wish I could put it all right, not just for me but for her as well.

'Whether you believe it or not,' she says, 'I so much wanted you to have a happy childhood.'

'I did,' I say. At least, until I was eleven. Heat and balconies, flower-trailing baskets, the sound of clapping, prayers dropping from the sky, the trickle of water into mossy basins, figs and parrots, indigo evenings, tall candles flickering under vaulted ceilings, the scent of incense. Childhood had been all that, yes, but it was also standing on the fringes, watching other children play, listening to voices in another room, trying to cope with languages I couldn't understand, wishing I wasn't always on the outside, wasn't always moving on.

'I just didn't know what to do for the best.' My mother chews at her lip. 'Maybe I should have kept you with me instead of sending you away – but when you were born, I wasn't much more than a child myself, and entirely on my own. I didn't know how to handle the situation.' She stares unfocussed across the room, looking at a past I can't see. 'Perhaps there was no good way to deal with things.'

'What things?' I don't begin to understand what she's talking about and I know that if I ask, she won't tell me.

'Things,' she says. 'Maybe if I could have the past all over again, I'd do it differently.'

'Not had me, do you mean?'

'Not had...?' She smiles. 'How could you think

something like that? You're my daughter. You're what's made it all worthwhile.'

She's slithering away again, slippery as a fish. I sense that I am going to leave here as empty-handed as when I arrived. The lost years are an unbridgeable gulf between us. 'All what?'

'Don't you realize that *you're* what it's all about?'

I raise my eyebrows. 'Really?'

'I have no rights over you any more, I know that.' Surprisingly, her voice shakes slightly, almost as if she is close to tears. 'I forfeited those long ago.'

'You used to accuse me of being middle-aged.' As a child, I had imagined myself misshapen, deformed by my inappropriate years, as though they were a club foot or a hare lip.

'I did, didn't I?' Another silence. 'That was unkind of me.'

But we're digressing. 'Look, I don't pretend to know what you're talking about, but why haven't you told me any of this before – whatever it is?'

'You've never asked. I'd hoped you'd never need to.' She reaches across the table again to touch my hand. 'There's no point in saying anything. You wouldn't believe me if I told you that you were ... are...' She wipes a finger below her eyes and fumbles in the bag hanging on the back of her chair. She brings out a pair of sunglasses and puts them on. Her voice trembles as she says, 'Look, I know I'm not the mother you wanted, but can't you accept that I'm the one you've got?'

130

'I don't suppose I'm the daughter you wanted, either,' I say.

'You are, Theodora. You always have been.'

'I still have to know about my father,' I say.

But however much I push at her, whichever direction I come at her from, she just shakes her head.

Finally, I stand. 'I don't understand why you won't tell me,' I say. My motherless decade drifts across my mind like a black cloud and though I want to tell her that I forgive her, I cannot force the words out of my throat. 'And I wonder if you've ever thought about how lonely I was when you disappeared, how neglected. Ten years, without a single word, nothing, no letters, no cards, nothing on my birthday or at Christmas.'

'Theodora...' she says. She reaches towards me but I ignore her.

'Just tell me this: was it a man that made you take off like that?'

These are not things I want to be saying. I don't want my past and my present to intermesh. I try to keep Luna's absence stored in the black depths of my mind, deep, deeply buried. Envelopes inside baskets inside cartons inside locked suitcases. Chinese boxes, not to be opened, except in my most secret moments.

'A man?' She gives a strange harsh laugh. 'Yes, in a way, I suppose it was.'

'I suspected as much.' Outside the windows, the street is wet and shiny, car tyres are throwing up sprays of grubby water, there's a distant rumble of thunder. I pick up a plate from the table and throw it hard against the wall.

'Oh, Theodora, I'm so...' Luna comes round the table towards me. She's wearing a red skirt which shows off the calves of her dancer's legs, with a patterned top in scarlet and black. She tries to put her arms around me but I push her away.

'Don't.' I turn and walk out of the room, leaving her there, glowing like a brilliant, heartless butterfly.

The only thing I take with me is the absolute conviction that, somewhere, my father is still alive.

TEN

Sitting on the narrow balcony at the back of Regis's house, overlooking the wasteland of her backyard, we discuss the revised set of plans I've drawn up. It's been several hours since I walked out on my mother but my heart still loops between my ribs; I am hyperventilating.

'Marvellous,' Regis says, and her voice seems to come from somewhere miles away. 'Simply marvellous, much more me, and very feng shui, too, which has got to be good, and I've just picked up this stone altar sort of thing which could go right *there*.' She points to the place with a purple-painted fingernail.

I force myself to concentrate. 'OK. But Regis,

I have to point out that if you want your garden finished this side of the next millennium, you're really going to have to settle for a design and stick with it.'

'Oh, I know I've been an awful nuisance, chopping and changing.' She clasps her hands to her non-existent boobs and says, without pausing for breath, 'Are you all right, Theo?'

'Absolutely fine, thanks.' I paste an unconvincing smile on to my face. She's probably going to tell me she's sourced some New Age essence of green-lipped mussels, guaranteed to restore your lost youth and put the zing back into your lovemaking.

'It's just you seem ... please forgive me for saying this, it's none of my business, I know ... but you don't seem to be your usual self. Have you had some bad news or something?'

'Nothing I didn't already know about.'

Her thickly kohled eyes widen. 'Is it something serious?'

'Honestly, Regis, I'm fine. Just very busy.'

'Or very unhappy,' she persists.

I put my hand on hers. 'I'm fine.' If I say it enough, it may even turn out to be true.

Crossing between traffic lights, I find my attention caught by the window of a bookstore on the corner. In the centre is a large photograph of Fergus Costello. Around it, a display of his books. To one side, a poster announces that the author will be talking about his latest work at seven o'clock that evening. I look at my watch. There's an hour to go. I tell myself I ought to get home, then wonder why. My usual imperatives

133

seem unimportant.

I find a coffee bar somewhere and sit with a cup of espresso, staring at nothing. Amid the hiss of steam, the clank of coffee machines, my mind roams free. Cricket on a green field, a green-and-white garden, Luna's panicked gaze. Since I'd wanted one so badly, she'd made me the gift of a father. Like it or not, that gift has now been stolen from me, and I want a replacement. I'm not giving up. I think of terriers with rats. I feel the snarling rottweiler of my determination.

Behind me, the coffee machine glugs and perks. I get out my mobile and dial my house. 'Theo Cairns' office,' a voice says, so crisp that I hardly recognize it as Trina's.

'How's it going?' I ask.

'Just fine.'

'Anything I should know about?'

'Nothing urgent. Someone in Lincolnshire moaning that half his garden died off in the drought. I said he'd have to take it up with God, not with you.'

'Trina!' Used now to her quirky sense of humour, I laugh.

'Not really. One of your suppliers rang to say the special order of containers you asked for is now ready. Plus that woman from London who sounds like Donald Duck on speed, saying she'd had a really brilliant idea.'

'Not again! I was only there this morning!'

'I told her the contractors were moving in next week and the date couldn't be changed.'

'Good girl.'

We chat for another five minutes, about

134

nothing very much, before I break the connection. At quarter to seven, I stand up. As I leave the bar, I catch sight of my face in the mirrors which line one wall and think how sad I'm looking. How worn.

By the time I get back to the bookshop, a considerable crowd has already gathered. I wander between the bookshelves, pick out a couple of Fergus's books and read the blurb on the front of the jacket. He's won several literary prizes, I note. The London literati have fallen over themselves to write plaudits. But isn't he one of them, all cosily writing reviews of each other's books? At the front of the shop, I pay for the books I've chosen. I'll start reading one tonight.

I find a seat at the back of the audience. A few minutes after seven, Fergus is led in by a person from the bookshop and introduced to the audience. I think how handsome he is, the straight black hair, close to navy in the overhead lights; the warmly blue Celtic eyes.

When he begins to read, I am enthralled. He uses his beautiful voice like an instrument, weaving a spell around the audience that is quite separate from the story he's telling. His Irish accent is stronger than it had been at Carolyn Cartwright's party; perhaps he deliberately emphasizes it on public occasions such as this. When he's finished, people ask questions, not so much, I suspect, because they want to know the answer, as because they want to hear his voice again. He signs books for those who've bought copies. I hang back. Finally the bookshop person indicates that it's time to bring the event to a close, and people begin to straggle away. I linger until everyone else has left then, ignoring the pointed glance at her watch from the minder, walk towards Fergus who sits relaxed, one leg nonchalantly crossed over the other, and say, 'That was wonderful.'

He looks up. 'Theodora Cairns! What are you doing here?'

'It seemed like one of those must-see-don't-miss things,' I say lightly.

'You're absolutely right.' He turns to the bookshop person. 'Is there anything else you need me for, Eileen?'

'No, thanks.' She smiles at him, flaps her eyelids up and down. She clearly thinks he's terrific. 'That was great, Fergus. It all helps to sell books.'

'Thank you so much for setting it up.'

'Always a pleasure,' she says, staring at me. Perhaps she's been hoping for a quick drink with him.

'This is Theo Cairns, the garden expert,' he says.

'Oh, yes.' Her face grows more friendly. 'We sell a lot of your books.' She hesitates. 'Maybe we could persuade you to come and talk about them one evening.'

'Contact my publishers,' I say, then, afraid that I've sounded rude, add, 'I'd love to.'

'Theodora's an old friend from way, way back.' Having offered her this kindness, Fergus raises his black eyebrows at me. Taking my elbow, he moves me towards the door. Outside, he takes both my hands. 'I shall be outrageously, stupendously, unimaginably disappointed if you don't have time for dinner with me,' he says.

'I'm banking on it,' I say, and mean it.

'How many books have you written now?' I ask.

'Six. In fifteen years. I'm not very prolific. And I do a lot of travelling, for research.'

I pat the bag lying on the banquette beside me. 'I bought two this evening.'

He looks anxious. 'I hope you like them.'

'Your friends give you terrific reviews; I'm sure I will.'

'Are you being caustic here?'

'A little.'

'You must tell me your honest opinion.'

'I can't imagine that you need it.'

'I'd like it because somehow I don't think you go in for bullshit. Also, I'd really like to...' He pauses. 'Got a bit of paper? Or a diary? I'll give you the number of my houseboat at Chelsea Reach. Not that I'm around much. It's just a place to hang my hat. I keep a change of clothes there, some books, my ten-speed bike – easiest way to get around London.'

The waiter comes and we order. *Bouillabaisse* for me, followed by scallops; *moules marinières* and lobster for Fergus.

'Read any good words lately?' I ask, as we wait for the food to arrive. 'Any specific words, I mean.'

'Alfalfa,' he says, pulling syllables from the air like a magician plucking scarves from his sleeve. 'Frankincense, plumbago, penumbra, Ovaltine.'

'Ovaltine?' I say, laughing.

'Yeah, why not? Apart from sounding nice, it has all sorts of resonances. Being a kid again, warm and cosy in one's jimjams and dressing-gown, bedtimes round the gas fire, Mummy reading a goodnight story, all the spurious safety of childhood.' His face changes. 'All the things I never had myself.'

'Didn't you?'

'Don't look so down in the mouth, my sweet. Nice little convent girl like you wouldn't really know how cruel the world can be.'

'You haven't the faintest idea about my childhood,' I say slowly.

'So tell me.'

I shake my head.

'I know about your mother from the Cart-wrights – what about your father, the military man?'

'I ... don't know.'

'Oh?' Questions crowd into his eyes.

'He's supposed to have died when I was a child.'

'Supposed?' He quirks an eyebrow at me, and I have to admit that put it like that, it sounds fairly bizarre.

I think of John Vincent Cairns in his cricket flannels, of the Siamese cat and the woman in the garden. My mother's lies. Fergus doesn't need to know any more than I've already told him. 'It's too complicated to go into. I don't want to talk about it.'

'One day, Theodora, I shall make you. When we're in Corfu, perhaps?'

I wrinkle my forehead. 'I don't remember saying I would come.' I concentrate on the excellent *bouillabaisse*.

He dabbles in his fingerbowl, squeezes the lemon slice it contains. Two tables away, a middle-aged couple is eating in a relentless kind of way, not looking at or speaking to each other. They must have loved each other once.

'When are you planning to go?' I ask, just for something to say.

'As soon as I've found a place to rent. I have feelers out. Maybe in a couple of weeks? A month?'

If I *were* to go, I could do that. A month would give me time to sort things out, separate the urgent from the postponable. Between them, Marnie and Trina could hold the fort while I'm gone, Marnie probably glad to come in an extra day or two, earn some holiday money. I think of warm nights, waking up each day at dawn with the pleasure of not having a single thing to do, no demands on me of any kind. Time to regroup.

Carpe diem, I tell myself. Go For It. I open my mouth to tell him that maybe I'll join him, after all, but the waiter arrives, puts one hand behind his back and with the other picks up the bottle of wine and refills our glasses.

When he's gone, Fergus clinks his glass against mine. 'So ... you said there's no man in your life right now?'

'Yes. No.'

'So there's nobody to tell you how beautiful you are?'

Who could resist? I laugh. 'I hope you don't

139

expect me to dimple prettily and gaze admiringly at your abs.'

'I couldn't tell my abs from my elbow.'

The press speculation has died down now, but I haven't forgotten his reputation. 'I also hope you don't think there's a blank space in my life that you could fill.'

He stares at me thoughtfully. Sighs gustily. Portrait of a man pretending he's disappointed.

'What about what you're working on now?' I ask. 'A book, obviously, but what's the setting?'

He looks evasive and I wonder if I've crossed some unacceptable line by asking. 'I'm still at the research stage,' he says. 'Which means I read a lot, think a lot. Look things up, make myself receptive, try to determine who the protagonists are, where to take them.'

'Any ideas?'

'Ideas are easy. It's finding one which can sustain me through the years it takes to write a book which is difficult. I'm finding it harder than usual to toss ideas around.'

'Isn't tossing ideas around something you do with someone else around?'

'Usually, yes, but I have this great relationship with myself,' he says. 'I mean, we can actually talk, have really meaningful conversations, me and myself. You must have had the same experience.'

'All the time.' I try to laugh, and suddenly, my throat is closing again, tears are juicy behind my eyelids, the room is blurring.

He looks at me with concern. 'Are you all right, Theodora?'

I swallow hard. This is all getting out of hand. If I could come up with a single reason why he might be interested, I'd tell him about James Bellamy's visit, my mother's refusal to help me. Maybe even try to describe for him those long barren years when I had no idea where she was, what she was doing. But I can't. 'Absolutely fine,' I say.

For some reason I can't quite define, the rapport between us is evaporating. 'How about dinner again sometime next week?' he says.

The invitation is given so offhandedly that I think he must be asking for form's sake only. On top of that, the burden of his possible expectations is too weighty for me to handle. 'Uh ... I'm pretty booked up at the moment. Can I take a rain check?'

Cautious now, just checking, he says, 'But Corfu is not rejected out of hand?'

'It *is*, Fergus.'

'Nonetheless, I shall call you on the off-chance, soon as I know anything.'

It's late by the time we've finished our coffee. Leaving the restaurant, he asks how I'm going to get home.

'I'm not going back tonight,' I say. 'The last train's already left.'

'In that case ... I was thinking of dropping in to a jazz club. Want to come?'

'Uh...' Jazz? It isn't really my thing. But I'd like to restore the free-and-easiness between us. 'Love to,' I say, sounding more enthusiastic than I feel.

The place is crowded. We squeeze in near the

back, listen for a while to someone playing the trumpet. The heat is intense. Fergus murmurs something about beers and pushes through the crowd towards the bar. The trumpet soars, wire brushes scramble across the surface of metal cymbals, snare drums growl. A few people are not so much dancing as moving, joined frontally at the hip, an excuse to have sex without the bother of taking off their clothes. I think of my mythical father, who has no existence except the one Luna has conjured up for him. Did he play jazz on his piano? Did he even *have* a piano?

Fergus returns with two misted glasses and offers me one. 'You look *distraite*,' he says.

'I am, a bit.'

'Even here with me?'

'Unbelievable as it may be, even then.' The red lights in the ceiling throw an unearthly light on the flat beautiful planes of his face. This is what he would look like if we found ourselves in Hell. What did my father look like? I still see him with the blond hair, the full mouth, in front of the garden my mother had told me he'd designed, but all of that is gone now. Someone pushes into me and I put my hand on Fergus's arm.

He puts his fingers over my hand and pulls me close to him. The music thumps through our conjoined bodies. I don't want to break the spell, but eventually, I stir, I sigh. 'I think I'd better go.'

'I'll come with you.'

'No. It's OK. I'll get a cab.' I begin to push my way towards the door,

'You can crash at my place, if you like,' Fergus

says behind me.

What, the love nest? No thanks. 'I've got a flat in Soho,' I say. 'I'll stay there. Catch an early train in the morning.'

'I'll see you home.'

'It's not necessary.'

'I'd like to.'

'You're not going to ask if you can come up for coffee, are you?' I say, as we get into a taxi in the street outside.

'And all that that entails ... no, Theodora, I'm not going to ask. Not that I wouldn't like to.'

We sit side by side, not speaking, our arms pressed together. I don't move away until the taxi stops outside my block of flats.

'No,' says Fergus, as though he's just finished his previous remark. 'I'll wait until *you* ask *me*.'

'That was a great evening.'

'How about giving me your telephone number, in case I need to get in touch when I know about Corfu?'

I smile. I enlarge my dimples until they feel like craters in my cheek. Dear God, I am actually flirting with him. 'I'm in the phone book,' I say and walk across the pavement, bat out the security numbers, push at the door when it clicks open, all without a backward look, though I believe I could draw him on the night air, trace the line of his jaw in the sky.

ELEVEN

Crap. Balls. Hogwash. How else to describe the nearly fifty pages he has produced in the past weeks? A pot of words flung in the public's face – except at this rate there isn't going to be a public. How can he ever have thought they were worth despoiling paper for? He is recycling, not creating. *The most original voice of his generation*? What a laugh. He's reproduced almost the same dilemmas, the same themes and characters as in his previous book. Not quite, but, reading the pages, discovering the parallels, he can see it coming. He's stopped being original. The energy, the muscularity, just isn't there any longer. A few good phrases wink and wave at him out of the maze of sentences, but the rest could be hieroglyphs for all the meaning it contains.

Like Irishness, Mexicanism is all too easy to parody and, to a large extent, that's what he's done. Caricatured. Cartooned. It is not what Fergus Costello's readers expect. The river laps against the sides of his houseboat as he flips through the pages again, every sharp-edged piece of paper a blade between the ribs of his talent. His *former* talent, his effervescing promise, razored in the crucible of a hellish childhood, even if someone once said a writer's childhood is his bank balance. Transformed into achievement, six books so far and little likelihood of a seventh. Maybe five per cent of it is worth keeping. The rest can be trashed. He bundles the pages into the wastepaper basket. Fuck it. How long can he keep on stalling? Agent sitting there with thumbs downturned. Editor finding more productive fish to fry. That guy in New York, huge advances for his second book, thirty years of procrastination and when it finally came out, it was rubbish.

Ever since his return from Mexico, he's been suffering from a total failure of nerve. A character based on Lennart Wells had seemed a great idea at the time, a strong idea, a journey to the heart of darkness, a raft-ride down the Mississippi, descent into the inferno, mouth of death, jaws of hell. He'd planned it all before he went. Done the research. Read everything he could find, gulping books down like beer on a sweltering day. Drunk with anticipation. Already enraptured by places he'd never seen. Telling the names like rosary beads, incantations of hope. Popocatapétl, Iztaccíhautl, Chihuahua, Tepoztlán – fabulous, magical, mythical names! Chicken *mole* and *chiles en nogada,* Mayan ruins and mariachi bands and chapels covered in gold leaf. Diego Rivera's murals in Mexico City and poor Frida Kahlo's peasant costumes at the Blue House.

Originally, he'd wanted to explore the reasons behind Wells's sudden departure. Why he'd taken off. What had been so compelling that a

145

man could stand up from the breakfast table one morning and go, just like that, slicing the umbilical connection between present and future, without so much as a farewell tear? What did it feel like to set off in search of a home elsewhere? Like men born into women's bodies, fully conscious of their maleness, hands beating at the fence of bone and flesh, let me out, I don't belong here. The same must have been true for Gauguin, for Wells.

He'd begun with that, with the Marie Celeste mystery of the pushed-back chair, the pot of tea on the table, a half-eaten slice of toast still lying on a plate, marmalade smears, damp towels on the bathroom floor, Wells's (not Wells, obviously, but some strong-syllabled name like that – say, for the moment, Fargo) dirty little habits plain for all to see, tissue full of cum by the bed, loo unflushed. Why would you do that, why would you just go? Maybe Wells carried around his own marlin skeleton, Papa Hemingway with the shotgun in his mouth, despairing at his shared humanity, Brendan's pale bruised face on a filthy cushion, marks up and down his arms, thin blue fingernails the colour of hyacinths, *that sanguine flower inscribed with woe*, ah, Christ, Brendan, leave me alone, *rest, rest, perturbed spirit,* another marlin skeleton.

He reaches down and takes the pages from the basket, spreads them on his desk. No two ways about it: this is bullshit. Dog shit. Twenty-pound note wrapped round a dog turd, jiffy envelope addressed to his da in Dublin. It felt good at the time, but he still shouldn't have done it.

Corfu – and a name leaps like a grasshopper into his mind. The man with a house there. Parker. Ian Parker. Parker, recently encountered at some gallery opening, paunchy in pinstripes, jaws overfull of flesh beneath the barber's shave, haw-hawing away, swift to reclaim acquaintance, met him at university, knew even then you were destined for greatness, old fruit, hah-hah, punch to the shoulder, reminiscence about those meadow-haunted punting-picnic Oxford summers which bear about as much relation to reality as a silicone-implanted boob. Fergus finds an address book. He's poised like a rocket, fizzing, frantic to go. He sees a white house, a bare table, square windows opening on the sea. He sees the muse, pale-eyed and beautiful, languid against the rolling waves, an unbifurcated siren. Impatience batters at him like the Greeks at the gates of Troy. Hurry, hurry, inspiration waits in the rock of the sea, the smell of thyme on the hillsides, he needs to be on his way.

He calls Ian Parker's number. Dulcet tones of operator lead to a secretary and onwards to the excelsior of a Personal Assistant, articulation rich as a Fabergé egg. 'He's in conference?' voice rising upwards into query, as though she isn't quite sure. 'I can try him, if you like?'

I do like, yes, indeed. 'If that wouldn't be too much trouble. It's Fergus Costello.'

'Who?'

'Fergus Costello.'

Tumblers clicking, numbers falling. Should she know the name, does this man run shipping empires, IT networks, smuggle people, run guns, is he FTSE, NASDAQ, NYSE, Nikkei? 'One moment, please.'

Then Ian comes on the line. 'Fergus, you old dog, what can I do for you?'

Pleasantries tennis-ball between them. Then to the kernel, the marrow of the thing. 'Last time we met, you mentioned you owned a place on Corfu.'

'Indeed, yes.'

'Is it, do you let it out? Or, if not, do you know of someone who does?'

'Always scribble, scribble, scribble, eh, Mr Costello?' haw-haws Ian. 'Going to write another of your damned thick square books?'

'Ha ha!' A craven response. 'Actually, yes.'

'If I can assist the Muse in any way...' says Ian.

Meaning what, exactly? Will I have to ask again? But no, the Parker is noseying his way towards completion. 'Want to go out there, old son? The memsahib and I'd be delighted to have the place lived in. What with one thing and another, we never seem to spend more than a few days there. As a matter of fact, we're thinking of selling the place, but you're welcome to use it, long as you like.' And on into exposition, a shop nearby, fresh milk, bread van, Spiros the gardener, Maria to come in and clean the place, look after you, yada, yada, yada.

It's that easy. Chest tight, breath palpitant, lemon-haunted dreams coming true. 'This is really generous of you, Ian. Name your price.'

'No, no. Be my guest.'

'I'd be more than happy to pay my way.'

'No, no, I insist. Consider it my contribution to

148

the literature of our age. Anyway, it's you who'll be doing me the favour, Fergus, keep the place lived in, scare away the spiders, all that.' Diffident pause. 'If you *really* insist, you could mention me, us, Daff and me, in the acknowledgements, please the wife, know what I mean, always fancied a slice of literary immortality, used to think I might write myself, haw-ha-hee.'

'The acknowledgement will be of the most fulsome,' Fergus says. Already his creative muscles are flexing and twitching, ready for a workout, ready to run a marathon. 'I can't tell you how grateful I am. Worth a drink or two, Ian. How about the end of the week, Friday?'

'Love to, but for my sins, I'm off to HK day after tomorrow, on to KL and then PNG, back via the US.'

'That's just initially, I take it.'

Digestive pause. 'Oh, hee-haw-ha, gct you now. Glad you're doing so well, Daff and I always watch you on the TV.'

'Would you mind if someone joined me out there for a few days?'

'Oh-ho, is this what I think it is?'

How the feck would I know what an eejit like you thinks? 'Just a friend.' Old boy, old egg, old fruit. 'Another writer. We're ... uh ... working on a project together.'

'Still the eternal bachelor, ha ha.'

'I'm ... like I said, Ian, I'm in your debt for this.'

'Let's hope I never have to call it in, ha ha.' Phones ringing behind him, personal assistant mellifluous in the background, 'Got to go,

Fergus. Look, we'll organize something when we're all back, yes? I'll get my girl to send on the details and information about the house. Be a day or three, up to the eyeballs at the moment. You're not thinking of taking off tomorrow, are you?'

'No, no.' Yesterday would be nearer the mark. Or the day before that.

After he's put the phone down, Fergus makes himself a mug of coffee and asks Directory Enquiries for Theo Cairns, somewhere in Hampshire. He has no idea of the address, but the operator finds it without difficulty. Dialling the number, all he gets is the answering machine. He rings several times in order to listen to Theodora's voice, low-pitched and brisk, more businesslike than she is in the flesh, telling him that she is not at home and inviting him to leave a message after the beep. He doesn't.

The fourth time, he slams the receiver back on to its stand. What the hell is the matter with him, obsessing about a woman he hardly knows and whom he is fairly certain he won't be getting to know any better? Granted, obsession is part of the way he operates, both as person and as writer, but Theodora Cairns is hardly the right object. He thinks of her sad eyes, like sunlit snow, like a frost-patterned window with a lamp behind. At Caro's party, she was wearing a floating dress of ivory silk randomly embroidered with flowers, flamboyant yellow-and-purple tulips, crimson camellias, sprays of forget-me-nots, pink rosebuds. Beautiful. But not as beautiful as she.

150

The yawning blank of his computer screen stares at him from the table, reproachful and hungry, but he ignores it. Instead, he goes through his shelves, looking for one of her books on gardening, and settles down on the futon he uses as both sofa and guest-bed. Reading, the classic displacement activity. And yet it is almost the most important part of the job, letting the mind roam free, accruing scraps, a tideline of flotsam washing gently on to the coastal plain of creativity.

He finds himself absorbed. Theodora writes about gardens as though they are pictures, painting them on to the page for her readers. Her descriptions are luscious, mouth-watering, warm. He reads aloud an account of a garden in Italy, savouring her use of language, walking with her down mossed steps, past trickling fountains, ducking under hanging branches of figs or myrtles, leaves clutching at his cheek like eager hands, lost in a paradise garden.

How different from the cool, wisecracking persona she presents to the world. He understands that only too well, knows all about the protective layer of relentless cheerfulness strapped over disintegration, lostness bandaged with a quip, the wounds of desperation concealed behind a joke. Laugh, clown, laugh. If you amuse them, people assume you're happy. No one bothers to look below the surface to the abyss yawning beneath.

What would Theo be like in bed? Would that air of aloof reserve break down, would she be avid and eager? Sweat on her upper lip, the musk of her, hands in his hair, on his back, pulling him deeper inside. Or, even in passion, would she still maintain her special mystery?

Stop thinking of her, Costello, she's not for the likes of you.

'I think I am falling in love,' he says aloud and feels suddenly afraid, because women like Theo Cairns are not easy, they need more than he is prepared to give, they refuse to settle for less.

Eager, impatient, he calls Theo's number again. Listening to the ring of the phone, he sees sails against a dazzling sky, the prim hooves of donkeys, silver-casketed saints. Be there, he wills, *be* there at the end of the line so I can tell you I'm in, I'm on, it's full steam ahead. An efficient voice this time, telling him Theo is away and not expected back for a while.

'How long is a while?' he asks. Rain jigs and prances on the wooden roof just above his head. 'Are we talking a day, a week, a month?'

'A couple of days. May I say who's calling?'

Anxious that Theodora won't know he's been rebuffed by her absence, he says, 'I'll call back.'

Phone replaced, he wonders if Theodora has left instructions that anyone with an Irish accent is not to be told of her whereabouts. Perhaps she was there all along, listening to him on an extension, and waving her hand, shaking her head, to indicate that she doesn't want to take his call.

Which leaves him with no alternative except to fill further pages with crap – and the world doesn't need any more of that. How has he come to this pass, thirty-nine years old and alone on a rainy Sunday afternoon, brain dead, idea-destitute, Sunday papers not even opened yet?

Can't keep moving forever, got to put down a root, tender and etiolated though it might be, got to hook on with trembling fingernail to the concept of staying put, got to let the restless earth spin without his pointed toes dancing on its rim.

Lennart Wells. Or Fargo. Far Go ... good name, *great* name, appropriate for the circumstances. Call him Gerard (for the moment) Fargo. Fargo caught in a moment of sudden departure, abandoning his present, walking away without a backward glance. Had a friend who did that once, drove to the far edge of Ireland and never even closed the car door behind him as he tumbled out into a new life.

Theo Cairns. Theo in her garden ... that's it, that's the thing! Excitement suddenly explosive, firework in the belly, start the book not with Fargo's abandoned breakfast but instead with Mrs Fargo, garden-loving Mrs Fargo, who sees the delphiniums and the dahlias but not the despair in her husband's eyes. Mrs Fargo, call her Griselda, Victoria, Charlotte, Jemima, call her Celeste even, with dirt under her fingernails and aphids in her hair. Mrs Fargo, raising flowers instead of babies, gone to visit mother, sister, cousin, returning home full of green thoughts, ensnared with blossom, to find the half-chewed toast, towels still damp with her husband's ablutions, bedroom ankle-deep in her husband's wet dreams, but no husband. Better? More of a story?

Sunday afternoon, sloping into Sunday evening. He picks up the phone and dials Theo's number again. Not back yet. He listens to her voice again. Wants her. Wants to tell her. Come back, he breathes into the dead phone, I need to plant my thoughts, my hopes in the receptive soil of your attention, water them, see if they germinate there.

Anal retentive, Charlie called her. Secrets. A different Theo underneath that buttoned-up voice. Imagines her unbuttoned. *A sweet disorder in the dress* ... his own wantonness kindles.

In his head, he sees it all so clearly. The table in Corfu waits for him. The blue square of window overlooking the sea. Dusk coming down as the words pile up beside his keyboard. At last, the drain cleared, the bowel unblocked.

He is growing weary of singularity, that's how it is. Thirty-nine, a burnt-out case. He doesn't have to be alone. There are women who would leave their hair unwashed for him, he knows that. There are friends who'd be glad to share a meal. There is a pub across the road, he could step inside, wrap himself in spurious warmth. Always afraid of that. Looming shadow of the Da. Reeling back across the road, later. Weaving between the cars, lurching down the gangplank to the concrete pontoon, stumbling on to his houseboat, muttering and cursing. The father in his blood, the passed-on ungainsayable DNA. Not a road he wishes to travel, afraid to meet the image of his da coming towards him, jug in hand, tainted genes, the dark at the end of the tunnel, and behind him, pale bones clacking, tufts of fair hair still sticking to his skull.

It's all coming out now, of course. Too late for Brendan, but more than time for the Church. Grave faces, a few token priests in jail, *'serious error of judgement'*, compensation paid. Not that the whole vile concept is exclusive to the priests. Tell me how you compensate for a life ruined, a life lost. *If you tell, you'll go to hell.* Did they seriously think they'd get away with it? Must have done. Move them on, that was the ticket. Move them on before the complaints snowballed into scandal. Move them on, and then on again, and forget the suffering of the little Brendans, God rest their innocent souls.

And here comes Brendan again, with his yellow curls and bright blue eyes and the pure shape of his boy's body. And the Da, the father, what of him? What would he do if the man showed up on the doorstep, hand out like a mendicant, shameless and abject? How long since he last went over to see the old boy – four years, five? If he's still bellowing round the back streets of Dublin, by now he'll be little more than the ghost of a whisky bottle, a shamble of a man. To seek him, or any of them, out at this stage – him or Father Vincent or that subtle little Jesuit inquisitor, Father Mahoney – where would be the point? Forgiveness isn't on the cards, nor should be, getting away with murder, the gardens of youth blighted and not a damn thing done about it.

TWELVE

Two days after having dinner with Fergus in London, I drive up to Yorkshire to see a client who has engaged me to redesign his garden so as to make it more Event Friendly (his phrase, not mine). He is loutish, uncooperative, not a man I want to work with, and I tell him so. The journey back is hot and sticky and I'm drained by the sheer nervous taking-your-life-in-your-hands experience of motorway driving. There is a major pile-up which we wait out through nearly two hours of delay, and several of those inexplicable traffic jams which, when you finally clear them, appear to have no cause.

On top of that, my mind is still churning with hostility towards my mother. How can I make her see how important my father's identity is to me? What right does she have to withhold the information? How can I find out without her cooperation?

By the time I am turning down the lane which runs past my house, it is nearly seven o'clock in the evening. I'm looking forward to nothing so much as sitting down with a cup of coffee and unwinding. So I am not thrilled, when I walk into the office, to find Trina still there. Although she's removed most of the metalwork from her face, her hair is still blue.

'Hi,' she says.

I drop my overnight bag by the door. 'What are you doing here? Shouldn't you have gone home at five?'

She shrugs. 'I been working in the garden, looking up plants. Didn't seem much point leaving early.'

Irritated, I want to point out that the place is also my home and I like it to myself after office hours. Instead I say, 'Did you cope all right?'

'Nothing to it. Wasn't anything urgent, except one letter, which I rang Marnie about and she told me what to say.' She sees the look on my face. 'Don't worry. I didn't screw up or anything, no spelling mistakes, made a kind of squiggle at the end and typed underneath that the letter had been signed in your absence.'

'Sounds like you've got it all under control.'

'Just answering the phone, really.' She laughs. 'Some old ratbag kept calling from Rome about every five minutes. In the end I told her to bug off.'

Luna, trying to get hold of me. 'You *what*?' I shout.

'Just kidding.'

Irrational annoyance boils inside me. 'For God's sake, Trina, whether you're kidding or not, this is all getting to be a bit much.' I press a hand to my head. 'And didn't I tell you to do something about your hair?'

'I'm going to.'

'Well, for God's sake do it *now*.' I'm losing control again. 'I do not want to come back and

157

find that ... that ridiculous hairdo in my office. Change the colour,' I say.

'Keep your shirt on, I—'

'I never wanted to have you here in the first place,' I say, my voice rising, the pressure building, my face reddening. 'It was only as a favour to Mick Haigh that I agreed to it. If you don't feel inclined to do as I ask, then perhaps you shouldn't bother coming back.' I hate myself but seem to have run out of self-control.

She squeezes her mouth into a thin line but doesn't say anything.

I stamp out into the kitchen. On the counter is a basket of fresh-picked runner beans, a bowl of strawberries, three courgettes. And, in several pieces, my favourite mug, sponge-ware, cream-coloured pottery with bunches of grapes stencilled on the side. It seems like the last straw. Marching back into my office, I say, 'Right, Trina. I'm sorry but I'm not putting up with having my things damaged. You'll have to leave.'

'What you on about?' She stares at me, her face closing, stiff with resentment.

'We said an initial month's trial and it's nearly that now. I'll pay you until the end of the week but don't bother coming back.'

'I won't, you needn't bloody worry,' she says. Under her breath she adds something which sounds like, 'Neurotic bitch.'

Slinging her bag over her shoulder, she steps out of the open French windows on to the path which leads around the side of the house. As I'm about to bang them shut, she says, 'If you're losing your bleeding rag about that mug, it was Marnie who broke it, not me.' And off she marches.

Marnie? Oh shit, shit, shit! Trina picks courgettes for me, harvests beans and strawberries, anticipating my pleasure. And I treat her like a piece of nothing, because of a stupid bit of pottery.

What's wrong with me?

As if I didn't know. The glue which has held my life together for years is melting. I feel beleaguered from all sides. For some reason I am, though I hate to admit it, aware that I am frightened. What of, or why, I cannot say. Is it something to do with a profound sense of loss because the Vernon Barnes portrait of a man who is not my father, and the subsequent loss of self? Or is it more tangible than that? Am I becoming as paranoid as my mother, seeing enemies all about me, like that hieratic figure outside my mother's hotel? Why does he disturb me? Why do I link him with my father, the painted garden, the hidden watcher at the window?

In addition, as well as alienating both Marnie and Trina, I've managed to screw up the two most significant relationships in my life: daughter and wife. Perhaps Trina's right and I *am* a neurotic bitch. I'm certainly acting like one. It's not a pleasant thought. I press the message button on the answering machine and listen to Jenny asking how I am, Terry sending her love, Elizabeth Crawfurd saying she hopes I hadn't minded her speaking to James Bellamy about the Vernon Baines painting and if he's upset me,

159

she's really awfully sorry, she had no idea that ...
I cut her off in mid-message.

Not only have I been both unfair and bitchy to
Trina, I've accused her of something she didn't
even do. Woman behaving badly. I change into
my grubby gardening clothes and go outside to
survey my small kingdom. The further away
from the house I go, the wilder the lushness of
grass and fern. I love this area of untamed
natural growth. Dozens of bulbs have been
planted here: fritillaries, daffodils, grape
hyacinths, lilies, wonderful tulips which push
their way through the fecund grass like
multicoloured ballerinas. As I walk, I recite the
lovely names of grasses: fescue and timothy,
fiorin and foxtail and Yorkshire fog.

Harry Lovage has obviously been busy down
by the spring; the last of the stone flags has been
set the way I showed him, and he's bedded in the
remaining hostas. Eventually the giant leaves of
the *hosta sieboldiana* will try to take over, if the
slugs don't get it first. I make a mental note to
topdress around it with a thick layer of sharp
grit.

In the area which will eventually be my
scented garden, I spend a couple of hours turning over the soil, jabbing my fork into the
ground and lifting huge chunks of heavy earth. It
all needs to be mulched and turned before I can
complete the plantings I have in mind. There are
no roses here. I prefer a dedicated rose garden.
Two springs ago, I put in an *acacia dealbata*; it's
not a hardy species and I'm delighted that it's
still doing well. The gorgeous perfume of

philadelphus drifts across the space, intoxicating and seductive, mingling with honeysuckle and lavender. This is open-air aromatherapy.

My suicidal self-hate subsides a little. Sitting on a curved stone bench beside the glorious pastels of sweet peas, I reflect that I myself am like an overgrown garden, where any number of delights may lie beneath the jungle of weeds and bramble, creepers, poison ivy, bindweed, the waist-high grass. Marble statues may be there, pools of rainbow fish, crystal-clear springs, beds of violets, heavy-laden fruit trees. But until I can clear away the creeper and the couch grass, cut down the brambles and scythe the grass, I shall never know.

Night-time scents – honeysuckle, jasmine, orange blossom, nicotiana – rise from the beds around me as I finally make my way back to the house. A neon city glow illuminates the horizon; nearer at hand, I can see the lights of the village through the trees. At the edge of the lawn, bushes quiver, shadows stir. A car engine thrums in the lane. A lone dog barks and is joined by a chorus from others. The image of that still, dark figure outside the Lotus Flower Hotel slithers into my head. Where have I seen him before? I shiver.

A lycanthropic moon hangs to one side of the sky and briefly I wonder why werewolves are always male when women, too, possess just as many of the baser appetites which inform the myth.

As if conjured by my thoughts, the telephone rings and it's him. 'I enjoyed our dinner together,' he says.

'So did I. Thank you.' I'm not just being polite.

'We could do it again.'

'That would be nice.'

'Or instead of dinner, we could go to the theatre.'

'Indeed.'

'Or skinny dipping, deep-sea diving, bungee jumping, Morris dancing. Anything you like.'

'All or any,' I say.

'Or none,' he says. 'We could go to Corfu, instead.'

'Fergus, I really can't take—'

'It's all settled, I've got the house sorted, I can leave as soon as I like. It'll be fantastic, especially if you come with me.'

'I'd love to Fergus, I really would. But honestly, I can't, I have far too much work to do here.'

'How can I persuade you to change your mind? What inducements can I offer?'

'Unfortunately, none. Really, I haven't time for holidays at the moment. Besides, I'm not ... not what you want.'

'How do you know what I want?'

'I don't know, someone bright, happy, enthusiastic.'

'And you're none of those?'

'At the moment, I don't believe I am.' Was I ever?

Abruptly he changes the subject. 'So, where have you been? I rang a couple of times but you weren't home.'

'I drove up to Yorkshire to advise someone about a garden.'

162

'Did he take your advice?'

'I didn't give him any. He turned out to be so disagreeable that I thought the hell with it, and drove straight home again.'

'Just like that?'

'Best way to deal with it.'

'I'd no idea you were so firm of purpose.'

'I'm not, usually. But sometimes life's too short.'

'Isn't there a danger that they'll look at the plans you've drawn up for them and then put them into practice without using you?'

'I took my design away with me. Of course, I'll have to send back the money he's already paid.' I sigh. Once that would have been a minor disaster, but now it merely seems irrelevant. 'Anyway, you can't patent ideas.'

I have an urge to confess my sins, tell him how mean I was to Trina, get from him some kind of absolution. But of course I don't. We talk for another ten minutes or so about very little. Tomorrow I will telephone Trina, apologize, beg her to come back. Ask her to talk over her garden plan for Holly Crawfurd. Praise her for the excellent job she's done.

I go to bed with one of Fergus's books. It's both clever and moving, a sensitive story about coming of age. But I am tired, both physically and emotionally, and fall asleep at chapter three. I dream I am dropping out of the sky, my parterred garden below me. I dream the flowerbeds are full of shrivelled plants; that the white pebbles have turned black and the unicorn is now a raging monster clawing to break in. I wake in a sweat of terror. I see the man at the window and he is not my father.

I dream again, this time of Luna, running, running, her red shoes clacking as she drags me behind her, running so fast that I flow horizontal in the slipstream of her passage, pursued by a black shadow. She is crying as she runs. So am I.

Once more I wake and toss around in the darkness, feverish, unable to get comfortable. Everything is breaking up around me, leaving me abandoned on the ice floes. My life is tilting, swinging, turning upside-down.

THIRTEEN

Fergus receives a padded envelope from Ian Parker. There are keys, photographs, local maps, directions for how to reach the house from the airport or the harbour. He can leave tomorrow, this afternoon if he wants. Suddenly Corfu has become a reality instead of a dream. His finger-tips are blocked with words, ready to jump on to the page. Time to go, time to write.

He telephones Carolyn Cartwright to tell her he is leaving. 'You sound lonely,' she says.

'I am.'

'Why don't you come round for supper? Spaghetti, a salad, the first bottle's just being opened.'

'Sweet Caroline.'

'Well?' Behind her, a squall of noise, fractious boy-voices, nordic soothings from the au pair.

'It's knowing that I *could* come round. Instantly, I'm no longer lonely.'

'Seen anything of Theo?'

'I have indeed.' He explains the sight of her at his book reading, the meal shared, the jazz listened to. Pause, sup at the opened beer, emotion fizzing in his mouth along with the hops and the yeast. 'Haven't met up with her since, Caro, and to tell the truth, I wish I had.' Wish I could stop thinking about her. Wish I could unlock the secrets she stacks so pack-rattedly inside herself.

'Are you going to say goodbye to her before you go?'

'I hope not.' Lungs filled. 'You may not believe this, Caro, but I asked her to come with me.'

'What? To Corfu?'

'That's right.'

'I'm gobsmacked! I don't know what to say.'

'Best to say nothing. Tell me more about her.'

'I don't know a lot. There's a dead father, some kind of war hero, I believe, and a slightly mad mother. According to Terry, the woman's a world-class dancer and choreographer, always on the move, but never seems to have had much time for her daughter. Disappeared for about ten years when Theo was twelve or so, resurfaced after Theo married Harvey.'

'Strange.'

'We all thought so.'

'She just took off? I wonder why.'

'She's ... weird.'

'Or running from something or someone.' His novelist's mind drums up possibilities: Mafia, murderer, stalker, debt collector.

He thinks of Theo's fingers so tender among the leaves of Caro's garden. Nurturing. The way she touched petals, stroked leaves. Bending her head to sniff at the flowers, hair falling away from the white nape of her neck, graceful. He thinks of love and its complications, how a person might be who suffers from a chronic lack of it.

'She's very like you, Fergus, in all sorts of ways,' says Caro. 'Which is why I knew you two would get on. You'd understand each other where other people might not.'

'Glass of wine, Caro?' Charlie's voice.

Fergus can almost smell the bolognese sauce, the sharpness of the fresh-grated parmesan, see the gleam of oil on green leaves, basil. All he has to do is walk out of the door and hail a cab.

'So, is something stirring between you?' Carolyn asks.

'Takes two to have a between, don't you think?' he says. 'Or a stir, for that matter. A person on his own couldn't manage it.'

'How can you get her to be the other person?'

'That would depend on whether I wanted to.'

'And you don't?'

You're not going to ask if you can come up for coffee, are you? Well, yes, as it happens, I *was* going to, as a matter of fact, since you're asking, actually I was, since I'm keen and growing

166

keener by the second, since I can't see the way into you and need to discover it, and while I have no expectation of sex or even a chaste kiss, I want to spend longer with you. And there was definitely a deliberate and derisive deepening of those dimples as she got out of the taxi. Laughing at me. No question about that.

'She'd laugh at me,' Fergus says.

'She's too kind-hearted to do that.'

'She already has, more than once.'

'She's normally rather solemn.'

'Solemn? I don't think so.'

'Why did she laugh at you?'

'I was being pompous. It's too embarrassing to be discussed.' Water-swell against the hull. Floor moving under his feet. Rocked in the cradle of the Thames.

'You didn't grope her, did you?'

'Of course I didn't.' Press of the cold beer's rim against his mouth. 'I'd better let you go.'

'Keep in touch. Don't be lonely. We love you.' Carolyn makes a kissing noise into the phone and switches off.

Theodora weighted down with chains ... Maybe something of the same for Griselda Fargo, patience made anorexic by her husband's indifference. But loves him still, the garden a substitute for the affection she yearns for, the chaos she can't control? He's gone, and seeking her own epiphanies, she goes after, follows (or pursues, there's a world in the difference) the hard-found trail to Mexico, a woman chasing a dream she never even realized she had, intrepid, yes, definitely better her story rather than his, would it work?

He picks up Theo's book again. Behind the words, at the back of his mind, Griselda – Charlotte? – begins to take shape and form as he turns the pages. An account of sixteenth-century gardens carved out of the forest of Tetzcotzinco. Medicinal gardens full of aromatic herbs. Blossoms raining fragrance from high, dark trees. Yes, Charlotte (or Griselda) Fargo (Victoria too hard, Jemima too dimity-sweet) travelling on her own account as well as her husband's, finds him eventually at the very heart of the jungle, and the work he's done without her, fierce and beautiful, a far cry from the stuff he produced in, where? Hampshire, Cornwall, Middlesbrough? Middlesbrough's good, got a rough-hewn sound to it. He's living in a tumbledown adobe studio, painting as though there is no time to say what he has to, canvas after canvas, meticulous facades starting up out of the undergrowth, temple ruins overgrown with creeper, antique faces inscrutable in sunlight, the luxuriant overwhelming undergrowth. She begins to see why he went, how marriage had brought him down, confined him, and yet he needs her. Has her own vision, a new garden springing, sprouting here in these rich forests.

It's emerging, it's coming, Aphrodite arising from the foam, Mrs Fargo spinning out of the brain-seethe, the mind-churn. Using Charlotte/Griselda as the mediator would remove some of the Gauguinerie of the thing. *Nafea Faa ipoipo,* Mexico not the same as Tahiti, but still a platitude-magnet, if care isn't taken. It'll have to be

168

looked into, have to be sought out, digested, in order to do it all justice. Him and Theo, following in Griselda's footsteps, great white hunters, questing beasts, searching for the beating heart torn dripping from the body, searching for the crock of gold.

Or of shit.

Griselda is a good name, but not good enough. Especially given the way she is pushing so breathlessly through the pages, stepping from obscurity, discarding her minor-character status, shouldering her way forward to the very centre stage of his mind. Charlotte wasn't right, either, not any more. What's in a name? A lot, since you ask. Just about everything. Fred Austerlitz and Ginger Rogers? Frances Gumm singing *Somewhere over the Rainbow*? I don't think so.

Joanna? Not bad. Julia? Always a problem, his phonaesthetic preference for names beginning with J, six or seven of them in the first draft of his third novel. Barbara? Not bad. Soft but determined. Go with that for the moment, see where it leads.

Cheep, cheep of the telephone again. And it's her! It's Theodora!

'Are you still going?' No introduction, no explanation.

He not sure what she means, needing it spelled out. 'Where to?'

'Corfu.'

'Ah, yes.'

'Or have you changed your mind?'

There's something wild and unsustained about her voice, a woman with something on her mind

169

that has nothing to do with holidays. 'No, it's all set, I'm planning to fly over any moment now.'

'I see...' Pause. Expectancy clotting the lines, both of them holding their eggshell breaths.

'Are you...' Croak in his throat, a clearing of the passageways. 'Are you coming with me?' He remembers his strictures about distraction, then thinks of her loosened by sunshine, running out of the sea, standing under a shower, lying on linen sheets beneath him. Would she, would he? Get thee behind me, he must not rush this, mustn't even consider the possibility, different beds, expect nothing.

'Yes. I'd like to. If you don't mind.'

'I don't mind. And let me tell you it's a palace. Swimming pool, little beach below, a boat, enough bathrooms for a harem.' Careless now, as though it doesn't matter. 'Bedrooms galore.'

Expulsion of the breath. She's been waiting for the bedroom quotient. 'It sounds great.'

'Belongs to a friend from my university days,' he says. 'He's lending it to us for auld lang syne.'

'Us?'

'Me.' Sweating, he adds, 'I'm so glad you've changed your mind.'

'About what?' Sharply spoken, conceding nothing.

'About coming with me.' Mistake, mistake, he's overdone the warmth, she's taken fright. In a rush, she's saying, 'Only for ten days, a couple of weeks. We go halves on everything. We have separate bedrooms. Do our own thing. No feeling that we have to do everything together, we're

170

not a couple, OK?'

'If that's how you want it.' Grace, he thinks suddenly. That's the name I'm looking for. Amazing Grace Fargo.

'I do.'

Times, dates, basic travel arrangements sorted out. He'll get the tickets, she'll pay him back. He puts down the phone. An irrevocable step taken, he is sure of it, though he can't imagine why.

FOURTEEN

'I'm taking a holiday next week, for ten days or so,' I tell Marnie. This is the first vacation I've taken in the more than three years that she's worked for me.

Her shapely eyebrows rise. 'Oh?'

'A chance came up,' I gabble. 'A friend's house, stupid to miss the opportunity, always wanted to...'

She holds up a hand to stop the flow. 'You don't have to explain,' she says. 'You're allowed. Do you good, I should think. You've been looking like death warmed up for weeks now. I don't know what's eating you, but something is and it's been worrying me.' She gives me a sideways glance. 'Where are you going?'

'Corfu.'

'With someone?'

'Yes.'

171

'Anyone I know?'

'I doubt it,' I say coolly.

'I see.' She adopts the kind of maddening I-Can-Put-Two-and-Two-Together smirk which gets right up my nose. 'You can rely on me and Trina to keep things going.'

'Well, no, I can't. Unfortunately I ... uh ... Trina and I had a bit of a falling out.'

Up go the eyebrows again. 'Oh?' She's already blaming me. And she's right.

I swallow. Accept Responsibility for Your Actions. 'It was entirely my fault. Long and the short is, I told her not to come back.'

'You flipping idiot.'

'I know.'

'What did you quarrel about?'

'It sort of started with her hair.'

'What's wrong with her hair?'

'It's blue, Marnie, in case you hadn't noticed. I can't have her looking like that when customers come.'

'Why not?'

'Because it's not suitable.'

'Don't be such an old stick-in-the-mud, Theo. That woman on the gardening programme's always flashing her tits about, and nobody seems to object. Especially not my husband.'

'What do you think of her?'

'The tit-flasher?'

'Trina, Marnie.'

'Very bright. Very efficient.' Marnie purses her lips. 'Remember I was talking about finding a like-minded person to help you expand the business?'

'Yes...'

'You could do worse.'

'A seventeen-year-old?' The idea is comic.

'Why not? Being young's an advantage, if you think about it. You could train her up. And she's really keen, really imaginative, works hard.'

'That's crazy,' I say.

She spreads her pretty hands, an action which makes me realize how unkempt my own are. 'I don't mean you should hand over the business to her, nothing like that. But you could think about taking her on full time, with a view to giving her a much bigger role. Share some of the work.'

'Thanks for the advice,' I say dryly.

'Just as a matter of interest, apart from the hair, what else did you and Trina quarrel about?'

'Oh, Lord ... well, if you really want to know, it was over that broken mug.'

'The one I dropped? Which I forgot to tell you about?' The look she gives me makes me feel two inches high. 'You *didn't*, Theo! You didn't accuse her of breaking it, did you? Tell me you didn't.'

'What can I say...'

'You could say you're a prize idiot. You could ask yourself whether a mug is worth making a fuss over. You could join a relaxation class or take up yoga – or you could spend this holiday in Corfu, with someone I don't know, sorting yourself out. And before you go, you could try to get Trina back. She loves it here and she does a terrific job.'

'Right on all counts.'

'And though it's got nothing to do with anything, she gets on really well with Harry.'

'Well, in *that* case...' I say.

We spend an hour sorting out my diary, stuff which can be put on the back burner, clients who need to be warned that I shall be away. Marnie and I run a tight ship, so the process is not too onerous, and in any case, I have a week to cope with the absolutely must-do things. As I work, the thought of being back on Corfu with Fergus floats like a calm sea at the back of my head. If I can hang on for seven more days without a major catastrophe, I'll be there, walking between olive trees, enchanted by wild lavender and sage, and maybe I'll recover some of my lost equilibrium. He'll be there, too. I shall have to think how to handle that. Not that I think that a holiday is a remedy for anything, far from it. Time off is like Valium: it may hide the symptoms, but it doesn't effect a cure.

A couple of days later, I drive over to where Trina lives. Her home is a terraced two-up, two-down place in a quiet backstreet. Motorbikes are parked halfway up the pavement. There's an Indian takeaway on one corner, a newsagent on the other, a Catholic church halfway up the street. The image returns of that silent watching figure standing against railings. Why did I find him so menacing, why has his image stayed with me?

I knock at the red front door and wait.

'Mr Hawkins?' I ask, when the door is opened.

The man in front of me is short, with a glint of bristle on his chin that implies he is normally clean shaven. 'That's right.'

'Trina's father?'

'Yes.' I can see a look of her about him, especially in the bright eyes and small face.

'Is she home?'

'Got herself a proper job, hasn't she? Junior down the hairdressers.' He frowns at me. 'Don't I know you?'

I can see along the passageway behind him to a sunlit rectangle, the doorway leading out into the backyard. There's an impression of roses, pink and crimson, of dahlias, of green leaves in the sun. 'Trina was doing work experience with me.'

His frown vanishes. 'That's right. She enjoyed that. You're the lady off the telly. Trina's always talking about you. Come in.'

I gesture at the open back door behind him. 'Are you a gardener?'

'Not me, luv. Leave all that to Treen.'

'Might I have a look?'

''Course you can.'

I follow him down the passage to the garden at the back. The house smells comfortably of fried bacon and old cigarette smoke. 'It's not much,' he says over his shoulder. 'Not to the likes of you.'

What kind of like am I? I wish he'd tell me because over the past few weeks, I have completely lost touch with myself.

We pass through a kitchen with the remains of breakfast on it, plus a cigarette lying half in and half out of an ashtray, a line of blue smoke climbing upwards to the ceiling. As we pass, he picks it up, draws deeply on it, lays it down

175

again.

We walk into what had once been a typical backyard. But instead of dustbins, concrete, old bikes, an outside WC, it's a bower of green, a riot of colour. It's flagged and bricked, turned into a secret garden among these little back-to-back terraces. Shrubs all round hide two brick walls and a fence, rose trees are trained against trellises, there are seats here and there, fitted into the tiny space, made of old brick with weathered planks set on them. Behind a beech hedge with a clematis trained over it is a small shed, smothered in roses. Water trickles into a stone basin. A big fig tree casts wayward shadows over all. Shallow brick steps lead to a second level of flower-crammed flowerbeds.

'She can't have done all this by herself.' I turn, to absorb it all.

'Gave her a bit of a hand with shifting stuff about,' he says diffidently. 'But yeah, most of it's down to her.'

'It's breathtaking.' I can see another book in the offing: *Backyards and Other Fantasies*, something like that, with Trina's name prominent on the cover. 'Anyone would think we were in the Mediterranean.' From here, the street noise is almost inaudible.

'Too small to do much with, see, that's what she said.' He gestures round his domain. 'She said no point trying to grass it, so we bricked it over, built the beds all round.'

He offers me a cup of tea and I accept. We sit companionably on the slatted seats. Sparrows chirp in the hedges. The fountain splashes. A

176

cloud of midges is dancing madly among the fig leaves.

'Trina says her mother wants her to go into hairdressing permanently,' I say.

He shrugs. 'A steady job, money coming in. Might end up with her own place, salon they call it, one of these days, she's certainly got the drive.'

'Nothing wrong with that at all. But it wouldn't be using even half of her capabilities. She's extremely intelligent, and very efficient. She should be going to college.' I gesture at the leafy space around us. 'And she's obviously got a talent.'

'That's what I think, too, always had a green thumb. But it's her mother ... you know women...' He shrugs, sighs. 'Can't tell them anything.'

'Trina should be going to a horticultural school,' I say firmly. 'She'd have no trouble at all getting taken on afterwards by one of the big growers or designers.'

'Anybody ends up with my Trina working for them is dead lucky.'

'You sound very proud of her.'

''Course I am. We both are. The apple of her mum's eye, is Trina. And mine. She's always been a good girl. And she's a real hard little worker. Clever, too ... ten GCSEs? You don't get that every day of the week, do you?'

'You should tell your wife that there's a lot of money in gardening these days. Television's made it very popular.'

'You mean she could end up on one of them

programmes?'

'Why not? She's got the looks for it, and the confidence. A lot more than I ever had.'

'Hmmm.' I can see him considering it, thinking that maybe gardening could prove as good a bet as hairdressing, if not better, at the very least be something to use on his wife.

'Does she come home for lunch?' I ask.

'Pops across the road from the salon, usually, grabs a sandwich or something.'

'I'd like to have a word with her.' I stand up. 'What's the name of the place she's working?'

'Lucille's.' He gives me directions.

She's inside, sweeping the floor. It's a week since I last saw her and she looks unhappy and defeated. I'm deeply ashamed of myself. Sins of omission; I should have come to see her before this. When I open the door, she looks up and her face grows stony; she hunches her shoulder, starts sweeping again.

'Have you got a minute, Trina?' I ask.

She leans on her broom. 'What for?'

'I want to talk to you.'

The woman who is obviously the owner of the place looks at me and then at Trina and once again at me. 'Go on, then, darlin',' she says. 'Almost your lunch-break, innit?'

Trina removes the PVC apron she's wearing and follows me across the road to a sandwich bar. I buy sandwiches and coffee for us both and bring them to the table she's sitting at.

'How'd you know where I was, anyway?' she asks.

'I went to your house and your father told me.

He showed me your wonderful back garden.'

'What do you want?' Her hair is now a defiant shade of green. Metal studs sprout like pustules on her face.

'First, I want to apologize.'

She just looks at me.

'Secondly, I want you to come back and work for me. *With* me.'

'After what you said? Right out of order, that was.'

'I know. I was rude, insensitive, unkind, mean, thoroughly—'

She lifts her cup and I can see she is trying not to smile. 'No need to overdo it.'

'I mean it, Trina. I should never have spoken to you the way I did. I can only say I've been going through a bad patch recently—'

'I noticed.'

'Still am, to a certain extent.' Never apologize, never explain, someone once said, and here I am, doing both.

'You got no right to speak to me like that.'

'That's why I'm here. Look, I really wish you'd come back.'

The look she gives me is inimical. She half turns away. 'I don't think so.'

'You've got huge talent, Trina. You're utterly wasted sweeping up people's dead hair. You need to learn as much as you can from me, and then enrol on a horticultural course of some kind.'

'My mum won't like it. And there's another thing...' She waves her left hand in front of my face and I see for the first time the small turquoise and diamond band on her fourth finger.

179

'Oh, Trina...' I feel defeated. 'Why?'

She gives the one-shouldered shrug I'm so familiar with, shutting me out. 'Seemed like a good idea at the time.'

'There are so many better ideas. Dozens of them.' Panic seizes. 'Don't do it, Katrina. Don't get married just as a way of getting back at me, or turning your back on all the possibilities ahead of you.'

Maybe it's the use of her full name. For a long moment, she stares me without speaking. Tears fill her eyes. Then she reaches for a tissue from her bag, and I can see it's hopeless to try and persuade her back. A life wasted. And it's my fault. Theo the Destroyer.

'You had so many plans,' I say feebly.

'Yeah, well...' We both fall into silence. Around us is the clatter of tea cups, voices murmuring, the whirr of the microwave, the slam of fridge doors. Is it my imagination or can I hear the sound of dreams shattering?

Eventually she turns away from me, gets up and leaves without looking at me. I watch her cross the road, back to Lucille's, and the pain I feel is almost insupportable. I think of my mother's face in the gloom of a hotel dining room, the way I shouldered away from her, the hardness of my expression as she tried to hug me.

I have to face the fact that my self-indulgent anger has precipitated Trina's engagement, the probable waste of a talent. What hurts me most, though, as I get back into my car and drive away, is the fact that she doesn't seem any happier about it than I am.

FIFTEEN

A seasoned traveller, Fergus guides us confidently through the journey. The flight to Corfu is free of snags, everything happens as it is supposed to; I don't have to worry about anything at all. It's a welcome change from most of my trips abroad. We take a taxi to the house that Fergus has borrowed from his university friend and are greeted by an ancient woman who establishes that her name is Maria by repeating the word several times and gesturing at her black-swathed bosom. She speaks rapidly in Greek, a language I don't know, Greece being one of the few countries where Luna never alighted. Luckily, Fergus seems to be fluent. The two of them chat away as Maria pulls open cupboards, demonstrates stoves, shows us where the spare canisters of Calor Gas are stored and how the washing machine works. Opening the big double refrigerator, she points at the contents and then at me. She pulls out a covered bowl and bats at her chest again, indicating that it's for me, that she made it herself. I smile and nod while Fergus murmurs gratitude.

She ushers us upstairs and flourishes at the view, the linen cupboard, the bathrooms. She leads us into what is obviously the master bedroom and makes gestures at the huge bed. Now is not the time to indicate that we won't be sharing it.

Downstairs, she shows us the garage where there's an old car, a motor-scooter, bikes. She mimes someone on a bicycle, arms pumping, legs stamping so vigorously I almost see the wind in her sparse grey hair. She points at Fergus, throws back her head and cackles, showing us brown teeth spaced haphazardly in her gums.

'So, what do we think?' Fergus asks, when she has finally gone, walking away up the stony track towards the road above the house.

'That we're very lucky indeed,' I say. 'That your friend must be exceptionally nice to let us have this place.'

'I'm in a state of total guilt. Ian's been incredibly generous, and I've been thinking the most uncharitable thoughts about him.'

'Who is he?'

'Some financial wizard I knew at university. A walking cliché. Always wanted to write the Great English Novel but instead took the easy glide into money-making, and ever since has felt that he betrayed his genius.'

'He knows I'm here, does he?'

'Yes, but I didn't mention your name.'

Contentment falls over me. From Fergus's description, I'd expected something between a castle in Spain and a piece of Hollywood schmaltz and it is undoubtedly very luxurious. Nonetheless, there's a comfortable feel about the place, as though it's a genuine home-from-home.

Ancient straw hats hang from hooks on the wall of the kitchen, there are ashes in the hearth where the scent of olivewood still lingers. I can imagine Fergus's friend and his family walking in for the first time each year, stepping out of their stiff English selves, taking on the relaxed personae that people do when they're away from the pressure of daily living.

I choose a bedroom. It contains one four-poster bed, one capacious wardrobe of iron-hard black wood, and one upright chair. The walls are whitewashed, the windows small to keep out the heat, the floor is tiled and wonderfully cool under my feet. Below is a swimming pool, set in the midst of burgeoning greenery. I can hardly wait to get into it. Tomorrow I'll try the sea, but for today, chlorinated water will do. I change into a swimsuit and run downstairs and outside. Despite the little onshore breeze, the heat is almost tangible, like a bronze ceiling above my head, as physically present as the chairs round the pool or the ceramic pots trailing flowering plants.

Fergus is already there, standing on the edge of the pool and looking down at the flat water, green with beautiful handmade tiles. I can't help noticing (and no reason why I shouldn't since it's right there on display) that he has a good body, better than you'd imagine from the fully clothed version. There's a tattoo at the top of his left shoulder, looks like a toucan from where I'm standing. Why would anyone have a toucan on their shoulder? Perhaps it's a guy thing. Un-accountably, uncomfortably, I feel a flicker of

183

desire. No – be honest, Theo – something more than a flicker. Something closer to a rush. It's been a long time since I was this close to a semi-naked man. A *gorgeous* semi-naked man. A man I ... face it ... really like.

'Last one in gets to –' he starts and I'm in before he's finished the sentence with – 'open the wine.' He leaps in after me, a boy's jump of splashes and spray, and comes clumsily after me. I've always been a good swimmer; he hasn't a hope of catching up.

It's moving towards dusk and birds are starting their twilight hymn to the coming night. A couple of swallows swoop across the water as I move smoothly from one end to the other and back again. On my tenth lap, I turn over and spread my limbs, floating like a starfish on the cool green surface as the still-warm sun beats down on me. I can feel stress sloughing off me and even though I know it can't last, it is none-theless healing. Energy flows into me, and a desire to move onwards. I experience one of those now-and-again moments of almost orgas-mic bliss, when everything combines into per-fection, though as always, it only lasts a nano-second. Then Fergus is thrusting out of the water beside me, his black hair clinging to his skull, his eyes reddened by the swimming-pool salts. He throws back his head to clear the hair from his face, scattering drops all over my warm body, and puts a cold hand on my stomach.

'Bug off, Fergus,' I say lazily.

'Come on, let's have a race,' he urges.

'I'll race you tomorrow.'

'Spoil sport.'

'Horrid, aren't I?'

'No,' he says softly, slipping away from me. 'No, you're not.'

Showered, easy in a cotton sarong and a white top cropped enough to show off my flat stomach, I stand barefooted on the terrace outside the salon. Cypresses and olives spread away to the left. I can see the roofs of the little town below, the fizz of neon lights. Occasionally, on the wind, floats the parp-parp of car horns and the sound of brash tourist-tempting music. The moon is rising over the edge of the sea, a great cheesy disk, dog-eared at one edge as though a giant hand has turned down the rim.

Fergus speaks behind me. 'Fancy a drink?' He is holding a tray, glasses, a bottle of wine.

'Wonderful.'

We stretch out on the generously cushioned chaises. He's also prepared a plate of *mezetés*: olives and a crumbly white cheese, smoked octopus. 'Maria said we must eat whatever's in the fridge.'

'It's a real bonus that you can speak Greek,' I say.

'I can't. Barely a word.'

'Didn't sound like that to me at all. Nor, as far as I could tell, to Maria.'

'Amazing what you can do with a classical education and a bit of Grecian gibbering.' He passes me a glass of wine. 'Are you hungry? We can raid the fridge, or walk down the hill to the town.'

'Let's think about that a bit later,' I say. 'How's

185

your book going, Fergus?'

'It's coming along.' He sounds evasive. Shifty.

'How far along?'

He shrugs. Busies himself with his wine glass. 'I haven't sat down and counted the words, if that's what you mean.'

'How long have you been working on this one?'

A long silence ensues. After a while, he says, 'Are you really interested?'

'I wouldn't have asked if I wasn't.'

'Well...' More silence, then, 'I've found this one more difficult to get into than I usually do.'

'Why's that?'

'Who knows. I've written a lot of it, and then junked it. It hasn't been coming out right. But ... the ideas are all there, all flowing, even if it's at the speed of a glacier. Any time now I'll start putting the words down on paper.'

I can see that he is telling me something which matters a lot to him. I suspect he doesn't often talk about his working methods. He fiddles again with his glass. 'Got any plans, now we're here?'

'Whoa!' I say. 'That nearly took my head off.'

'What did?'

'The speed with which you changed the subject. Anyway, since you ask, tomorrow, I'm going to do absolutely nothing except go down to the beach, swim, eat and read.' And try to overcome my demons. The memory of myself shouting at people who are in no position to shout back makes me hot with shame. 'How about you?'

'Pretty much the same. After that, I must work.'

We both sip our wine. He clears his throat. 'Look, since, as you pointed out, although we are entirely independent, we are nonetheless together...'

'Yes?'

'This beach...'

'What about it?'

'Am I allowed to occupy it at the same time as you? If I showed up and you were there already, could I spread my towel near yours?' he asks humbly.

'If you promise not to flick sand in my face.' I'm smiling. 'Though...'

'What?' he says, leaning forward to refill my glass. 'You're staring at me.'

'From what I read in the gutter press, you must be used to that.'

'If you believe that...' He spreads his hands. 'The occasional crazy bag-lady might try to catch my eye, but beautiful women gawping, drooling slightly as they do so, have so far been a little thin on the ground. Callypygian women even more so.'

'Callipygian?'

'Beautiful-buttocked.'

'If this were a Doris Day movie, that would be my cue to slap your face.'

'If this were a Doris Day movie, the word "buttock" would have been censored. You should be flattered; it's one of the attributes of Aphrodite.'

'Consider me flattered. And for the record, I

187

am not drooling.'

'Drooling is in the eye of the beholder,' he says.

I laugh. I feel entirely at ease even though I hardly know him. Fergus demands nothing from me. Not yet, at least, though I suspect he may later.

'You're looking very pretty.' He gazes at me with an expression on his face that I can only describe as hopeful. But I'm here to try and sort myself out, calm myself down. I've made my intentions perfectly clear. I'm paying my half of this holiday; I don't owe him a thing.

Of course I know that's not true. This place alone, I owe him that. And the peace which is dropping over me, the perfumed air, the shimmering sea below us, all that is a debt – but I do not intend to repay it with my body.

'There's a garden I want to go and see,' I say quickly. 'On the other side of the island. One of these days, while you're working, I thought I might hire a car, drive over and look round.'

His face droops and I feel mean, knowing he would like to come with me. But we've established the ground rules and we ought to abide by them.

Later, we put together a meal from the contents of the fridge and the stone-shelved larder. Fergus lights the barbecue. I find rosemary growing wild on the rocky slope outside the kitchen, and thyme. We sit out on the terrace and watch the mysterious movement of the sea. There are long candles in glass shades, another bottle of wine, *yoladze dolmas* out of a tin. The covered bowl

188

pointed out during Maria's introductory tour proves to contain a rich green soup whose ingredients we can't figure out, though I recognize fennel in there, and dandelion leaves. We eat fresh tomatoes sliced and seasoned with coarse salt, dribbled with green oil. We grill a piece of anonymous white fish on the barbecue, with rosemary, thyme, garlic. Above our heads, little purple grapes cluster among vine leaves.

'Maria was saying her husband caught this fish for us this morning.' Fergus lifts a forkful to his mouth and chews it with relish.

'But you don't speak Greek.'

'I know.'

'So she could equally have been saying that she's read all your books and loathes them.'

'Or that the fish is part of a fertility rite which has to be completed by sundown.'

'Or even that it belongs to the family cat.'

'Which hasn't yet – supposing it even exists – put in an appearance. It's the early cat that catches the fish – and we got here first.'

Some of my blood has been replaced by wine, and I'm enjoying the feeling. The smell of rosemary drifts from the barbecue and as the wind turns, we briefly hear Elvis belting out 'You Ain't Nothin' But a Hound Dog'.

'I know the two of us are acting as separate entities,' Fergus says. 'I know we are not in any way bound by the fact that we are here together, sitting across a table from each other, grown fat on the cat's supper, having gazed upon the wine when it was red and also when it was white but...'

'What's your point?'

'Tell me about your father.'

My father suddenly seems irrelevant. 'Do I have to?'

'Sooner or later, yes, so why not now?'

'The thing is...' I hesitate. Where to begin? How much should I tell this man who seems able to prise secrets from me as though he were opening oysters?

'Is your presence here something to do with him?'

I reflect on this. 'Yes,' I say carefully. If James Bellamy hadn't arrived to destroy my illusions, I probably wouldn't be here now. 'I think it is.'

'You said you thought he'd died,' prompts Fergus.

'That's what my mother always told me. And then I discovered...' I explain about the portrait of Thomas Bellamy. 'And suddenly I feel as if my foundations have gone and I shan't be able to function until I know the truth.'

'Can't you ask your mother?'

'I have. And she won't tell me. Says I'm being unreasonable. Says I don't need to know.'

'But you do.'

I am vinously eloquent. I gesture into the firefly-studded night. 'Is it unreasonable,' I demand, 'to want to know more about the blood which flows in my veins, the genes which have been handed down, the lines of my story which stretch back to grandparents and great-grandparents? I can't see it. None of us exists in isolation, but my mother has wished exactly that kind of isolation on me.'

190

'She seems fairly unusual, your mother.'

'She is.' I look towards the town and the lights of some nightclub flashing a hectic blue in the darkness. 'Come to think of it, I don't know much about her either, beyond a few details.'

'Such as?'

'Her own mother died when she was quite young. Her father left her to be brought up by a housekeeper, before shunting her off to a series of boarding schools from which she was expelled for "inappropriate behaviour".'

'Like what?'

'I've never found out. She's never been receptive to personal questions. Most of what I know I've gleaned from Terry Cartwright. They met at school in Canterbury. She's a dancer, maybe even a choreographer now. That's almost everything I know about her. Not much, is it?'

'Not a lot.'

'I don't have a close relationship with her,' I say.

'I gathered that.'

'I used to. I used to love her ... oh, God, so much. We used to be absolutely inseparable.'

'What happened?'

'When I was eleven, she sent me off to boarding school.'

'That's not so terrible, is it? Lots of middle-class parents do the same, especially if they're moving around a bit.'

'There was much more to it than that.' Why is it all still so sharply painful? 'She ... she just completely dropped out of my life. Disappear-ed.'

Fergus sits forward. 'Why would she do that?'

'That's just it ... I don't know. I lived with the Cartwrights; to all intents and purposes, they became my family, but they didn't know where she was either.'

He frowns at me, considering. 'Could she have been in prison?'

'I've thought of that, but it doesn't seem very likely. What for, anyway? I mean, ten years? That's practically a life sentence, isn't it? She can't have *killed* someone.'

'Could she have been running away from some threat?'

'Ye-e-es...' I say slowly. I remember her insane notions about spiders and fire-setters. 'Maybe that's what it was.' My languid mood is dissipating. I'm starting to panic again. I drop my shoulders, breathe in deeply, try for calm. That man in the black suit: was it him she was running from? Was he a policeman, a private detective tracking her down? Had all her paranoia, our constant moving from place to place, been due to some crime she'd committed? 'Trouble is, if she goes on refusing to tell me anything, how will I ever find out?'

'Let's think about it while we're here.'

Her head droops and he wants to hold her, support her. Sad Theodora, fatherless, motherless. He knows about all of that, both of them orphans of the storm. Perhaps Grace Fargo is an orphan too, her husband all she has, which explains her long trek to find him in the Mexican jungle.

His own father, the whole grisly business of

his mother's slow disintegration as her body putrefied from the inside out. Never spoken of, except the one wretched and retching time, to Carolyn. It pulses inside him now, a boil, an abscess.

'At least you still have her. I had to watch my mother die,' he says suddenly, launched upon a sea of troubles before he can think too hard about where he might land.

'What did she die of?'

'Bowel cancer.'

'Horrible, horrible.'

'My brother and I had to nurse her. I was eight, he was six.' Just to think of it set his teeth on edge. Jesus, the stink of her rotting flesh and the slime on the sheet under her wasted buttocks, the shame he felt at such thoughts, this was his *mother*, and the two boys trying to clear up the vile mess and make her a little less uncomfortable, the father worse than useless, leaving them to it, leaving them memories which would sour the rest of the future.

Her eyes are round with horror. 'Wasn't there an adult, a doctor? A hospital? Someone you could ask for help?'

'We didn't know any better. Thought it was what we had to do. How would we know where to ask? Besides, our father was still in the house; no one realized we needed help.'

'A neighbour? School teachers?'

'Looking back, I can see that help must have been around. But we'd learned not to talk about our home life.' *If you tell, you'll go to hell,* whether it was a priest's probing fingers or a mother's cruel dying.

'What about your father now?'

'He still lives somewhere in Dublin. I've no reason to think the old soak is dead yet.' He picks up a fish bone, marlin bone, *those are pearls that were his eyes*. 'I'll tell you what the truly terrible thing about it was, the real killer of it all. Just after I'd buried Brendan – that's my brother – my first book was published, with the usual inflated releases about the big advances I was getting. You wouldn't believe it, but my father had the gall to get in touch, saying he always knew I'd do well and could I give him the loan of a tenner.'

'What did you do?'

'Wrapped twenty quid round a lump of dog shit and sent it to him.'

'Seriously?'

'God's honest truth.' Fergus grimaces. 'I'm not proud of that.' The thyme they'd cooked with is on his tongue, wine is in his nostrils. The moon is higher in the sky now, and smaller.

'When did you last see him?'

'Four or five years ago.'

'Don't you want to find out how he is?'

'He'll be drinking himself into a pauper's grave. If he hasn't already done so.'

'All the same, it would bother me not to be sure.' She's thinking of her own non-existent father. 'Have you ever written about it?'

A sad cadence of the heart. Brendan... 'That's the book I don't want to write.'

'Maybe it's the book you *ought* to write.'

'I've left the past behind me.'

194

Small etch of lines between her heavy brows. Arctic eyes full of pity, which he doesn't want from her. From anyone. Pity in the eyes of the neighbours who finally offered help, pity in the face of the doctors and the undertakers, pity from the social workers. But none from the Brothers, the holy fathers, which was when he first understood what he and Brendan were up against.

'That's nonsense,' she's saying and how right she is. 'You know it is. How can you leave the past behind, when it's always there, when it shaped you? You are the past as much as the present, like it or not.'

'I know.' He can't write about Brendan, won't *use* him like that. Besides, emotional self-flagellation is always suspect. When the time comes, maybe, but it won't be yet, not while there's unfinished, maybe unfinishable, business still to be dealt with.

Absorb it. Let it become part of you. As if he hasn't tried to do that already.

'I thought I'd had a hard time,' Theodora says, leaning across the table to touch his arm with her rough gardener's hands. 'But it was nothing like you. What happened after ... after your mother died?'

'Our father dispatched us to an orphanage run by the so-called Christian Brothers.' Face darkening, crow-black, bible-black, cassock-black. 'The only thing Christian about them was the fact that they hadn't been circumcised. They were liars, hypocrites, sadists, perverts ... They nearly killed us both.' Breaking off, breath

195

coming faster, fury like a steam engine boiling. Swallowing the thick black phlegm of hatred. 'They *did* kill Brendan.'

'Your brother? Oh, Fergus, how?'

'Me, they just thrashed the bejasus out of. Brendan was more unfortunate – he was pretty.'

'I don't understand.'

Her childhood less fraught. Emotional abuse, maybe, but not physical. Which is worse? He takes her hand in his. Wounds bandaged by dreams. Clinging to the wreckage on the stormy seas of the past. Rugged hands, remnants of gardens under her fingernails, calluses on the palm, sees her digging, thrusting the spade in among the beetles and worm-trails, men have died and worms have eaten them. Squeezes the green fingers, feels the sprout of seedlings in them, the potpourri of roses, the plump of peaches.

'Basically, they buggered the poor little sod to death. Not literally – he got out of there alive, more or less. Went on the streets for a bit, sold himself where he could – it was all they'd taught him – got into drugs. Last time I saw him, he was lying dead on a pile of newspapers in some filthy squat in Ballymun. OD'd on heroin, so thin I could count his ribs.' His mouth a bitter curve. 'A bag of bones. A bodybag of bones.'

'Poor, poor Brendan.'

'Poor all of us. The human condition, what a crock.' Shrug. Reach for the wine. Drown your sorrows, except there can't be too much of that, not with the father an exemplar, *there's* an unexamined life, all right. As she's said, we're all weighted down with the past, the trick is to organize a life where the baggage becomes light-weight. 'I'm sorry, Theodora. I had no intention of burdening you with my life story.'

Her face is smooth. 'I'm not burdened, Fergus.'

But I am, of course. In my bedroom, two doors away from his, I undress slowly, wondering whether it is possible to unload the past or whether we are doomed to carry it forever on our shoulder. A small black spider hurries across my pillow and I flick it away, remembering the way my proud, courageous mother had stood, white and shaken, looking down at another spider. Why have I been so unforgiving? So many times I've envisaged myself taking care of her, but it was always for some neatly-broken ankle or dislocated shoulder, never for the messiness of mental breakdown.

Why did she run?

I climb into bed and lie beneath a linen sheet, its turned-down border hand embroidered with blue and white flowers, and try not to think of those two small boys attempting to ease their mother's passage out of life. No wonder Fergus is ... is what, exactly? Reluctant to put down roots, to commit to someone, to the present? I wonder whether he has talked of this before, and why I find it so easy to tell him things. Perhaps it's because we are more alike than we realize. At some point during the evening he'd said I ought to be trying to discover more about both my parents. But I know it's pointless. Luna has rarely talked to me about the past and now I doubt that she ever will. How much of that is my own fault? She abandoned me, so when she finally came tiptoeing back into my life, I abandoned her. Tit for tat.

There's a sound and I hold my breath, straining to hear. Is it the settling house, a creaking branch, the supperless cat? Is it Fergus, making a move on me, hoping to surprise me into succumbing to his blandishments? Because I'm not going to pretend I haven't noticed that he fancies me. Just as I fancy him. I know I stand teetering on the edge of a cliff, at the foot of a ladder, and all the warning signs are marked 'LOVE'. I stare at the black shape of the half-open door, longing for him to come in.

Just let him try it, I think. Short shrift is what he'll get. 'Short shrift.' I breathe the words into the empty air and hear the sound again. A voice, a moan. It *is* Fergus, but not with seduction on his mind, more like the beginnings of a bad dream. I can sympathize. I've had them myself.

I get up and walk the short distance between our two rooms. It's very late, but there are still faint bursts of music from the cafés along the shore. At the door of his room, I stand for a moment. In the moon-coloured light, I can see him lying on top of his sheets, limbs cast to the four corners of the bed. He's wearing cotton boxers and sweating, his body gleaming with it. Sturdy, rather than elegant. A deep chest, narrow hips. The tattoo on his shoulder is just a dim blur. Tiptoeing further into the room, leaning closer, I can see that it is not a toucan but another kind of bird, long-legged, a flamingo perhaps, or a stork. As I watch, he gives a little shriek, twitches,

198

reaches for something with one of his curled hands and grips it tightly, although there's nothing there. Shrieks again.

I don't know what to do. You're not supposed to wake sleepwalkers – but he's not sleep-walking. He looks delicate, almost fragile – and after what he's told me this evening, I suppose he is.

Tentatively, I take one of his hands and stroke it, then move up from the palm to the wrist, from the wrist to the elbow, gently, gently. After a while, he calms down.

I'm about to lay his arm carefully back on the sheet when he says, 'Don't stop. That feels good.' He's obviously been awake for a while.

'You fraud!' I say indignantly.

'Why are you here?' he asks.

'You were keeping me awake.' I drop his arm heavily on to his chest and step away from the bed.

'Maybe you should stay.'

I want to but... 'Why should I do that?'

'In case I have another bad dream. I'd hate to wake you up again.'

'I'll be sure to shut my door so I can't hear you.' As I leave him, I am smiling.

Theodora, a whisper in the night. The feel of those rough hands caressing him, a tingle in the spine. Nothing sexy about it, wouldn't have touched him if she'd known that he had woken the moment she came into the room, senses alert, the habit picked up quickly in Mexico in case the *muchachos* sent someone to visit him, the usual calling card a stiletto in the heart, a machete down on the wrist.

He struggles into a sitting position. He can see a piece of moon at the edge of the window, hear the sigh of waves down on the beach. Getting up, he leans from the window into the warm darkness. Black cypresses puncture the landscape. It's quiet up here, but there are lights still on in the town, ugly concrete blocks, just as he'd expected, villas, red roofs bleached by the moon, white walls charcoaled with, what, geraniums, hibiscus, plumbago, bougainvillaea? He's no idea which is what but he's read enough books about places like this to know they'll be one or another. A cloud seeps across the moon, which is yellow here, not silver. He could go and swim in the pool, there's enough residual light, skinny dipping, water sinuous round his limbs, herbs seasoning the night, but he'd wake her up again. Or find her there already, drawing herself up, glowering from under those black eyebrows, ill met by moonlight, proud Theodora. She'll think he is trying to come on to her – which, no point denying it, he wants to do. Wants? A mealy-mouthed word. *Aches* to do. But she doesn't. Isn't it always the way, the shadow falling between the idea and the reality?

He is drawn by the secret caves behind her glass-clear gaze, by the quirk of her mouth as she sieves his sentences for meanings, the way she leans forward, eager as a lighted match, when he offers words on the platter of his wide vocabulary, *moufflon*, she echoes, *dendrophile*, egging him on, waiting for revelation.

Leaning on the window sill, he thinks of the words he would smell and polish, were he in love with Theodora.

The next morning, I'm up early. I go quietly out of the house and take the stony path down the edge of the bluff above the beach. The sun is low on the horizon, splashing the sea with gold. The promise of heat rocks on the water and the air smells of sage and thyme and wood smoke. If tourists use this beach – and I see evidence that they do: cigarette stubs, a flattened plastic bottle, a scrap of newspaper – they haven't yet arrived. I drop my towel on the sand. I'd drop my swimsuit too, if I weren't afraid that Fergus will follow me down. Aphrodite arising from the foam with her buttocks on display is one thing, a naked Theo Cairns is quite another.

The water is sweet and crisp. In a fast crawl, I swim three-quarters of a mile out to sea before turning back. A hundred yards offshore, I turn on to my back and look up at the house. It sits back from the edge of the low cliffs, protected from its neighbours by an olive grove on one side, a patch of meadow on the other, gnarled trees standing deep in lush grass.

Fergus is on the terrace and I wave, not sure if he can see me. He waves back. He's a good companion. He's more than that. If I'd stayed in his room last night, hopped in beside him, would it have been good between us? I don't need to ask the question.

In a minute I'll swim back to the beach and climb the path, brush beneath the generous falls of pink geranium, the clumps of iris, past the lemon tree with its white-painted trunk, and round the back of the house, ignoring the faint whiff of sewage, the implacable smell of goat, though so far I have seen none, only their droppings. We'll have breakfast together: yoghurt, honey, figs, the coarse Corfiot bread. We'll do nothing in particular; maybe walk down to the town and shop in the market, have a lemonade somewhere, if we can find a tourist-free café. We can stroll through the narrow backstreets, light a candle in one of the square-towered churches, eat something at an outdoor café, seafood, or grilled fish, lamb, whatever.

There's an ache somewhere close to my heart. How different it would be if I were here with a lover. I wish I were in love. At least, I think I do. I never have been. Harvey, to my shame, was expedience. Who does that leave me? Jenny, whom yes, I love, but with whom I am not *in* love. Terry, who has always folded me into her warm embrace when I most needed it. My mother, whom I no longer know.

What is love? A construct, that's all. The word which describes that delicate flutter in the heart. That thump in the blood. That heat between the thighs. I suppose that were I able to define it, it would imply a private universe of two: me and one other. If it were, say, for the sake of argument, Fergus, we'd hold hands, we'd kiss in the shadow of a white wall, our finger ends would spark as we moved, we'd exchange looks full of tumbled sheets and lingering pleasure, memories of the night before and the days to come, anticipation and recollection burning along our bodies.

But we're not in love, and that's all there is to it.

SIXTEEN

Wearing a battered straw hat, she walks through the meadow at the side of the house, knee-deep in grass which is studded with wild flowers. Yesterday she had taken his hand. 'Come and see, Fergus, it's like perpetual spring. Look at this: jonquils, anemones, cyclamen.' She'd parted the stems of grass. 'Look, such beautiful leaves.' Red stems, dark green leaves patterned in grey. 'There's even a patch of bee-orchids. Amazing, isn't it?'

'Fantastic.' He barely knows a daffodil from a dandelion. 'Lovely.'

He'd never seen her so animated, so softly erotic. Now, she picks a bunch of wild flowers and puts it into a blue pottery jug in the middle of the table where they sit drinking coffee. Crumbly white cheese on a blue plate, crimson lubricity of a quartered fig, liquid topaz of dribbled honey. One strap of her blue top hangs down the tanned polish of her shoulder.

'Tell me their names again,' he says, to hear the love in her voice as she recites them: campanula, willowherb, honesty, buttercup.

'I keep an uncultivated patch at home, in my own garden,' she says. 'I like to let it have its head, so it's only touched once a year, when a man comes in to scythe it. I tried to do it myself, the first year, but the scythe was too heavy and I couldn't get the rhythm of it at all.'

'How much ground do you have?' He pictures her in a sun bonnet, the far-from-grim Reaperess, flushed with sun. He pictures Grace Fargo, knee-deep in grasses.

'An acre, at the moment. But I'm hoping to increase it.'

'An acre...' It seems excessive, immodest. He owns nothing but a houseboat, and the nearest he's come to a garden was a flowerpot which once held a bushful of tiny pink roses. 'One of these days I'll have to come down and inspect it.'

'Yes, you will.'

Not much conviction there. Don't expect a hand-engraved invitation any time soon. She glances at him. Uh-oh. Already he's learned to be wary of that look. Mouth firm, grey eyes determined. 'May I ask you a personal question?' Why does she bother to make the request, since she intends to ask it even if he says 'no'?

'As long as you're prepared not to have it answered.' He touches a patch of sunburn on his arm. Five days of Corfu sun and when he looks in the bathroom mirror a blue-eyed Mexican flamenco-dancer stares back, skin coppery-red, black hair flaming round his skull.

'Why haven't you got a woman, a wife, a partner?' she asks. Lifts a piece of fig to her red mouth, encloses it.

'You asked me that at Terry's party.'

'And you said it was because women didn't

204

like the gypsy in your soul, or something equally evasive.'

'It's not evasive, it's the truth.' The past few days of early pearly mornings will go down as among the most magical of his life. Even though the words aren't coming yet, not yet, he can feel them marshalling, stepping into line, ready to march on to the page as soon as the time comes to switch on the laptop.

'The truth is that you've never actually fallen in love with anyone, isn't it?' she persists, inquisitorial as a Stasi interrogator. 'Because if you had, you'd be willing to settle down for her sake, at least a little.'

'The world well lost for love, is that what you mean?' Is she implying that if he were more grounded, more dug into stability, she might consider him?

'Sort of.'

'There's a possibility you don't seem to have considered. Suppose someone fell in love with me.'

'Yes?' She fiddles with her hair, pulls up her strap. 'So?'

'In that case, why shouldn't *she* give up everything to follow me to the ends of the earth? Why does it have to be *me* doing the changing, rather than her?'

She's obviously never thought of that. 'Good point.'

'Have *you* ever been in love?'

She hesitates. 'Not really. Not yet.'

'For the sake of argument, let's say that you have. Let's further say that, hypothetically, I'm the lucky guy,' he says.

A blush spreads beneath the tan. Her blue strap slowly falls down again. She puts her hand to her hair, presses a finger to her lips. Picks up her coffee cup. 'All right,' she says. 'It's ridiculous, of course, but let's say that, just as an example.'

'My point, Theodora...' Pretty Theodora with her sun-kissed shoulders and the lascivious fall of her strap, groin responding, life of its own, jasus, if only she ... Back off, he tells himself, she's a needless complication in your life at the moment. 'My point is, if that were the case, would *you* be able to change, to keep starting over, keep putting down tender little roots only to pull them up again when the fancy took me to move on?'

'I ... uh ... I...'

'No, is the word you're searching for. But why not? You'd expect me – if it *were* me – to stay put, but you don't seem to believe that maybe it could be the other way round and you – if it were *you* – should move on.'

'You're right...'

'Of course, the interesting thing would be to see what happens when two people with dia-metrically opposed philosophies, like, for instance, in this extremely unlikely scenario, you and me, when such people try to make a life together.' He's talking in order to have an excuse to go on watching her.

She blinks at him, clear eyes startling against her tan. She licks honey from her fingers and he watches the slide of it down her throat, keeping his face neutral. If she were to suspect the white

206

heat of his thoughts, she'd be away out of there quicker than a bat out of hell. 'I don't know, Fergus. I never thought about the other side of the coin. That there'd have to be give, as well as take.'

'As a matter of fact, *a chuisle*, neither have I.'

'What's that mean?'

'An Irish term. Just slipped out.' One thing he's not ever done is trade on the ould blarney-stone nonsense, agenbite of inwit sub-Joycean thing, not that there's anything wrong with it in its place and if he were to ever set Brendan down on paper, he might be tempted. Brendan the Voyager, barely navigating his coracled way through the shoals and reefs, waves swamping his frail bark until he finally foundered.

She tugs up the strap again. Gazes out to sea. 'But you're right, Fergus,' she says. 'You're absolutely right.'

The two of them have fallen into a semi-routine. Shopping in the morning, lounging around, swimming, working, and then, when dusk begins to fall, wine on the terrace followed by the shared task of cooking garlicky herby dishes that linger on the lips. They do the laundry, talk when the spirit moves or stay silent, read together, watch the news on the uncertain black-and-white television in the salon. It's how he imagines marriage to be, were it not for the celibacy. Don't think about that. For the moment, but only for the moment, it's enough just to be with her, getting to know her, worming his way under her skin. Sometimes, in the warm nights, he imagines he can hear her quiet breathing, breasts lifting beneath the virginal sheets, dark crotch musky in the heat; wonders if she sleeps naked, not his business, not his concern – separate entities, independent, simply chums sharing a holiday, that's all.

If he is honest, he has to admit that the island is not the paradise he had hoped for. His dreams of a bare table, a white wall, the timeless Odyssean sea, have been shattered, or not so much shattered as stretched to breaking point by noise, tourists, the constant thutt-thutt of the caïques carrying visitors round the point to unluckier beaches than theirs, the unrelenting music from the cafés. It can only be a matter of time before there'll be a taverna down on their own little bay, concrete lavatories, brutish British beer-swillers, farting and fucking. He thinks of the Durrells, of Edward Lear. That idyll is slowly vanishing, is almost gone for ever.

Meanwhile, as the days pass, he watches Theodora change. Seeing her unwind is like unwrapping a mummy, eating an artichoke, layer after layer of whatever it is she has encased herself in slowly sloughing off to reveal the soft tenderness at the heart. He wonders what precipitated that phone call to say she would, after all, come with him. He thinks he has unfathomed her mystery: she is afraid to be happy in case it's snatched away, as it must have been when her mother dropped out of sight. She's so different now from what she was a week ago: languid, loose-bodied, her mouth tender in the warmth of the candles she lights each evening, eyes secret in the semi-dark, shadows jumping on her smooth skin. He wants to take her to bed, wants to kiss every part of her, wants to savour her. He knows that he must be careful. He feels he is moving closer to her, taking tiny unhurried steps nearer. Softlee, softlee ... Sometimes, standing in the kitchen while she pegs out her bras and knickers on the washing line strung across the courtyard outside, he feels explosive with desire. Too erotic, too intimate, do those nylon (silk or maybe cotton?) garments take on the tang of the air in which they've dried? When she puts them on in the morning is she assailed by syringa, lapped in lavender?

'Do you have an address for your father?' she asks. It's another of the evenings spent eating a long, slow meal by candlelight, under the stars, mournful moon higher now, paler, less of it as the days go by, sage and sea-smells brought on the breeze.

'I know where he used to live. Which isn't to say he's there still.'

'But if anything had happened to him, you'd be told?'

'There are enough people who would make it their business to let me know.' Thinking of the man, he experiences the familiar mix of fear, regret and rage.

She holds her glass thoughtfully by the side of her mouth. 'I think you ought to go and find him.'

'To what end? All it will do is rekindle old hostilities.' Start stirring, and who knows what will float to the surface, what debris lies buried in the thick sludge at the bottom of his heart. 'I

209

can't see the point.'

He mustn't let her sense the fear. How can he bear to meet his father face to face again, with Brendan intolerable between them, draped across his shoulders like the flayed skins of Aztec victims? He's done all right for himself, he's slipped out from under, but his brother was captured. He has to be avenged, can't let that go. Easier to stay away, fall instead into the fictional jungle where Gerard Fargo paints his huge canvases, far from prying eyes and amazing Grace.

'He must be getting on a bit, isn't he?'

'So?'

'If I knew who or where *my* father was, I'd go and see him. Besides, you might get a book out of it.'

'It's too much of a cliché, too common an Irish story. In any case, other better people have told it already.'

A silence falls. He is aware of a happiness so intense that it could burn him up like a martyr at the stake if it were not also fleeting, gone almost before glimpsed. 'Theodora,' he says, 'in Corfu Town there's a saint that has the same name as you. We should go and visit the shrine.'

'Years ago my mother told me there were lots of Saint Theodoras.'

Below them, in the darkness, the sea surges against the edges of the shore. 'Want to walk down to the beach?' he asks.

'Why not.'

The kitchen is well stocked with torches and we take one each, make our way down to the little

210

bay. The shimmering dark is full of scent. Waves lap softly at the pebbled beach. The night is warm, hot even. Sweat breaks out under my arms and along my forehead. We can hear music from the cafes beyond the point; tonight it's the Beatles and Tom Jones. It's intrusive, but not unpleasant. '*Yesterday,*' croons Paul McCartney. Fergus takes me into his arms and we sway together beside the silver water.

Corfu has seduced me. Despite the serpents in this Eden, it enters me like a lover to whom I willingly give myself up, it runs through my blood. For this moment, I concentrate on nothing, am simply content to be. Is Fergus finding this holiday as productive as he'd hoped? I've heard the meaty thunk of his computer keys when I pass the room he's using as an office, but not very often, and not for very long. Maybe that's how it works with creative fiction, periods of thought interspersed with intense activity on the keyboard.

Why, Delilah? Tom Jones demands muscularly from the next bay down. Fergus's arms tighten round me. I can smell his skin, the wine he's drunk, candle smoke. I am weak with desire. 'Want to swim?' he says into my ear, tickling me.

'We didn't bring our—' I break off. Lighten Up, Seize the Day, Go For it. 'All right.' I disengage from him, pull off my shirt, my shorts. I hesitate a moment, then I step quickly out of my panties and run wincingly across the pebbles into the cool embrace of the sea.

He follows me. I can see the pale swing of his penis against the dark bush of hair as he splashes

211

untidily through the shallows, staggering as the pebbles punch the soles of his feet. As he comes nearer, I plunge beneath the waves and swim strongly away. When I surface, he is peering through the moonlight for me, his wet body shining as though made of quicksilver. 'Fergus!' I call, before submerging again. I swim underwater towards the pale columns of his legs and push out of the water beside him.

'You look like a mermaid,' he says. 'A siren.'

His eyes are on my breasts and I turn and swim away once more. The moon throws a gilded path across the dark sea. The sensuous feel of water against bare skin is almost indescribable; my whole body is given over to silky sensations. I can hear Fergus behind me. Sirens lure men to their deaths with promises they have no intention of fulfilling. Is that what I'm doing? Does he think that because we're both naked, there's a tacit agreement that we will make love? Why am I so reluctant to do something which I know will be all I've ever wanted, read about, longed for? I know the answer to that: I cannot afford to be subsumed in someone else.

As soon as I can, I make for the shore and run back up to my clothes. Clumsily I pull on my T-shirt. The breeze has more than a touch of chill in it.

He comes up the beach and flops down beside me. 'Don't be afraid,' he says quietly. And it's this gentle sentence which undoes me. Had he touched me, I could have risen to my feet and walked back up to the house, but his words disarm me, leave me defenceless.

'Fergus...' I give an involuntary sigh, a sound so full of desire and passion that I am embarrassed.

He puts his hand on my still-wet thigh. 'You're shivering,' he says.

'So will you, if you don't put some clothes on.'

'Not yet.' He pulls me closer, puts his mouth over mine. He is warm, and I instinctively move into his arms. He puts his hand under my T-shirt, holds my breast. I ought to tell him not to but it's lovely. I want him to touch my other breast and when he does, I find myself moaning with pleasure. At what point do I call a halt? I remind myself that I am thirty-one years old, not a schoolgirl, not inexperienced, this is just a bonk, a screw, a fuck, it carries no significance and I can stop whenever I please, but somehow I don't seem to have done so as his hand inches lower and then he is on top of me, and the sweet ache of desire floods me, it's been such a long time since I did this or wanted it as much as I do now, just the act, no involvement, nothing like that, and I am urging him onwards, and then he's slipping into the warm wetness of my body and despite all my intentions, I am not pushing him away, but already exploding as I welcome him.

'You told me I should go and see my father,' he says. They're sitting at a table outside a taverna in the town, eating grilled lamb, courgettes stewed in oil, fresh tomatoes. The wine is rough and red. Under the table, their legs are entwin-ed, one of her feet resting between his thighs. Around them is music and bustle, the slap of tourist flip-flops

213

echoing back from the tall Venetian façades, clop of donkey hooves, cries from the owners of shops and stalls along the street.

'Yes.'

'You ought to do the same.'

She thinks about it. Chews slowly. Crumbles bread on the tabletop. 'You could be right. But it's not possible.'

'Why?'

'Where would I start? My mother won't tell me the slightest thing. It's as though she's deliberately tried to expunge him from our lives, every last memory, every clue as to who he was – or is. I'm so angry with her, so furious...'

'You have a right to be.'

'Then why do I feel so guilty?' She lifts her glass towards her mouth then stops with it in mid-air. 'You don't think he could be somebody important, do you? Like, the prime minister or ... or a presidential candidate? Or royalty?'

'Could be. From what you've said, the possibilities are endless. Whatever it is, I think you need to find out.'

She slumps in her chair. Shakes her head. 'I don't want to.'

'But...' He's confused. 'Didn't you say you needed to find out about him?' He takes her hand and holds it tightly enough that she can't pull away without a struggle. 'How come you're so ready to tell me what to do, but won't take your own very sensible advice?'

She shrugs. 'Maybe I'm afraid of what I might discover.'

'Where would you start? If you're not afraid,

214

that is?'

'If you think about the timing, she'd have found herself pregnant with me by March of her second year at college in the States. So there would seem a logical place to start looking.'

'If you go, I could come with you.' He can't let her go, now that he has found her. 'I could chauffeur you around and buy you iced coffee at the Dairy Queen and slay any dragons who are bothering you.'

'I can slay my own.'

'I could carry your bags.'

'I travel light.'

She's deathly afraid and he doesn't know how to help her.

He's asleep, my lovely troubadour, my wandering minstrel. I look down at his sleeping face, the non-aligned eyebrows, the dark hair, and feel dampness between my thighs, heat in my lower belly. I've never felt anything like this sexual closeness; I am famished, ravenous for him. I want to wake him, arch over him, lower myself hard and fast on to him. Instead, I touch the tattoo on his shoulder. Standing on the edge of the bottomless pit of love, I am afraid.

'I think I love you,' I murmur. But how can I love someone else when I don't know who I myself am? Do I dare to love someone else when the last time, I was left alone? And of all men, how sensible would it be to fall in love with this one, a man without commitment? Enjoy it, Theo, I tell myself. *Carpe diem.* Seize the day, and then move on.

Move on ... something I've never been good at!

I don't want to go back to what my existence seems to have become: responsibilities, sudden rages, panic attacks. Not yet, not ever. I need to change things. A thought ricochets around my skull, something never considered before: the wrenching up of tap roots is like pulling a tooth or severing a limb, but no more painful, surely, than a wanderer forced against his will to stay put.

I press my hands against my flat stomach. Will I ever swell as pregnant Jenny does, walk with that proud jut, cradle my belly in both hands as though shielding the child inside from harm? I move closer to Fergus, run my hands down the front of his body, stroke the feathers of dark hair across his chest, in his groin. Even in sleep, he thickens for me. I throw my leg over his hip and guide him into me.

'I'm having the most fabulous dream,' he murmurs. His gypsy fingers touch my breasts, my nipples, and turn me into liquid silver as we move together, slowly at first and then with increasing passion.

'I think I am too,' I gasp, as I roll over on to my back, and he groans above me.

Later, curled in his arms, I say, 'I have to go back to England.'

'No.'

'I'm going to follow your advice and really try to find out who my father is. But to do that, I need to go back to the beginning, to where it all started, to the point at which I must have been conceived. I already called the airline. There's a flight to Gatwick I can get a seat on, one o'clock this afternoon.'

'Don't leave me, Theodora.'

'I don't want to. But I have to sort myself out.'

I have to plug the cracks which have appeared in my life before I can grow. I have to decide whether the new-found expansion of my heart is something more than a simplistic physical harmony.

SEVENTEEN

I make a phone call. 'Are you at home tomorrow?' I ask, when Hugo answers.

'Come for tea,' he says. 'That way, depending on how long it takes you to pick my brains, I may be granted the privilege of taking you out for dinner.'

'How did you know that's what I was going to do?'

'I've always expected that, if you hadn't done so before, by the time you were thirty you would insist on knowing who your father was. And besides, I've been speaking to your mother.'

From that first meeting at the airport, my love for Hugo has been absolute and uncomplicated. When I appear at his flat the following afternoon, he leads me into his comfortable bachelor sitting room, full of books and pictures and pieces of sculpture. Hugo collects art deco bronzes: nymphs leaning into an invisible wind with their skirts blowing behind them, women bent lithely backwards with a crystal ball balanced on the palm of one heaven-flung arm, odalisques with alabaster vases on their shoulders, tippy-toed girls with bronze scarves streaming from their outstretched fingers. In my opinion, all of them are hideous.

A bottle of expensive red wine stands on a copper tray incised with a swirly art deco design, alongside two glasses. A photograph album – mock red leather with a tasselled silk cord to hold the pages of black card together – sits on the arm of the chair I usually occupy when I visit. Hugo pours us each a glass of wine and hands one to me. He smiles faintly and folds himself into his own chair.

'*Allons*...' he says. 'I know your mother isn't being helpful because she told me so.' He hands me a dish of salted almonds.

Hugo, impeccable, civilized, alone. Hugo meeting a little girl off an aeroplane, taking her to fancy restaurants, squiring her around London, watching over her through the years. A question which has been hovering on my tongue for as long as I can remember suddenly materializes. 'Why haven't you ever married?'

'Because the person I fell in love with, years and years ago, has always been in love with someone else.'

'That's so sad.'

'Not really, Theo. Believe it or not, there are compensations.'

'Such as?'

'I still have a dream. And there's even the faint possibility that it might one day come true.'

I should have seen it before. 'It's my mother, isn't it?'

He leans his head against the back of his armchair and drops his elegant eyelids. 'Yes.'

'And the person she's always loved was – is – my father?'

'Unfortunately, yes.'

'My unknown, undiscoverable father.'

'The very same.'

'Oh, Hugo,' I say, wrenched. 'I wish he was you.'

'So do I.'

'Is that why you live in England?'

'Partly. It's a more civilized place than America. And, of course –' he smiles – 'it's nearer to my heart's desire, even though she's not here very often.'

I reach across the gap between us and put my hand on his. 'Oh, Hugo. Darling Hugo.' He means so much to me. He matters far more than any father I might discover. Why can't that be enough?

He strokes the navy cashmere sweater draped over his shoulders. 'Some people might look at me and think what a waste of a life mine has been, but they'd be wrong,' he says. 'I'm a born dilettante. Never settled down to anything much. Never really wanted to. I pretended to practise law for a while, but not very seriously, because I hated it – I only went to Harvard Law School to please my parents. I grew coffee in Brazil for

219

eighteen hellish months. Toyed with the idea of becoming an architect or an art dealer. But once I came into my inheritances and trust funds, I just spent my time enjoying myself.'

'So fuck 'em.'

'Precisely. And it's not your mother's fault that I fell in love with her. Nor hers that she didn't love me. We're both people with a fixation we can't shake off.'

'What a pity that you couldn't have been each other's fixation.'

'Isn't that the truth? And of course I should have gotten over her years ago, gone on to other things, other women. But she ... she enraptured me from the moment I first saw her, running across the rough grass in her yellow swimsuit and diving into the lake. She looked like a streak of sunshine. I've never forgotten it. Nor have I ever found anyone else who could give me even a fraction of the pleasure that she does on the rare occasions that we meet.'

'Maybe that's a definition of happiness.'

'Very possibly.'

'OK, Hugo. Since you're not my father, do you know who is?'

'No.'

'Do you know anything about him?'

'Not a thing.'

'Do you think he's English?'

'I have absolutely no—'

'Do you think –' I lean forward with my hands between my knees – 'he's alive?'

He doesn't answer.

'The way my mother's behaving, I'm pretty

220

sure he is,' I say.

He looks relieved. 'So am I. Though again, I'm guessing.'

'I always believed everything she told me about him.' I take a sip of wine. 'When she told me he'd died before I was born, it never crossed my mind that she was lying.'

'She can be very convincing.'

'Maybe it's stupid of me to want to find out. I mean, in the end, what does it matter who a person's father is?'

'It matters very much indeed.' He, too, leans forward. Carefully he puts his glass down on the table beside his chair. 'Your adorable mother has many faults,' he says. 'The chief one being that she's never fallen in love with me. Among the lesser ones, is a strong tendency to bully people. Or to be so absolutely certain of her opinions that it amounts to the same thing. So before we go any further with this discussion, I'd like to register my disapproval of the way she's always insisted that you call her Luna. It's ridiculous. She's your mother, and in any case, her name is Lucia. Nor did I ever approve of her dragging you all over the world. Furthermore, I believe you have an absolute right to know the identity of your other parent. I've told her that many times.'

'And?'

'She disagrees.' He shrugs. 'You should stand up to her, Theo.'

'I tried it, last time I saw her, and got precisely nowhere. What I can't understand is what she's trying to hide.' I pick up the photograph album.

'Why is this here?'

'I thought you might find it informative in some way, though I've no idea how.'

I open the album and there, unmistakably, is my mother, aged maybe sixteen or seventeen, standing with a group of other young people at the edge of water. She holds her fists clasped under her chin, as though she is cold. I turn the pages and see her again and again, by the lake, or against a tree, caught in some private moment. She dances alone, arms raised, her body sways as though she moves to inner melodies, and despite the years which separate *then* from *now*, I can almost hear the same music as she does, the pine needles under my feet, the breeze off the lake on my bare legs.

The poses she strikes reminds me of something. Looking up, and then around the room, I understand for the first time that each of Hugo's dancing girls and zephyr-kissed nymphs are versions of my mother.

I turn a page – and freeze. 'Who's this?' I say carefully, turning the album round so Hugo can see the black-clad figure standing motionless in the shadows of a tree, watching as the girl who is my mother climbs out of the water. He wishes her ill. Whoever he is, and I can only see him from the back, I am suddenly certain he would like her dead. And suddenly Luna's paranoia no longer seems like madness. Is it this man from whom she fled for all those years? Was this what she was trying to escape? And if so, why?

Hugo looks, shrugs. 'No idea. Some friend of my parents, I should imagine.'

'Why was he there?'

'People were always drifting in and out. My parents kept a hospitable house, and of course the Americans love France, so our place became a fixture on the summer circuit among our friends.'

'He looks kind of sinister.'

Hugo considers the photograph. 'I can't see him very clearly but he seems more lecherous than sinister, if you ask me.'

'I know why you've come,' Terry says. She's sitting in the long conservatory which runs across the back of her house. There's a pitcher of iced tea on the glass-topped table in front of her, a pile of old magazines from which she is cutting out recipes. Terry collects recipes but seldom uses any of them. I think she gains a certain security from knowing that if she absolutely had to, she would immediately be able to whip up a flourless chocolate-and-almond cake or produce *teriyaki* or *spanokopita* without even blinking.

'That's very clairvoyant of you,' I say.

She stares at me over the rimless magnifiers she's recently taken to using. 'Your mother telephoned. She said you'd be coming round, asking questions.'

'Yes, well...'

'She told me not to tell you anything. She said I had to stop you trying to find out about your father.'

'What did you say?'

'Basically that though I knew absolutely nothing, I still couldn't see any reason why you

223

shouldn't be told.' She pours me a glass of iced tea. 'Why has it suddenly come up?'

I describe Liz Crawfurd's visit, the thunderbolt James Bellamy had delivered, Luna's responses to my questions about my father. I don't tell her that I feel as if I'm cracking up. I don't tell her about Fergus.

When I'm through, she says, 'Knowing who he is won't change anything, sweetie. The past's over and done with.'

'It may be over, but it's never done with, and the thing is, Terry, until recently, I thought I'd come to terms with it all. But I haven't. And now, until I've sorted it out, I don't see how I can get on with the future. Nor with anything else.' Ice cubes chunk against the side of my glass. I can smell the cool freshness of mint sprigs and lemon slices. 'Why did she lie to me? Who is he, if he's not the man in my painting?'

'She's kept it secret all these years – does it really matter any more?'

'*Yes!* Now more than ever.' I rest my head in my hands. 'I believed everything she ever told me, and now I know it's all lies, all I can wonder is what else is completely untrue.'

Terry's face crumples with sympathy. 'It can't have been easy, her vanishing like that.'

'Where do you think she was?'

'We were all as mystified by her absence as you were.'

'Did it have anything to do with my father?'

'Who knows? Max and I often discussed it. Hugo, too. Was she dead? Had she been thrown into jail somewhere on a drugs charge? Had she

224

been abducted? We had no idea.'

'What about her getting pregnant?'

Terry spreads her hands. 'I knew nothing whatsoever about it until you were about three and she got in touch with me again. And though I've asked and asked, she's absolutely refused to say who your father was.'

'What was this place she went to in the States?'

'A Catholic girls' college – St Margaret's, in Maybury, Vermont. Her mother was there as a girl.'

'So that at least is true,' I say bitterly.

'Don't be like that, Theo. You can't stay angry at her for ever. You mustn't go on carrying this kind of stone in your heart.'

It's not so much a stone as a chrysalis desperate to break out and spread its wings. 'I don't want to be angry,' I say dejectedly. 'I don't even *feel* angry, though I obviously must be. Recently I've been yelling at people, going way over the top about nothing at all, and I hate being so out of control.' My hands are trembling in my lap. 'I want to let go, and I can't. Ever since that man told me the painting wasn't of my father, nothing else seems to matter, even my business or my friends.'

'Darling Theo...'

'If you look at the timing, it almost has to be someone she met over there, doesn't it?' I ask.

As Terry nods, I stand up, too restless to remain seated. 'I can understand why she kept his identity secret back then, but what's the point now, all these years later? I don't even know what nationality he is. I mean, I always assumed

225

he was English, because of the painting, but he could be anything. American, most likely.'

'Not *any*thing.'

'I still don't understand why she kept me.'

'Ever thought that maybe she *wanted* you? She told me once that you were all she had left of your father. All she'd ever have.'

Terry gets up too and stands behind me. Her hands are strong as she kneads my shoulders. 'Don't blame your mother too much. If it's any consolation, I don't think she's been happy for years. She wants to be. She *tries* to be. Just can't make it, somehow.' Her fingers work on the tight muscles at the top of my spine. 'Let's face it, sweetie, God moves in a mysterious way.'

'It's not *His* mysterious way I'm bothered about, it's Luna's. And so-called John Vincent Cairns's.'

'Who?'

'My father. John Vincent Cairns.' She's staring at me quizzically now and my stomach constricts. *'What?'*

'Is that what she told you?'

'Yes. What's wrong with that?'

'Cairns was your grandmother's maiden name,' she says slowly. 'She used to sign herself Lois Cairns Caxton, the way American people do. Your mother was Lucia Caxton, when we were at school. I hadn't realized she told you Cairns was your father's name.'

My father moves further and further away from me. The layers of obfuscation Luna has laid down over the years seem increasingly impenetrable. 'Why would she lie like that? She must have known that I might find out from you. They probably weren't even married.' I can't keep the sense of betrayal out of my voice. 'She's always said it was a whirlwind courtship.'

Terry gazes at me thoughtfully then shakes her head.

'What?' I say.

'There *is* someone who might know who your father was.'

'Who's that?'

'Her confessor, Father Francis. I remember her writing to me about him when she first went over to the States, saying he was kind of scary, all the girls were terrified of him.'

'Even if she did confess what she was up to, he's not going to tell me, is he? Secrets of the confessional and all that.'

'So that's not much help, is it?'

'From something Luna said – or didn't say – I think my father's still alive.'

Terry doesn't seem nearly as surprised as I thought she would be. 'I've often thought that,' she said. 'That line she handed us about him being killed in a car accident before you were born somehow never quite rang true. But if he is ... what then?'

'I have to find him.'

'Do you really, Theo? Suppose he's got a wife and kids. Grandchildren. Maybe he doesn't even know you exist. Maybe she disappeared without telling him.'

'Why would she do that?'

'I've no idea, but if you find him, are you just going to barge into whatever life he's living and

227

maybe destroy it?' Terry is shaking her head. 'I told Lucia years ago that by keeping silent, she was storing up trouble for herself and for you. It looks like the trouble's here.'

'I just want to know, that's all.'

'Why does "that's all" always mean so much more?' she asks sadly.

It's time I left. I squeeze her hand. 'I don't think I've ever said it before, Terry, but thank you for all you've given me. For taking me in, raising me, for everything.'

'Believe me, sweetie, it's us that are grateful.' She pats my cheek. 'You know how much we love you. Max always wanted another little girl. Think how sour and wizened he and I might have become if we hadn't had you.'

'Oh, sure.'

'But you might also think about this,' she says slowly. 'We took you in, but we didn't do much raising. Most of that was down to your mother.'

I think of Luna criss-crossing the globe with a child in tow. I remember the places I've seen, the people I've met. Luna may not have taught me to cook or sew or run a house, but she taught me to read, she showed me paintings, she discussed things with me. I remember evenings in whichever rickety room we were currently occupying, laughing as we concocted ever wilder pseudonyms for ourselves. I remember her charming spiky sketches. I remember distant happiness.

'She did, yes.'

'And even though you feel pretty down now, you're a strong woman, a strong person. Isn't that enough of a gift from her? She hasn't been the best mom in the world, in the conventional sense, no question of that. She's always had broader horizons than the rest of us, and that's why her friends value her. Maybe you should try looking at her that way too, as a friend rather than parent. I loved her because she was a one-off, an original. She was witty and warm and when she walked in, the room lit up. Like I said, she's not like other people, never has been, she always – what's that quote – marched to a different drum.'

She's right. I know that. But I still need to find out who I am.

As I am leaving, I say, 'By the way, were you serious about giving away Nancy's shoes?'

'Why, do you want some?'

'I'd love to take a couple of pairs.' If apology doesn't work with Trina, maybe bribery will. Not that now is the optimum moment to try. I'll have to leave it for a while.

'We're not talking an Ugly Sister thing here, are we? Because after all those years of buying school shoes, I know your feet are several sizes larger than Nancy's were.'

'Several? Are you joking?'

'Three, then.'

'They're for someone else.'

'Help yourself. Otherwise they'll only end up at the Oxfam shop.' She takes my hand, pulls me close, kisses me. 'What you need to do is enjoy the things your mother *did* do, instead of resenting the things she didn't.'

'I know.'

Which doesn't make it any easier.

EIGHTEEN

I spend the next two days making phone calls. When Marnie comes in on the third morning, I say, 'Look, I know I've just been away but I'm going to take some more time off.'

'Fine by me.'

'So I'm going to the States tomorrow.'

'You were there just a few weeks back.'

'I need to go again. I shan't be more than a few days. You shouldn't have any problems while I'm away. There's always the mobile, if something really urgent comes up.'

'Fine.' She is dying to ask questions, but manages to keep them to herself. 'Is this business or pleasure?'

'I doubt if it will be pleasure,' I say.

'But not strictly business, either?'

'That about sums it up.'

'Take good care, won't you?'

'Maybe,' I say, 'I should learn to take less care.'

She fishes a chocolate bar out of her bag and puts it beside the telephone. 'Good point. By the way, did you ever catch up with Trina?'

'I did.'

'So why isn't she outside?'

I can hardly bring myself to explain. 'Basically, because she's got engaged.'

'That's not good. I knew the boyfriend was itching to get a ring on her finger. He's probably had it ready for months, just waiting for the right moment.'

'Which would never have come if I hadn't shouted at her. As you said, she was really happy here.'

'Looked like it to me.'

We stare at one another. 'Maybe I could visit her while you're gone,' Marnie says. 'See if I could do better than you.'

I ignore her expression, which says plainer than words that she could hardly do worse. 'It's worth a try.'

Another two-hour delay. What is it with these airline people? If I ran my business as inefficiently as they do theirs, I'd be out of a job in a New York minute. I wander round Heathrow, buy a paper, drink endless cups of ugly coffee. For a while, I slip into a kind of trance, seeing no other way to pass the time. In one of the airport bookstores, I pull out an atlas and open it at the page marked Eastern United States. I try to calculate how long it will take me to drive from Boston to Vermont, give or take a hundred kilometres or so. I buy a book to read on the plane, written by a much-touted American woman.

Finally we board the plane to Boston. Once I've been served drinks and something to eat, leafed through some magazines, I doze off. I hate to think how much later I wake, to find myself canted sideways in my seat, head almost resting on the shoulder of the woman next to me.

231

She is wearing a blue shirt and well-cut jeans. Please don't let me have dribbled all over her shirt, I pray. I straighten up. I take a surreptitious peep but can't see any suspicious stains, and get out the paperback I bought at the airport.

My neighbour stretches her arms above her head and makes a series of grunting sounds. It's one of the hazards of air travel, in these post DVT-scare days. Then she pulls one of her knees up to her chin in a lithe kind of way I couldn't duplicate in the privacy of my own home, let alone in an airline seat. 'I'm Gemma, by the way,' she says, seeing me watching her.

'Theo.'

I look out of the window beside me. The plane skims across piled clouds, towers, castles, battlements, all as solid looking as rock. 'Hard to believe that if you stepped into that, you'd plummet to earth,' I say.

'That's what they *tell* you,' Gemma says darkly.

The flight attendant pauses by our seats, offering drinks. I ask for red wine; Gemma orders a gin and tonic. 'And boy, do I need it,' she says, drinking half of it in one swallow. 'I'm on my way to see my mother, and the first thing she'll do is stare meaningfully at my totally naked ring finger. She *so* wants me to get married – or at least engaged.'

'Anybody in the offing?'

'Actually, and at last, yes, I do believe so. But it's still early days, so I shan't be telling Mother, unless she drives me to desperation.' She rolls her eyes. 'Mothers! You gotta love 'em.'

'When she's scoped out the ring-finger, what else will she say?'

Gemma puts her hands behind her head and bends sideways from the waist until her face is almost in my lap. 'That she doesn't like my hair like this or that blue never was my colour. That I've put on weight. That I obviously don't care about her any more or I'd have visited ages ago.' She smiles. 'And then she'll hug me till my ribs crack, and tell me she's fixed fried chicken for supper, and when we get back to the house, there'll be a welcome banner hanging across the porch, which my sister and I made about a thousand years ago, and a pecan-caramel coffee cake will be cooling in the kitchen, my all-time favourite, and it'll be ... it'll be *home*.'

Dozing again, as the plane drones across the Atlantic, turns over Greenland and comes down the east coast of the United States, I think of Fergus. I never asked him why there was a stork tattooed on his shoulder, and now I probably never will. My mother's image floats behind my eyelids, with blossoms in her hair, a wild child long before anyone gave them a name. *Mothers ... you gotta love 'em.*

You do.

It is mid-afternoon by the time we stumble off the plane in Boston. Although I'm not into random hugs, I nonetheless find myself returning Gemma's brief embrace with something more than perfunctory politesse. 'I think you look great in blue,' I say.

I watch her pass through the barrier and into the arms of a plump brown-haired woman who is dabbing at her eyes. She holds Gemma away from her so she can check her over, pulls her back again into an even tighter embrace, pushes her away again to look at her hair, her face, her size, and all the time she's talking sixteen to the dozen. Gemma turns back to me and winks. I wink back.

When I ask how to get to St Margaret's Junior College, they tell me at the Tourist Information Center to take the road out of town towards Burlington and turn off after five kilometres, that I'll come to St Joseph's first and, two kilometres later, St Mag's. I drive slowly, taking in the landscape of my mother's college days, the first piece of her past that I've ever knowingly encountered. I think of those cute-as-a-button Doris Day or Debbie Reynolds movies I've seen on the television and wonder if Luna ever sat at the counter of the ice-cream parlour with a root-beer float in front of her, wore her hair in a ponytail, owned a pair of saddle-Oxford shoes. Not that I know for certain what a root-beer float is, let alone a saddle-Oxford. In any case, since it was the late sixties, she was more likely demonstrating against the US presence in Vietnam, in skirts which barely covered her fanny, skinny-rib sweaters and white knee socks.

I pass signs to St Joseph's and sure enough, two kilometres later, come to a tasteful dark-blue board with *St Margaret's Junior College For Girls* painted in gold letters, *founded in 1902*. I drive down a road which leads to another sign and a pair of red-brick gate posts, and follow the boards leading me to the reception area. The

234

driveway winds between smooth lawns and mellow oaks, past a series of red-brick buildings in Gothic style, all narrow-pointed windows and granite turrets. On the left, a stream flows under a bridge into an artificial lake.

More buildings back away up a hill to culminate in a chapel with stained-glass windows, its front portico dominated by a huge white statue of a melancholy woman in a marble mantle. St Margaret herself, of course. From my school days, I recall that St Margaret was swallowed by a dragon and then brought forth from the belly of the beast without a scratch on her, thus qualifying her to be the special patron of childbirth.

Beyond the chapel, where the hill dips again to the other end of the stream, the buildings become less decorative, more functional and modern. Knots of people stand about under the trees, some with books in their arms, others with packs on their backs. Still others move purposefully along the paths. A woman with flowing grey locks sits with her back to a tree trunk, plucking at a guitar and singing.

At the Administration block, I park and get out. I go in and push open a door marked *Reception*. The room is small and very crowded: file cabinets, two desks, bookshelves, computers, and a thousand photos of groups of girls in white gowns and caps on Graduation Days, going back for generations. Since she left at the end of her second year, without graduating, my mother won't be among them.

Behind one of the desks sits a fresh-faced kid in a little white blouse with a rounded collar and

235

embroidery down the placket. Fingering the pearl stud in her ear, she smiles at me, and asks what I want.

To find my father seems too direct. 'I'm from England,' I say. 'I'm looking into my family background and since my mother was here at college, I thought I'd stop by and see if there was anyone left who might remember her.'

'What years was she a student here?'

I tell her, and she doesn't even have to think about it. 'You want Sister Mary Immaculata. She's the only one who was around back then.'

It is more than I've hoped for. 'Could I speak to her?'

'I'm afraid not. She's on vacation.'

'Oh.' For some reason I've imagined that any nun who'd taught my mother would by now be incapable of much more than lying in bed in a black robe and white wimple, bathed in the odour of sanctity, weakly raising a frail finger in blessing as other nuns crowded round her, sobbing at the prospect of her imminent demise. But of course she wouldn't have to be more than a few years older than Luna.

The girl grins, as though she's read my thoughts. 'Not all nuns are elderly, you know. And we don't experience anything like the physical wear and tear that our lay sisters do. How old do you think I am?'

'Twenty-four, twenty-six,' I say, though she is probably younger. *We?* It hasn't occurred to me that she is a nun.

'I was thirty-four last April.'

I'll have whatever she's having. Her face is as

smooth and unlined as a teenager's. 'I'm sorry to have missed her,' I say. 'Anyone else I could talk to?'

'Not really.' An idea strikes her. 'You could always try St Joe's. I know we were sharing facilities with them by the time your mother must have been here. They had much better-equipped labs than we did, plus a very sophisticated theatre. And they had a terrific sports facility.'

'Anybody in particular I should speak to?'

'I suppose Dom Francis is your best bet.' Terry had mentioned him, too. My mother's confessor. 'He's the abbot now, been there for donkey's years. But he's a very busy man and I don't suppose you have an appointment, do you?'

'No.'

'He's a bit of a...' She wrinkles her nose while she tries to think of the right word. 'He can be a bit ... uh ... difficult.'

'So can I,' I say.

The campus of St Joseph's is similar to that of St Margaret's, but older and richer. The landscaping is more lavish, the chapel bigger, the lawns greener, the dormitories larger, but the same stream runs through the grounds, straddled by an identical stone bridge, leading to a similar lake. The buildings, too, though in some indefinable way more masculine, are pretty much the same: early nineteenth-century Gothic, augmented by fifties Expansionist Modern dorm blocks, featuring layers of uncompromisingly bare rectangles of glass accented by plastic panels in unattractive shades of yellow and blue.

The reception area here is not a modern office but housed in a graceful Colonial building which has been restored to such a peak of pristine perfection that it might have been completed that very morning. Inside, what look like priceless oriental rugs lie over an expanse of polished oak planks. Through an archway, a staircase rises gracefully to upper floors.

A young man in a clerical collar and black shirt, tucked into pale chinos, identifies himself as Father Patrick. He's a dead ringer for Tony Perkins in *Psycho*, so much so that I nearly ask how the motel business is doing. Instead, I tell him I'm hoping to speak to Dom Francis, and explain why. After listening to my spiel, he pulls forward a pad of paper and a pen. 'And your mother's name?' he asks.

'Lucia Cairns.'

He lifts the receiver of the phone on his desk and speaks to the abbot. 'Ms Theodora Cairns,' he says, twinkling a complicit smile at me to show that we are all feminists now. 'That's right, her mother was at St Mag's.'

He listens some more. 'Yes, Cairns.' Another listen. 'C-A-I-R-N-S, I imagine.' He raises his eyebrows, checking to see if he's spelled the name right, then replaces the receiver. He shakes his head. 'Sorry, but he's busy.'

'Ask him again. My mother wasn't called Cairns, back then,' I say belatedly. 'She was Lucia Caxton.'

'But if he's busy—'

'Try again,' I say. 'Please.'

Something in my voice persuades him. He

rings the abbot again, gives my mother's maiden name, raises his eyebrows, replaces the receiver. 'You're in luck,' he says. 'Dom Francis is having a coffee break.'

We walk past a statue of a benevolent St Joseph and climb the elegant stairs. I follow him down a polished-oak passage, past windows which look out on to a hedged garden very like the one in my painting of Thomas Bellamy. I stop. *Very* like. Hedges, pebbles, a white seat. Stone urns in the corners, obelisks, a fountain in the middle. In fact, it is identical. I stare down at it – there has to be a connection here, there just has to be.

Tony Perkins stops outside a door of highly polished wood, on which he taps respectfully with the knuckle of his forefinger. He lays an ear against the panels. Obviously someone tells him to come in because he turns the big brass knob and stands politely to one side to let me in.

It is an impressive room. Painted a deep Prussian blue where it isn't panelled in mahogany, it has tall windows with fold-away shutters, overlooking the campus. The floor-length curtains are of heavy red damask tied back with thick tasselled braids of crimson silk, matching the reds in the huge Persian rug on the floor. If Dom Francis has taken vows of poverty, he must have forgotten them some while back, though to be fair, the man himself is considerably less sumptuous than his surroundings. He sits at a large partner's desk, beneath a heavy wooden crucifix, and my first guess is he's anorexic, my second that he is starving. All the spare flesh has gone from his face, leaving only beautiful bones under olive skin stretched so tight that it shines, as though it is buffed up each morning with chamois leather. It is the face of an ascetic, or a saint. I have no trouble imagining him in a cave somewhere, living off wild honey and locusts and getting friendly with the local lion.

And my heart rate quickens until I feel I might begin to hyperventilate as, with absolute conviction, I recognize him. He's the sinister-looking man in the photograph of a long-ago summer in France. The same man who waited so patiently by the railings of a London public garden. A man I have seen before, many times, in another existence. A man who haunts my dreams, and stalks my mother across the globe.

I say nothing but I am gripped by something primitive and evil.

The sight of me jolts him. He is far too smooth and secretive to show any change of expression, but I see the flicker far back in his eyes. He indicates an antique carver chair in front of his desk and I sit.

'How can I help you?' His voice is suave, a little weary as though, in the years that he's been supervising generations of Catholic youth, he has seen it all and there is nothing that can surprise him. He is wearing a long black robe with a black skullcap over a fluff of white hair, a heavy gold cross on a chain. The college might be contemporary, but he seems determined to cling to the Middle Ages. In front of him is a tray with a white coffee jug, a pitcher of milk and a white porcelain coffee cup, all of them decorated

240

with a single silver cross.

His eyes are flat and black, the pupil almost filling the eyeball, like a lizard's. Something radiates from him which I am fairly sure is hostility. Not generalized hostility, but very me-specific. Is it because I am female, in this bastion of maleness? Can he sense that I'd started my period the day before and am therefore, in some primitive way, unclean? Or is it my likeness to my mother?

'This is a male college,' he says, the words dropping from him like flakes of ice. Fergus would hate him. 'What makes you think I can help you?'

'My mother was at St Margaret's, thirty or so years ago. They told me that you might possibly remember...'

'Lucia Caxton, I think Father Anthony said.' He pretends to mull it over, though it's obvious he has no difficulty at all in recognizing the name. He picks up the coffee cup and sips from it as delicately as a cat. 'I know the girl you mean. From England, wasn't she? I believe her mother had been here before her.'

'That's right.' What did Luna do, to imprint herself so strongly on his memory? 'I'm amazed you remember, after more than thirty years?'

'It's part of my job to remember those who were once in my pastoral care. I was, after all, her confessor at the time, though my place within the college then was very much junior to my present position.' He closes his eyes. 'Is it really thirty years ago that she was here? One begins to feel so old.'

'Do you remember all the girls who came here to confess?'

'Of course not. But Miss Caxton was an ... an exceptional young woman. The sort who would go on to become an exceptional wife and mother.' He opens his eyes again and smiles thinly. 'Which I'm sure she is.'

'Mmm.' I nod.

'And is she well?'

'Yes.'

'And ... I never heard what she went on to do ... a promising artist, was she not?'

'She may have been, but she's a dancer now.'

I can't swear to it, but I think his bloodless face goes even paler. Two small dots of white stand out on either side of his nose. 'A dancer? But I always understood...' He draws in a hissing kind of breath. He's let out some information though I can't imagine what it is. Unless he thinks dancing is less respectable than painting. 'But I imagine she didn't continue that after her marriage.'

'She's not actually married,' I say.

'Your mother, not married?' he echoes.

'That's right.'

'Then you are...' Again the jolt, his collarbones shifting momentarily under his gown. Do I see fear in his face? Or merely contempt for a woman who could so far forget her privileged upbringing, waste the care spent on showing her the paths of rectitude, as to produce a child out of wedlock – and then further compound her sin by not setting things straight and making it legitimate? 'I thought ... didn't you tell Father

Patrick that you were researching your *parents'* background?'

'Yes, well, I was a little economical with the truth.' I smile at him but he doesn't smile back. 'Basically, my mother left St Margaret's because she found she was pregnant.'

'*What?*' He leans towards me, and this time there is no mistaking it. For some reason, he is frightened. His teeth clench together. Maybe he thinks I'm going to sue. 'She was pregnant? Are you sure?'

'And unmarried,' I repeat, rubbing it in. 'There was nobody she could turn to: her parents died about that time, and I don't suppose she expected the nuns to be sympathetic.'

I sound confident but the truth is I don't know a great deal about my mother's early life; much of what I've learnt has come from Terry Cartwright.

He leans back against his chair and presses his lips together so tightly that it looks as though he has no mouth at all. Although his face remains impassive, he can't do much about the tiny flicker which has started up under his left eye. 'If they'd known of her plight,' he says, 'I'm sure they would have done everything in their power to help her.'

I can't imagine that the average nun would have been much help but I'm not going to get into a discussion about the different ways you can handle desperate adolescents. 'As far as I can make out, she didn't tell anyone at all,' I say.

'Except, presumably, the father?'

I shrug. 'Perhaps not even him.'

'You mean he might not know you exist?'

'That's very possible. Just as I know nothing about him. Which is part of why I've come here, in the hope of tracking down someone who could help me find him.'

'Why would you think it was someone from St Joseph's?'

'I don't think anything, Dom Francis. My mother has consistently refused to tell me anything at all about him. In fact, she invented a completely spurious father for me – it was only by accident that I discovered the man she claimed was my father had nothing whatsoever to do with me.'

'Interesting.'

'As far as I can work out, she must have discovered she was pregnant with me sometime during the summer semester that year – her second year at St Margaret's. She dropped out of school then, and –' I spread my hands – 'temporarily vanished. According to her friends, when she resurfaced, she had me in tow. She always refused to tell anyone about the father.'

The narrow face relaxes imperceptibly. 'How do you think I can help?'

'It's at least possible that it was one of your students.'

'It could have been someone from Maybury. Or Butterfield. Someone she knew from another college in the area – there are dozens of them round here. A friend from England. Or even someone met after she had left here.'

'Unlikely, although I have no preconceptions,' I say. 'Why else would she drop out of school?'

He makes a stiff little gesture. 'And obviously your mother didn't put you up for adoption?'

'Yes, she kept me. She brought me up, provided for me, all on her own,' I say, and if his voice is chilly, then mine is positively arctic.

Somewhere outside the window, a bell begins to toll.

The abbot looks at the clock on the mantelpiece and then checks his wristwatch. He takes another cat-sip of his coffee and closes his eyes again, this time for so long that I start to wonder if he has fallen asleep. He looks at me eventually. 'Does your father's identity matter that much?' Something about me disturbs him profoundly. Is it the likeness to my mother? Am I stirring up old guilts he'd rather forget?

'Yes, it does.'

'Can you not accept our Lord God as your father?'

'Not really.'

'Your mother hasn't spoken of the man to you?'

'She refuses to. Says there are compelling reasons why I shouldn't know.'

Another flash of something I can't identify shines at the back of his non-reflecting eyes. For a wild – and I admit, horrifying – moment, I wonder if he himself is the man I'm looking for. He bows his head. 'Perhaps you should respect that.'

'I don't think it's her secret to keep.'

'It's a wise child that knows its own father, as they say.'

'Do you know yours?'

He parts his narrow lips. 'Of course.'

'And isn't that knowledge part of what makes you who you are?'

'I would like to think that what I am is what I have made myself – with God's help.'

'Nonetheless, you've never had to worry about your own identity, so you may not be able to understand how very disconcerting it is to discover that you don't know where you come from.'

Another long pause. Another bend of the head. 'Tell me, Theodora Cairns,' he says eventually, 'what would you do if you acquired the information you seek? Would you accept the knowledge gained as sufficient in itself, or would you want more?'

'I guess I'd like to meet up with him, if only to see what kind of a man he was. Except that, according to my mother, he's—' I am going to say 'dead' but Dom Francis doesn't give me the chance.

'You think you have the right to trespass into this man's life?'

'I don't know why not.'

He thrusts his head forward, like a snake. 'You would actually try to make yourself known to him?'

'Why not?' My voice is so tart it sets my teeth on edge.

He frowns again, two fine lines appearing between the stretched skin above his nose. 'Has it occurred to you that he may have another life, a life in which he is not your father, a life which could be *profoundly* disturbed if you intruded?

246

Perhaps you should do so. Perhaps you should remember that all actions have consequences.' I am suddenly aware of power, and of danger.

'Indeed they do. And *I'm* the consequence of an action taken thirty years ago, possibly by one of your students.'

I watch the skin on his face wrinkle and return to smoothness. 'I can tell you categorically that you are mistaken,' he states flatly.

And as he says this, a number of things become shiveringly clear. First, that the abbot knows exactly who my father is. Second, that my father is indeed alive. Thirdly, that the abbot would burn in hell before he'd tell me anything that would help me track him down. And finally, that until I showed up, he had no idea that the liaison with my mother had produced a child.

He comes to some decision and stands up. 'I'm sorry I can't be of more help,' he says, not sorry at all, glad, if anything that, as far as he is aware, I am leaving with no more information than I'd arrived with.

'It was good of you to see me at such short notice.' I too can be gracious.

He comes round his desk, fleshless as a skeleton, and opens the door of his room. He bends his head towards me. 'If I think of anything that might help your search, I'll let you know.'

'Thank you.' I hope he'll be going to confession very soon, if only to admit to the lie he's just uttered.

When I reappear downstairs, Norman Bates jumps up from his desk, smiling that shy *Psycho* smile of his. 'Any help?'

'Not a lot.'

'I am sorry you've come all the way from England and ended up with nothing.'

'I wouldn't say nothing. But a lot less than I hoped.'

'Oh, well.' He grins so sweetly that I start wondering if his mother is OK. He walks me to the door. I stop in front of an oil painting which shows a jolly-looking man in black robes. Behind him is a garden I recognize. As I recognize the artist's style. The garden is formal, hedged in box, with the same white bench and plashing fountain. And, as in my painting, beyond the confines of the formal garden, the artist has mixed realism with magic: incongruous among Vermont hills is a palm tree from which are suspended scarlet coconuts; on the painted sea is the wreck of a two-masted schooner, and goats frolic among the fronds of a luxuriant pearl-hung jungle in which, when I look closer, I discern a kind of goat-skin-clad figure that is recognizably Robinson Crusoe.

'Is this a Barnes?' I ask, although it's not really a question.

'Yes, an early one.'

'How early?'

He peers at the canvas. So do I. And seeing the year on the frame, realize that Luna was here at the time. I'm immediately interested. Could Vernon Barnes possibly have known her back then? Can that have been how she got hold of the portrait which she'd passed off as my father? 'Oddly enough,' I say slowly, 'I own a Barnes myself.'

'Is that right? It's probably worth a fortune now.'

'So I've been told.' I'm still staring up at the portrait, wondering why Barnes should have used exactly the same garden in this painting as in the one of Capt. Thomas Bellamy Bt.

'That's Father Dominic Campbell, the last abbot but two,' Norman Bates is saying. He turns to me with his cute Tony Perkins smile. 'Did you know that he lives not that far from here, up near the Canadian border? Barnes, I mean, not Father Dominic.'

'Does he, indeed? Would you ... would you by any chance have a phone number for him?'

'Indeed.' He consults lists, writes down the number, hands it to me.

An idea is forming in my head. I look at my watch. 'Listen, I'm a professional gardener. That's the same garden you have out the back, isn't it? Any chance I could take a look at it?'

He hesitates, looks at his desk, picks the cordless phone off its stand. 'I guess so.'

I follow him round the building and through a narrow gap between the hedges. At last I smell the box, the tobacco plants, crunch across the white pebbles, hear the plash of the fountain. Stepping into the landscape of my painting, the landscape of my dreams, is surreal, like something out of *Alice in Wonderland*. How many times have I imagined myself in this very place?

I feel unaccountably sad. Finally, I turn. 'Many thanks for your help.'

'Have a good day now,' he says.

But I doubt that I will. If my conclusions are

correct, then the man who is my father was almost certainly a St Joseph's college alumnus, someone who'd made his confession to Dom Francis, done his penance and been absolved of any further sin. While my mother had been left with me.

As I drive away down leafy Vermont highways, I have a strong conviction that Dom Francis is still sitting at his desk, weighing up pros and cons, working out the best way to proceed. Because proceed he most certainly will.

NINETEEN

Back in my hotel, I call the number I've been given. The phone is picked up by Barnes himself. He has one of those nasal Bostonian accents which remind you of the late President John F. Kennedy. 'Could we meet? I own one of your paintings,' I say.

'Which one would that be?'

'A man called Thomas Bellamy.'

'Bellamy, Bellamy? Aha! Look, are you anywhere near here?'

'I will be tomorrow.'

'Come and have lunch with us. Around noon.' He gives me an address and rings off.

So, here I am, on what is certainly a wild goose chase, driving along a road cut out of the forest, which stretches endlessly before and behind me, unbroken by signs, gates or driveways. There is no traffic, either. No semis, no RVs, no vacationing senior citizens in matching petrol-green shell-suits, or college kids mooning from the windows of beat-up jalopies. Nothing.

I mull over what I've indirectly learned from Dom Francis. Even if I could get hold of a list of students who'd attended St Joseph's while my mother was at St Margaret's, it wouldn't be of any help, since I have no idea what name I'd be looking for – if indeed there is a name to find. The only thing I can be sure of is that it won't be either John or Vincent. And, as Dom Francis pointed out, she could have been involved with someone who had nothing to do with St Joseph's. But I don't believe that: I'm still convinced that he knew who I was talking about.

I've asked for directions at no fewer than four different filling stations but only the last one, five miles back, has been of any use. 'Just keep on till you see a metal postbox,' the guy said, wiping his hands on an oily rag which only made them more oily. 'Says five-four-seven-eight on it, clear as day.'

Indeed it does, when I finally find it. It seems strange that I've passed no mailboxes displaying any of the other numbers prior to 5478, but maybe it's a New Hampshire thing. I turn off the highway and bump up a wheel-rutted track between a close-packed growth of maple, pine and birch, until I reach a grassed clearing. I can see glimpses of lake between the trees to either side of the house in front of me, a Frank Gehry sort of building of strange angles and impossible

251

roof-lines, with hints of field-stone here, glass sheeting there, cedar shingles and breeze block elsewhere, the whole given a forest-green trim.

Apart from the tick of hot metal cooling, the sigh of wind in the trees all round me and lake water lapping behind the house, there is no sound at all. Nothing to indicate the presence of other people in the vicinity: no voices, or music, no noise of radio or traffic, no distant speedboat buzz, none of the sounds we've learned to take for granted, even in the wilderness.

A porch sits in front of the house – and so, I suddenly became aware, does a man. Not only is he in an Adirondack chair painted the same forest-green as the trim, he also holds a shotgun pointed straight at me. My insides flutter with fear. I've seen my share of gangster movies but nothing can really prepare you for the unnerving reality of a gun barrel. It would take him no more than a nanosecond, long before I can fling myself to one side or another, to plug a hole straight through my heart.

'Oh, hi!' I say, nervously clearing my throat. 'I'm—'

'Since I just got a call from St Joe's, I got a pretty good idea who you must be.' He stands up. 'And likewise, I guess you realize I'm Vern Barnes.'

'I hope so,' I say. 'Otherwise it means I'm out here in the woods with a maniac pointing a shot-gun at me.'

'I've been blasting squirrels.' Carefully he breaks the weapon and lays it down on the wooden floor of the porch. He is a very big man, six foot six or seven, in paint-stained jeans and a checked shirt open over a grey T-shirt. Grizzled: the word was invented to describe his weather-beaten face, wild grey hair, untamed eyebrows over piercing blue eyes. He advances towards the top of the three shallow steps up to the porch. 'Miss Cairns, right?'

'Right.'

'Come on up.'

I step up on to the porch and collapse into a chair. 'Jesus,' I say, letting out a gust of relief. 'Do you have the slightest idea how scary it is to find yourself being faced down by a gun?'

'Sorry.' He opens a screen door. 'Get you a drink?'

'A strong one, please.' I close my eyes and palpitate quietly for a second or two until he re-appears with two glasses half-full of something that is definitely the right shade of brown.

'Bourbon,' he says, handing me one. 'You use water?'

'Only for my pot-plants.' I swallow a large slug of the alcohol and almost immediately feel better. Blue sky blinks between the crowded leaves; sunshine casts bars of light on to the forest floor. 'What a lovely place this is.'

'Peaceful.'

'Your house has an ... interesting design.'

'In other words, it's an eclectic hodgepodge of styles, don't you think?' He smiles. 'Built the whole thing myself, without a blueprint or even a spirit level, would you believe?'

'I would indeed.'

He scratches at a mosquito bite on his arm,

then tilts his glass and knocks back what's left. 'So, what did you want to discuss with me?'

'It's just a shot in the dark, but...' I explain the question of my father's identity, and the faint link with the portrait of Thomas Bellamy he painted before I was even born. 'The garden,' I say. 'Was Bellamy at St Joseph's?'

'Not as far as I know.'

'But the garden in your painting is identical to the one there.' Even as I'm speaking I can see what a pointless journey this is. If there ever was a connection, Luna has covered her tracks far too efficiently.

He makes a rueful face. 'Sheer laziness, I'm afraid. Back when Connie Franklin asked me to paint the portraits of her and her husband, I was about as respectable as I was ever going to get. Married, a couple of kids, established as a –' his face contorts in a grimace – 'society portrait painter, for God's sake. Jesus, what a phrase. A self-fulfilling prophecy, really. Some big cheese in the merchant banking world that I'd played squash racquets with at Exeter and Harvard commissioned me to paint his wife and kids, to show he could afford to, and then everyone else wanted in on the act. Keeping up with the Rockefellers. Worst of it was, the more I charged them, the more they thought I was worth it. I won *prizes*, would you believe? How to dig yourself into a hole. Terrifying. I went along with it as long as I could, and then I just lit out for the territory. Never regretted it for an instant.' He waves a hand at the trees and the silence. 'But when Connie – or the Honourable

Constance, as she then was – when she asked me, for old time's sake ... and she was prepared to pay handsomely for it...' He breathes in sharply through his nose. 'Selling my soul to the devil, I suppose.'

'And the garden?'

'Oh, that. Like I said, laziness. I'd just painted a portrait of the current abbot – I'm going back a heck of a long time here – using that garden as a backdrop, and since Connic hadn't even begun the restoration of the gardens at that place she lives – Sheepsfleece or something – I just used the same one.'

It seems too mundane an explanation for the place which has haunted my dreams. 'I see.'

'Other than that, do I have any information which could help you?'

'I guess you don't remember my mother. Not that there's any reason why you should.'

He shakes his head. ''Fraid not. I never really went for girls in bobby socks.' He cocks an untamed eyebrow at me. 'You say she won't tell you anything?'

'Nothing.'

'Hmm. I wonder what she's trying to hide. Or who she's trying to protect.'

'It *is* the obvious assumption, isn't it?' I look round at the gently stirring leaves, smell the resinous aroma of the cedar shingles. Thirty years ago, Luna would still have been a teenager. A nicely brought-up Catholic girl, she must have been terrified to discover that she was pregnant. How long had it taken her to formulate a plan of action, where had she gone once the semester

255

was over? Had someone helped her, and if so, who?

'Wish I could be more help.' Getting up, he walks back to the screen door and holds it half-open, beckoning me with his head at the same time. 'Another drink?'

'Oh,' I say. 'Why the hell not.'

'Come in and have a look around.'

The door leads into a burst of light, sun reflecting off water through tall pointed windows. A cathedral ceiling arches overhead, pierced by a fieldstone chimney breast. Knee-height bookcases run right round the room and provide seats for the many windows. Such wall space as remains is covered with huge abstract paintings, swirls of gorgeously violent colour. There is only one room, a large open space which serves as living room, dining area and kitchen. The place is unkempt; piles of books jostle with newspapers and magazines, there are empty coffee cups on the floor, dust lies thickly over what furniture surfaces can be seen. Nonetheless, it looks like a loved and lived-in place.

I kneel on one of the window-seat cushions and look out at the dancing water behind the house. 'Where do you paint?'

'There's a shack out back,' he says. 'Want to see?'

Below the house the ground slopes gently down to a narrow creek which runs into the lake. Sunlight dapples the ground through the trees. Another eccentric building stands on the other side of the house, a sort of cross between an aircraft hanger and a filling station.

'More of your architectural work,' I say as we step through aluminium sliding doors into the studio.

'All made from stuff picked up at the salvage yard,' he says. 'Cost about the same as a car port.'

'Very impressive.'

Trees have been cleared in front of the back wall to let the light in. There are counters for his paints, a couple of wooden easels, a pile of driftwood in one corner, a bed-base made out of planks set on bricks with a foam rubber mattress covered in a Mexican serape. Surplus scaffolding has been fixed to the walls at intervals, and holds canvasses, for the most part. Otherwise the space is empty.

A car pulls up. 'There's Larry, he just slipped down to the store to get some more raspberry vinegar for the salad dressing or some other damn thing. He's very anxious to talk with you. Probably hoping to get some free advice on our backyard.'

Vernon's rugged face lights up as we walk out to greet a handsome, slightly raddled man a few years younger than Vern himself. 'Nice to meet you,' I say. Larry has a big Hey-I-just-won-a-million-dollars! kind of smile. His eyes lock with Vernon's and I'm aware of the sexual currents between them. They've been together for twenty years and each still looks as though someone just switched on a lamp when he sees his partner. I envy them.

Vern pours wine from what looks like a hospital specimen jar. 'Theo wants us to help her to trace her father,' he announces.

Larry looks puzzled. 'Call me stupid, but why would we know any more than she does?'

'We don't,' Vernon explains briefly. 'Seems to me,' he continues, 'that it's an inalienable right to know who your parents are; otherwise how can you ever know who *you* are?'

'That's way too philosophical for me,' says Larry. 'In my case, I'd much rather *not* know who my parents are. A dental nurse and a realtor?' He shudders delicately. 'Too gross.'

I wonder where Fergus is, whether he thinks of me, whether we could ever have reached the same level of loving familiarity that these two have. I'm dejected, cast down by the hopelessness of the task I've set myself. Coming here has been a waste of time, nothing more than an exercise in making me feel I was doing something. The more I probe, the frailer seems my own identity, the further it recedes.

And then I remember the abbot's face. I clear my throat. 'There's a possibility he might have had something to do with St Joseph's Academy.' I explain why.

'You mean that Catholic boys' school, in Vermont?' asks Larry. 'I'll tell you, those holy guys give me the creeps.'

'Too butch for you, darlin'?'

'It's not just the dreary black frocks they wear. It's the way they look at you, as if they'd bat you out of the way without even thinking about it. And all in the name of God, which makes it even worse. Remember that head honcho we met a couple of years ago, Vern? Cruelty on a stick.'

He dances lightly across the room and refills our glasses. 'Matter of fact, wasn't there a rumour that he more or less drove one of those kids at St Mag's to suicide?'

'Drowned herself in the lake, wasn't that the story? For love of one of his protégés?'

'That's it.' Larry shakes his head. 'The bastard.'

'I had a commission down there once,' says Barnes. 'Jeez, more than thirty years ago.'

'Way before I was even born,' Larry says.

Vernon laughs. 'I'd hate to see the portrait in *your* attic.'

Larry bats his thick eyelashes. 'Oh, you *men*! You're so *mean*.'

Vernon looks at me. 'Given the lack of any information whatsoever, your mother must have put a lot of thought into how best to cover her tracks. In fact, she must've planned it from the first moment she realized she was up the spout.'

'Must have been someone her family might have disapproved of,' Larry says. 'You get someone's darlin' girl-child pregnant, kiddo, the family's going to disapprove if it was the pope himself.'

'*Especially* if it was the pope himself,' says Larry.

'If you want *my* opinion,' Vern says. 'It's what I said earlier, she's trying to protect someone.'

'She had me in India,' I say. 'If nobody knew when I was born, it'd be easy for her to lie a little, wouldn't it?' I look from one of them to the other. 'Especially out there, where people might have been less rigid about the registering

259

of births and filling-in of documents. My mother could easily have fabricated most of my significant details. I might not even be the age I think I am. When she met up with her friends again, she only had to say that I was big for my age, or small for a five-year-old, and who was ever going to question her further?'

I am even more profoundly depressed by this.

'At least she got away. That other poor kid didn't.'

'How do you drive someone to kill themselves?' I ask.

'Way I heard it, you convince them that nobody loves them, especially the boy in question. Then you point out that they could ruin the boy's career if there was a scandal. And you repeat this over and over again. It's called brain-washing.'

'And the gossip says Dom Francis was responsible?'

'That's the word on the street.'

As I'm leaving, Larry says; 'You said you'd be in Boston tomorrow. Me, too. Let's do lunch.'

'OK.'

'I'll take you to my favourite of all restaurants and we can go shopping afterwards.'

'Shopping?' I say.

'You have *heard* of it, doll, haven't you?'

'Retail therapy doesn't do a thing for me, Larry.'

'I'll hold your hand. Where are you staying?'

I give him the name of my hotel.

'That dress is so *fabulous* against your skin, doll. You should never ever wear anything but red.'

260

Larry peeks inside one of the carrier bags dangling from the end of my arms, at the hideously costly dress I've just bought at his urging.

'Campbell's tomato soup isn't really how I see myself,' I say. 'I feel like a red pepper or something.'

'A red-hot *chili* pepper, honey. Trust me: the guys'll be queuing up for a chance just to look at you.'

'So, where to next?'

As well as the dress, I'm weighed down with a completely impractical jacket of champagne-coloured suede, which Larry said I simply had to buy or he'd kill himself right there on the shop floor. Undies, too. Green satin, the exact colour of holly leaves in spring, trimmed with pewter lace, with a matching set in scarlet. Along with that there's an evening dress in brilliant green, the bodice exquisitely beaded in a design of leaves leading to a single glorious pink rose, with shoes to match. 'I don't know when you think I'm going to wear all this,' I complain.

'Cometh the frock, sweetie, cometh the man,' says Larry. 'Though not the one over the other, I *do* hope.'

'I know it's an alien concept to you,' I say, 'but I'm perfectly all right on my own. I don't need anyone else.'

'Who do you think you're kidding?' He nods at a guy coming towards us in tight leather trousers and a grandaddy shirt, a preppy blond haircut emphasising the strong line of his manly jaw. 'Hi, how are you?'

'Hi.' The guy pauses.

261

'Lookin' good,' says Larry, flashing a big smile.

'Feelin' good.' The guy stares at the two of us. 'How're you going?'

'Just fine. You?'

'Never better.' He smiles uncertainly and moves on.

'Who was that?' I ask.

'Haven't a clue, hon, but he was too pretty to pass up, don't you think?'

I laugh. His happy-go-luckiness is tempting, seductive. I wish I were more like that. Terry had said how sad Luna was, how hard she tried to be happy. I was close to becoming the same.

'I want to go back to the dress department,' I say suddenly.

Even though I've reached a complete dead end with regard to my father, I'm feeling a lot better by the time I'm in the cab, heading for the airport. I haven't even maxed out my credit cards. Maybe there's something to this retail therapy stuff, after all.

Luckily the flight is half empty, and I'm able to have three seats to myself. I put up the arm rests and stretch out, try to sleep, but all I can think of is Luna. Nineteen years old, her parents dead, the stigma of an illegitimate child. She must have been terrified. Vernon Barnes had suggested she had lied for all these years in order to protect someone. Two questions nagged at me. Firstly, who was she protecting? And secondly, what was she protecting him or her from? Could it really be Dom Francis? And if so, why? There is a mystery here and I need to unravel it if I am ever to achieve peace.

I picture Luna in the dramatic evening dress I've just impulsively bought her, a simple sheath of black satin with cut-in panels of brilliant red, expensive and beautiful. It's years since I bought her a present. Even if she never wears it, I shall feel good because I bought it for her.

In that hotel dining room, she'd held out her arms to me, and I'd turned on my heel, though the yearning in her face had wrenched my heart.

Oh, Luna, Luna, mother, enchantress ... I miss you so, the way we were, the way we could have been, I miss you, warm as a flower in your rosy scarves, cinnamon-skinned in moon-coloured silks, gorgeous with your pale black-rimmed eyes, magical, with a scarlet bloom behind your ear and your long hair shimmering at your waist. Without you, I wouldn't be the person I am. You shaped me with your careless disregard for the rules of the game – whatever game it was that you were playing. I have become your negative, the inverse of you. Where you are free, I am tied, where you are open, I am shut tight. Where you dance, I falter.

I cry all the way across the Atlantic. Once we were so close but then we became no more than adjacent countries in an atlas, next-door neighbours who don't speak, Siamese twins joined at the hip but facing opposite directions. I fashioned myself to be as unlike her as I could but as I learn more about her, we are gradually merging again, our colours running into each other.

How can I have allowed myself to be so

hostile, so crippled with resentment? Perhaps the answer, for both of us, lies in the identity of my father. Yet, as we circle over London, I start to wonder whether I really care who he was or is, what difference it would make if I knew.

TWENTY

Fergus books in at the Shelbourne, on St Stephen's Green, mostly because he can. The priciest of the pricey. Haunt of the gentry, of the lettered classes, of the Dublin literati. Of which he is now one. He stays there because it is a poke in the eye for the past, a snook cocked at poverty. Walking the grey pavements, brushing up against the lives of the people mobbing round him, he thinks that almost anywhere else on this earth would have been more congenial to him, *I do not want to be here,* childhood sitting like an ape on his back, misery swathed like a choking scarf about his head.

Not just because of his father, but Theodora, too. Which is why he *is* here. No point staying in Corfu without her, it's not the same. Never will be, the zest gone out of it. At long last love, is that the size of it? He's tried to keep her out of his head and his life, but she's there, whether he likes it or not. After she left, he packed up his stuff, paid Maria to clean the place, followed hard on Theodora's heels, though she doesn't know it. She's right, he shouldn't have left it so long before visiting the old man. It can't be put off any longer.

After breakfast, he sits in the lounge with a final, procrastinating coffee. Glances at the papers. *Telegraph, Guardian, Irish Times.* Same old same old. War, destruction, angst, gloom. Prime Minister this, President that, Queen the other, salacious details of mistresses murdering rich lovers, or rich lovers murdering mistresses, some poor yachtsman drowned with his two sons, a wee girl's body found murdered in a field, the Irish paper full of the visit of a Yankee Cardinal doing the rounds, drumming up support, Mass at St Patrick's, at Notre Dame, Westminster and San Marco, why does he bother, makes you fecking sick.

His father has moved. So what else is new? Over the years there've been so many new addresses, so many steely-eyed landladies all akimbo. But tracking him down is no more than a matter of making his way via the last address he had for him, and following directions to the next. It occurs to him, with surprise, that the man will probably not be much more than in his late fifties. Remembering his best-forgotten years with the Christian Brothers, Fergus wonders where his da had been then. Had he sometimes stood at the school railings and picked out his two sons from the snot-snuffling crowd of wretched boys?

Suppose the man is already gone – but no, he'd have told enough people, landladies, garbage collectors, bus conductors, creditors, every gobshite and fuckwit at the local drinking hole, of his son, the famous novelist, your man on the TV, always knew he'd do well, gets it from me, so he does. Someone would have got in touch.

He comes to the top of the road and stops. Small brick terraces. Trees at the edge of the pavements. Whitened doorsteps. He walks slowly along the street, looking for Number 27. Green-painted front door fitted with brass, Rooms To Let neat in the net-shrouded window, tiny pebbled area in front, surrounded by multi-coloured concrete flags, a half barrel set dead centre with a dismal pointy-leafed plant in it. Uncompromising respectability. Surely some mistake. Or has some luckless landlady given the man houseroom and not managed to move him on ever since?

He rings the doorbell, knowing already this is going to be a cliché, or, possibly, a series of them. Money owing, a daughter got in the family way, rage or indifference, *he's away to America these past three years*. Down the passage comes the clack of boots, clip *clop*, clip *clop*, dot-and-carry-one, and Fergus steps back, sweating suddenly, memories swaddling him, holding up his hand as though to ward off the oncoming traffic.

'Yes?' He is small and stocky, powerfully built, muscles bulging under the short sleeves of his shirt. Lodger turned landlord; how can this be?

'Yes?' There's the birthmark at the base of his throat, familiar as Fergus's own thumbs, heart-shaped, liver-coloured.

'Can I help you?' Red face, abundant with the

266

morning's bristles. Eyes of a watered-down blue. Broken boxer's nose.

'Look, fella, do you want something or shall I be shutting the door and going back to my breakfast?' Lips pursing in annoyance for a moment and then a gawk, a gawp, realization settling into his face, an understanding, the prodigal father with the fatted calf come home. 'Is it Fergus?' And when there are still no words from the man who uses words for a living, 'It is!'

Thank the good Lord there's none of that cod-Irish malarkey: *Sure and is it me darlin' bhoy come home again at last?* Dumb as a dustbin, Fergus steps over the threshold, wipes his feet unnecessarily on the spiny WELCOME mat and follows the gimpy limpy knit-one-purl-one of the father's gait. Down the clean, tiled passage they go, between furniture shine and carpet pile. Into the crack-tiled kitchen, dresser against the wall, geraniums on the window sill, scoured pans hanging from butcher's hooks. Cold hum of refrigerator, drip of tap, everything used but scrupulously clean. Books piled on the edge of the dresser, *his* books. Paper folded beside a plate, kettle whispering steam on the stove.

The past years, guzzling off the skewers of hatred and anger, all come down to this, a red-faced man in jeans and trainers, not a whiff of liquor about him, not so much as a hint.

Tea poured, a plate fetched, bacon and eggs, baked beans and a potato cake glistening with lard. And at last, above an empty plate, Fergus finds his voice and says, 'That was good.'

'And it's good that you're here.' There is

267

curiosity in those washed-out, Monday-morning eyes. 'I was reading about you in the paper.'

'Yes, well...'

'Sounds like you're leading quite a life in London.'

'Not a life, not really. And you mustn't believe all you read.'

'Still, that woman, Lady Someone...'

Not down that route, please. 'Do you get a lot of people looking for a bed?' Fergus asks.

'A fair number. I have my regulars.'

'So, explain.' Fergus waves a hand at the neat kitchen.

'Roisín. You didn't meet her but she was the making of me. She rescued me, no more and no less. St Georgina, I used to call her.'

'Used?'

'Dead these two years. Pneumonia. Always was a chesty woman.'

Fergus ashamed that he didn't know, didn't offer, at the very least, lip-service comfort. 'How did you meet her?' How did you meet my mam, for that matter, what farm or village did you charm her away from, what shop or counting house, for the dubious honour of being your wife?

'I fetched up here one evening, looking for a place to stretch my limbs for what was left of the night, and she took one look, said she had rooms to let but they were for decent folk, no filthy spalpeen like me was going to use them.'

'Sounds like a woman of strong views and not afraid to air them.'

'She was that, all right. Anyway, she told me I

could sleep in the garden shed, if I was so minded, just as long as I was gone by nine in the morning.'

'And did you take her up on the offer?'

'I had no choice.'

'Were you gone by nine?'

'One second past, she's whipped open the door where I'm lying in a daze of last night's drink, toes twitching, shoes under me head, mouth on me like a rotten egg, and she's thrown a bucket of water over me. Ah, jasus, it was the coldest water I ever felt in me life, including the day the priest plunged me up to me neck in the font.'

'And you've been drying out ever since.'

'Nice way of putting it. Drying out ... that's good.' The father sucks at his teeth, gathering together the facts of his story. 'Roisín got me off the booze, d'ye see? Changed my life. I couldn't ever begin to thank her.'

Shaking his head. Slipping into *temps perdu*. 'Ah, Fergus, I hope you'll never know what a grand thing it is to have the drink taken. Roaring through the city, drunk as a fiddler's bitch, the taste of it swilling round behind your eyes, half-seas over and more, ten sheets to the wind. Worth all the shaky hands, I'll tell you, all the next-day headaches and clamouring tongue, the way the floor flies up to greet you when you finally get your head up from the last place you laid it down. The drink may be washing the marrow from your bones, you're falling to pieces in front of your very own eyes, but you can't give it up.'

'Not even for a sick wife, and two young

sons?'

'Not even for them.' The father fiddles with the brown-bellied teapot. 'I'm not denying the shame, or the guilt you feel at falling headlong into the arse of the rat. There's plenty of that, I'll tell you. Don't think I haven't been there. Don't think Brendan's not standing in front me eyes whenever I close them. I'm not even going to try to say I did it for the best, showing me heels to the pair of you, but at least I did it from something more than just nothing.'

'And that would be?'

'Education. Simple as that. There was I, twenty-six years old on a bright morning, a hundred and six when it rained, two boys needing things I couldn't give them. Caitlín, God rest her soul, gone. I gambled that if I went, too, they'd put you with the holy brothers, who'd do more for the two of you than I ever could.'

Anger flames, roars. 'Do you have the slightest idea what they—' Fergus breaks off. Tears flooding. Weariness hanging off the end of his tongue, his fingers, his heart. What point in going over it yet again? And the man was right. They'd been given an education, even if, in Brendan's case, he learned things no one needs to know. 'I saw him dead,' he announces.

'Brendan, is it?'

'Dead. My brother. I can't get him out of my head.' He is weeping now, black pain seeping from his pores.

The father wipes a palm across his sweaty brow. 'I'm not about to excuse meself. What I did was wrong. Me own flesh and blood – and of

270

course that included you – for better or worse, abandoned to...' He waves a hand to indicate that for once he can't think of words to express what he wants to say.

But words, unexpressed, are worming their way into Fergus's ear. 'Included me, you say?'

'That's right.'

'Meaning?'

'Meaning what do you think?'

'Meaning I've not the slightest idea what you mean.'

'I took you on when I married her—'

'Took me on?'

'The shame of it. The parents not speaking to her for all those years, ever since they found out she ... Nobody uttering a word in her direction. Dumber than the beasts of the field. She was glad to find a man who didn't ask too many questions. And I was glad to rear you like me own, lively wee thing that you wcrc, four ycars old and a mouth on you like Mount Etna.'

'Jesus Christ a-mighty!' explodes Fergus. He rises to his feet and spreads his arms, touching plates and saucers, cactus plants and the BVM framed in gold, salt cellar and honey pot and tea cosy hanging from a hook like an old lady's workaday bonnet. Touching walls, reaching through brick and plaster to the front gate, to the trees along the street and further, long King-Kong arms reaching for planes to pluck from the clouds. 'After all these years, are you telling me, that you're not my real father?'

'Didn't you know?' The old boy looks up, a sorry Rustem to Fergus's Sohrab, a flabby Laius to the father-killing Oedipus. 'Are you t-telling me you d-didn't know?'

'You silly old codger. Of *course* I didn't.' Reprieve, release, emancipation, thick as cotton in his throat. Restored to life. Edges of the wound cauterized, closing up, a miracle of healing.

'D-does it make any d-difference?'

'All the difference.' Fergus throws back his head. 'All the fecking difference in the world.'

This man is not his father, which is all that matters. Brendan rocks against his side in the quiet sea-swell of the past, creaks, turns slightly, *those are pearls that were his sighs*, loosens. He owes the man nothing, all debts paid by the upward scramble of another man's ovum-seeking sperm, no quarter given, no gifts exchanged.

Or maybe so. Maybe so. The gift of the gab, the way with the words. He looks at the no-longer-father. Who'd had a name, once.

He smiles. 'Any more tea in the pot, Sean?'

'You've a fine mouth on you,' Sean says later, tears mopped, shoulders thumped, not friends, never friends, but compatriots, brothers in arms. Nodding at the books on the dresser. 'I've read all your stuff.'

'Thank you.'

'The fourth book, now there you were really moving,' Sean says. 'Really getting into the heart of the thing.'

'And will be again.' And here I never even knew he could read, let alone offer comment. Cogent comment, the fourth easily my best book

– so far.

Everything is suddenly coming together in the shrubbery of his mind. Into his head she strides, Grace Fargo, grey-eyed and fiercely eyebrowed, maybe even faintly moustachioed, the Frida Kahlo *de nos jours*, Grace stepping through the windows with a whatdoyoucallit in her hand – a trog? A trug? – pannier filled with flowers, to mangled toast and cooling tea, 'Where are you, Gerard?' and from there swings the whole wild story, Gerard running through the jungle with the woman in pursuit, dragging his own personal marlin-skeleton behind him, the reason he left in the first place, it's all coming clear.

Sean flips a switch and there's an unearthly voice singing on the radio. *'I dreamt that I dwelt in marble halls, With vassals and serfs at my* side...' and Fergus recalls the pitiless Jesuit at the piano, Mahoney drunk as a fart, lifting his narrow serpent's head to the ceiling, cruel eyes oh-too-briefly closed, *'But I also dreamt, which pleas'd me most, that you loved me still the same...'*

It's all anyone ever wants, to be loved still the same, come hell or high water, no altering when it alteration finds, a steady burn of heat in the heart, Brendan, I've carried you around with me far too long, he's not heavy, he's not even my brother. And he is weeping again, snivelling, I loved you, Brendan and now I let you go, I'm done with sailing on the puddles of the past, go back into your father's arms because I cannot carry you a minute, a second, not even a split second longer, I'm through, I'm free.

He thinks of Theodora, caterpillar-eyebrows above her beautiful arctic eyes, timidity masquerading as briskness, and he's pushing back his chair, 'Sean, it's time I was away, I have a book to write.' And a life to find.

'Will I be seeing ... will you come again, Fergus?'

'I will.'

'And you could, if you've a mind, send me your next book, see, with your name written in the front, it would be a grand thing to have.'

Smiles, nods. 'I'll do that, so I will, Sean, and you can let me know what you think of it.' Another smile. 'Maybe you'll be in London one of these fine days, we could get together, share a pint and a pie.'

And maybe he won't, but it's good that he asked.

So, finally, 'It's been...' The non-father eyeing the non-son, hesitating as he, faltering, rummaging for the word. Good? Not really. Real? Nearly. Great? Sort of. 'It's ... it's been...' whatever it's been. Hand out, fingers clasped, a clumsy sidestepping move towards an embrace as civil as a chamberlain's.

He's back in London. A new man, burdens lifted, future clear. Sun beats down as mail thumps and bumps through the letterbox. Invitations to this, requests for that, will you take part in, we would like you to, books to be reviewed, opinions to be given. Ego-plumpers, no doubt about that, shows somebody still values him even if Theo does not ... oh, what kind of a self-pitying eejit has he turned into?

274

Among the envelopes and packages, a crumpled brown one, fresh label stuck over former addressee's name, postmarked Dublin. Scrawly, unfamiliar writing repeats itself on half a piece of lined paper inside.

Thought you might be interested in this. It was ~~grate~~ great seeing you the other day now. Sean

This is an article from *The Irish Times* on his own work, native son, spellbinding, blah blah, weaving myth and actuality, magic realism, crap and bollox, arty-farty the lot of them, kissing each other's backsides. He imagines Sean carefully cutting it out of the paper, finding envelope and sticky tape, tongue cornered, doing up his message to the man who's not his son, all the son he has now.

On the reverse side is part of the story about the visiting cardinal he'd read while he was in Dublin. He reads further, the man brought up in Oregon, youngest child of seven, studied here and there, shooting up the hierarchy from teaching to bishopric and onwards to archbishopric and cardinal, ending up in Rome with the future bright around him, damn him and all who sail in him. There's a bit of a picture of the man, eyes as pale as moonlight, ringed hand raised to bless the cringing multitudes, embroidered this and gold-fringed that, must have cost a fortune while, all over South America, people starve.

And then he's looking again at the man's face, he's rereading the accompanying text, he's thinking, have I stumbled over something here, is this a secret of which only I am aware? Me, and one other person on the planet? And if I am, what do I do with it?

I could take it to her, he thinks, an excuse to see her again, and if she shows the least bit of reluctance there, so much as an iota of hostility then I back away with my dignity intact, as if dignity is what matters.

TWENTY-ONE

Back from Boston, I'm too tired to bother with the stuff Marnie has left for me in the office. Dumping my bags in the hall, I scroll through the messages waiting on my private line. There are only three. One from Jenny. One from my mother. One from Regis Harcourt. Nothing from Fergus. Why do I expect there might be?

Jenny's message asks when we can meet. Luna says she'll call me back. I dial her number but no one answers. I long to talk to her, even if she is not prepared to tell me what I want to know. At this stage, any kind of conversation with her means another brick removed from the wall which divides us.

Although it's early, barely ten o'clock in the morning, nowhere near lunchtime, I fix myself an open beef sandwich, lavished with butter and mustard, a pot of strong coffee, gather up the scatter of mail on the doormat, and carry the lot out to the pergola at the end of the flagged walk. The sun throws an amber light over the borders which stretch behind the house. Birds chitter as I reflect that I ought to do some deadheading of the roses, that the wisteria needs tying back. There's a buzzing sound, either a large bee close at hand or a distant plane preparing for its descent into Heathrow. Dew glimmers on the bending spikes of orange lilies and lies like glass beads in the cupped leaves of lady's mantle.

The mail is mostly bills, but there is also a stiffened manila envelope, addressed in my mother's handwriting. I toy with the idea that she's relented, that inside will be certificates, photographs, papers that prove my father's identity. I hold it in my hand and try to gauge whether its contents are hostile or friendly, but in the end all I have is a brown envelope which tells me nothing and probably contains even less. I put it to one side.

Fergus was right to insist that the best thing I could do was go searching for information in the States, and I feel, perhaps unjustifiably, that in some way, I have taken two or three steps closer to my goal. Yet, apart from the St Joseph's connection, I've come back with very little more information than I left with. The abbot, Dom Francis, stalks skeletally through my mind, hugging his knowledge close to his chest. Is it him my mother's been afraid of all this time? Did he offer her eternal damnation in return for her earthly sins? Did he threaten her? Is that what frightened her thirty years ago, set her on the run?

Half asleep, I linger as the sun climbs above the old brick wall and catches the roses I've trained over the pergola. *Wedding Day. Mermaid*. I look down to my herbaceous borders – slowly recovering from the drought – and note that the old *Albertine* needs to be dug out. I wonder if Fergus is still on Corfu, how his book is progressing, if that's why he hasn't left a message on my machine.

I remember how perfect we were together, the look on his face as he waved me off on the caïque, and suddenly I am afraid. Fergus, the Love Rat. I remember the scandal earlier in the summer and feel terror in my loins. Did it, *could* it have meant as much to him as it had to me? And if not, then the least I can do is not to let him see that I am affected. If nothing else, I can maintain my dignity. As though dignity mattered...

Perhaps my precipitate departure from Corfu signalled the end of something which had scarcely begun. Perhaps I have lost something more valuable than I realize.

He has a habit of entering my mind shortly before he enters my world, and when I hear the distant peal of the doorbell, I know already that it's him. I run to let him in.

'Good afternoon,' he says, formal as a judge, when I open the door.

I feel shy. He is tanned and fit, his black hair plastered down on his skull. 'I thought you were still on Corfu.'

'I came back three days ago then flew straight on to Dublin.' He's so brisk and businesslike that I realize how foolish my fantasies have been. Men like Fergus don't fall in love.

278

'Did you see your father?' I ask coolly.

'I did indeed. I came down to tell you how I got on. And hear how your own trip went. And–' he looks over my shoulder – 'to have a look at your garden, if that's OK.'

I motion him into the house. 'Since when did you get interested in gardens?'

'All that talk we had in Corfu about roots. It was interesting.'

'Right.' I lead him out into the neutral territory of my garden. Any emotion, whether good or bad, is easily buried in talk of mulch and wall building, the merits of one hybrid versus another, the problems of keeping a garden going year-round. He is – or appears to be – fascinated by my greenhouses, where I nurture the multitude of miniature plant versions which I use in my Decorations.

'As you can see, this,' I say, 'is the orchard. Mostly apples past their prime, some marvellous Victoria plums, two kinds of pear and several cherries. There's even –' I wave at a big trunk – 'a wonderful walnut tree.'

'So you're practically self-sufficient?'

'With the stuff from my vegetable garden, I guess I nearly am. I just need a few hens and a cow.'

'And a sheep or two, then you could spin your own wool and make your own clothes.'

'Indeed.'

The crumbling old wall at the end is covered in clematis and *lonicera fragrantissimna* and as we pass it, I close my eyes, breathe in the deep perfume.

'No peaches or apricots?' Fergus asks.

'I thought about it, this wall's obviously perfect for them, but I couldn't bring myself to train them up.'

'Why not?'

'Maybe it sounds stupid, but espaliering always seems so cruel, kind of like crucifying them, torturing them, as though they were just fruit-producers, not trees.'

He nods. 'I can understand that.'

At the edge of my meadow-wilderness, he stops. 'Even I could manage this kind of gardening,' he says.

'It's a lot harder than you think.'

'What, just to stand back and let the grass grow?'

'No, to make the grass appear as if all it's doing is growing. It may look like a piece of meadow to you, but it all has to be carefully monitored. There are bulbs in there, and different kinds of grasses, you have to plan when to cut, and how much to leave, you have to keep down the things like nettle and dock which can take over if you give them half a chance. I'm constantly experimenting – for instance, this year I seeded part of the area with hay rattle, which reduces the richness of the soil.'

'Why is that good?'

'It takes a lot of its nourishment from the plants round it, so it means that the other grasses and meadow flowers don't grow so vigorously.'

'You know a lot.'

'I know about gardens, you know about novels.'

'I used to.' He looks down at me and then quickly elsewhere. 'You are such a beautiful woman.'

I'm not going to fall for it again. Already I am packing my heart away. I smile up at him. 'Thank you.'

'I brought some wine.' His eyes whisper to me but I pretend not to hear. 'Want a glass?'

Into my head flashes a brief image of the two of us tumbling among the rich green stems of knapweed and bent, while grasshoppers and crickets chirrup above our heads. 'It's too early for me, I'll stick with water.'

Settled on a bench in the orchard from where we can hear the trickle of the spring in my bog-garden, and the frogs croaking like a Greek chorus, he describes for me his trip to Dublin. 'And Theodora,' he says, his eyes alight, 'when he told me that he wasn't my father, it was extraordinary. I literally felt a burden drop from my shoulders.'

'Why was that?'

'It meant that since he isn't my father, I can be free of him.'

'He was still your brother's father.'

'Yes, and for that he deserves condemnation, I know that. But life goes on, doesn't it, such a cliché, yet so bursting at the seams with truth. Brendan's dead, yes, and he shouldn't be, but I can't go on holding it against Sean for the rest of my life.'

Something in the expression on his face tugs at my heart. There is a lesson for me too here. 'Sean?'

'That's his name. It wasn't his fault that my mother died. I saw that I just had to let go. There are so many other places in this world that I don't need to be in that one.' He chuckles. 'I can't thank you enough, Theodora, for persuading me to go and see him. If I hadn't, I'd never have found out.' He hums a few bars of *Amazing Grace*.

'If Sean's not your father, Fergus, don't you want to know who is?'

'Some farm lad in County Clare, no doubt, or a roving tinker passing through with a nice line in fake pearls or cheap watches. False promises of marriage. It doesn't matter. Who he was isn't important to me. I am who I am. Now –' he leans towards me – 'tell me about *your* trip; I want to hear every last detail.'

He takes my hand and the mood changes. Colour creeps along his jawline. 'I was going to bring you flowers,' he says, awkwardly, 'but it seemed like coals to Newcastle, since you're bound to have a gardenful already.' A creamy-pink petal has fallen from the roses on the table where we're sitting and he picks it up, strokes it, raises it to his face. 'Tell me about it,' he repeats as though he really wants to hear.

'At my mother's old college,' I say rapidly. 'I was put on to a Catholic liberal-arts college called St Joseph's. An all-boys' school.'

'Ah.' Thoughtful sip from his glass. 'And where would that be?'

'Vermont.' I describe Father Francis, the conversation we had, my conviction that he knows something. I tell him about Vernon Barnes, and

282

the garden in the portrait which still hangs above my hearth. I imagine the weight tumbling from Fergus's back, and wish my own could as easily drop from my shoulders.

'The upshot is,' I say, 'I'm not really any further on than I was. And much more than that...' I pause. How to put this without sounding neurotic at worst, melodramatic at best? 'I think – sounds ridiculous, I know – but I think I may have put myself in danger.' I explain my feelings about the abbot, my strong impression that I am in some way a stumbling block to his plans, my belief that he could eliminate me without a second thought. The surge of something close to terror that seized me at the sight of his face.

'Are you serious?'

'Perfectly.'

'But...' Fergus wrinkles his brow. 'He's a Catholic priest.'

'So? Look at the way they treated you and your brother.'

'Surely you don't imagine he'd come after you, like some hitman in a thriller.'

'Perhaps not. But...' This is my home, my sanctuary; I wonder if I will ever feel safe again here. Or elsewhere. I imagine the creak of floor-boards in the night, a car screeching behind me, the shove of a hand in the back as I wait to cross the road. 'Look: I suffer from an overactive imagination.' I try out a laugh. 'By the way...' I tell him about the Lennart Wells exhibition I'd read about on the plane, to be held in San Francisco in a few weeks' time. 'Are you still working on that book you talked about?'

'I certainly am.' He looks excited. 'I must go to that.'

'Good idea.'

'We could go together.'

Is this another of his carelessly tossed invitations? Does it mean anything? I am nonchalant. 'Right.'

The two of us sit in silence for a while. Frogs croak at the edge of the pond beyond the thickets of may and bramble. A combine harvester whirrs in a neighbouring field, reminding me that summer is ending, the harvest must be safely gathered in, nature is regrouping in order to face the challenge of the coming winter.

'It's beautiful here,' Fergus says. 'You've made it beautiful. Tranquil. I can see why, if you were to meet Mr Right – which we're emphatically agreed is not me – you might be reluctant to up sticks.'

'People invest a huge amount of themselves in a garden.' For a moment on Corfu, I'd truly believed there might have been things worth leaving a garden behind for.

The edge of his shoe has mud on it and he leans down to brush it off before he takes my hand in his. After a while, I pull gently out of his grasp.

'Theodora, I think you need to understand something.' He looks at me properly for the first time since he arrived.

'What's that?'

'What happened on Corfu was an absolutely natural event, a man and a woman getting it together under the moonlight. There's absolutely

284

nothing wrong with that.'

'For most people, perhaps, but not for me.'

'Lighten up, Theodora, for God's sake. It was no big deal.'

I stand up. How right I was about him. I'm shaking with something between anger and regret. 'It *should* have been a big deal.'

'Sex between two consenting adults? Come on, woman, you're not a starry-eyed teenager any more.'

'I don't think I ever was, but that's beside the point.' I want to be more to him than just a consenting adult. But that's all I am, all it meant, just another conquest, another fuck.

'So what exactly *is* the point?' He sounds so cold.

How can I explain that for the first time in my life I felt that I'd met a companion, that sex – fucking, bonking, call it what you like – had put a gloss on the relationship for which it was not ready. The chance to grow slowly, to mature naturally, had been removed. I shrug, visualizing all the tender little roots which were never given the chance to hook themselves into the soil of our friendship. 'Never mind. If you can't see it...'

'I'll tell you what I can see and that's that you're – to say the least – deeply immature.'

Anger conquers regret. 'And you're an arrogant sod with writer's block,' I shout.

He gives me one of those How-The-Hell-Did-I-Get-Into-This? looks. 'I came down here with absolutely no ulterior motives. I wanted to show you something, talk about it, something you

285

might be extremely interested in, and you start acting as though you belong to a closed order of nuns.'

'I didn't ask you to come. You could easily have telephoned.'

'Actually, no I couldn't. You'd need to see it.' His mouth twists angrily. 'You think I only showed up here in the hope of getting into your knickers again, don't you?'

'You ought to have known *that* wasn't going to be on the cards,' I say, 'not now, not ever.'

'Well, fuck you.'

'Not if I can help it.'

We glare at each other. He lifts his shoulders, spreads his hands like a Frenchman. 'All I intended was to invite you out to lunch and see how your trip to the States went, maybe tell you about my visit to Dublin.'

'You've done that.'

'Mission partly accomplished. Right. Well, I won't hang about, I'm sure you've got better things to do.'

'I most certainly have.'

He walks back towards the house while I watch him go. From the set of his shoulders, I can see that he is not only angry but also hurt. He is a gentle man, and I have made him fierce. I know that I ought to call him back, drink wine with him, talk about other things. If we're going to part, it should be as friends.

Instead, I just let him go.

Story of my life.

What a mess I'm making of things. When I hear a car start up at the front of the house, then

286

move along the lane and finally out of earshot, I get up and walk unsteadily into the house where I splash brandy into a balloon glass and drink it down neat. Pour another slug. Medicinal purposes only. The room shimmers, although there are no tears in my eyes. Only in my heart. I pick up a piece of glass shaped like an egg, and set it down again. I plump up the cushions of the sofa. Straighten a picture, reposition a photograph.

Somewhere I'd read a letter in which a woman explained that the reason she had so loved a man who had just died was because he never expected her to be anything different from what she was. That's it, I think. That's Fergus. I can always be myself with him, stroppy, irritable, lazy, comfortable. Even when we are together, we are still able to maintain our own separateness. The woman killed herself eventually, unable to face life without her beloved.

And then I wonder why I am thinking such things when Fergus and I aren't in love and now are not even lovers.

TWENTY-TWO

I spend the next couple of days working furiously at my desk or in the garden. Trina is gone, Harry doesn't show up, Marnie phones in to say she has a summer cold and won't be back until the beginning of next week. I wonder if she is really sick or simply trying to avoid me.

At night, I stand under the shower for long enough to rinse the dirt out of my hair and the sweat from my body, before collapsing into bed. The phone is unplugged, the house locked up. On the second afternoon, someone knocks at the front door in a fairly persistent manner before finally giving up. The postman pushes mail through the letterbox. I suppose I must have eaten something during that time, gone to the loo, possibly even brushed my teeth. I resolutely shove Fergus to one side.

But I am no nearer to a resolution. In fact, I'm in an almost worse state than before. Let it go, I tell myself. You've come this far without knowing who your father is – what difference will it make? Then I think, no, I ought to know, it is my right, just as it is my mother's right not to tell me. But she's not going to.

Right...

Deep breath.

Onwards and upwards.

Clean sweep, new brooms, fresh starts.

The community garden is bustling with activity, despite the fact that it's gone six thirty in the evening. Three kids are working on the banked flowerbeds and wave when they see me. A couple of young black girls with somnolent babies in pushchairs are giggling together. An old man with trousers tied round the ankle with string, wearing one sneaker and one brown leather brogue, is drinking beer and reading the paper.

Carrying a bag of bulbs, I join the kids – a boy and two girls – and for a while we weed in companionable silence.

'How's Trina Hawkins going, miss?' the boy asks after a while.

'I ... uh ... I don't know.'

'Wasn't she doing work experience with you?'

'Yes.'

'She's working at Lucille's,' the other girl says. 'You know, where I had my hair straightened.'

'What, she there long-term?'

'Dunno. Can't see Treen being a hairdresser for the rest of her life, can you?'

'If Trina's left, you going to be looking for another work experience person?' the boy asks me.

'I don't know. I haven't thought about it.' I'm more interested in what the girls are saying.

'Only I was kind of thinking of the same sort of thing, when I leave school,' he says. 'Something agricultural, you know? Horticultural?

Maybe I could...'

And maybe he couldn't. I've got the message. Only a few months ago, my life consisted almost entirely of work and solitude. My spare hours were my own, to do with as I wished. Now, it seems like everyone in the world wants to marry me and have my babies.

'I'll think about it,' I say, 'but it won't be this year, I'm afraid.'

'I still got another year at school,' he says.

'Good.' I envisage my quiet house filling up with stray dogs and lame ducks, needy people demanding things from me which I am not qualified to provide.

'I'd really like the chance to work with you, miss.'

'Leave it out, Kev,' says one of the girls. 'Don't push yourself in where you're not wanted.'

'Get stuffed,' Kevin says.

'Miss doesn't want you, can't you see?'

'I didn't say that at all,' I say quickly.

'No, but it's obvious, innit?'

'Stands to reason,' the other girl says.

'Yeah, like you'd know all about it,' says Kevin.

They bicker amicably among themselves.

I dig in my spade and lift some earth. 'Bulbs,' I tell them. 'For next spring.' I push in the firm teardrop shapes, visualizing narcissi and daffodils spilling white and yellow down the bank to the edge of the pond.

'I been growing stuff in our back garden at home,' Kevin says. 'Planted a clematis over my dad's toolshed.'

'Did he like it?'

'Reckons it's right poncy, pink flowers and all, but my mum's dead chuffed.'

'Talking of Trina Hawkins, did you hear she broke it off with Mick Roberts?' the first girl says to the second. 'Give the ring back and all.'

'Yeah? Wonder why.'

'She's got more brains than him, that's why.'

'He's all right, though. Wouldn't mind a bit of that myself.'

'Go for it, girl. He's still available, last I heard.'

Trina's no longer engaged? Maybe this is my chance to persuade her to come back. I look at my watch. 'It's time I left.'

'Got a hot date tonight, miss?'

'Sort of.'

'Don't do anything I wouldn't do.'

'Gives her a lot of bleeding scope, that does,' says Kevin.

'Oh yeah, like you would know, you total zero.' The girls laugh scornfully. Kevin doesn't appear to be crushed by their apparent contempt.

All three of them grin and wave again as I leave.

The front door of the Hawkins house has been painted a bright egg-yellow since I was last there. I lift the knocker and let it drop against the plate. My hands are sweaty; if Trina rejects me again, I fear that I shall burst into tears.

Mr Hawkins opens the door on a wave of cigarette smoke and fried fish. 'You'll be wanting to speak to Trina,' he says.

291

'Yes.'

'I'll tell her you're here.'

'Mr Hawkins...' I put out my hand to stop him turning away. 'I understand she's broken off her...her engagement.'

'Good thing, too. Her mum's not best pleased, mind you. She's got grandchildren on her mind but I say Trina's much too young to be settling down.' In his eyes are the broad highways down which he wishes his beloved daughter to travel. 'Anyway...' He smiles at me and turns down the passage. I hear him call Trina's name, and I turn to look across the road, praying that she won't refuse to see me.

She's behind me. 'What d'you want this time?'

'I heard that you broke off your engagement.'

'What's it got to do with you?'

'Nothing. That's not why I came.'

'Why did you, then?'

'I wanted to give you the present I got for you when I was in the States.'

That stops her. It's difficult to maintain hostility in the face of kindness. I delve into my bag and bring out a package.

'What is it?' she says suspiciously, as though she thinks I might have brought her a gift-wrapped dead rat or a severed hand.

'Open it and find out.'

'I don't mean that ... why you giving it to me?'

'Correct me if I'm wrong, but didn't you recently have a birthday which I didn't know about so I didn't give you anything? Call it a belated birthday gift. Besides, I thought you'd like it. Simple as that.'

She bends her head and concentrates on pulling at the ribbon. Her movements are slow and reluctant. She pulls out the box, reads the label, takes off the lid and stops again as she sees the swathing white tissue paper. She says something I can't hear.

'What?'

'Why you being nice to me?' she mutters.

Because I want to nurture you, I want to say. Because if you are watered and mulched and encouraged, you will grow straight and tall. Because you are loved by your parents and that has made you beautiful. Because I wish to step inside your magic circle and be allowed to love you, too. 'Why shouldn't I be?'

'You don't know me or anything.'

'I know enough.' There is soil under her fingernails. Her shoulders are hunched. Such a little thing. She yanks at my heart. 'Besides,' I continue, 'people have been nice to me over the years. Maybe I just want to pass some of it on to someone else. And also...' It's hard for me to say this, 'I want you to forgive me.'

She uncovers the handbag I'd purchased for her in Boston. Draws in a breath. 'Hey. That's *well* cool.' She rubs the fine blue suede gently with the ball of her thumb. 'Classy, innit? Gorgeous. Feels more like silk than leather.'

'The reason I bought it was –' I reach into my bag once more and bring out a cotton drawstring bag – 'it matches these.' I hand it over. 'I'd have given them to you earlier but ... the timing wasn't right.'

She grins at that and I am encouraged.

'They're not new,' I say, as she pulls out a pair of Nancy Halloran's lovely shoes. 'And they might not even fit but if they do ... There are more where those came from.'

'Jimmy Choo! *Wow!*' She looks up at me for the first time. 'I've read about him. His shoes cost a fortune.'

'They belonged to my best friend's grand-mother,' I said.

'Pretty groovy kind of grandmother.' Trina examines the beautifully made blue shoes. 'These are really ace!'

'Nancy collected shoes. Expensive shoes. She must have had like a hundred and fifty pairs. Also, she had tiny feet, like you.'

'I'm size three.'

'Same as Nancy.' I smile at her. 'Try them on, Trina.'

From the end of the passage her father calls. 'Aren't you going to ask the lady in, Treen?' he says. 'Can't stand about on the doorstep all night.'

She looks at me, then with a quick little twist of her mouth, indicates me into the house. We go into the kitchen and sit at the table where Mr Hawkins is drinking a beer from the can and reading the racing page. There's no sign of Trina's mother or the three brothers. In the mid-dle of the table is another container garden, pebbled paths running across moss into a copse of sedum and tiny firs, a flat piece of lawn lead-ing to bushes where a miniature Venus de Milo stands on a plinth. It's absolutely charming.

Mr Hawkings looks up. 'Can I get you something?'

'No, thank you.'

'What you got there, Trina?'

'New shoes.' She takes off her boots and socks and puts the shoes on her feet. She slings the bag over one shoulder and begins to sashay up and down the kitchen floor, swaying her boyish hips. Take it from me: cut-off shorts and Jimmy Choo are never going to figure high on any What's-In? list – at least, not together – but on Trina they look pretty good.

'Oh, la di dah,' she says. *'Pretty Woman*, eat your heart out.'

'Funny kind of an outfit.' Her father takes a swig of his beer and wipes his mouth with the back of his hand.

'They'd have gone perfectly with your hair, if you hadn't changed it.' I begin to laugh.

'Fashion victim, that's me.' She laughs too, bending from the waist. Laughs and laughs. Her top rides up her back, displaying the thin white knobs of her spine. It's so good to see her laugh again. 'I'll go back to the blue, if you like.'

'Why not?'

She eyes me. 'Thought you wanted it natural.'

'Maybe I've mellowed.'

'That'll be the day,' she says, but there's no sting in it. 'Look, you know the border just outside your sitting room.'

'What about it?'

'Harry 'n' me was – were just talking about it the other day.'

'The other day?'

'Yeah. While you were in America. There's a

rose there, up against the wall—'

'*Albertine.*'

'Whatever. It needs to be cut right back – or better still, taken out.'

'I know.'

'Well, I was reading this catalogue and I saw this new rose which it would be fun to put there instead. Sort of pale purplish. There's already iris in front and delphiniums and lavender. And that blue prickly stuff like thistles...'

'*Eryngium*. Sea holly.'

'It'd be lovely.'

It's an olive branch. It's a hand extended. I give her a worried frown. 'Trouble is, I'm going to be frantically busy over the next few weeks. And Marnie doesn't know a delphinium from a dandelion. I don't know when I'm going to find the time to deal with it.'

'I might have an hour or two spare,' she mutters.

We both know what she's really saying. I'm careful to stay businesslike. 'You'd have to organize it with Harry. The *Albertine*'s an old plant so it'll take some shifting.'

'OK.'

'And once you've put in the new rose, you could walk up and down in front of it in those blue shoes.'

Her relief is palpable. 'Yeah.'

'Rhapsody in Blue,' I say, and then we both start laughing again, while Trina's father watches us bemusedly before licking his thumb and turning the page of his newspaper.

It's dark by the time I get home. The automatic

296

light comes on as I turn in to my drive, crunch across the gravel, open my door and close it firmly behind me. On the kitchen table is the envelope Luna had sent me and I pick it up, hold it against my chest. I can't put off opening it. Be Prepared, I warn myself. Life May Be a Test but You Don't Have to Pass. This is absolutely not going to be the proof positive you seek. You will know no more, after you have opened it, than you do now.

Thus armed, I tear off the end, although, in some secret corner of my brain, I still hope that I'm wrong and there will be birth certificates, photographs, documents. A declaration of some kind: *this is my beloved daughter, in whom I am well pleased.*

What am I, crazy? Of course there is no such thing. Instead, from between two protective sheets of cardboard, I pull out a number of drawings. I recognize the spiky cartoonish style. For the most part, they're little watercolour sketches, dashed off in odd moments on scraps of paper. All are of me. Cradled at my mother's breast, her white sleeve against my cheek. Aged two or so, in a blue smocked dress with a daisy chain slung round my neck. Four or five, with a band holding back my unruly hair, and an ice lolly in my hand. Eleven, twelve, fifteen. In my school summer frock of yellow-checked gingham, all elbows and bony knees, awkwardly adolescent, half turned away. As a bridesmaid at Charlie and Caro's wedding, in rose-coloured brocade. Running along a cliff, during my last year at school, my hair buffeted by the wind off the sea. Standing in a bathing costume with my hands on my hips. Bending among flowers to pull something from the earth – a weed, a blossom – white shorts riding up the tanned length of my legs.

Where had she been, to capture these and the other images? They are so much more revealing than photographs. I look through them again and there I am, a new bride in ivory satin, a pearl necklace, white flowers wreathed in my hair. I hadn't invited her because I had no idea where she was. Yet she must have been there, she must, because how otherwise can she have drawn me holding Charlie's son, Ricky, by the hand – there are no photographs she could have copied it from. Where was she? Lurking behind a pillar, hidden behind a tree?

I suddenly understand that all those ghostly visitations really were her. Watching over me, sharing my life after all. She *was* there. If I had, after all, followed her, gone to meet her, would she have turned and run, or would she have put her arms round me, given me the love I so craved?

I feel sick. For years I've nurtured my feelings of rejection. Wallowed in them. But I'm at least as much to blame as Luna. All those sightings, which I convinced myself weren't really her ... blood rolls like lava through my body. I remember one particular time at school, when I was sitting in a coffee bar and saw her watching me from across the street. I must have known it was her and yet I turned away, laughed at something one of my friends was saying, acting unconcerned. I'd *known*. And next time I looked, she was gone. Across the years, I feel the pain she must have felt and the sad humility which let her walk away from me. Why hadn't she said something, next time we met?

Pressing my hand against my mouth, I sniff back the tears but they keep on coming. 'Luna,' I say, in a kind of primeval wail that comes from the deepest part of me. 'How could I? How could you...' I can hear my own bewilderment and shame.

I see her red shoes dancing across cities and continents, dancing until her feet bleed, over thorns and briars, dancing from one city to the next, doors always closing in her face. Although I don't understand why, I realize that it was *me* she was trying to protect though I have no idea why or from what. And once again the closed face of the abbot sidles into my mind. Was it him she was running away from? How does he fit into this story?

'She loves you,' Terry had said. More plainly than any words could say it, these drawings show me how true that is.

In among the scraps of paper there is a note from her.

Theodora, my gift from God, the gift He gave me in return for the gift I gave to Him. I'm sorry I can't tell you what you want to know. It could be disastrous if I did. I've cheated you of a father and, in many ways, of a mother. It was unfair of me. It was wrong. I was wrong. If I could put it right, I would. The saddest thing is that it was myself I cheated. I think we could have been friends.

I love you more than you will ever know.

I read it over and over again. I don't have the slightest idea what the first sentence means but the rest of it seems obvious. Plainly she wishes she could have been something other than she was – but how many of us manage that? At least she has recognized that there were things which should have been different. *Could have been friends* ... the phrase stands like a gravestone, marking the lack of connection between us. Is it too late or can something be resurrected?

I turn the page over and there is a sketch of a by-now-familiar face, so lightly pencilled in that it scarcely marks the page. I hold it against the light and it's him, younger, dark haired, with the same inimical expression, the same flat black eyes. Why? What does he mean to Luna or she to him?

My fingers shake as yet again I dial the number she has left me, but of course she is not there and there is no answering machine on which I can record my need, my hunger, to speak to her. I dial the Lotus Flower Hotel, but they tell me she left a couple of days ago and no, they have no idea where she went.

I imagine her talking to Terry on the phone, asking how I am; I envision her listening with envy to Terry's descriptions of family outings, picnics, holidays, while she is cut off and alone, always an outsider, her nose pressed to the window of other people's celebrations. But it was her choice. Nobody forced her to keep travelling, to dance until her feet bled. She could have come in from the cold, any time she wanted to.

Surely she could.

I'm always alone, she told me once. *I've learned to be lonely*. I never stopped to think how deeply sad that is.

I sense that if I am not careful, I will learn the same thing. Unless I finally make myself vulnerable, I will shrivel, wither, die. If I step forward, take the initiative, take a risk, offer myself to opportunity, then maybe at last I can begin to flower.

TWENTY-THREE

The Embankment lies ankle-deep in fallen leaves. They float down from the plane trees along the river as the bus trundles past the Physick Garden and I reflect that one day I must bring Trina here. There are so many things to show, to teach. I'm eager to get started. Marnie's words come back to me: *you could do worse ... train her up ... a like-minded person.* I could indeed do a lot worse. With my help, like an apple tree, she will develop and mature, grow into lovely shapes, produce the fruits of experience combined with imagination.

I'm thinking of these matters to avoid considering the others which press so urgently upon me. I have other responsibilities now. My mother. Myself. Most of all, Fergus. Last night, I dreamed that he made love to me. I felt his

301

buttocks in my hands, the sweat of his body between my breasts. He thrust into me again and again, and I responded, aching with pleasure, knowing this was what was meant to be.

The bus jolts to a stop and I get off. Across the river are yellow high-rise blocks, surreal in the pale sunshine, blank black windows, apocalyptic shapes against the sky. I think of the myriad people occupying them: insurance companies, detective agencies, government bureaux, illegal immigrants, weeping children, barbers and stockbrokers, neglected wives and lonely pensioners, singers, acrobats, lion tamers, geologists. The multiplicity of the human race is invigorating, euphoric.

Below me, boats heave solidly at their moorings. A ramp slopes down to a concrete jetty, from which wooden gangplanks lead to individual houseboats. One of them is Fergus's. A quick trawl through my limited naval vocabulary produces a word.

'Ahoy!' I shout, over the rumble of buses and churn of cars from the road above me. 'Ahoy there!' It's the wrong word for this place. 'Ahoy!' needs anchors and gleaming brass, horizon-eyed men in blue blazers drinking pink gins, a smell of diesel, the wheel's kick and the wind's song, all that kind of stuff. Instead, there are taxis hooting above my head, and pieces of styrofoam nudging at the jetty.

I call again, less vigorously this time, feeling foolish. The only response is from a tabby cat lying on the roof of one of the boats, which stretches one leg impossibly far, the way they

302

do, trebling its overall length. Most of the sterns have a chain across the end. I deduce that this means the owners are not at home. On the other hand, it could mean that the occupant hasn't been out that morning. I step on to the deck of one of the three boats which are not chained up and rap at a surprisingly suburban-looking door.

Again nothing happens. I regain dry land and walk further along to the next unchained boat. A mountain bike is on the deck, fastened by two thick padlocks to the guardrail. A dead geranium sticks gauntly from a dry pot. Inside, someone is singing *Amazing Grace*. Who else could this be but Fergus?

'Ahoy!' I bang loudly.

'I once was lost –' goes the soloist and then the door opens – *'but now I'm found.'* He is wearing a white shirt, the sleeves rolled up above his elbows, and there is a stain of some kind on the breast pocket, too red for ink, too blue for ketchup. Either he's been out in a Force Ten gale in the not-too distant past, or he's been raking his hands through his hair.

'Hi,' I say, a smile on legs. Oh, Fergus. My hands tingle. I love him. Fergus...

'Was blind, but now I see.' He is singing, but his eyes are cold.

He's wondered if he would ever see her again. And now she is here. The birthday of my life. Strong but timid, eyes like ice sparkling on a frosty day, hair like a cloud of blackbirds. She is here, in his life, in his book, Grace Fargo made flesh. What does she want? It doesn't matter, she's here. He has never felt awkward with a woman before this one. He wants to grab her, kiss that full red mouth, feel her breasts against him. He knows better than to try. Now then, Costello, none of that, keep it cool. Don't go overboard. Don't frighten her away.

He is less than effusive. 'Good morning, Theodora.'

Uh-oh. This is not a man who is glad to see me. This is a man who hasn't forgiven me for shouting at him the other day.

'Can I come in, come aboard, whatever?'

He moves aside. I step over the lintel, if that's the nautical term, to find myself in a space flooded with light from the river. The space is full of strong and complementary colours: lilacs, crimsons, purples, blues. A white lily stands in a tall earthenware vase on the floor. There are a couple of woven cotton kilims on the bare, blue-painted floorboards, three mugs on a low table, a folded newspaper. And books. Hundreds of them, on makeshift brick-and-plank shelves all the way round the room, piled against the arm-chairs, neatly stacked under the table. A copy of a Frida Kahlo self-portrait is Sellotaped to the ceiling, above the sofa. I imagine him lying there, staring up at her, dreaming of Popocata-pétl, exploring the secret landscapes inside his head.

'Coffee?' He removes the mugs and comes back with freshly filled ones from a galley kitchen where I can see stainless steel appliances and dark-blue handmade tiles. 'So ... what can I do for you?'

I'm embarrassed by the chill in his voice. 'I

just came to find out when you were leaving for California.' It has to be one of the most obviously lame excuses of the century.

'Can't wait to see me gone, eh?'

'Quite the opposite. I need to organize things.'

'What for?' He looks into his mug.

'Uh ... Mexico?' Suddenly, it is all I ever wanted, to ride beside him through clear mountain air, to smell the damp richness of the jungle, to learn a world far wider than the narrow one I've so painstakingly built for myself. I hear a tiny tearing noise, a painful little rip, and know it is the sound of my roots finally loosening.

'Ah,' he says. 'Yes.'

'You asked me if I wanted to join you.'

'I see.'

He doesn't want me to go with him after all. I shouldn't have come. I'm mortified at having put us both in this awkward situation. Time to change the subject.

'This is wonderful,' I tell him.

'The boat or the coffee?'

You, I want to shout. You, Fergus, with your glittering eyes and your burning enthusiasm and your strong, beautiful body. But after that stilted little exchange, there doesn't seem much more to say. 'Both.'

'Want to see the rest?' He doesn't sound as if he cares either way.

I'm grateful for the change of pace. I'll let him show me round, and then get back on dry land as fast as my feet will take me. I'll head off back along the Embankment and hope the tears will hold until I can reach the cold harbour of my flat.

We shan't meet again, I know that. The bleakness of my Fergus-less future is frightening. 'Love to,' I say.

'Come on, then.'

I follow him along a passage, past a bedroom and a cubbyhole with a computer in it, papers and books, his study, I guess. Past a bathroom. Another bedroom. It's extremely civilized, neat as a pin, tastefully idiosyncratic. I think how much I'd like to live in a space like this, waking up each morning to the light on the river, the sound of water against the hull.

He pauses at the door of another room. 'And here we have the master bedroom. En suite, you'll note. Not just a bedroom but a lifestyle.' There is a mocking note in his voice. He's getting at me. My desire for stability. My narrow mind. My fear of the unexpected. The room is mostly bed, under a skylight. There's a pile of suitcases in one corner, the sort which used to make my heart sink when I was a child. By the door is a small chest of drawers.

'Fergus...' I place my coffee mug carefully on the chest.

'What?' He is wary.

I take a step towards him and his eyes change colour, still the same brilliant blue, but warmer now, delphinium-blue, the colour of the sea in Corfu on a sunny day, indigo. I put my arms round his neck. I kiss him full on the mouth and he pulls his head away.

'Jesus, Mary and Joseph,' he says.

'You said you'd wait until I asked you.'

'I did so.'

'Well ... I'm asking.'

For a moment I am terrified that he will reject me; my palms are sweaty with fear. But then he draws me in to him, so close I can smell the coffee in the weave of his shirt, the soap under his jaw, the sweet scent of his skin. His hands are under my shirt, on my bare skin. Together, we fall on to the bed. 'Is this what you want?' he asks. 'And this?'

'Utterly. Totally. What about you?'

'This is what I want,' he says. 'And this.' He starts to kiss me. My lips first, my neck, my breasts. It is as though this is the very first time, each separate particle of my skin yearning to be touched so I can at last understand how it feels. I look up at him, and there are tears in his eyes, the tears a man might want to shed on seeing his home again after a lifetime's absence. 'Theodora,' he murmurs. 'How much I've longed for this. From the very first moment we met.'

And as he moves above me, I'm thinking, me, too. I'm thinking how short life is, how quickly it passes, how easy it is to waste. Roots are not the only way for things to grow strong, I realize, as I think of all the lovely things still to do and that this is one of them, kissing this particular man, learning the weight of his body, the curve of his shoulder, the scar below his collarbone, the way his eyelashes lie on his cheek. We are so attuned that it is as if we have been lovers for years and as he enters me, as I give myself up to him, I'm inside his head and he is thinking the same thoughts that I am, of Mexico and parrots and lime trees, of silver nutmegs, golden pears, gardens in the jungle, pleached beech hedges with each leaf rimed with frost, I'm thinking of sunshine and warm seas and I'm arching under him, begging him to give me something I've never had because I've never allowed myself to feel like this before, never surrendered, never let myself loose, because I'm soaring, on the verge of a thousand rings of light, diving into a galaxy of spectacular constellations, grateful, calling his name again and again, no longer in control, 'Fergus, Fergus,' but he doesn't hear me for he is calling too, my name on his lips like a roll of thunder, lightning, star-shine and moonshine, as we drop away at last into the easy flowing oceans of love.

And he is thinking that his hunger is at last assuaged, the castanet-rattle of bones finally stilled, he has come home, his restlessness submerged in the still places at her core. He is thinking of dolphin-haunted seas and clipped box hedges, of parrots harsh among vine-hung branches, of this feel of her breast in his mouth, the flutter of her heart against his lips, the sweet shake of her mouth as she comes, the disbelief in her eyes, as if she shouldn't be doing this but oh, oh, she can't help herself, his prim and passionate Theodora, dizzy with love as she cries out, loose-limbed in his arms.

The sun through the skylight is warm on his back. Then the mounting urge again, the hunger, her hands taking him, delicate as mice, showing him where she wants him to be, bold as a hoor, sweet as a virgin, Theodora, *a cuisle,* pulse of my heart, gift from God. He sees the two of them then, in the love-dabbled future, walking over white sand, ducking into doorways for a kiss, raindrops like diamonds on her hair, standing on top of mountains with the world spread before them, riding green oceans, and then he is roaring her name once more, 'Theodora ... ah Jesus,' a steam engine, a jet plane, his climax boiling inside him now, an ever-rolling stream, shooting like stars from his joyful body, melodies stereo-ing round him, he shall have music wherever he goes, the amazing grace of it, her mouse-cries in his ear, lips flushed, fleshed with desire, love is the sweetest thing, Agas in his future now, babies tumbling about his feet, the upthrust of his seed, ah, ah, oh, sweet Jesus...

We sit looking out at the river. He is holding my hand, I am holding his. We are wearing towelling bathrobes because we know there is no point getting dressed again just yet. Though I know they will return, the fears of the past weeks have receded so far into the distance that I can hardly perceive them. The river glides past us, fiery with the noontide sun.

'Your tattoo,' I say lazily. 'Why a flamingo?'

'It's a crane,' he says.

'OK, why a crane?'

'Very strange birds, cranes. Revered in all kinds of mythologies as symbols of strength and endurance, longevity, even wisdom. That seem-ed to fit.' He grins at me. 'Not that I knew any of this at the time. It was the result of a hard night's drinking and the need to sit down somewhere which wasn't a cobbled street. So I went into a tattoo parlour...'

'As anyone might.'

'...and chose the crane. What I also discovered later is that in ancient China, a crane is the symbol of the relationship between a father and his son. It seemed serendipitous.' He presses my hand against his heart so I feel the strong beat of it under the skin. 'You're going to come to Mexico with me, is that right?'

'Anywhere. Anywhere.' I'm thinking I could understand how my mother could follow a man to the ends of the earth, because I will follow this one, anywhere he leads. It's called love.

'Kilderkin,' Fergus says. *'Desuetude.'* He presses my fingers again, pulls back the edge of my dressing gown. *'Lollipop, oriole, amorous.'* He leans over and kisses my shoulder. *'Love.'*

'Love,' I repeat. 'The best word of them all.'

'The only necessary word.'

There is so much to learn, but this I already know: it will not be a conventional life we share. But then, try as hard as I might, I never quite managed conventional.

Maybe I'm too much like my mother.

Looking at her, he sees his book rush towards him, Grace Fargo settling herself, drawing her skirts about her, big bosomed or flat chested, she would tell him when the time came, and, too, his mother's thin blue-veined eyelids as she drew her final breaths, and Brendan's soiled hair on the filthy pillow, goodbye Brendan, your head against my breast, *moi croidhe,* my friend, lost forever now in the waters of death, *and there shall be no more pain, neither shall there be any sorrow.* Mexico gleams like Aztec gold, but next

310

time he – *we* – visit the place, it will be different. The cold eyes of the *muchachos* had frightened him, now he could admit it, had terrified him, if truth be told, a bullet to the heart, a drag of the heels and himself buried in the all-devouring jungle, never a soul to know or to mourn, let alone care, *Author Disappears on Mexican Trip*, an obit in the papers and that's that. With his once-and-future Theodora beside him, it will be another thing entirely.

'By the way...' He reaches behind him for the newspaper on the coffee table. 'Sean sent me this from Dublin. It's something you should see.' His fingers run up her arm, reflexive action, purely unplanned, can't help himself, and she pushes her mouth towards him, kisses him lightly, eyes blazing like stars.

'What is it?'

'I came down to your place to show it to you. Thought you might find it ... intriguing.' Unfolding the newsprint pages, passing them to her, the Prince of the Church with his beringed hand raised to bless the multitudes. No reaction, except she's wondering why she should be interested. 'Is this something to do with your brother?'

He's shaking his head.

'Do you want me to read the whole thing?'

He points at a paragraph halfway down the page.

...left the seminary in Boston and taught at Boston College for a year before being appointed as Head of History at a small Catholic liberal-arts men's college in Maybury, Vermont. He was plucked from there to become coadjutor

311

to Bishop Juan Martinez, then appointed bishop himself, before being elevated to his own metropolitan arch-diocese. In the seventies and eighties, he made a name for himself through his firm pronouncements, often taking up a position directly opposed to both the current administration and, indeed, his own superiors. He was also responsible for spearheading the 'Get Your Hands Dirty!' initiative, a new social agenda aimed at shaking out the calcified orders of monks and nuns. A man of unshakable principle, independent and widely admired for the moral authority which underlies his work, Cardinal O'Donnell seems to have been marked out from the first as one destined to make a rapid rise through the hierarchy. Thirty years on, he appears poised to take up the very highest office of all, when events require...

Words fling themselves at me, a hail of unnecessary information. *Coadjutor, calcified, social agenda, moral authority.* Only one phrase is of any importance ... *a Catholic liberal-arts men's college in Maybury, Vermont* ... It can only mean St Joseph's.

Fergus's arm is around my shoulders. 'Look at his photograph,' he says. 'And then look at yourself in the glass.'

'There's no need.' I am staggered, dumbfounded, gobsmacked. Is this, after all, the man I have been looking for all along? If so, it explains so many things, why my mother wouldn't tell me who he is, what the compelling reasons she'd spoken of were. How frightened she must be that with one word, I would destroy the

312

construct of decades.

'The man's saying Mass at Westminster Cathedral this afternoon.' Fergus's face is very gentle. We stare at each other. I lean forward and kiss him hard on the mouth. 'I think you should be there.'

'Fergus,' I say. And pause. I've never said it before, not to anyone. Never felt it. My bones are soft. 'I love you.'

We turn down Victoria Street in the direction of the river. As we approach the Piazza, we can see a crowd gathered outside the Roman Catholic cathedral.

As I hesitate, Fergus takes a firm grip on my sleeve and pulls me after him. He asks a women with a rosary in her hand what everyone is waiting for.

'It's Cardinal O'Donnell,' she says. 'The American cardinal.'

Fergus pretends surprise. 'I read about him in the paper.'

'He's celebrating Mass inside,' says the woman. 'He'll be out soon.'

Through the loudspeakers which have been rigged up outside the cathedral, I can hear voices chanting. The congregation inside murmurs in response, as do many of those standing round me. Most of them have dropped to their knees and are crossing themselves.

'Come on.' Fergus is pushing his way right up to the front of the crowd.

I am anxious. Not sure what to expect. A bolt of lightning, clouds parting and a heavenly finger pointing at the cardinal's head? A celestial voice announcing that this is my father? Of course not. My stomach flutters with apprehension. Even if he looks as similar to me as the picture in the paper does, it will not prove anything. Now that we're here, I would rather be somewhere else.

The mood of the crowd is upbeat. People are laughing, talking, hugging. I don't know if this is the clappy-happy sort of stuff you read about in the papers, or some truly momentous event. I turn to the middle-aged man beside me. 'Is there always a crowd like this for visiting cardinals?'

'Not always.' He is American, white hair cut *en brosse*, one of those black macs favoured by tourists from the States.

'If it's not a rude question, why are you here?'

'Well, now.' He smiles. 'How many reasons do you want? First off, I'm a Catholic, a professor of law at Notre Dame. Second, this guy's supposed to be something special.'

'Is that why there are so many people here?'

'That and because he's relatively young for a cardinal. Thirdly, the buzz is that he could become pope, one of these years. If so, he'd be the first American to fill the office. I'd like to be able to tell my grandchildren I saw him way back when. My personal audience with the pope.'

'He's a truly great man.' A woman joins in. 'We're from Chicago, aren't we, hon?' The man beside her nods. 'He did an enormous amount for the Church while he was there,' the woman says, while her husband nods again.

'An American pope,' the law professor says.

314

'What an honour. Unbelievable. A man born and raised in the States.'

'Not because he's ambitious,' the woman from Chicago said, as though reading from a press release, 'but because he truly wants to do good.'

'Is ambition so bad?' It's Fergus, of course. 'If you have great aims, you'd have to be ambitious in order to fulfil them, whether it's world domination you're after or world peace.'

'I hear what you're saying,' says the law professor, 'but it's his humility that's been his defining characteristic.'

'And his compassion,' puts in the woman.

'The point about Cardinal O'Donnell,' says the Chicago woman's husband, as though sensing a fight in the offing, 'is that nobody's ever been able to dredge up the slightest hint of scandal about him.'

'And believe me, with the kind of problems currently plaguing the Church, they're looking,' says the professor. 'Not just the gutter journalists, but the people in the Vatican. If they're going to back him to the top, the last thing they want is some skeleton coming out of the closet, five years down the line.'

'What kind of skeleton?'

'You know: paedophilia, or homosexuality, or illegitimate children or an alcohol problem. But he's absolutely clean.'

'Being gay is a problem, is it?' Fergus asks aggressively.

'In a future pope, I'd say it was, yes.'

'It's splitting the Anglican Church even as we speak,' says the husband.

315

'His reputation is spotless,' Chicago Woman says, her tone decisive. 'He's totally committed to even the lowliest of God's creatures and always has been.'

'Like worms, do you mean?' says Fergus.

'Worms?'

'They're about as lowly as you can get. How concerned is the cardinal about worm welfare? Vermicular rights?'

'Shut up, Fergus,' I say, squeezing his arm.

'He's a *saint*,' the woman insists loudly. She turns towards her husband who gives his wife a why-do-the-fruitcakes-always-latch-on-to-us? look and they both edge away.

It's another fifteen minutes before the crowd starts shifting and sighing, gathering itself for the appearance of the cardinal. Through the open doors comes the sound of an organ recessional as a procession of splendidly robed clergy appears. There are altar boys swinging smoking censers, sending up aromatic smoke, and more priests. A lot of lace and gilt, which gleams in the sunlight. The cardinal himself emerges, splendid in cranberry silk robes and mitre and the crowd utters a kind of muted roar. He seems taken aback, as though wondering why they are all there. As he comes towards us, Fergus sinks to his knees, dragging me down with him. We are right at the front of the crowd.

I've always thought that the senior hierarchy of clergymen is, almost by definition, elderly, somewhere on the doddery side of sixty-five. This one can't be much older than his middle fifties. There is vigour in his expression and a

316

spring in his step. His face is serene and beautiful. He turns enquiringly to the crimson-robed prelate walking beside him. The prelate extends his arm, as though to guide him on his way, but instead, the cardinal takes a step towards the crowd. He touches someone, murmurs over them. Moves down, stops again. And then he is in front of me. I've seen him before. Not just someone like him, wearing similar vestments, not the generic priest offering up the Mass, but this man. In Spain, in Hungary, in Mexico, in Rome. I've followed him around the world. Wherever he's been, I've been there, too. I recall my mother's face, the tears on her cheeks while smoke from the swinging thuribles thickened the air, and far away from us, a sonorous voice intoned.

And now, standing on the steps behind him, is another familiar figure. Unlike the other attending clerics in their lace surplices and scarlet silk, he is black-robed. His sinister reptile eyes flicker across the crowd, searching for something. For someone. Who ... my mother? Me?

I shrink back but too late. He has seen me. In a controlled but rapid movement, he has run down on to the paved concourse and towards me. There is murder in his face, his mouth says words I cannot hear, one hand reaches into his robes as though he has a gun concealed there, or a knife.

Before I can stand and melt away into the crowd, the cardinal is laying his fingers along my forehead. *'In nomine Patri, Filii et Spiritus Sancti,'* he murmurs softly. 'Bless you. Bless

317

you, my daughter.'

The longing to announce myself, to ask him if he is my father, is almost overwhelming, but the black presence of the abbot, standing almost at his shoulder, ready to strike like a snake, kills the urge stone dead. But imagine it. The consternation, the stepping away, memory winding back thirty years while the crowd heaves and surges, the puzzled look, the final realization...

Do I feel anything at his touch? Do I feel that I am in the presence of holiness, sanctity, whatever you want to call it? I feel an interior shift, as though one half of my heart is grating against the other. There is a stillness, a serenity inside this man which is almost palpable. I could lie down in it, feel safe for aeons as his tranquil soul wraps itself round me. *My soul there is a country, far beyond the stars*, we used to sing at school and I am there now, swinging from a thousand sparkling silver points, as his ice-grey eyes embrace me. His Icelandic eyes, exactly like my own. I am pulled towards him. Is this what they call charisma? Is this the quality which has taken him to the College of Cardinals, which causes people to announce that he is a saint, a possible pope?

I look up at him and for a moment, his smile falters. How many million people does he see a year? How many does he touch with his saintly fingers, offering them hope? Although I recognize him, he can't possibly have recognized me. I want to seize his sleeve, make him stop, but after the briefest hesitation, he has already moved on to someone else in the crowd. Dom

318

Francis follows in his wake, turning his head to watch me, ready to move like a bodyguard between me and his charge.

Around me, people are holding up crucifixes, fingering rosaries. As I get to my feet, a woman reverently touches my shoulder, as though the force of the cardinal's blessing might pass from me to her.

My forehead sweats. Is this how Christ himself recruited his disciples? Is this what my mother felt, all those years ago? Is this why she and I wandered the earth, followed unknown in his footsteps? What I want more than anything else at this moment is to ask her if it was worth it.

I turn and start pushing through the crowd towards the road. Before I can get clear of people, someone catches me by the sleeve. Fingers dig into my arm. I feel a cold satanic breath against my cheek.

'Should a momentary lapse be allowed to jeopardize the hope and salvation of millions?' a voice murmurs in my ear.

I say nothing.

The fingers tighten abruptly. 'One word, Theodora. Say one word, and I swear that I will kill you. And then your mother.'

I sway, the pain of the abbot's grip almost makes me reel. 'That's not ... not very Ch ... Christian,' I gasp.

'I have to do this,' he continues tensely. 'For the sake of the Church. And then I will kill myself, to pay for my sin.'

'Two mortal sins, Father Francis?' My arm aches and throbs. 'Let me go, please.'

319

'If you speak out, he will feel compelled to resign and the world will lose a man who can change it. I cannot allow this to happen.'

Around us the crowds push and swirl, oblivious to the drama taking place in their midst. I try to prise his fingers off but they bite even harder into my flesh. 'I shall ... not speak,' I manage.

'If only I could rely on that, Theodora.' His voice is soft, sibilant, and infinitely ruthless.

'Rest assured, you can.' But as he turns to catch up with the cardinal and his retinue, I wonder if I shall ever feel safe again or am doomed to spend the rest of my life looking over my shoulder.

Fergus catches up with me. He takes my hand and holds it against his heart. 'Theodora, this father thing really doesn't matter. You are who you are.'

'I know.' I bite my lip.

'Remember that I love you.'

'I know that, too.'

We gaze at each other and I see the years ahead in his eyes. The two of us walking the earth, rootless yet grounded. My worries drop away. As he says, whether or not Cardinal John O'Donnell is my father doesn't matter. What matters is Fergus and me, a couple, a partnership. What matters is that after all the wandering, the two of us have found a home in each other.

And then, on the other side of the square, I see my mother. She is staring at me, her mouth open. She has seen it all, the cardinal stooped over me, the confrontation with the abbot. Alarm, terror, despair, are written all over the prominent bones of her face. The streaks of white in her hair blaze in the sunshine. She looks ephemeral, as though one whisper would waft her up into the air. Her eyes are sunk deep into their sockets. But it's not really my mother, I tell myself, it's her ghost, her essence, it's a woman with the same cast of features or a similar way of holding her head. If I push my way towards her through the procession and the crowds, if I reach her, touch her on the arm, catch her attention, I will find that I am backing away from a stranger, apologizing for the intrusion.

Stop that, Theodora, I tell myself. You *know* it's her. As it has so often been. It's your mother, watching over you in her wounded, awkward way. Your mother, who didn't know how to be a mother, never really learned. Who wanted you to be safe from whatever demons surrounded her. Safe from Dom Francis. Because I see at last that *he* was the danger we fled. And realizing that, I understand what this has all been about.

All her adult life she has been pulled by two kinds of love. One for me, helpless in her arms, unplanned, not really wanted on voyage but taken along because to leave me behind was unthinkable, because she loved me. And the other for the man who is my father, who is as far away from me in this moment as he had always been, even though at last I know who he is. I *think* I know.

My mother is in pain, I can tell. One hand is pressed to her side. All my pretences drop away. My sense of self is crumbling, falling from me like a rotten branch. It is time to start being a

321

daughter. It is time to relearn my mother.

The procession of robed clerics moves slowly between us, croziers glinting, mitres gleaming, a shiny tide of religion, she on one side, me on the other, as if we stand on opposite shores of a vast ocean.

Fergus is saying something but I don't want to listen. I want to be with my mother, who is moving away, who is disappearing. I can only see the top of her head now, where the dragonfly clasp in her hair catches the light. I've let her go too often; this time I shan't give up until I reach her. I start pushing after her through the crowd, moving so rapidly that Fergus falls behind.

'Theodora,' he calls, plaintive.

'I'm sorry, Fergus, my darling Fergus,' I say over my shoulder. 'I have to go.'

'Where?'

'I don't know yet.' I remember then that if it weren't for Fergus, I wouldn't be here now. 'I'll ring you,' I call, across the heads which divide us. 'I love you.' And I blow him a kiss, which falls like a moth into his outstretched hand.

I'm only a few yards behind my mother when suddenly she steps into the street and flags down a taxi. Although I shout her name, she doesn't hear me – or chooses not to. Before I can reach her, she is gone. I rush to the kerb, my arm raised, but she seems to have found the only empty taxi in London. Long after it's far too late to catch up with her, I stand at the side of the road, tears running down my cheeks as I wait for a cab which never comes to carry me to my mother's side.

TWENTY-FOUR

'Where is she?' I demand, as soon as Hugo opens the door.

'Where is who?'

'Luna ... Mother. My mother.'

'Ah.' He starts to murmur something noncommittal but I push past him into the hallway. A gilt mirror hangs on the wall above a Sheraton table, and in it I can see the reflection of a crazy woman, my mother, *me*, features slanted out of the true, mouth twisted, eyes full of wildness. 'Is she here?'

'No.'

'Then where? I need to know.' I'm shouting.

'I can't tell you.' His shoulders sag. He seems defeated.

I take a step closer. 'But you do know, don't you?'

'She asked me not to say.' He backs away and if I didn't know myself to be unscary, I would almost think he is frightened of me.

'I'm her daughter, Hugo.'

'Yes, you most indubitably are.'

'I think she needs me.'

He nods. 'There's a house,' he says slowly, hands flat against the wall behind him. 'On the south-east coast. Near Dover. She's down there.'

'She told me that she was dividing her time between Stockholm and Rome.

'She's...' His refined eyelids droop. 'She hasn't been well recently. She's ... she's over here for some tests.'

'What kind of tests?' A shroud of alarm wraps itself around me. Her hand like a claw on my arm. The unfleshed oval of her beautiful face. 'What's wrong with her?'

He doesn't want to answer,

'*What*, Hugo? Is it ... cancer?' The word is monstrous.

'We don't know.'

'But it's definitely something.'

'Yes.'

The blood clogs in my veins. With infinite slowness, I put out my hand and reach for the table. It feels like several centuries before it connects with the edge. My eyes are as heavy as stones. 'Is it ... life-threatening?'

'That's what she's here to find out.'

'I just saw her, Hugo. At Westminster Cathedral.'

'She said she was going to stop off there on her way to Charing Cross.'

'Why was she there?'

He hesitates, torn between truth and lies. He clears his throat. 'I can make an educated guess.'

He knows too, I think. All these years, he's known who my father is. Or, at the very least, suspected. 'Whose house is this one near Dover?'

'Mine. I bought it a few years ago. Lucia stays there sometimes.'

324

'Give me the address, Hugo.'

'She doesn't want to be disturbed. To see anyone.'

'Too bad. She's going to see me.'

For a long minute he stares at me. Finally, reluctantly, he finds paper and pen, and writes it down. I'm out of the door almost before he's finished.

I have to wait for a train and, when it arrives, the journey is long and tedious, full of unexplained halts and delays. I reflect upon the chain of events which has led me to make this journey. If Fergus hadn't gone to visit Sean Costello, Sean would not have sent him the newspaper cutting which gave a clue to my father's identity, and then I would never have gone to the forecourt of Westminster Cathedral and seen the man for myself.

I hug against my chest the dress I bought for my mother when I was in Boston. It's by the same designer as the one I bought for myself, but hers is scarlet, the colour of the shoes I dream of her wearing as she runs, runs. My gypsy mother, in her crimson-beaded dress; is she running towards someone, or away?

By the time I reach the salt-fresh, seagull-screaming railway station where I'm to get out, the sun is casting a golden glow over tall chimneypots and slate roofs. There is a sense of summer drawing to a close, as the taxi drives through streets full of guest houses, past boarded-up whelk-stalls and ice-cream parlours, a Tudor castle, a lifeboat station.

Two miles out of town, I am dropped at the end

of an unmade-up lane which runs past a row of seaside cottages set behind privet hedges and fronting a pebble beach which spreads for miles on either side. The shingle is like bones, bleach-ed and scoured by uncountable tides. In the distance is a headland – white cliffs topped with bright green grass. A grey sea stretches to where a low hump of land squats on the horizon.

Seaview is the name of Hugo's house. Pebble-dash painted white. Brick chimneys at either end of the roof gables. A balcony along the first floor and casement windows, all wide open to catch the brisk evening air. It's almost dark as I walk to the front door between scrubby bushes. Clumps of coarse marram grass and pinky-purple valerian push up between the pebbles which make up the front garden. Beside the door is an unkempt bush of fuchsia.

Since there's no bell, I rap at the glass panes of the front door – deep, rich blue round the edges, a ruby-red central pane with an elaborate star cut into it – and after a while, my mother appears. She looks exhausted and, at the same time, tranquil. As though she has at last found peace. As though she has been dragging at a heavy weight and has finally let it go. At the sight of her, I am overwhelmed with emotion. I put my hands to my face. She is so familiar to me, so loved, yet still so unknown, though more known now than she ever has been. She opens the door and I stumble into the house. 'Mother...'

'Theodora,' she says. Her voice is soft.

'Oh, Mother,' I say. 'I've missed you so much.' I stare at her, pulling her into me, reassessing all the memories I've kept locked up for so long. 'I tried to pretend it was your ghost,' I say. She won't know what I mean, of course. But she does.

'It really was me.'

'Keeping watch.'

'Sometimes the need to look at you was too...' She doesn't finish the sentence.

I see, suddenly, a woman, a mother, not knowing how to erase the past or bridge the chasm which divides her from her daughter. 'I guess I was pretty hostile,' I say. 'And always so darn sorry for myself.'

'You had good cause.'

We gaze at each other for a timeless fulfilling moment. 'This is for you,' I say, handing her the dress in its protective cover. 'It's a dress.'

'A dress?' She takes my hand. 'Come inside, Theodora.'

I follow her into the house and she gazes back at me over her shoulder. 'Theodora. Such a lovely name. Given the circumstances, it was the only possible name I could give you.'

Inside, the sitting room has been knocked through so that it faces both to the sea and to the garden behind the house. A slate-floored kitchen ends in a circular conservatory where there are rattan chairs softened by plump cushions. Otherwise, the house is furnished like any other holiday home. Neutral, well-used sofas. A couple of armchairs. A bookcase along one wall crammed with paperbacks and board games. Tall seagrasses have been pushed into a spaghetti jar. A basket of driftwood sits beside an unlit hearth;

on the mantlepiece above it, a fading shabby-edged postcard of the Virgin of the Rocks. One of the icons of my childhood.

'I'll be back in a moment,' my mother says.

I watch the way her dancer's calves flex as she walks, and the thinly frail set of her shoulders. My chest aches. Through the open windows, I can hear the endless suck and sigh of the sea, the push as the waves surge in, the grinding of shingle as they recede. Far away on the horizon are lights, a glow in the sky.

Then she is standing beside me again. 'That's France,' she says. 'It's so exciting to be here on the edge of England, looking across at another country.'

She reaches for a bottle of white wine standing on a teak tray, already open. There are two heavy crystal glasses beside it, a dish of macadamia nuts. It's very different from the way she used to be when we lived together.

'You were expecting me,' I say.

'Hugo rang to warn me you were on your way.' She pours me a glass and hands it to me. 'It's an Australian Chardonnay. Your favourite.'

How does she know? 'Your very good health,' I say formally, raising the glass to my mouth. Her face changes. I put the glass down on the counter, very carefully, as though it might shatter at the slightest knock. I want to take her into my arms. Behind her, I see a world closing in where she no longer exists and wonder if I can bear it. 'How bad is it?' I say.

A shadow passes over her eyes as she decides whether to lie. 'Not particularly good.' Her fingers flutter towards her breast and fall back. 'But it's under control. If it happens, it won't be yet. Not for a long while.'

She's still trying to protect me, I think, but this time I know what from. My mind rejects the information but already I'm making plans. I'll take her back with me tomorrow, get Bob Lovage to start converting the downstairs rooms immediately. Or maybe wait a couple of weeks until the work is finished, and then bring her down. And I'll have to ring Fergus. There's definitely no way I can go to Mexico, not now that my mother needs me.

My mother needs me.

She puts her hand to her throat. 'I think it's time we talked.' She too drinks her wine, sipping slowly, savouring it. 'So you know what's at stake.'

'I already know.' I walk over the slate tiles to stand at the window overlooking the sloping back garden. In the early-autumn fade of the light, the sky is darkening. I look out at bushes, flowerbeds, rocks.

'The garden's nothing,' my mother says. 'I'm not here often enough to get it into any real kind of order. And I know so little about...' She speaks quickly, as though she is embarrassed and I realize she wants my approval but at the same time is guarding against the possibility that I will find her wanting in this matter of growing a garden.

'It looks great from here.' I can see my reflection in the window and then hers, as she comes to stand beside me. How alike we are.

How very much I do not want her to be ill. She has changed into the black silk dress, which flows over her breasts and hips. The beaded red flowers curve around her slender waist. She looks beautiful, even more beautiful than I remembered. Very carefully, she puts her hand on my shoulder, light as a leaf, and I reach up to cover it with my own. Her little crabbed hand, already signalling mortal illness. We stand like that for a long time.

'I'd better feed you,' my mother says. 'You've come a long way.'

Our sentences are laden with double meaning. 'Such a long way,' I agree. And it's true. I have come a long way from those days when all I would acknowledge was what she *didn't* do.

She sets white dishes on the table. 'It's not much. There's soup in the fridge if you'd like.'

'This is more than enough. I had lunch.'

'With that writer?'

'Fergus, yes.'

'An uncommon man, I would say.' She eyes me sideways. 'Very much your sort of person.'

'A man who never stays in the same place for more than a few months is my sort of person?'

'You love him, don't you?'

I think for a while about the answer. How do you express the totality of love without descending into cliché or sentimentality? How do you convey the completeness of two people perfectly, infinitely, attuned, or the burn and throb of desire which transcends time and distance and yet is only one of the links which bind you together? But she knows about that. She has loved, still loves. 'Yes,' I say. 'I love him.' Why say more?

'Does he love you?'

'Yes.'

'Then you'll work it out.' She puts a loaf on the table. A slab of creamy cheese. Cold sliced chicken. Tomatoes. Apples, yellow flushed with crimson. 'Sit,' she says. She refills my glass, straightens the cutlery at my place, lights the candle in the centre of the table.

She is my mother again, the woman who used to sweep me against her, the woman I used to think about at five o'clock each evening, until resentment pushed the habit away. I remember Gemma on the plane to Boston, the certainty of her connection to the woman who gave birth to her.

When she has seated herself opposite me, I raise my glass. 'Let's have another toast.'

'To what?'

'To us. To ... love.' Looking at my mother, I appreciate her in a way that I have never done before. A child – a daughter – can never fully know her parent. This moment of recognition, the acceptance of fallibility, is perhaps as intimate as we shall ever be.

She smiles at me. 'To love.' She lifts her glass and sips. Picks up her fork and looks down at the food in front of her. 'I wanted you to be strong and certain,' she says. 'I wanted you to be independent. I wanted you to be confident. You're all those things and I'm proud of us both for that.'

'I know who my father is,' I say.

Her head goes back. The olive tones of her face fade to ivory.

'This afternoon, in London...' Other scenes come back to me. Memories. Candles and incense. Gold-embroidered robes. A presence so beneficent that it embraced the world, drew people after it like Orpheus's lute.

'Oh, God...' She covers her face with her hands.

'When I saw his photo in the paper ... You always said I had my paternal grandmother's eyes. I'd already begun to wonder whether my father might not be a priest of some kind. And then this afternoon, when he blessed me, I knew it was him. It had to be.'

She places both her hands flat on the table as though she is about to stand. She looks frightened. 'You're jumping to conclusions.'

'I looked into his face and it was like seeing my own reflection.' I am strong and certain. As she wants me to be.

'No.'

'I think yes,' I say. 'It explains so many things. I can see why you didn't want to tell me.' I watch her absorb what I am saying. Very gradually the tension drains from her thin shoulders.

'I might have done.' She sips thoughtfully at her wine. 'Maybe eventually I *would* have done, if only for your safety's sake.'

'I went to St Joseph's, in Vermont,' I say, and her head comes up again, rigid with alarm. 'I spoke to Dom Francis.'

'Oh my God. What did you say?'

'That I was your daughter. That I suspected my

father was one of his students.'

She is rising from her seat, hands fluttering with tension. 'What have you done? What have you...?' She gazes wildly around. 'All these years I've tried to protect you and now you say you ... Oh God, what have you *done*?'

'Luna, Mother: what is all this about?'

'He'll kill you,' she says wildly. 'He would stop at nothing, for John's sake. When he found out about ... about John and me, he threatened me. He said I must never contact him or John again, that if I did, the consequences would be fatal. He was always there, somehow, in the background ... I was so terrified, for your sake. And then I came face to face with him in Rome, and he must have realized that I was there because of John. It was Easter – you probably won't remember–'

The day my mother went mad ... 'I remember it as clearly as if it were this morning.'

'–you hadn't come with me, for once, thank God. If he'd known about you, I can hardly bear to think what he might have ... He recognized me, of course he did, and I knew he would try to follow me, find out about me, maybe ... I know this all sounds a bit far-fetched ... maybe even kill me. And you, too, if he ever found out you existed. And those other times, when I was pushed into the roadway, and almost run over by a car, I knew it had to be him, or organized by him.'

'It's all right.' I try to soothe her but she's too wound up.

'Maybe I overcompensated. I was so fright-

333

ened, so alone. The one thing I couldn't let him know was about you because I was certain he'd have tried to harm us both. That's why I sent you away to school, why I didn't get in touch.' She laughs, awkwardly. 'Maybe I'd read too many crime novels, but I was terrified that he – or his people – were tapping my phone lines, opening my mail.'

'But why would he do that?'

'Darling Theodora, he'd been grooming John for years, pushing him onwards, making the right contacts, rooting for his boy. Although John's now a cardinal, there's another step still to climb. And we two are the only things which could ruin the work of three decades.'

'I still don't really understand.'

'Think about it. If the world found out that John had an illegitimate daughter, that would be the end of all his hopes. And Father Francis's ambitions, too. Because if John does ever get to the very top, you can be sure the abbot will be at his side.' She looks at me fondly. 'Why do you think I always walked on the other side of the road from you? Why did I make you call me Luna, rather than Mother or mom or even Lucia? Why did I send you away from me, and not get in touch with you for so long? I was so desperately afraid he would harm you. It would look like an accident but I would know. I simply couldn't afford to let anyone ever know the connection between the two of us. It wouldn't have been fair to John.'

'Why not?'

'Because...' She sighs again. Pokes at her food

then carefully puts a crust of bread into her mouth, a sliver of cheese.

I realize that she is forcing herself to eat in order to keep up her strength. 'Was it fair that you had to deal with ... with an unwanted pregnancy all by yourself?' I demand. 'To fend for both of us, without any help?'

'He doesn't even know that you exist. I've made it my business to see that he didn't. By the same token, that meant you could never know about him, just in case.' A faint smile plays round her pale mouth. 'I was so afraid, Theodora, of what you might do. You were always so sure of yourself, far more so than I've ever been. I was sure that if I told you, you would make yourself known to him. And because of what he is, that would have forced him into a terrible dilemma: his duty towards his God versus his duty towards you. He's a good man. An exceptional man. His destiny was plain to see and he had to be allowed to fulfil it. I couldn't risk jeopardizing that.'

'His duty to me? He has none. I'm an independent woman. I don't need anything from him.' Except, I suppose, recognition, love. I have to accept that I'll never have either.

'Nonetheless...' My mother crumbles a piece of the bread on her plate, forks up the tiniest shred of chicken.

'How did you meet him?'

'On a picnic. When I was at St Margaret's, in Vermont. We joined forces with the boys from St Joseph's. He was teaching there.'

'How old was he then?'

'Twenty-four. One year out of the seminary.' She wipes her mouth with her napkin. 'Oh, Theodora,' she says. 'I never wanted this, but it's the most enormous relief that someone other than me knows about him. I've never been able to talk about him to anyone, ever.'

'Don't forget that we aren't the only ones who know,' I say. I tell her what happened earlier, at Westminster Cathedral, the abbot's threats, my promise never to speak.

'Dom Francis. That evil man,' my mother says. 'Don't trust him. You must be careful.' Her palms are pressed against her narrow chest. 'I can't handle this,' she whispers. Her eyes are huge in her pale face. Candlelight catches the beads on the crimson panels of her dress.

'As soon as he'd confessed about being in love with you, the cardinal must have been sent away, out of reach of the evil temptress,' I say.

'Who'd already decided to remove herself for much the same reason.'

'Is that what you meant about the gift you gave to God?'

'Yes.'

'Fergus told me that John O'Donnell had taught at St Joseph's as a young man.' I explain about the article Fergus had seen in the newspaper. 'When I actually went there and looked down at that garden, things began to make a little more sense.'

'It was because of the garden that I bought the portrait from Tom Bellamy.' Her voice is so low I can hardly hear it. 'It meant pawning my mother's pearls, but I had to have it. The garden reminded me so much of the place where I last saw John, where I made my decision to leave him, to keep you. The place where,' she says, without any hint of melodrama or sentimentality, 'my heart broke in two. It was only much later I realized I could use the picture to comfort you.'

'Keep me quiet, you mean.'

'That, too.' We smile at each other.

'I made him British,' she says. 'A professional soldier, as far from the truth as I could manage, just in case they ever caught up with you.'

'Was anything you told me true?'

'He plays the piano,' she says. 'He loves gardens, just like you. But otherwise, not very much.'

A flash of the abbot's expression comes back to me. I'd thought he was seeing the young Lucia Caxton in my face, but it was the likeness to the young priest which had really alarmed him. *If this should ever get out* ... I remember the headline I'd read weeks before. *First American pope?* Can my father really lighten the darkness in which so many believers currently stumble? I've seen him elevate the Host above the altar, the light streaming from above to illuminate his golden robes. I've seen the absolute goodness which radiates from him. I've felt his hand on my head. The hand of my father.

'He called me his daughter,' I say.

My mother's face is full of hollows. Her eyes are fearful. 'I truly believe that given the chance, he could change the world for the better,' she says. 'You can ruin all that, if you want to. If he knew about you, his conscience would force him

337

to resign.'

'That's what the abbot said earlier.'

'It was never John's fault, always mine,' said my mother. 'I fell in love the very second I saw him. I threw myself at him. He knew nothing about sex or love or women. Nothing about the world, really. Nor did I. He'd been in a seminary since he was eight years old, being fed the doctrine. Can you imagine that?'

'Yes.'

'He didn't know how to handle me. For six months we...' She covers her mouth, speaks from behind her fingers. 'Oh, God ... it was beyond anything either of us had known or could imagine. He was in spiritual agony the whole time. When I discovered that I was pregnant, I knew I'd have to disappear. He'd said several times that he'd leave the Church for me, but I couldn't put him in a position where he'd have to choose. So he never knew about you. I couldn't risk him making the wrong decision.'

'Nobody forced him to sleep with you.'

'Except me. He was innocent. And in love. We both were.' She presses one hand to her heart, in a gesture I've seen many times before. 'First love is a powerful emotion.'

'Why did you keep me?'

She is silent for so long that I wonder whether to repeat the question. It's almost dark outside now, just a line of summer sky resting on the horizon, a lightship flashing its beam intermittently across the fading sea.

She picks up her glass and holds it cupped in her hands. 'When I discovered I was carrying

338

you, I was distraught,' she says. 'I decided I couldn't go through with it. I didn't want to make do with John's baby, when what I really wanted was John. Trouble is, it was difficult for a girl like me – Catholic and innocent – to know what the processes were. I used to press my stomach against the wall, as hard as I could. I made myself sick on gin. Naturally, it didn't work. In the end, it seemed it would be easier to kill us both. I drew up a list of the different ways I could do it – a gun, a rope, poison, jumping off a cliff – and tried to decide which would hurt least.'

'What stopped you?'

'While I was making up my mind, you moved,' says my mother softly. 'It was like having a tiny bird trapped inside me. Or a firefly. I imagined you dancing there, in the dark. At that moment you became my world.'

'And afterwards?'

'Afterwards...' Her head droops. 'I didn't know how to handle you. My own mother died when I was young, so I had no guidance, no precedents. I did what I thought was best, but it usually wasn't, I can see that now.'

'You made me strong,' I say. And it's true.

What is also true is the fact that she chose his life above her own. Above mine. I think of the churches, the cathedrals we visited, the voices at the altar, the tinkling bells and clouds of incense. That's why we were there. She had followed him wherever he went, dragging me along. And he never knew. Sometimes there were tears on her cheeks as he celebrated the Mass. That was all of him she allowed herself. I am angry about the way she has wasted her life.

'Has it...' I clear my throat. 'Has it been worth it?'

In the windowpane which holds back the night, I see her head move. 'If I am honest, probably not.'

'You say you never stopped loving him but you ... had other men.'

'Had?' She laughs. She finishes what is left on her plate. The bones in her throat constrict as she swallows. 'That's my Theodora,' she says. 'Still so prim. Yes, over the years I slept with other men. Even loved some of them. But I've only been *in* love once, and that was with John.'

'What about Hugo?' My voice is begging her. I want there to be a happy ending. In the black glass, I can see our reflections, our similarities. Love, passion, the sacrifices women make for their men. 'He's loved you for years.'

'Hugo has come to mean more to me than I could possibly have thought.'

'Perhaps that's love,' I say. I, who, until now, knew so little about it. 'Just a different love from what you expected.'

She hesitates, the glass of wine in her hand. Light falls through it, casting a lemony shadow on to her skin. I can see light through the frail bones of her fingers. After a while, she says, 'You may be right.'

She rises in a fluid motion from her chair. The black silk of her dress moves softly around her legs as she walks into the sitting room, and looks out at the invisible sea. A breeze, salty and fresh, blows through the window, stirs the candles she has lit, ruffles her hair. It's hard to believe that something deadly and terminal might have taken hold of the secret places of her body.

Questions spill through my brain like loose gravel. 'Why did you send me off to convent school?'

'I've never been good at talking.' She nods slightly. 'I thought it was the best thing for you. I could see how much you wanted to be still for a while, whereas stillness was the last thing I wanted, because if I ever stopped moving, I would have to examine the pattern of life I had chosen, face up to the pain – the absolute futility of it.'

'What do you mean?'

'Oh, Theodora. There were so many times when, if it hadn't been for you, I would have killed myself. You were what kept me alive. You were all I had of John. I didn't want to let you go, but I knew I had to, for your sake. And you know what? Letting you go was the biggest relief. I've never been able to forgive myself for being so glad that you were elsewhere.'

'Not wanted on voyage,' I murmured.

'It was that without you, it was easier to keep moving, to keep one step ahead of Dom Francis, to follow John, to be where he was.' Her eyes are warm. 'You look so like him. So very like. And I do understand why you felt you had to find him.'

For a long moment we stare at each other. I've lived nearly all my life believing he was dead. To all intents and purposes, for me he still is. But

I have my mother back. Like a ticking clock, I hear the minutes rushing by into oblivion and I seize her hand, crush it between my own. 'Mother,' I say. She has rebuffed me so many times in the past that I hesitate to speak in case she does it again. 'What I really wanted, *always* wanted, was you. I thought of you at five o'clock nearly every single night of my life.'

'As I thought of you, my darling. As I still do.' She makes a breathless little sound, somewhere between a laugh and a gasp.

'Are you in pain?' I ask, alarmed.

'No.' She shakes her head. 'No.' Images of a house of cards, an overblown rose, come back to me. She is so fragile. If I'd taken the time to recognize it, I'd have seen that she always has been.

'I was always so afraid that if I got in touch, you would reject me.' She falters. 'I don't think I could have borne it. And then you met your husband and got married and I thought that at last I could maybe come back into your life, now that there was someone else to look after you.'

Silence lies like a bowl between us, full of possibilities. We can either spill them out, or we can carry it carefully between us for as long as we feel the need. She is still standing by the window, looking out to sea. The lights of France above the horizon stain the sky a dull yellowy-grey. A gull shrieks in the darkness.

She turns towards me and I hold out my arms. I don't think I expect her to embrace me. But she's changed. We both have. She comes to-wards me.

'I'm so sorry, Theodora,' she whispers.

I put my arms round her. I am taller than she. I hold her tightly, the way a mother might hug a child. I smell her, breathing in the good scent of her hair, her skin. And the very faintest tang of her mortality. I am aware of her body against mine; I paste the present feel of my mother on to the past. In the days, the years ahead, it will be my task to conflate the two. It will take time. Perhaps the rest of my life. I have to learn that nobody, no parent, can ever achieve a perfect score; no child should expect that. 'You can't be anywhere near as sorry as I am.'

Her cheek is against mine. Mine against hers.

'I promise I won't tell,' I say. 'I won't seek him out. I won't destroy him.'

'My darling daughter,' she says.

Finally I release her. 'How much longer have you got, Mother? Tell me the truth.' I reach forward and push a lock of her hair back behind her ear. Our roles are already changing back to the way they used to be.

'I told you before. It's under control. If, when, it's a while from now.'

Not long, then. But time enough for healing. Time to be friends.

Headlights move along the unmade lane between the house and the beach. A car pulls up outside and my mother's face lights up like a lamp. We hear footsteps along the path, the sound of a key in the lock, the closing of the front door. 'Hi,' someone calls.

'Hugo,' we both say. We turn to the door as he comes in, stooping slightly against the low

343

ceiling.

He stands there, looking at us. His face is gentle. He gazes at my mother and she smiles back at him, like a young girl, the way she must have when he first saw her in her yellow swim-suit, a beam of sunshine, lighting up his life. I'd thought his love for my mother had meant a wasted life, but perhaps it hasn't been. Any more than her love for my father has been.

Hugo comes across the room. 'Lucia,' he says, and his voice is so tender that I want to weep. He is part of my past. And, I think, of my future. I understand then that I am not wanted on their voyage, but only because I'm not taking the same journey as they are. These two will be together now, for as long as it takes, and I shall be included.

Hugo turns to me. 'I thought I'd better drive down here, in case either of you needed me.'

'I think we're managing,' my mother says. She takes his hand and pats it.

'I'll find a hotel in the town,' I say. I am look-ing at a man whose dreams have finally come true.

'There's room here for you.'

'I need to leave early in the morning.' I put an arm around each of them. 'But I'll see you very soon.'

Before I leave, I take the Da Vinci postcard from the mantelpiece and put it in my pocket.

On the train, I think about my Vernon Barnes portrait. Once it was crucial to my well-being but now it means less than nothing to me. There is someone, however, who wants it and I can see exactly how to turn that to my advantage. One day soon I will take Trina and the portrait over to Shepcombe Manor and negotiate with Constance Bellamy. Trina's training in return for my picture, because Lady Bellamy is a fine gardener. Only a few weeks ago, such a proposal would have been unthinkable, but now I feel no emotion whatsoever at losing the portrait. If Lady Bellamy has any sense at all, she'll jump at it.

From Charing Cross, I call Fergus. 'I'm back in London,' I say. 'Can I come to you?'

'Only if you promise never to leave me again.'

'I promise,' I say.

Outside the station, I take the postcard out of my pocket. It's all I will ever have of my father. But the Vernon Barnes portrait, this postcard, have both lost their point. Slowly I pull it into smaller and smaller pieces until they are too tiny for tearing. Finally, I locate a trash can and drop them into it.

Then I join the queue and wait for a taxi to carry me into the future.

He stands by the window, recalling a summer day more than thirty years ago, this same garden, scarcely changed since then. Clipped hedges, white benches, a girl in a wide-brimmed straw hat and a white dress. The girl he has never been able to forget. When she looked up at him from the garden that afternoon, he'd known at once what her decision would be. He remembers exactly how his heart had cracked with loss – and, yes, shamefully, with relief.

It is strange to be back here after so many

years. To remember his youthful self, ignorance and determination equally strong in him, the promises which had lain ahead, the path he has had to tread in order to reach his expected destination. He is almost there now, at last, ready to take up the burden if it should fall upon him, content enough if it does not. He has fulfilled his destiny, spread the Word, done all the good of which he is so far capable. As Dom Francis said, all those years ago, it was unthinkable that a single lapse should jeopardize so much. God Himself knows that he has spent his life ignoring the hypocrisy, trying to make up for that momentary fall from grace.

Where is Lucia now? There is a place in his soul where she still exists. Every time he celebrates the Mass, he wonders if she might be among the congregation. He looks for her sometimes. Occasionally he even thinks he has seen her, sitting at the back of some cathedral, lighting a candle, walking round a corner, through an archway, on the other side of a window. In Venezuela, in the great Metropolitan Cathedral in Mexico City, even in Rome. It's not her, of course, but a distillation of his own longings. If he were to meet her now, he would probably not even recognize her.

Under his robes, his heart knocks with resurrected grief. Is she happy? Does she have the loving husband she deserves, the children she wanted? The children he would have given her if she had asked.

It is all as clear to him today as it was then. The June picnic. St Margaret's girls, St Joseph's

346

boys, staff from both colleges. They'd taken buses to the lake. There'd been laughter, music, barbecue smoke drifting between the trees. Sweetcorn sizzling on the grill, yellow kernels browning. Hot dogs. Spare ribs glistening with sauce. Potato salad and coleslaw. They were all so young, so certain that the future was rosy. Theirs to conquer.

She was wearing a yellow bathing costume. She moved like a flash of gold between the trees as she dived into the lake. For the first time in his life he had known carnal desire, felt the unbearable tug of sexual longing. Unappeasable, unquenchable. Love, like a gift from God. Love, transfiguring, altering the shape of everything. A force no more resistible than a volcano or a tidal wave. One moment, he was one person and the next, someone entirely different. Later, she'd told him it had been like that for her, too.

The temptation to throw aside all his ambition for the sake of that sinful sweetness had been overwhelming. If the choice had been left to him, could he have resisted? Because of that, he'd left the decision to her. She had been strong for both of them.

Can one man change the world?

He will, given the chance. Already, approaches are being made. There is so much work to do and he will do it well. Not just well, but gloriously. A clean sweep. A clear direction to those who falter. The winds of change are sweeping through the corridors of the Vatican. It is necessary, if Mother Church is to recover from the mortal blows at present assailing Her on every

347

side. Why had they ever thought it could be kept hidden? That it wouldn't eventually catch up with them? Abused children grow up into damaged adults. They clamour for their revenge – and who can blame them? Even though the abusers are only a tiny minority, in one sense they are not even the most guilty. It is the bishops who knowingly moved them on to a new parish, a different diocese, tacitly gave them the opportunity to offend again. And then again. Saving face was everything.

We must acknowledge our shortcomings, he thinks. We must be seen to have rooted out the abusers. No excuses, no cover-ups. If we refuse to make a clean breast of things, the laity will grow ever more mistrustful. We live in an increasingly secular world. Even the faithful no longer blindly accept the rules laid down for them. Everything is questioned – and quite right too, for only by moving with the times will the Church survive.

If he were in charge, the first task he'd undertake would be to rid the Church of the abusers, the – call them what they are: paedophiles, pederasts, ephebophiles, whatever name they want to give to their cravings – either by suspension or by forced resignation, certainly by exposure. If they would only admit guilt now, not only would it render Mother Church more human in the eyes of the laity, he believes it will make Her stronger, not weaker.

But he must never forget that he too has sinned. He is as guilty as anyone else.

London last week, New York this, Brazil next

weekend. He has taken time from his busy schedule to drive up here, spend a last night at the Academy. He's talked with Dom Francis. They have spoken of that long-ago sin. He did not mention the fact that he still thinks of Lucia with regret and longing, that he often wonders what happened to her, that he hopes she is happy. The abbot had shrugged, and they moved on to other, safer topics, as though she had never existed.

A man's heart is not like a man's soul. The soul can be disciplined, trained the way you wish it to grow, like the topiary in the garden below. Like the peach trees espaliered against the wall in Rome, a sight which always disturbs him. The heart is different. The heart is wilful. At his age, in his position, he should no longer have room in it for Lucia. It was on these hills, beside these lakes, that they had made love and nothing had ever been sweeter nor ever would be. It was a sin of which he cannot repent.

A bell tolls. Dom Francis will be fetching him soon to conduct the Mass. It was the abbot who had arranged that final meeting with her. 'You have to make a choice, John,' he said. 'And once made, you must never falter. Look to the future, not the past. You think now that you want the happiness of an ordinary man, but you must never forget that you are not an ordinary man. You have been chosen, set apart.'

'My heart is breaking,' Lucia said, as they walked in the garden. 'I shall never love again.'

'You don't know that.'

'Oh, John, I do.'

And he believed her. 'Lucia...' She looked so beaten down. A small creature, wounded to the core. She had laid her fluid dancer's hands on her stomach, as though trying to contain her pain. He'd seen in her face the woman she would become in the future. He had wanted to be her future. 'I'll do whatever you ask of me.' So craven. So weak.

'I give you back to God,' she had said savagely. Her long fingers had pushed at his chest. 'He may forgive us, but I shall never forgive Him.'

The words had shocked him.

How might it have been if he had not accepted her decision, if he'd gone with her, after all? All the ordinary joys, home, family, children. It is the children he regrets most. A son, tall, a basketball player like himself. A daughter, dark-haired, like Lucia, with his eyes, his mouth. Last night he'd played the abbot's grand piano, Chopin nocturnes, Debussy, sung Schubert lieder, röslein, röslein to the sterile air, the way he used to sing to Lucia, imagining that in another life he might have sung for his daughter.

There'd been a young woman in London, a few days ago. He was processing out of the Cathedral, walking between the crowds. When he stopped in front of her, she had looked up at him and his heart almost stopped beating. If he and Lucia had had a daughter, he had thought, this, this is what she would have looked like. Lucia's hair. His own mother's strange Icelandic eyes. He'd thought back to this garden, the woman in the white dress, a green ribbon lying across her shoulder. The way they had been together, body

350

embraced by body, the sweet, sweet ... Oh, God, the young taste of her, the joy.

He rests his head against the window. His shoulders shake. As always when he grows agitated, his thoughts return to the little farm-house outside Rome, and the garden he is build-ing there, green and bowered, leafy, scented. Herbs and roses. Olives and oranges. Increas-ingly, his garden has become his refuge. So dif-ferent from the fruiting trees outside his window in Vatican City, tortured apples, distorted apri-cots, espaliered and cordoned like so many crucified victims.

How often he has been transported since he was last here at St Joseph's, lifted out of himself as he raises the Cup, as he accepts God's will. He shouldn't think this, could never confess it, but increasingly it seems as though nothing, nothing can compare with the ecstasy he'd found with Lucia. From our vices, God makes whips to scourge us ... He'd learned that as a young priest in Boston, and never realized the truth of it until Lucia walked out of his life forever.

Behind him, the door opens. Footsteps move across the carpet. He turns. And is shocked by the look of the abbot's face. The change, even from yesterday, is profound, as though the black wings of death are about to bear the man away at any moment.

'How long, Francis?' he asks.

The abbot shrugs. Carefully, to avoid the pain. 'Only God can know that.'

'Months? Weeks? Days?' He knows it cannot be years.

'Weeks, if I'm lucky. Days, if not.' The abbot's hand is on his shoulder. 'You made the right choice, John.'

'Did I?' He looks at the garden below. 'Did I really?'

'You must always believe that.'

He doesn't answer. A fifty-eight-year-old man, among the very youngest of the cardinals, destined for glory. Even now, he cannot be certain that if she were to come to him, he wouldn't trade all of it for the touch of her hand, her lips on his.

Does she ever give him even a passing thought?

His punishment, his penance, is that he will never know.